BLURB

His Love For Her Was Alive, Even If He Wasn't
Astra
I never knew there was a life after death.
A world beyond the Veil.
I also never knew I had a stalker, one who watched me from the shadows and vowed to protect me forever.
Or that he died saving me.
Now I'm haunted.
A ghost lingers in the darkness of my sanctuary and I find myself with no escape.
Because you can't escape the dead, you can't fight them either.
So afraid, and at his mercy, confusion follows when I come undone for an aspiration. From the feathered kiss of a touch that seeps beneath my skin.
No Straitjacket will stop my ghost from coming for me, or possessing all those who dare to harm me.
Hunter
I saw her once.
The girl with ocean blue eyes and a problematic smile.

She was a deviant under the surface.
Mischief dwelled within her troublemaker's heart.
So I decided she'll be mine.
Only I forgot to tell her that.
I became obsessed and transfixed by her wicked smile.
I hadn't meant to become her stalker.
But I did.
And I regret nothing.

HAUNTED BY DESIRE

LIFE AFTER DEATH

EMMALEIGH WYNTERS

Hunter & Astra

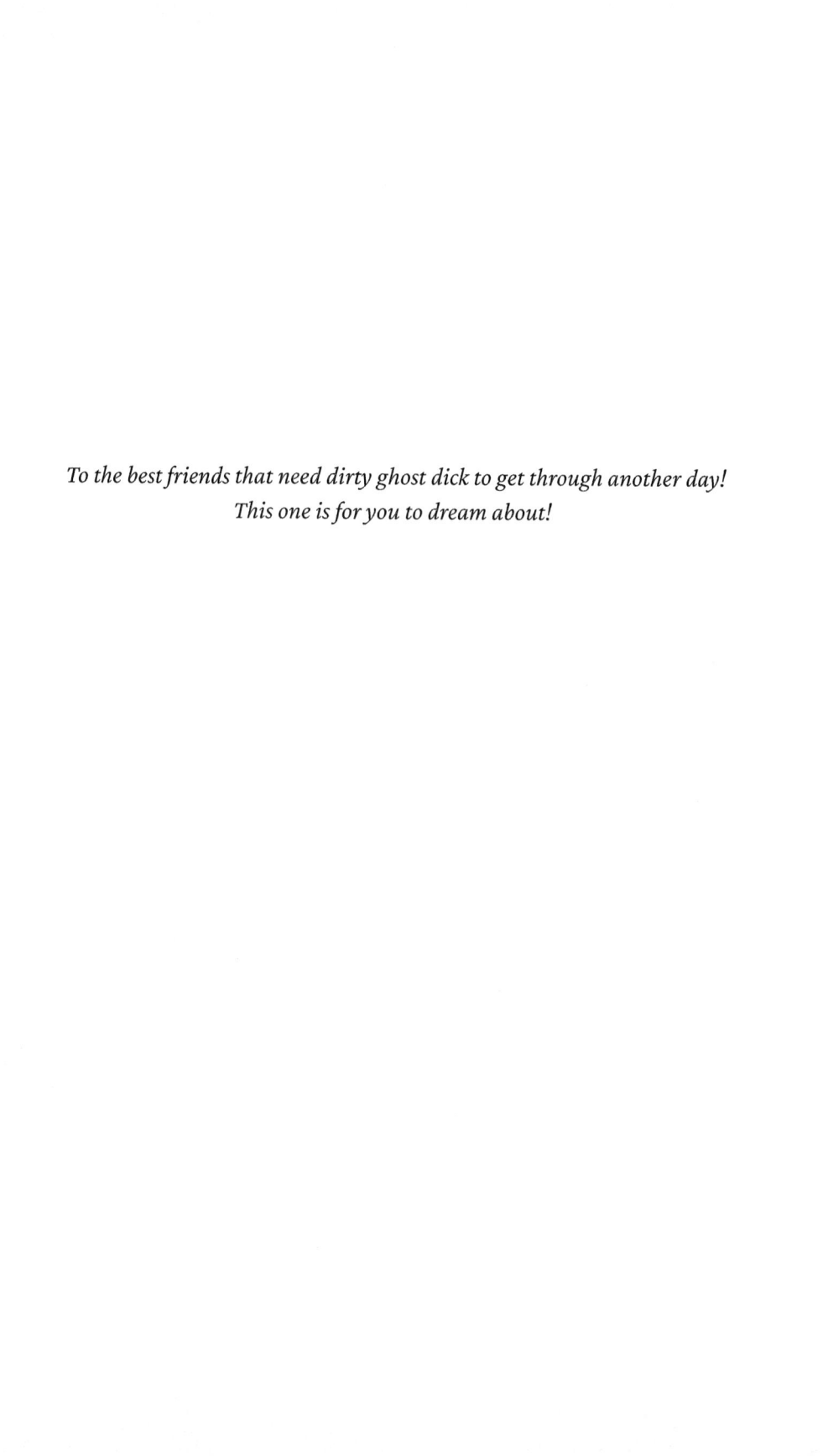

To the best friends that need dirty ghost dick to get through another day! This one is for you to dream about!

SONGS

Ava Adore - Smashing Pumpkins
This Mess - Tyler Posey
Cry Baby - American Avenue
What's Going On - The Snuts
Ocean Eyes - American Avenue
Every Breath You Take - The Police
Dark Can Be Beautiful - Alec Chambers
Dancing After Death - Matt Maeson
Blood On Your Hands- Veda
Cravin - Stileto
Burning House - Cam
Scars - I Prevail
How Villains Are Made - Madalen Duke
Rest In Peace - Dorothy
In Case You Don't Live Forever - Ben Platt
Carry You - Ruelle
Don't Forget About Me - Emphatic
Game of Survival - Ruelle

Crazy in Love - Eden Project
The Hunted - The Rigs
Middle of the Night - Elley Duhé
Another Life - Motionless In White
I Found - Amber Run
Parachute - Kyndal Inskeep
Bury - Unions
Kill the Lights - Set It Off
Addicted to You - Picture This
Ghost of You - Mimi Webb
@ My Worst - Blackbear
Now We're Alone - The People's Thieves
Desire - Meg Myers
Stitch Me Up - Set It Off
Catch Me If You Can - Set It Off
The Lines Begin To Blur - Nine Inch Nails
Ghost - Justin Bieber
Monster Made of Memories - Citizen Soldier
I Found - Amber Run
Moonlit - Rivals
I Don't Deserve It - Lisa Cimorelli
Hell's Coming With Me - Poor Man's Poison
Never Stop - SafetySuit
House On A Hill - The Pretty Reckless
Love U To Death - DeathByRomy
Mad Hatter - Melanie Martinez
Drag Me To The Grave - Black Veil Brides
No Saving Me - Framing Hanley
I'm Sorry - Joshua Bassett
Naked - Jake Scott
Ghost Town - Layto & Neoni
Bring Me to Life - Evanescence
If Today Was Your Last Day - Nickelback

War Of Hearts - Ruelle
Heaven - Julia Michael
Afterlife - Hailee Steinfeld
See You Again - Whiz Kahlifa

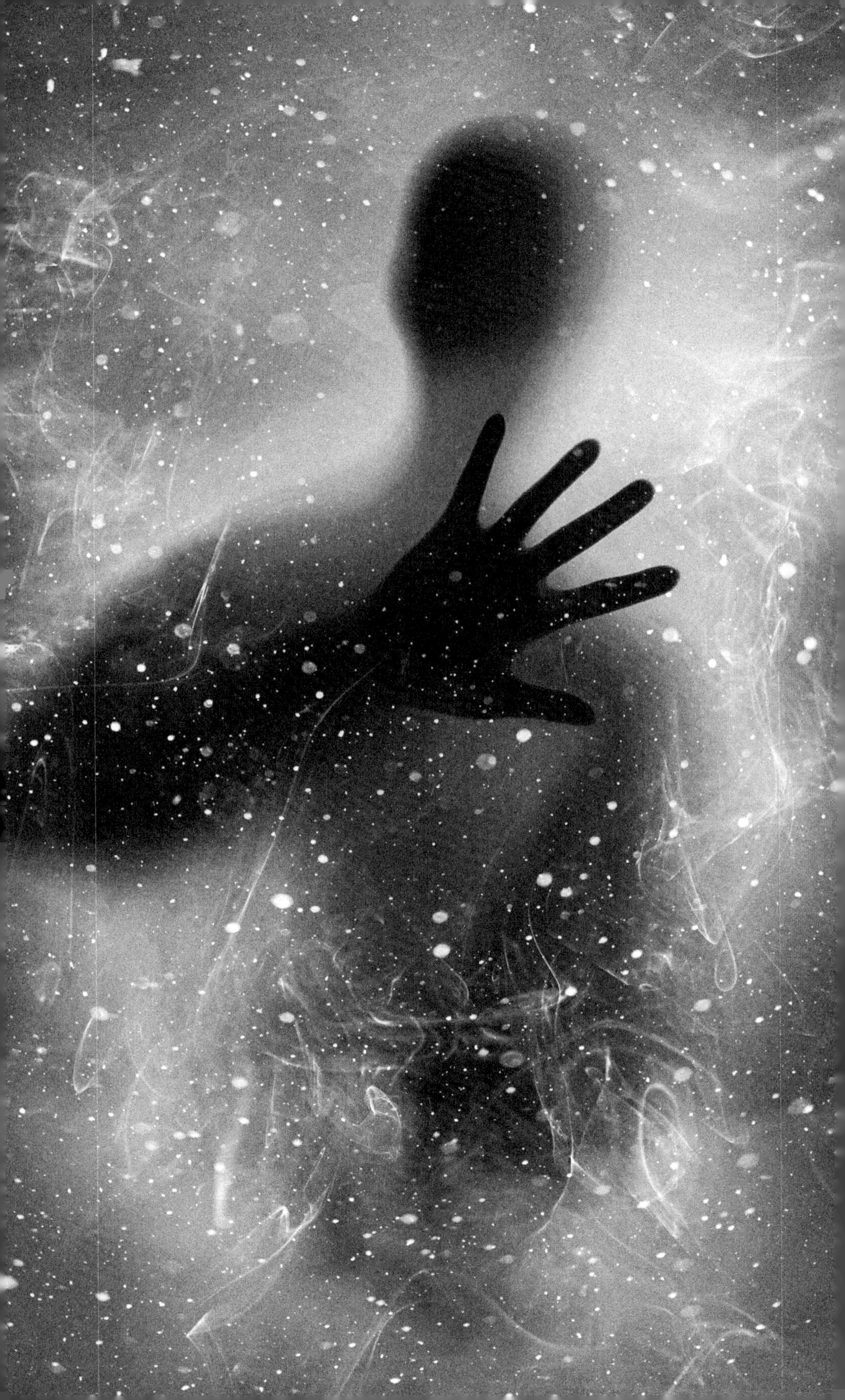

PROLOGUE

Hunter
Ava Adore - Smashing Pumpkins

Enamored. That's the only apt description.

Never have I been struck silent. Rendered immobile by such a simple touch.

She leans over my bicep, so entranced in her craft, she doesn't notice the strands of her black hair brushing over my chest. I glare at the white cotton separating us, vowing to incinerate this damn shirt the instant I get home. Never mind it's my favorite, it has sinned against me now.

Keeping me from my darkest desire.

There's nothing for it.

It has to pay.

Pain digs into my skin a little too deep, coiling around my bones and I hiss.

Not in anguish.

The opposite actually, but then those ocean blues flash upwards and I'm stuck again. Pinned against the recliner, a lightning bolt of electricity spearing my heart. Blood seeps from the wound, draining me of everything I thought I knew. Everything I had thought that I wanted and have been working towards. Yet I can't regret a single brutal moment that has brought me here...

Because it's all brought me to her.

After a beat, her eyes lower and my lungs collapse on a harsh exhale. I can't breathe when she's looking at me, can't think, can't respond. She's oblivious to the agony she is causing me. So damn right, innocent about the sinful ideas she's implanted in my mind. The turmoil she inflicts on my soul turns me into a shell of necessity.

When she is here, I'm no longer a man. No longer the billionaire playboy I'm portrayed as in monthly magazines or hierarchy society.

I'm merely her willing victim.

I refuse to protest. Refuse to argue against her touch once it's placed on my skin. To taint the artwork she draws against my flesh in crimson silk.

Whatever she wants to do to me, whatever mark she wants to leave on me, I merely lay here and grit my teeth, stopping myself from not getting up and walking out, but instead getting up and making her mine.

Incapable of words that can express the need to have me branded with her authenticity, I sigh and lean my head back on the table.

Tilting my forearm further in her direction to better access my inner arm, her clinical fingers follow my veins upwards. I reckon she doesn't even realize she's doing it; the journey of her fingertips tracing the raised network of lines brings her a sense of satisfaction that I encourage. Straining against my zipper, I don't try to hide the visceral reaction she draws from my body. Then she dives back into her sweet, rapturous torture, leaving me to ponder my fascination for the next few hours to come.

Too soon it's over. My jacket is back in hand, my loyalty card stamped and my fleeting looks ignored as she cleans her workstation. Not one look back or word of recognition that I'm still standing in her vicinity. The receptionist handles my payment and books me in for my routine slot next week.

A deep sigh catches my ear, and she drops onto the stool, her face downcast. A rare moment of vulnerability that has my chest turning inside out with turmoil. My fingers twitch to tug her into my hold. Yet when those blue eyes rise to me again, a steely coldness has glossed over her emotions and a raised eyebrow asks why I'm still here.

It's a reasonable question, but I can't bring myself to leave.

The bell above the door rings out behind me, a fake smile pulling at her lips in welcome. I find myself coldly dismissed. Not a soft moment warranted from what she has just done to me. Only the continued harsh brutality she has shown from the beginning. Week after week.

Then I'll be back and she'll be mine once again.

Doesn't she feel what I feel? Does she remember me at all?

Just another face in her crimson room of pain?

Spinning on my heel, I leave and cross the street. Even in the height of a summer's afternoon, the opposite alleyway is cast in shadow. The place I come to battle with the war between my head and my heart.

A direct line of sight through the arched window that outlines her hourglass figure settling onto the same spot it always does. Leggings hug her rounded ass, mocking me with their snugness. The black T-shirt that appears normal at the front is exposed in the back, revealing an array of artwork amongst the corset-style laces.

Drawing her silky long hair over one shoulder, she throws her head back in laughter. The first I've seen. The one I've yet to experience myself. A dulled sting across my knuckles is the only sign I've broken something, my arm extended into the brick. This has gone beyond basic attraction.

We're bordering on *fatal* attraction from here on out.

I crave her every smile. Yearn for her undivided attention. Ache for her every breath to fan against my pebbled skin. To go through life without knowing the ferocity of my need for her may be a shame, but the time isn't right. To successfully win her will be a result of knowing her.

Fucking up isn't an option.

Vibrations filter from the pocket of my slacks, the twittering ring alerting me to the incoming business call that I shouldn't be receiving at all today. As if a note in all of my diary's stating that I'm out of the office isn't enough. I've given my life to my companies. This is my time for... *whatever* the fuck this is.

My target smiles again. My jealousy is raw and wild as it gnaws at the slushy thing inside of my hard chest. My blood boils. My breathing labored. I could stomp back over there and take out the prick slouched in her recliner, drawing those sweet smiles from her lips, and stab him with the pen in my jacket pocket. But a better idea filters into my mind.

A much more productive one.

The more my phone continues to ring, the more my fury grows.

I draw it out from my pocket with a meditated calmness.

There's only one call I need to make. Hitting the speed dial without ever taking my eyes from her curvy frame, I lift the cell.

"Huntie? Where are you?" The feminine voice coils around the shell of my ear. The slight squeak hasn't irritated me before, since usually it's silenced by my cock filling her throat, but now...

Now my balls shrivel up, cutting any form of circulation from my body and severing any hopes of an heir to my fortune.

Not that a shrewd bastard like me would deserve one.

"Huntie baby? Are you there?"

"Get in the jet, fly home. We're over, I never want to see your face or hear your name again," I bark. Hanging up the phone, I release my grip and it smashes into the concrete. Slamming the heel of my dress shoe into the screen, I put an end to any following calls and return to the task at hand.

From that moment on, I silence all logical reasoning. All

thoughts, in fact, that dare to pull me from my mission. I refuse to let this ungodly woman out of my sight.

Because let's face it.

Once I sink my claws into her, she won't be anything other than unholy.

Whether I'm deluded, or my heart has simply settled on its prey, I won't break this infatuation.

I'll thrive from it.

Lean into it.

The slight sway of her black hair as she works, a trance.

The soft hums that escape her lips as she sings to herself, a lullaby.

The wide eyes that pool with the deepest blues, a new reality.

It's all meant for me, just as *she* is.

You're in my sights now, Little Siren, and I'm not letting you go.

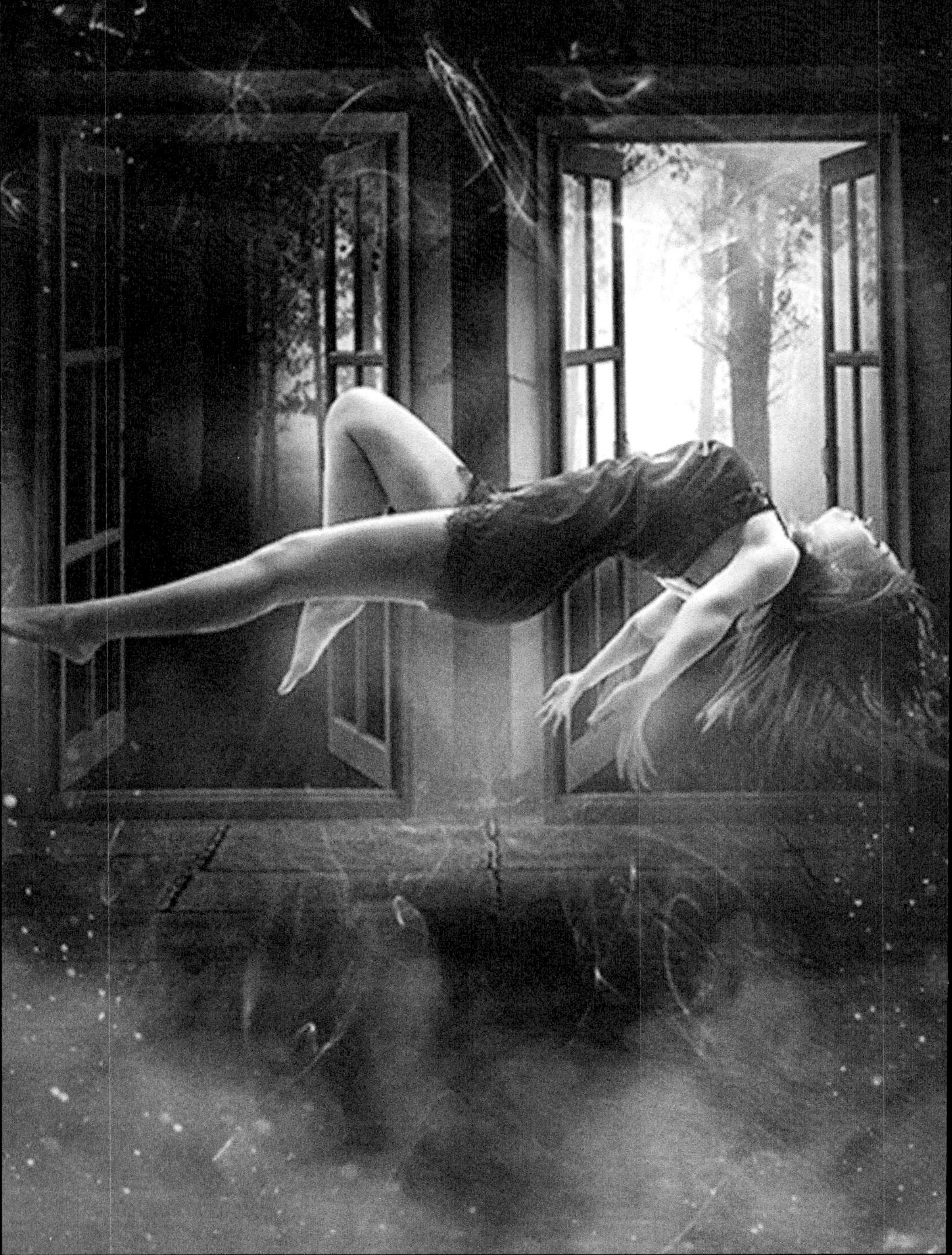

CHAPTER ONE

Astra
This Mess - Tyler Posey

"Touch me again, and the only thing you'll be swallowing is my fist shoved down your throat," I hiss, my eyes filled with the fury of my venomous words trained on the fuckwit that just asked me to sit on his face so he could swallow my sweet juices. He then thought it would be a good idea to touch my ass. Now his face is pressed against the stone wall in Benny's.

Naturally, I've had a long fuck of a day and my stomach is cramping with empty rumbles, and all the assholes of Krosslife City are out on the prowl, hitting up a range of the nightclubs along the strip. Not my usual Friday night plans, but not even the temptation of a luxurious meal with Jess at our favorite booth in the Empire could convince me to stay away from my bed a moment longer.

Seriously not after today.

I woke up late, then my car-choked for half an hour before it started and I got to work. My clients were tedious and squirmy. I usually like the squirmy ones, it's fun to watch their discomfort, but today, all I wanted was my bed. It called to me like a starving lover and I wanted nothing more than to sink into its embrace.

So I canceled on Jess for our weekly dinner date. I'm now picking up takeout and I should make it home just before the storm hits so I can sit in the bay windows and watch as the heavens riot against the lands.

My favorite thing.

Living in the outskirts of Forest County in the suburbs, the commute from work will be delayed enough without dickheads pissed out of their minds thinking they can touch my ass without permission.

"Woah now, pretty lady! He never meant no harm by it," one of his pals drawls, intending to touch my shoulder before I turn scornful eyes on him. His hand hovers in the air before he lets it fall back to his side with a shrug. "Okay, maybe he did. But how about you just let him go and we leave, aye?"

"How about you learn to respect women?" I counter. "I'm not yours. I will never be yours. Guess what that means?" I twist the man's arm higher up his back and he yelps, crying out from the pain that has a smile gracing my lips and his two friends turning white. "You don't get to touch what doesn't belong to you. Now fuck off, I've had a shit day and you're only making it worse." I step back and let him go. He slumps forward and the three of them flee for the street like out there will treat them any better.

I highly doubt their night is going to be trouble free, but they are gone now and I'm hungry, so fuck them. I turn back to the counter and the young girl standing behind it looks at me sheepishly. "Are you okay?" she asks with such a timid voice, it angers me she has to deal with things like this. Especially for how young she looks.

"I'm fine." I smile back at her, hoping to ease the trepidation I see in her brown doe-eyes.

"I'm so -"

"- Don't," I cut in, a little harshly. She draws back, eyes round. "Never apologize on behalf of a vile man, sweetie. This world will swallow you whole and spit you out, only once they have chewed you, you'll be nothing but shreds of the person you once were if you let them." I lean forward, dipping my head so my eyes hold hers. "Don't let them. Don't show them."

"Show them what?" she breathes, trembling more now than when I was assaulting the douchebag who seems to be a regular around here. To break the hold of my stare, she meekly tucks a strand of hair behind her ear and reaches for the bag sitting on the hot plates.

"Don't show them your fear. Or you'll never know what it's like to be unafraid ever again." I finish strong because this moment could be the game changer in her fate the next time that, or any, dickface rolls back around. Taking the bag from her, the heat warms my hands as the smell of all the things bad for my heart waft around me, making my mouth water and my tummy growl.

"Have a good night, and tell the prick checking his phone out back to come deal with the drunks."

Then I leave, the door dinging closed behind me as I walk toward my car with a headache and starvation souring my mood. Yanking open the car door, I settle into my seat and place the bag on my lap, diving straight in. I can't wait until I get home, or I'll likely chomp on my steering wheel. Flicking on the engine, the heated seats turn on at the same time as the stereo.

"Won't Go Back Again" by Megan Mckenna bursts throughout the car and I roll my eyes thinking of my best friend Jess. She's a bleeding heart and *"I will never go back to that asshole again,"* her favorite phrase. Turning it down to background noise, I open the compartment and pull out some napkins before pulling out a sticky BBQ rib.

Fuck me, I have one hell of a saucy orgasm whipping up for this bad boy.

I'm a curvy girl, a figure to be desired. But that wasn't by design. I eat like a trucker and drink like a sailor. Have a mouth like one too.

But meat?

The food of the gods as far as I'm concerned. I suck the bone, savoring the juices as I chew the succulent and tender meat, then reach for a wing. Just as I'm able to devour it, a scream tears through the night and I narrow my eyes. Twisting in my seat, I search the shadows but as quickly as the horrifying shrill of pain reaches me, it just as quickly fades into nothing. Furrowing my brows over sleepy lids, I question whether what I heard was out of pain or pleasure. Either way, no fucker ever looked out for me but myself so I'm not about to go hunting for trouble that doesn't concern me. Instead, I make the smart decision to pack away the rest of my food for home, clean my hands and pull out of the lot, driving deeper into the shadows that seem to follow me.

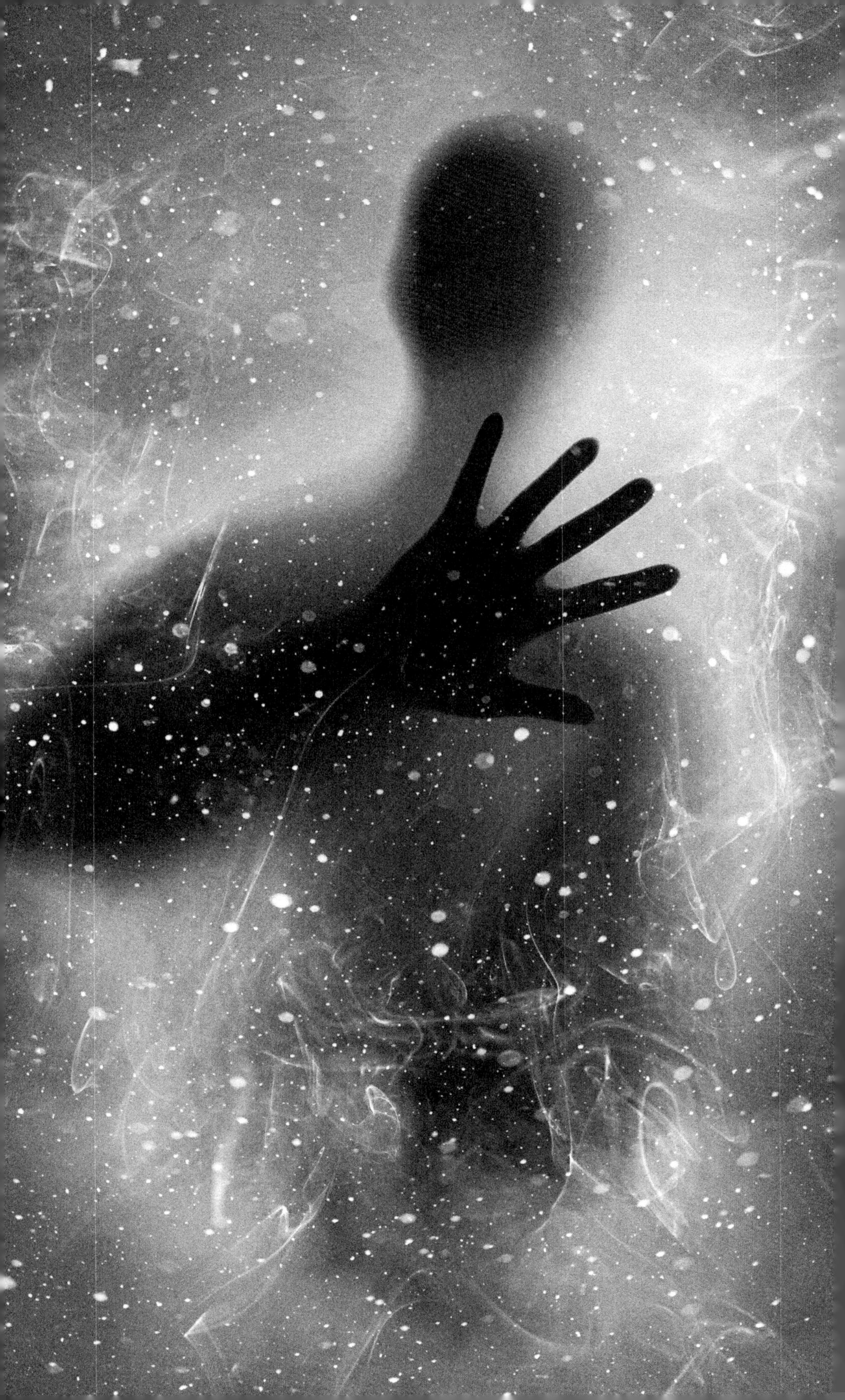

CHAPTER
TWO

Hunter
Cry Baby - American Avenue

They scream like cowards.
　　　I guess that is because they are.
　　　Squealing, snorting cowards praying to a God they don't believe in just to be freed from my wrath. That in itself is a wickedly beautiful thing.

The sound of terror.

And it's all fucking mine.

Only sleazy cunts grope a woman with no issue in violating their personal space as if they were entitled to it.

As if it was their right to violate my girl in the first place.

Unlucky for them, I have no issue in violating the space of pervy bastards. So, I guess we were all doing things tonight we shouldn't be.

Because I most definitely shouldn't be killing in the name of obsession.

I most definitely shouldn't enjoy it either.

I bleed from the shadows, my frustration growing by the second as I grit my jaw and crack my neck.

"Get up," I demand, stalking my prey like a vulture. "Fight like a man."

"Why are you doing this?" The drunk who touched my woman asks from his knees, hands clasped behind his head as I point my gun directly at the back of his skull.

"I-I, please! *Don't*," one of his pals sobs. His blond hair darkens in the lack of light in the alley, his fearful eyes turn to mine and he shudders in horror when the only thing he sees is absolutely nothing but the darkness that harbors what used to be my soul.

All that's left now is a nightmare.

"I'm growing tired of the back and forth. You will kill each other and be thankful I'm allowing you a semi-honorable death at each other's hands. Men like you, don't deserve to walk the earth. Touching what doesn't belong to them," I end on a low growl.

Patience waning, I sigh. Weary of the tedious time I'm spending here when I could be in Forest County, watching my woman as she sleeps like an angel cocooned within the veil of silken shadows that befalls the dark corners of her bedroom.

"The winner," I add with a hike of my dark brow, "gets to walk away with their life." The incentive is enough to get the reaction that I want. Blondie starts throwing punches with a vengeance, the brown-haired man with golden highlights not standing a chance in hell from the flurry of a vicious assault that has blood spewing from his mouth and the once sturdy bones of his face now shattering under the heavy fist which knocks him out cold. He flies backward, head thumping on the concrete with a stomach-churning whack as his skull cracks.

But that doesn't stop the monster on top of him.

Blondie rains down malicious punch after malicious punch and it's fucking glorious. I tilt my head, watching as he heaves every breath. As the sweat glistens along his tanned skin, his muscles ripple and flex under each controlled moment of his attack.

"Leon, stop!" The guy on his knees screams as I push the head of the gun deeper into the back of his head. "Stop it! That's Brady, man, you're killing Brady! He's your brother!"

Well, I never saw that one coming.

That is the thing about mental warfare, though. Once you play with the strings of the mind, you can easily reroute the basic survival instincts that linger there.

Tonight, I gave them an option.

To survive the hands of death, or to give themselves over to the man himself.

Like most people, this man feared what he never could understand.

So many people misconstrue what it means to die.

They feel like it's the end, instead of the beginning of eternal life without burden and worry.

Without turmoil and anguish.

On the other side, there is nothing but peace without the emotion of a harrowed suffering that suffocates you with every passing day from the infliction.

I chuckle, shaking my head. "Little more, dick. I'm not sure he's dead yet."

"You're a sick fuck! Why the fuck are you doing this?" the poor excuse for a man at my mercy screams, the cogs in his inebriated brain finally starting to work. "Touching what doesn't belong to us? That woman? Are you talking about that fucking bitch?"

I pull the trigger, watching with cold contempt as the back of his skull bursts wide open like the unleashing of a bear trap. Blood gushes from him, spraying in a large arch as fragments of skull dance within the night air like tiny specs of dimly lit stars before they tumble to the ground.

For a moment, he sways, unsteady on his knees, slurring his words before he slumps forward and thunders to the ground. Leon shrieks, flying backward as if he was recoiling from the hit himself. Cowering, he covers his head with his arms as he cries uncontrollably, too lost in his terror that even if I tried talking to him, he wouldn't even notice. He quivers, trembling like a leaf in the wind so I stalk closer to him and pull the trigger once again.

Tossing the gun on the ground, my leather-clad hands tug on the sleeves of my shirt as I right myself once more. The Devil's hitman, handing him yet more scum from these vermin-ridden streets. Knocking Brady with my shoe, he groans and I quickly bring the heel of my loafer down on his forearm. I wasn't lying when I said the winner would walk free, and in my world - I always win.

My breath billows before me as I prowl from the alley, into the night and toward my Mustang, ready to hunt down my Astra.

My Siren.

The woman I just killed for. *Again.*

I pull out my phone and thumb on the screen. It lights up as I scroll looking for the number that I need. After one ring, someone answers, "Blue Orchids, twelve dozen delivered by six am tomorrow? I know the place." The elderly woman reels off my usual order without me needing to much more than grunt. I hang up and pocket my phone, breathing out slowly.

After tonight, I think my love will need a little pick-me-up. Every girl loves a romantic as much as a loyal protector, and I'll be damned if I'm not the thing that picks her up when she falls.

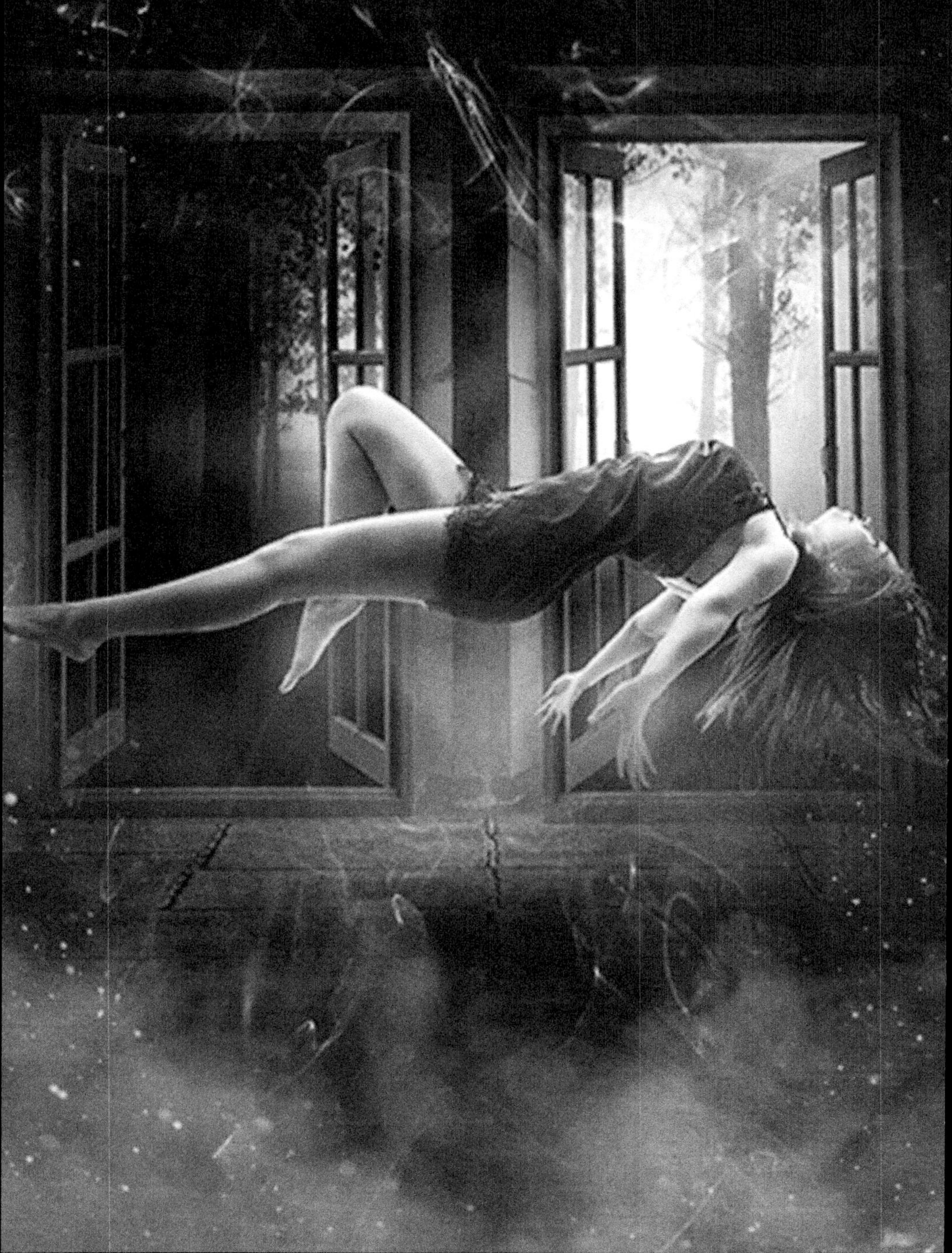

CHAPTER
THREE

Astra
What's Going On - The Snuts

"For the love of all things cars, would you fucking start already?" I growl, turning the key one last time as the engine turns over and chokes to a stuttering stop.

I seriously don't want to catch the bus. I was able to bail on dinner last month when that creep touched me in Benny's due to exhaustion and now this month, I'm just as tired. I want to bail again tonight, but if I have to take the bus, I know I'll cave for the simple fact that by the time I lock up the shop, I'll have an hour to kill before the next bus even arrives. I'm a good girl, I know how important our dinner dates are to Jess, but sometimes I'm too tired to even open my eyes let alone deal with people.

I just don't like people.

I huff in frustration and slam my tiny fist against the wheel. Accidentally knocking the horn, I scream into the wail of it, allowing the blare to conceal the shriek of my stress. Reaching over to the passenger seat, I grab my handbag and throw it over my shoulder.

I'm not usually a handbag kind of girl, but this beauty was a gift from one of my clients, and not even I can deny the call of red leather with chain detailing along the sides. If only I knew which client in particular dropped it off, I'd have been able to thank him or her properly.

Riffling through the contents, I pull out my headphones, shove the port into my phone and bring up "Dr. Feelgood" by Motley Crue. After one good slam to my driver's side door, I stomp the two-mile walk to the nearest bus stop pissed as all hell.

The dark clouds bleed into a cherry red and the first rays of the morning sun breaking through the gloom are the only things keeping me from allowing my day to start off with a looming cloud over my head. It's too artistic not to find beauty in, and I have the sudden urge to sketch the spectacularly soulful elegance of mother nature.

Bobbing my head and mindfully rocking out with the Crue, I pull out my sketch pad and pencil. I know the route to the bus station by heart, and as usual there is low traffic around the suburbs, so with one deep sigh I start to draw. Looking out toward the skyline of the city that sits far off into the distance, hidden behind the morning fog which coils higher, I find a moment of calm. The trees surround us with a forest that makes the perimeter of Forest County. It's stunning and full oaks become a lush contrast to the brooding sky above, in comparison to the city.

So tall and aged, withered with deep knowledge. Every time I look out into the mountains just beyond the woodlands, my heart soars with the flight of a majestic bird. One that could soar so far from here, my tiny insignificant life would be but a spec behind me.

Dropping my head, I opt for losing myself in my art for a while instead. That's about the best I can manage with my two feet rooted to the ground. Before I know it, I'm sitting on the bus and heading into the city. I almost miss my stop, but luckily for me this is as far as the bus goes. We only have one direct line from Forest County into Krosslife City, then it shifts over to the city buses that get you anywhere else you need to in lack of a hurry.

"Ma'am, this is your stop," Daniel tells me politely as he looks over his shoulder from the driver's seat.

"Come on, Dan. How many times do I have to tell you? My name is Astra," I chastise as I place my things away neatly into my bag and stand. As I walk down the aisle, I narrow my eyes and shake my head in displeasure. "How many years have you been driving this bus? How often do I take it?"

"I have been driving this bus for as long as you have been born, young lady. Yet, you will always be ma'am. My mama raised me right." He winks with a firm nod and those aged eyes of his settle any turmoil I had from the start of my morning.

I chuckle softly and reach over to pat him on the shoulder. "Have a good day, okay? Don't work too hard and tell Shelly I said hey."

"Will do. The Mrs. is cooking pot roast tonight, so I'm counting down the hours till I get back to her."

I smile at him as I step down from the bus with a few other passengers and stand on the sidewalk, waiting for him to pull away with a genuinely warm smile on my face. He's a good soul, has always been kind to me on the days my ass has become all too familiar with the bus seats. My car is pretty reliable, but we get into a spat every now and then because I'm too cheap to take her somewhere nice like the service station.

I screw up my nose and exhale harshly. The air still carries that wet dog smell that comes after a heavy rain. It poured in the late hours of the night, the puddles still ankle-deep along the streets. It rains a lot here and I freaking love it.

A car comes zooming down the road and I frown, not quick enough to get out of the way of an oncoming shower as the prick drives straight into the pool of water and sends a torrent of its waves high into the air. I gasp, sucking all of the morning's cold winds into my lungs and tense my body tightly. My eyes snap shut and I hold my breath, waiting for it to hit me.

Instead, a dark shadow falls across my face, eclipsing the early rays of the morning sun and I slowly blink open my eyes. The arch of an umbrella conceals me, as the handle spins in ungodly hands. Masculine and large, they twirl the end of the umbrella artfully as they shake off the excess water and I watch in amazement as the droplets sprinkle back into the air, falling flat along the ground while I stay nice and dry.

I turn to look at my savior, but all I see is the suit-clad back of a man who quickly draws a veil of darkness over himself, hiding from my sights as he walks in the opposite direction.

My brows furrow and I pout, shouting, "Well thanks!"

Would it have killed him to just look at me?

How can a man be so arrogant and so thoughtful all at once? Maybe he had a business meeting or something, but he could have at least given me the chance to say thank you properly. Jeez, my frustration is back in full swing.

That's what this city does to me, but hey, I have to earn money somewhere.

Blowing out a chilling breath, I make my way toward the store and groan when I see Hazel waiting outside for me. She wasn't supposed to be in for another hour.

"You're early," I state as I place the key in the lock and jiggle it open.

"And you're not - which can only mean you've had car trouble again. So I knew you'd be cranky, and I thought I know what'll cheer you up - coffee and my dazzling conversation for an hour before my shift." She grins offensively as she hands me a massive coffee blast from Joy's Diner. It's a two-liter thermal coffee mug she sells for ten dollars.

It's a heavenly fucking addiction and when the smell of caramel drifts to my nose, my shoulders slump and I groan for a whole other reason.

"Thank you," I mutter genuinely.

"You're welcome," she singsongs. "Bad morning?"

"Understatement," I grunt as I take my bag from over my shoulder and throw it onto the receptionist's desk. "As you've already guessed, my car wouldn't start. Then an asshole, driving like a prick, almost drenched me in a puddle, until some mystery man saved me and walked off before I could even thank him. Not to mention last night." I blow out a breath as I flip the sign hanging in the window to open.

"What happened last night?" Slinking into a seat, although not behind her desk, I pout at the fact that she is actually not going to work for an entire hour but bug me instead.

Don't get me wrong, she is an honestly nice person and a better employee than I could have asked for. I'm just not, nor would I ever be, a people person. God, the thought of speaking to people gives me anxiety. I don't know what it is, but there is something about a social life that has always chafed wrongly against me and I guess that makes me a freak. People should love having friends and enjoying their lives, but honestly?

I've never rated it.

There are so many emotions that plague a person outweighing the moments of good that could ever possibly happen. Dark thoughts spiral through my mind, my eyes falling heavy and all too quickly, the anguish of the life I've never truly mourned twists my heart painfully in my chest. Tears well against my lash line and I bat them away, refusing to let the sorrow in.

Refusing to drown under the ocean of grief that will kill me dead, if I ever let it in.

It may not be healthy, but when the alternative to grieving is dealing with the desolation of a loss impossible to bear, a girl has got to do what a girl has got to do in order to survive another day.

My phone buzzes and I pull it from my pocket. Seeing *mom* flashing across the screen with a photo of her from a different time, a different version of herself, I throw it onto the counter and disregard it when it skids across the surface and falls to the ground on the other side. Hazel looks at me in confusion but when she sees the look on my face, she closes her open mouth. If I answer right now, with the dark demon that has taken over my soul, it will only end in an argument worse than the last.

Truth is, my mom is not the person I once knew, and after we lost *them*...neither am I.

The bell above the door rings and I can't bring myself to put on my game face, so as I glare down at the papers on the desk, I don't see who walks in.

"Oh, wow," Hazel breathes, and with such awe, it has me snapping my eyes toward her in curiosity.

An ocean of blue fills the doorway and it takes a moment to see the courier underneath the plethora of Orchids. He walks in, shuffling on his feet as he struggles with holding the shit ton of flowers in his arms. *Not this again.*

"Excuse me?" I start, walking around the desk and toward him. He stumbles forward and I catch him, relieving him of a bouquet that covers his face. "I've already had this conversation with your manager. You keep bringing your bouquets to the wrong address. Unless these Orchids need some ink, this is the wrong store."

"Astra? Astra Stone?" he stutters, the weight getting too heavy for his frail bones to handle.

"Oh for God's sake," I sigh. "Hazel, take them from him before he falls over and we end up with a lawsuit." Together, we remove some of the flowers and place them gently on the floor by his feet.

"Oh, thank you, thank you so much! Who knew one hundred and forty-four flowers would be so damn heavy. Last time I deliver a baker's dozen, that's for sure!"

"I can see that, but as I said, sir, you have the wrong address." My clipped tone betrays any politeness I was attempting to portray.

"I don't think so," the kid, no more than twenty, shakes his chestnut-covered head. "Astra Stone at Sirens Ink. This is Sirens Ink, isn't it?" he questions with furrowed brows as he looks around the parlor looking for a sign. "You're the only parlor in the city, right?"

He was right. Not long after I opened the doors a little over a year ago, all of the other tattoo parlors went out of business. I mean, there were only two others, but it sure did make me question if I could make this store a success. Especially considering it was so sudden and mysterious. They almost seemed to disappear into the night.

But so far so good.

"Yes, but who the hell would continually send me blue orchids?" Besides the fact they are my favorite flowers - they remind me of the sea - there is also the small fact that not a soul alive would know that.

Not even my own mother would know that.

"No other details have been left I'm afraid. It's an anonymous delivery, but there is a card." He bends down, shifting through the bundle of flowers until he finds a card.

Passing it to me, my frown deepens.

To a better day, Siren.

I hiss through my teeth, inhaling a quick and brutal breath at the note. I am too enraptured by the words to notice the man leave or Hazel falling to her knees to smell the stunning array of petals. Circular puddles of the purest blue beckon me to stroke them as much as I want to reject them. Yet something urges me to look up, glancing through the windows, and search the shadows. I feel drawn there, but only darkness greets me.

"Who sent them?" Hazel breaths.

"Like I said, wrong store. I'm nobody's Siren."

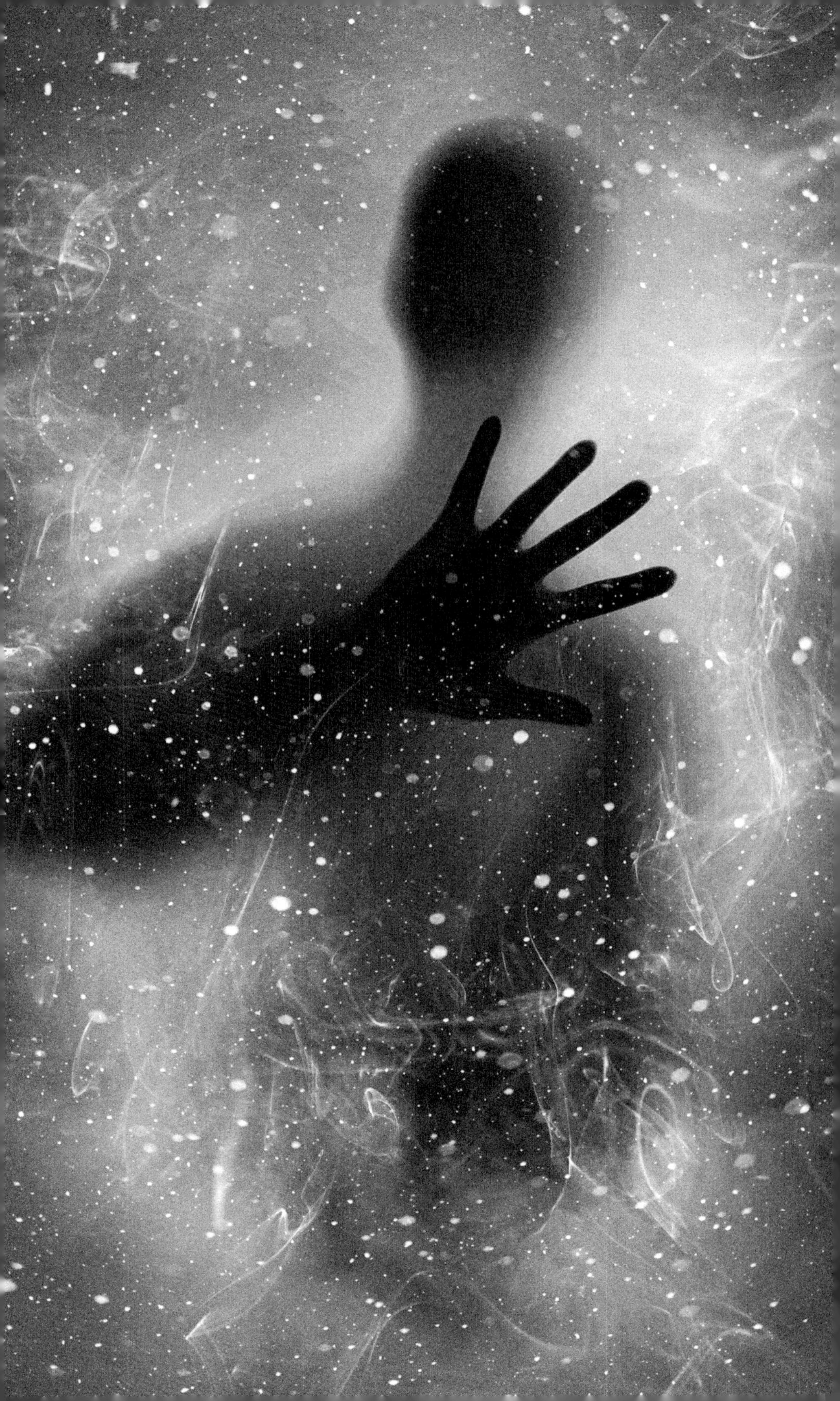

CHAPTER
FOUR

Hunter
Ocean Eyes - American Avenue

The baker's dozen of blue orchids sit dotted around Astra's cozy cottage home. The smell is potent in the air as I stalk through the shadows, keeping to the corners of the darkened rooms. Half a sleep, she lazily lolls her legs about as she raises them and leaves them hanging in the air, tired from another hard day working her sweet little ass off in nothing but tiny shorts and a cami. Her dark and silky-looking locks sit tussled at the back of her head in a messy bun and she couldn't look more endearing, more captivating to a man who is never so easily enthralled.

Most of the lights are off, all apart from the dragon lamp sitting on a side table in the sunroom that she's using as a dim light to read another one of her dark and spicy romance books. The floor is covered in multiple throws and fluffy pillows as she lays on her back, gazing up at the stars between the lines of the page she is reading. Her ample breasts rise higher on her chest, threatening to spill from the cups of her bra as she hums softly. I'm enraptured as her breathing grows heavy, the heaving of her jumping tits almost a real delectable taste that sweetens the air.

I lick my lips, biting back a groan that vows to roar free.

There is something so sensual about being here, a few feet away from her, and her not having any idea about it. I'm a deeply penetrating abyss that follows her everywhere, encloses her like a cape wrapped around her head and she has absolutely no idea that I even exist. That I'm the moving silhouette she sees in the darkness.

That I saw her and declared to never, *ever*, let her go.

Oh, the fun games that we play.

She is the unsuspecting little prey and I'm the big bad predator that she wouldn't be safe from even if the bars of a cell separated me from her.

My intense focus bleeds through her skin, watching as a delicate hand caresses the length of her curves before she dips them between the valley of her thighs. She moans, back arching and head thrashing as she circles her tight little numb with a firm stroke of her thumb. My breathing grows coarse and thick, aching throughout my chest as I fight to keep myself quiet.

To my own ears, my harsh breaths sound like a steam train pulling into the station. I shiver, my entire body unable to calm as my reaction and my mind war with one another. I sweat, cold and clammy as I inch forward a little closer to the light, forced from the shadows and compelled to witness her lust. The potent scent of her sweet, sweet cunt hits me and I grunt, tight eyes snapping wide open in panic hoping she never heard me.

She doesn't.

She is too busy, hand dipping beyond the waistline of those tiny shorts right now as she plays with herself. My eyes burn a hole through the fabric, imagining what it will look like to see her wet fingers slipping with ease inside her slick pussy.

Watching as her tight walls flutter around her digits, holding her close. Refusing to let her go until she owns the release I can sense is brewing in her core.

I beat my dick harder, faster as I abuse it with my impulsive strength. The crown of my thick head bulges, the shiny skin stretched tautly as I give my foreskin little room to move. Imagining her tight mouth wrapped around me, holding me back so the delicate shaft of my raging cock feels the raw sensations of her tongue licking against me, has my eyes rolling back in my head.

This is it, Sweet Little Siren. This is it.

I think to myself as my eyes sting, wide open and refusing to close so I won't miss a second of this glorious woman stretched out before me.

Those damn shorts are in the way of what I need to see most.

"Oh fuck, fuck. *Knox!*" she exclaims in sensual delight as she comes all over her hand, screaming the name of the man in the book she's reading. It lays open on her stomach, her ass rocking her hips into her hand more forcefully, steadily slowing down as her release ebbs.

The fuck did she just say?

That's it, the book gets it too. As soon as she's out, that fucking book and those damn shorts are going to meet the flames of hell.

Nobody gets my woman's screams. Not even a fictional book boyfriend.

Hunters never share their prey and this Hunter is no fucking different.

My release dies in my hand and my fury only grows. I'm a man of ill temper when it comes to what belongs to me. But I can't deny how beautiful my girl looks all hot and flushed, her soft cheeks scarlet. A trash can clatters to the ground somewhere outside and my whole body gets snatched taunt. I narrow my eyes, searching for a threat.

Astra barely glances over her shoulder, looking out into the darkness, and with a sigh, rolls to her knees and stumbles to her feet heading towards the kitchen.

I follow quickly, making sure to stay in the darkened shadows as I round the corner and duck under the staircase she hardly uses. Peering out, dick still swinging free in the wind, I watch as she leans over her waste disposal and opens a window. I narrow my eyes when a small fluffy head pops from the bleak background and meows.

Scoffing, I shake my head.

"Come on, you little shit, you know the drill. Two seconds then you're back on the streets getting the word out that a crazy woman lives here and instead of loving on cats, she boils them for stew," Astra mumbles and I smirk, knowing how much shit she is talking right now.

She bends, thick ass sticking out as she opens a cupboard under the sink and pulls out a bag of cat food and a bowl to fill with water and heated milk. Placing it on the ground, she firms her back to the unit and slides down it until her ass hits the cold floor. Reaching out a tender hand, she strokes the gray cat while she devours her food and laps up her heated beverage.

Astra always talks a big game, she's an absolute anti-social chick if I've ever seen one, but it's all an act to hide that big heart of hers. One that's been broken one too many times. I growl, thinking of the one person on my kill list who I just haven't yet been able to quite reach. I know enough by watching their interactions to know that someone who hurts her frequently is her rich-bitch mother.

But I need more information than that before I can slit her throat.

I mean, most people argue with their parents. But the look in Astra's eyes every time she gets off the phone with that woman is gutting. Something so deeply rooted that looks like anguish takes permanent residence in her gaze and I hate it.

"I don't know, Gray. Maybe I should just bite the bullet and become a crazy cat lady who loves on them instead? I mean, it's not that I don't love your fluffy ass anyway, it's just it would hurt a lot less if you decided to leave me, y'know?"

The cat she named Gray, simply because the thing is gray, purrs at her, trotting to her side to butt her hand with her little head. "I know, I know. But they all say that. *I'll never leave, I'll be around forever* and then bang, in a flash of smoke, I'm alone again."

A forlorn expression consumes her soft features and my heart wrenches in my chest knowing exactly what she's talking about. I never knew her then. There was nothing I could do to save her, but I can protect her from feeling that pain again.

Gray mewls, her chest rumbling. "Hey hey, yeah, listen. This is about me right now, kay? Keep your street life to yourself," she pouts and I chuckle silently at her quirks. "Anyway, you little shit, that's your two minutes up. I'm going to start billing you for these damn therapy sessions. Out you go." She stands, picking Gray up and snuggling her close to her chest, taking a moment to kiss the top of her head and just hold her before she places her on the ledge and watches her slowly stalk back into the night.

Once she closes the window, she heads for her bedroom and I whisper to the shadows, *"I'll never leave you, Siren."*

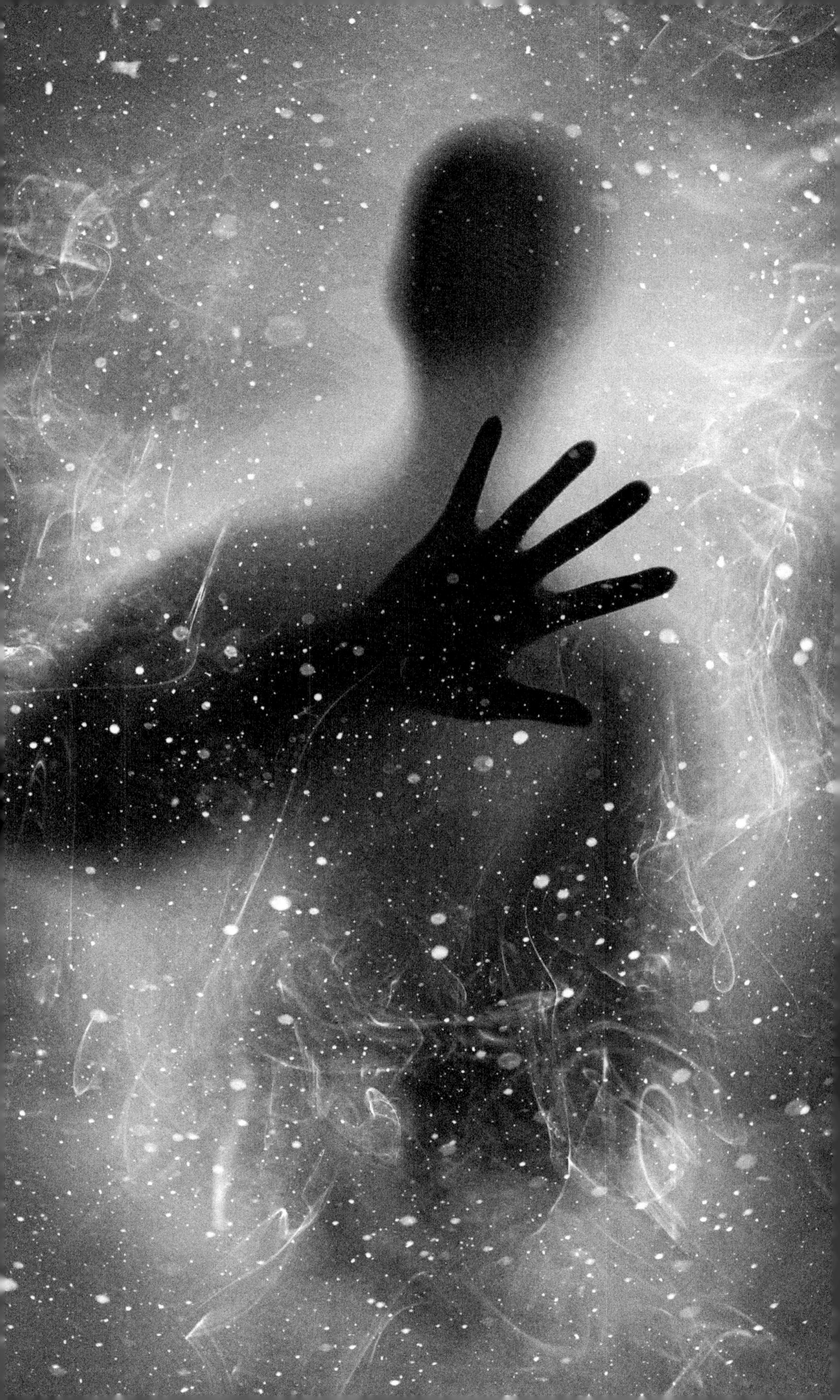

CHAPTER
FIVE

Hunter
Every Breath You Take - The Police

The moonlight cuts through the baleful clouds as they part like a laced veil. They highlight the angelic beauty of the goddess that stands spotlighted under the low street lighting. She appears to me as a wicked angel with a glowing yellow halo wrapped around her raven black hair. My heart hammers within my chest, beating a pattern of desire into the ribs that encase it as I move like a silent sentinel within the shadows and follow the woman that has ensnared me within her enchantment for over a year.

It's been months now. Months of watching and wishing.

Wishing she knew I was here. Wishing I could tell her.

Tell her that I'm paying attention, that I *see* her, and always will keep her safe.

But she doesn't know.

She'll *never* know who I am.

I'm too enraptured with her to break the trance, step forward into the light and introduce myself as her savior and her nightmare.

It would be so easy, only there isn't enough time. Even a mere second will take away from the tender moment of me tracing the lines of her features and sketching them forever into the walls of my dangerous mind.

My *memory*.

If I look away... I might forget.

I might miss a new tender look she'll have in those ocean blues, or a different kind of world-awakening smile she may have sparking grace across her lips. She is often sullen, hidden in a sense of sadness I don't know how to explore. She flutters about in her day-to-day life. But sometimes, when she thinks nobody is looking, a moment of calm bleeds in through her armor of defense.

She could fade from existence if I don't hold onto her with a vicious grasp. If I break the trance, the moment I'm looking at her now could very well become my last.

No, I can't have that.

She locks the door behind her as she leaves Siren Ink Tattoo Parlor on another unsuspecting day, a Friday evening, and heads out into the night.

She's a vision.

A dark and tormenting dream I just can't wake from.

My little siren.

How beautifully she lures me in.

No, I'm happy like this.

Stalking, learning, watching...

She's my prey and I'm the wicked predator that becomes the danger your mother warns you lurks in the shadows.

I'm fine with being the protection that lingers in the veil of darkness and the whisper that echoes throughout the night. The uncertainty that she feels feathering down her spine. The eyes prickled at the back of her nape.

Nothing but a sense in the back of her mind that the air around her is displaced, shared with another presence.

The breeze drifts past and takes with it the billowing strands of her raven black hair. She stiffens, looking out into the darkness as she senses the primal man that skulks there.

I smile, cruel and savage at the thought of her sensing me without ever seeing me at all. Those watchful eyes of hers flicker back and forth along the lines of the abyss. They land on mine and all the air stills within my burning lungs. I hold my breath, wondering, waiting...

Has she seen me?

The moment seems to stretch on forever until she sighs deeply in resignation and continues on her way.

In a rush, the stifling air is ripped from my agonizing lungs and I grin darkly, matching her step for step.

What a fun game we play.

Tonight she's dressed up, her full and thick lips are painted in a deep crimson red that has my cock straining in my tented jeans. I groan painfully as I reach down and readjust myself.

Tight blue jeans wrap around her curvy thighs and sit a little short around the ankle, hinting at her silken, tanned flesh hidden beneath the fabric. Flat-soled pumps sit comfortably on her feet as a black blazer, rolled up at the sleeves sits on top of a red, low-cut blouse.

She's going out tonight.

It's a good job I'm here.

Who else will keep her safe? Who else will slay the monsters that dare to convince themselves they could steal a quick taste of what belongs to me? She's been mine for over a year, and she'll be mine for many more years to come.

Until death parts us.

I'm just preparing, for the moment that I can claim her properly. Until I can give her the world, placed at her feet to run or crush beneath her heel as she sees fit.

So that I can step free from the darkness and show myself to her for the first time, in the *right* way.

I needed to know her first.

To learn everything there is to know about her so that I can never get it wrong and I can never mess it up.

It's too important.

I need her to know that she is the center of my world and to do that, I need to learn every single part of hers. She walks for fifteen minutes before she stops outside the Empire - a local, high-class bar and restaurant that's the place to be on a Friday night.

She frequents here with her best friend Jessica once a week so they can catch up. My girl is pretty anti-social, and not in a bad way. She just enjoys her own company and sketching ominous and frightfully beautiful drawings.

The first time I followed her here, I knew it was her favorite. She lit up the room with her stunning smile. She was comfortable and at ease and if that wasn't enough to make me buy the building on the spot, it was when she sat her ass down into one of those booths.

I had it removed the second she left and placed it inside my apartment.

Nobody was going to sit on the same seat that had those succulent rounded globes of hers imprinted into the leather.

Mine.

I growl at the thought and she stops with her hand hovering above the door handle to stare over her shoulder, back into the darkness before she once again dismisses me and turns to walk inside.

One day, when the time is right, I'll gift it to her. She can become the owner and do whatever it is she likes to the place.

The first token of my love.

But definitely not the last.

Written within the lining of the deed to the property, she'll be the queen of it all.

It was one place to start anyway.

The air around me stirs menacingly and I frown, the displeasure heavy in my furrowing brows as I sense another predator close by. I turn my head slowly like a feline in the wild and tilt it to the side. I stop breathing, stilling the world around me as my ears twitch for any sign of movement, any sound that doesn't belong.

There.

Along the street, standing in the yawning mouth of the alley stands a man with a cigarette hanging from his lips and a leering look of evil and filth lingering in the darkness of his eyes. I follow his line of sight and notice him watching my girl.

Interesting.

If he thinks he's going to lay a hand on her, I'll be more than happy to show him what it will look and *feel* like detached from his body as I beat him with it. He steps from the darkness and into the street light as he heads toward the entrance of the Empire. Pulling open the door, he flicks the butt of his cig into the street and heads inside and right on over to my Siren's fucking table.

Fury boils in my veins and a vicious sneer is forced to whisper past my lips as I step forward, ready to expose myself and rip his head from his shoulders all until he reaches their table and leans over to place a soft kiss on Jessica's forehead. She tucks a strand of brown hair behind her ear as she peers up at him through big deep pools of dark brown eyes. It's more of a chaste kiss than a passionate one, not that she seems to notice as her face lights up when he approaches.

But I see him though.

I see *through* him too.

As he takes a seat beside her and slings an arm around her shoulders, it's Siren he watches intently with eyes that must feel like fire ants to her skin if the uncomfortable squirm she does in her seat is anything to go by.

The fire burns hot in my veins as I bide my time. I'll catch him when he leaves, have a few words with him and warn him to stay the fuck away from my girl.

He won't like the man I'll become if doesn't heed my warning. I've killed for a lot less than the sense that this man could be a serious threat to Astra.

The entire evening consists of him gawking at my woman in an insidious leer and the entire *night* consists of her looking away in disgust.

She must sense me. She must feel that I'm here. She *has* to feel it too. How could she not when the connection between us is cosmic? It burns in the stars and lights up the night sky. It filters across galaxies and exists in every plane in the universe.

It's a connection stronger than time itself and will age just as gracefully.

It does something raw and primal to me watching her reject other men. It awakens the carnal need within my core that becomes doused in the sensations of intoxicating lust.

Beyond the veil of light, concealed in the darkness and peering through the abyss, I watch her keenly. Taking my hard and heavy cock in hand, I begin to stroke myself back and forth, imagining it's her that pleasures me.

A reassurance that *I'm* her man.

She'll be on her knees, looking up at me coyly through those ocean blues as she teases me into madness. She'll look so doe-eyed and innocent and when I stare back into those still waters, I'll see the world reflect back at me because *that* is how she will see me.

As her fucking *orbit*.

I'll pull free once she works me into a frenzy, lift her from her knees and bring her to me with my strength. Placing her on my cock, I'll bounce her with ease, hand coils in her thick strands as we gaze longing into the eyes of each other.

Until the aspiration of sweat begins to taunt me with the sensual caress of sweet oblivion, at the moment right before it turns into beaded drops that trail over the ink of my tattoos and down my naked chest as she worships me.

Fuck.

I can feel her everywhere.

Within the walls of my mind, in the thumps of my erratic heart, under the veins of my arousal. In my very dark and twisted fucking soul. She's present like a live entity within my very core and every time I close my eyes, she brands me over and over again with those sinful lips like the burning embers of a steel cattle prod.

I hiss, almost feeling the burn like a flame to my dick as I begin to pump myself even harder, with much more aggression. I become almost hyperactive with the need to dive over that cliff into the sea of burning passion.

I need this.

I need *her*.

"Siren," I breathe, the sound rough and raw as it scrapes free from my dry throat. "Fuck, yes! Siren! That's it, Astra, a little harder. That's it, baby, fuck! I'm so fucking close. Take me, baby, into the back of that fucking pussy, capture me in that sweet fucking womb!" I detonate, exploding all over the worn and weathered brick walls which mark this occasion.

The occasion of my desire, set in brick for all of history, to age like our love throughout the times.

Every time I do this, I leave a part of myself behind. It would be much easier to wear a condom and much less messy. But fuck me if I didn't want the mess. If I didn't want history to know that I was here, with her name on my lips.

I'm a powerful man.

The second I found her, I had to know everything there was to know about her.

So I hired a PI.

The best in the business and he delivered in aces.

My heavy breathing mingles with the cool night air and I shudder, my release rushing through me like a live wire as I salivate at the look at her beyond the window. Laughing musically as she throws her head back at something Jessica has said. The creep next to Jessica smirks, like he's feigning humor just to pass the seconds they remain seated at Siren's regular booth.

Downcasting her head, her hair falls like a veil around her face and those dark ocean eyes peer up into the shadows. The smile cracks and the tiredness creeps in around the edges of her wise eyes.

She normally holds a spark of mischief in her wicked gaze and a problematic smile on her thick lips as she strives to cause a little chaos. But tonight, she looks like she just wants to crawl into bed and the mere act of being energetic and engaging is a chore. After a deep sigh, she turns back to Jessica and smiles, getting up to kiss her friend goodbye, then walks back out into the night. She wraps the blazer around her curvy frame and tilts her head back, breathing in deeply before turning and heading in the direction of her house.

I'm about to follow when the man from the alley kisses Jessica and gets up from the table. She sits, hands folded into her lap as he steps out front and pulls a smoke from the inside of his jacket. He gives her a little wave and smiles back at her as she beams at him with undiluted devotion in her gaze. Right before he steps forward into the shadows, hiding from her sight, her gaze falls to the table.

He takes off after Astra, and follows her down the street, keeping to the edges of the sidewalk as she walks on blissfully unaware of the monsters that are hot on her heels.

Wild frustration collides with vivid anger and I follow the cunt who is following the love of my life, through the night.

He lunges from the shadows and fists a hand into the back of her dark head of hair while he shoves her forward into the brick wall and tries to wrestle her into an alley. She puts up a fight, latching onto the corner of the wall like her life depends on it. Blood pools along her cuticles as she digs into the harsh brick that burns the flesh around her fingertips.

He holds her in an unrelenting vice making it impossible for her to turn around and face him or to get the upper hand in warding off her unsuspected attacker. She cries out in shock. The sound does something horrid to a person. It's like a chime that coils every emotion inside the human body into one huge, vile, and violated shudder that has a person's very soul trembling. It's a sound so raw, and so unexpected, that even the devil feels the waves of it down in the depths of Hell.

Thrashing wildly in his unforgiving grip, she stamps down a heavy foot on top of his with the furious intent to leave a mark. He bellows, yanking her back before thrusting her face first back into the wall even harder than the first time. The harshness chafes across her cheek leaving savage marks that bleed.

She shrieks, the sound fading away into the cool night air that is growing chiller by the second, disorientated from the second assault she falls slightly limp in his arms.

I tear from the shadows, a demon in the night, and throw myself at him. We both fly through the air in a brutal collision, his hold on her head gone as quickly as he held her in his hands. She stumbles on unsteady feet and takes off down the sidewalk choking on a sob without even looking back.

I don't blame her.

She must be terrified, the only thought in her mind is one of survival, especially when she has been hurt, made dizzy and afraid. Just the thought of what he was planning to do to her is enough to make bile churn within the pit of my stomach as it somersaults in revulsion. We land with a loud thud, crashing into the dumpsters down the alley he was trying to drag my Siren into. I throw a hurried look over my shoulder, making sure my girl is safe and out of harm's way before I turn back and let the monster out.

"Want to hurt what's mine?" I sneer, spit flying from my lips in my uncontrolled rage. "Let's see how you like it when you become the plaything to a savage beast like me." Bringing my fist back, I pummel his face with barbaric and murderous assault.

Thundering punches that shatter his human structure.

They are ruthless as I aim for blood. I bring my fists down like the crack of a skin-flaying whip. Bones crack and reshape under my knuckles and I chuckle darkly at the carnage beneath me. Blood splatters, spraying my jaw in crimson speckles and I lick my lips as some of his plasma lands on them.

I hum, run my tongue along my bottom lip, and smile like a crazed loon. "Hmm, tastes just like strawberries and cherries. Is this lip balm?" I ask casually like we're old friends as I look to the sky and think about it. "Dude, are you wearing lip balm?" I choke on another dark and humor-filled laugh as I begin my assault once again.

His eyes fuse shut and swelled beyond the point of balloons as his skin splits and his welted flesh curdles.

I lift his head, my thick and brutal fingers threaded through the strands of his hair as I pound his head into the unforgiving ground.

Over and over again, until the firmness of his skull loses its tension and softens, like a deflated ball as the air is dispelled as a sacrifice back to the earth.

"This what you wanted to do to her, sugar?" I singsong in a southern accent. "Let me guess, she would have loved it, right? What about you? Do you love it?"

He doesn't answer. Not that he could. Instead, he splutters and chokes, vomiting on his own blood as it mingles with the bile that bubbles like acid from his split lips. Something sharp pierces my side, a stitch that filters through my muscles like a vicious ache and forces me to fight to regulate my breathing.

It only takes me a moment, then I finish the job.

Glossy eyes round, bulging from his skull as they turn a lifeless kind of yellow, and the spluttering stops abruptly as he has no more air left in his lungs to fight for. I'm still blinded by the rage, in shock that somebody would even have the sick and twisted thought to hurt a woman like Astra.

Doesn't he know women are gifts?

A perfect package sent by the gods until her man can find her and seal the deal?

Reborn and re-birthed soul mates that go on a journey to find their twin flames in another life?

I found my soul when I found Astra and this man would have tainted that. Destroying it and throwing it away like it was nothing.

I'd kill him all over again if I could.

I'll kill anyone that threatens her.

I'll *kill* to *protect* her.

I stand up from his limp corpse and swipe the back of my arm across my face, trying to wipe away the blood and evidence of what I have just done.

All I can think about is my Siren.

I have to make sure she's okay.

As I stand, I stumble and fall forward. It feels like I've just missed a step and the ground hurries towards my face at a rapid pace before I catch myself.

"What the fuck was that?" I ask, just as I turn to see my body sprawled on top of the dead man and a knife sticking out of my ribs.

The fuck?

My mind is so consumed with Astra, that one moment I'm trying to make sense of the crime scene in front of me, and the next, I'm standing in the shadows of her bathroom listening to her cry, watching her tremble and trying to pull herself together as she cleans the scrapes along her cheek which prickle with little tendrils of blood.

The quick change startles me, and I reach up to place a hand over my racing heart and notice that I'm a pale baby blue, and utterly eerie.

Almost incorporeal.

Like a fucking ghost...

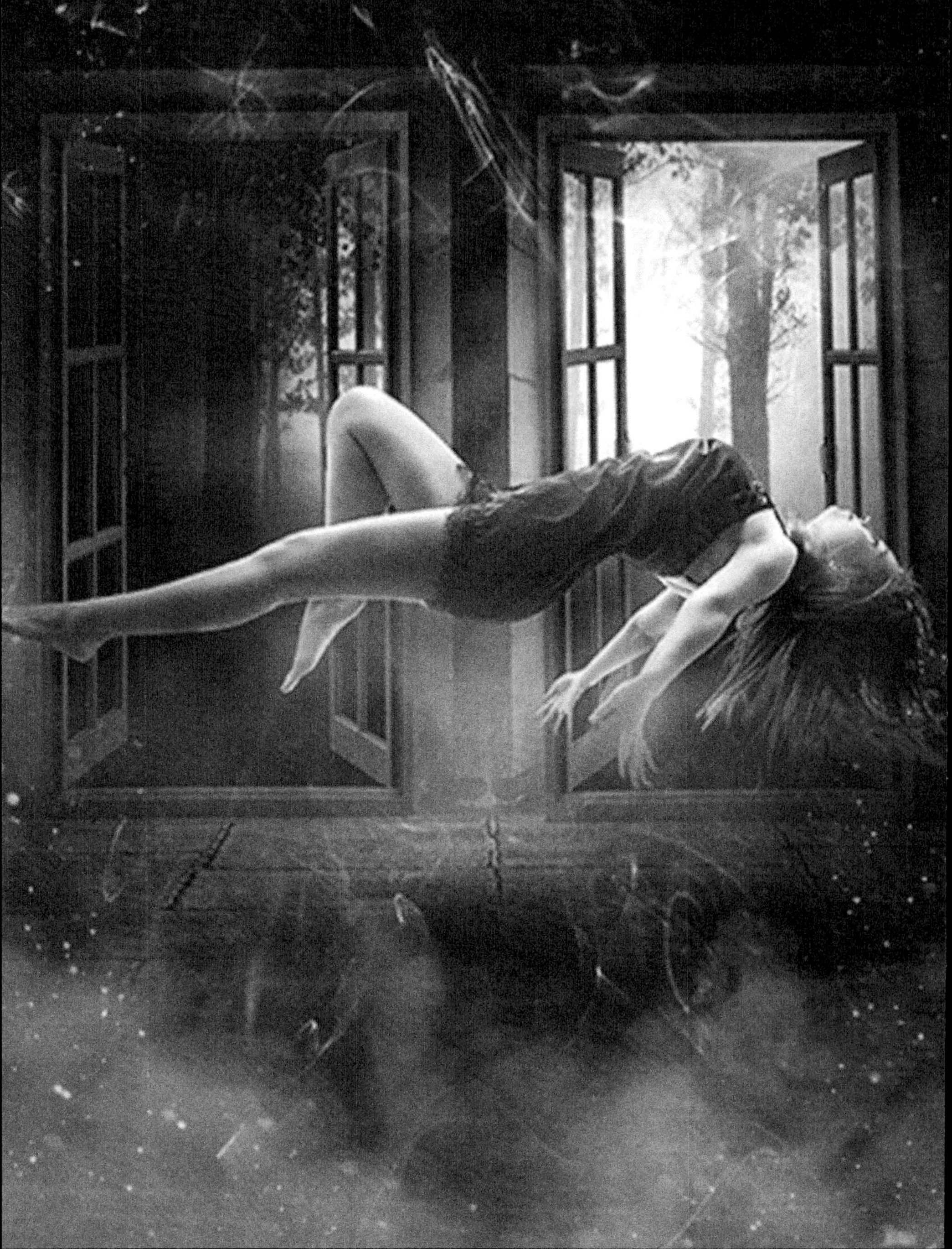

CHAPTER SIX

Astra
Dark Can Be Beautiful - Alec Chambers

Switching off the lights, I pause to rest my forehead on the cool wooden door. Just like that, my phone buzzes in my blazer pocket and I know who it'll be.

My best friend Jess, telling me she's already arrived at the restaurant.

When I try to convince her to skip the club part of our Friday night after we eat, she chants *'but it's Friday'* on repeat and it did nothing to lure my headache into fucking off following a nine-hour session with a wriggly screamer. Being a tattooist is my passion, if only my crippling debts would permit me to be fussy about my clientele. I've been evading paying the bill for months now. until I could save up enough to pay off a hefty sum all at once.

I also couldn't really be a bitch to undeserving customers in truth, no matter how much I hated being around people who gave me these horrible mind-anguishing headaches.

Especially since I'm the only parlor for miles.

It definitely gives me an advantage and I earn a lot of money from the store, but since I'm still saving to pay off medical bills and funeral costs, health insurance, and all of the rest of it, I won't be seeing a profit for a while.

I plan on making my first payment in a few weeks because I already have a good few grand saved. Not all of it, but a good dent of it.

Emerging from the small parlor I'm incredibly proud to own, I lock the door when a shiver of trepidation tumbles down my nape. It's been happening more and more often lately, that sixth sense warning me something's not quite right. Yet as I look over my shoulder to search the shadows, I see nothing.

The same leering corner beside an alleyway, the same abandoned BMW that's now missing all wheels and its wing-mirrors still idles. Even if there is someone lingering back there, they will be far more interested in claiming a piece of scrap metal than touching me.

Shaking my head at myself, I start the walk toward my favorite spot. The recent downfall of rain glistens across the sidewalk, another reason I'm glad I opted for flats tonight. The other is a very real concern I may drift to sleep standing up and have further to fall.

There's a visible shift between the less affluent neighborhood where my parlor happens to be the best I can afford, and the part of town frequented by those who won't blink at their wallet being stolen. They'll just pull out a backup and continue enjoying the nightlife of Hook-Up Street.

Yes. That is the legal government name for it, as documented on any map in my world.

The irony.

The sidewalks become wider, the buildings stretch higher and soon enough I'm faced with the Empire. A structure made entirely of glass that spears the sky like a lone, broken shard. The club/restaurant I've come strangely attached to has three floors open to the public, and apparently, the owner has a penthouse suite above that but I can't say I've ever seen him.

Bracing my hand over the golden brass door handle, that prickle of self-awareness comes again. Twice in the space of fifteen minutes? Maybe it's a sign I should be curled up in bed with my sketchpad tonight. I'd be a recluse if Jessica let me. Hence our weekly meetups, to make sure I don't spiral down the route of dying alone and no one coming to find me. But the fact I've never been a people person has kicked up a notch in the last year. I can't help feeling like I'm being watched. That there is a darkness that follows me around and it's the hands of death waiting for the last frays of my sanity to snap so that I turn into some antisocial serial killer or something.

Everything feels ominous and nowhere feels safe.

All of the weird occurrences, the gifts, the unexplained encounters.

They all play on a loop in my mind and I have to sigh and push them away.

Like my life would ever be that interesting.

Forcing my gaze away from the street behind me, I exhale at the sight of my best friend waving me over and plaster a smile across my face.

"Bitch, where's your dancing shoes?!" Jess half-jokes, raising from the booth to pull me into a tight embrace. I fight to not lie across the red leather and rest my eyes, despite the hustle and bustle of the restaurant. Upstairs, the city's hottest nightclub is the regular talk of Hot Bark's magazine, and above that, a gentlemen's club that is by invite only. All sorts of rumors fly about what happens up there, from prostitutes to gambling, but who really knows and who really cares?

The tabloids will say anything for a story.

Even if it does bring a lawsuit from the rich and the fancy when they end up featured in it.

"On the house, ma'am," the waiter appears like clockwork. Placing a glass of Pinot Grigio on the table in front of me, I thank him with a genuine smile.

Ever since my first visit, I've been welcomed here as if it's my second home. It takes me all week to afford the menu prices, but I can't help the attachment that brings me back time and time again. The only place in town that stocks my favorite wine, the recent renovations bringing the restaurant to life in my favorite shades of dark aubergine and dusty pink, almost rose gold, and the booth in the corner that always seems to be free has become my regular spot.

Sipping on my wine, I sigh and melt into the booth, my eyes flickering back and forth, up and down the street beyond the window at my side. There's nothing much to see when the chandeliers reflect my own image back to me, but when a car passes, that brief glimpse of a headlight awakens the shadows like a habitat untouched. A figure looming here, a stray cat strolling there, couples walking by arm in arm that makes my heart squeeze.

Loneliness is a fickle trait. I love my space as much as I love my freedom, but a girl can only get too far into her thirties before deciding I just might not be lovable. Any dates I've had this past year suddenly blow me off for a follow-up, and any cute clients that flirt with me never return to the parlor.

"Hey, where have you gone? You look lost," Jessica reaches over to touch my hand. Opening my mouth to reply, ready to let every inner doubt fly from my mouth, a figure appears in my peripheral, and Jess's whole demeanor changes. "Oh, babe! What a surprise!"

Gone is the fun-loving best friend that turns up at my house in her PJs and slippers with movie snacks at the ready. Instead, her eyes light up at the sight of Theo, completely besotted with the way his jeans hang to the backs of his thighs and the stale scent of cigarette smoke clings to his body. She always was one for a bad boy.

But in this case, this bad boy wanna-be is just an arrogant ass who thinks he's God's gift to women.

Leaning down to kiss her hastily, Theo drops into the booth and my hackles rise. This is girls' night, a dick-free time to unwind with good food and better company.

"Couldn't let my best girl out on a Friday will all these jealous men around," he sneers like he's being protective. His eyes rest uncomfortably on me. The tone is so apparent that I narrow my eyes at the fact it flies straight over her head. Now, if I were her, I'd be questioning the term *'best girl'* which implies there's a whole fan club out there but it's not my place to tell Jess what to do. Not when she's so smitten and frankly, needs to learn from her own mistakes. I've mentioned it to her once and she brushed it off so I tapped out. There is only so much a girl can do before even she wants to tell herself to fuck off from the unwanted advice.

I'd love to say I'm the friend that would go ham on her ass, freaking out until she listened about what bad news he is. But I'm not, because the only thing it would do is tear apart our friendship until she wises the fuck up and comes crawling back with her tail between her legs. By that time, the damage is already done.

As I said. She will learn by trial and error.

"We were just discussing how Astra doesn't appear herself tonight. Don't you think she looks down, babe?" Jess pouts and I spear her with narrowed eyes that could kill.

I don't want this bastard looking at me.

I don't even want this bastard uttering my name let alone sitting across from me.

"Just tired, that's all," I mumble, grateful the waiter appears at that very moment to take our order. Not so grateful Theo asks if they've got anything close to a burger and settles for a steak tartare. Guess that means the playboy is staying, despite us all knowing he has as many dollars in his pocket as slits in his left eyebrow.

Three, to be exact.

"Must be draining, working all those hours for yourself," Theo comments, picking up a bread roll from the basket to point at me. "Need to find yourself a man to take on the hard work." Jess beams up at him, her arms snake around him as if he's the center of her universe.

She's always like this, ride or die for every two-week fling that leaves her in a crying mass of brunette hair and darker eyes that leak like waterfalls. The worst part is she's so damn gorgeous, caring, and funny if she'd just believed she's worth more she would have already found the one.

"If I were to *'take on a man,'*" I lift finger quotes into the air and sneer at him like a pissed pitbull. "It'd be purely for the company, Theo. Not every woman needs a man to hold her hand," I snap and Jess's eyes widen. She knows I hate this man. Yet I always try for her sake. But there is only so much of his egotistical ass I can take. "Besides. I am the talent. The artist. What could he do aside from sitting there and looking pretty? I've built my business from the ground up and I won't let anyone waltz in to take credit for that."

"Alright, don't get your panties twisted. Just saying there are men out there that'd kill for a pretty, curvy thing like you, is all."

There are *so* many issues with everything he just said. Starting with referring to me as a thing, addressing my weight, but mainly the sheer audacity of an utter waste of a man trying to tell a working woman she should lean on somebody else.

Despite the casual hunch of his posture and lazy grin, there's a laser sharpness to his otherwise dull eyes that tells me he knows exactly what he's doing. Trying to rile me up, divide me from my best friend, and be able to blame it on the fact I never liked him in the first place. As our starters are delivered, Jess holds my gaze across the table, imploring me not to make a scene with a small shake of her head.

"Mmmm," I wonder out loud, reigning it in as much as I'm able. "There are also men that think leeching off vulnerable women will get them everything they want in life." This time, Theo's smile turns mechanical and if I didn't need any other proof that he's taking my best friend for a ride, there it is.

If there was any chance at salvaging our night out, it's well and truly dead. Throughout the awkward silences, multiple glasses of wine, and the duration of our main course, my eyes grow heavier and my patience wears thin.

Every awe-filled look Jess gives the asshole who spends the night staring at me instead, makes me what to kick her under the table.

Damn, I should have worn my heels. A broken leg and the realization he'd bail as soon as she needed support during physio would wake her up to the harsh reality - her choices suck.

Hmmm there's a thought.

I twist my ankle and ready my foot for the strike of a lifetime when she starts talking again.

I mean damn... it isn't like I was going to do it...

"So, Theo and I were talking," she drawls and I cringe inside. "We're thinking of moving in together. Theo was having some... issues with his mom's partner and asked if he could stay at mine for a while so I said why not make it official." She shrugs, beaming a smile so pure, I could weep for her. But instead, a blurt of roaring laughter leaves my mouth, my head dropping back with the miserable hilarity of it all.

"Good luck with that." I dab my mouth with my napkin and toss it onto my empty plate. Rising to my feet, I almost crash into the kind gentlemanly waiter who looks at me in confusion. "Oh, compliments to the chef. Please pass the bill onto my chivalrous friend here, he's going to *take care of it.*"

"Astra? Where are you going?" Jess gasps. I sigh, noting the concern in her gaze, and lean over to kiss her goodbye.

"I'm just tired and cranky. You do you, boo. I'll be here to pick up the pieces when your ivory tower falls." A growl sounds from Theo, whose chest is far too close to mine, and as I straighten, the dark glare in his eyes can't be ignored. A snarl catches the top of his lip so I make sure as I spin around, the length of my black hair slaps it off.

The cold air outside is a balm to my senses, even if I'm forced to tighten my blazer around my chest. Inside, an inferno of disappointment swirls until my hands are fisted in the lapels. Why can't Jess see she's better than that asshole, better than all of them combined? Stepping out into the street, the blare of a horn jolts me back to my senses. Dammit, Astra, this is why you don't have loads of friends. You can't control people and you especially can't help them if they don't see the problem in the first place.

Once safely across the road, I stick to the sidewalk. There are noticeably fewer people around, the clubgoers already queueing around the block of the street behind me. Scrubbing a hand down my face, wishing for my bed, a firm tug on my hair has my head reeling back. I scream on instinct, the blaze of pain exploding through my scalp as my face is shoved against the wall. My chest opens up, swallowing the sensation of fear whole and planting it inside of me. It dips and somersaults, then that feeling that you're falling takes root inside my chest. Absolute sheer, unyielding terror consumes me.

Rough brick grates the flesh of my cheek, the stale scent of cigarette smoke washing over me. I gag, both with the invasion of my senses and the realization of who might be pissed off enough to attack me out here in the open. I lose all of my sensations, all of my coherent thoughts and reactions had I seen this attack coming, and instead, I'm left with nothing but panic.

Screaming, crying, and screeching, I pray for a guardian angel to save me. For the devil himself to reach a hand through the earth and free me from this hell that walks upon it.

I never pray for anything, but I've also never been a victim before. A savage perturbation takes me in its chokehold as alarm burns through the veins of my blood.

It's easy to have a devil-may-care attitude until the demons that serve him come for your sanity.

Because never feeling safe again, in the streets or in your home, is the definition of a true shut-in. And that feeling only comes from those who have survived at the hands of a monster.

I pray for someone to give enough of a shit about the woman pinned against the wall against her will to lend a hand, instead of thinking it would be easier to not get involved.

Because let's face it, that is the world we live in. Bystanders have become too afraid to help the victims for fear of becoming a victim themselves.

The harrowing cries of innocent people are a normal tune that echoes through the night.

But this is a cruel world and no one is looking out for me.

Nobody is coming to save me.

Swinging my arms back wildly, I make a last-ditch attempt to dislodge him by stomping my heel into his shoe. This gains me the smallest amount of freedom, his grip loosening as I rush forward. The sound of my hair ripping free from my scalp makes me wince but then he's on me again, shoving me into the wall. Gasping for air through the panic attack that threatens to kill me off quicker by resisting my lung's standard function. The weight of another body colliding with my attacker throws me off kilter. I stagger aside, not sparing one second to look back.

Yelling louder than I thought possible, I run.

My throat burns and I swear I can taste blood as it slicks to the back of my throat. Pounding my flats against the concrete, I make it two blocks before my voice is scratched raw. My throat is like sandpaper as I make it to the street I get the bus from.

I clamp a hand over my mouth, trying to keep the sickness threatening to spew from my lips at bay.

There weren't any other houses along the way. Nobody I could turn to for aid in the darkness being in the center of the city.

Fuck.

My bus is waiting at the stop up ahead, preparing to leave until another one comes on the hour, but I can't board public transport looking like this. The stares, the questions. I tremble, ducking back from view until it's pulled away, sobbing to myself. The sting of scored flesh beneath my fingers mixes with my salty tears as I slink away from the city.

It doesn't take as long as I expect, the swiftness of my feet defying the numb tingle crawling up my limbs. I can't slow, I can't stop. The suburbs are desolate, the cottage I inherited from my grandparents sitting alone amongst the hedges. It's only when I'm locking myself behind my front door with a shaky hand do I flop into the hallway and let the emotions consume me.

I was...attacked. My body was overpowered. The *'What ifs'* wrack my mind, the realization of how close I came to find out what it means to be a real victim heavy on my chest. Crawling the rest of the way to my bathroom, my shoes get kicked off along the way and I struggle out of my blazer.

My legs feel numb like I'm unable to make them work and the thought terrifies me even more.

I'm letting the fear in and I don't know how to shut the door that will lock it out.

What if he comes back?

What if I'm unable to move, helpless, overpowered?... *Again.*

What if I'm frozen in time while the toxic feel of his touch burns like acid through my flesh? What if I'm immobile while he violates me and all I can do is lay here and cry? What would have happened if I hadn't been able to run?

Would I still be breathing right now?

Switching on the hot tap over the bathtub, I slump against the white porcelain. Tears trail down my cheeks, diluting the blood that drips onto my already red blouse. If there's a way to lose myself in the steam billowing around me, I will find it. I'll scrub myself free of the cigarette stench that clings to my flesh, the layer of grime and shame coating my skin. At least no one is here to see me at my weakest.

I'm not this girl.

Who am I kidding? Everyone is this girl when faced with the unexpected.

It's easy to live in bliss, knowing of the horrors when they don't affect you directly.

It's easy to hum and ah in shame and regret, nodding your head and offering your heartfelt condolences when it isn't you that feels like the monsters will eat you alive, then go back to sharing your Sunday roasts like tragedy doesn't live in this world.

Then when it attacks you, you can never forget it.

After a long while, I bring myself to switch off the tap. Stripping, I slide into the clawfoot tub in the center of the room. Water pours over the sides, gushing across the tiled floor, but I don't care.

It doesn't matter that the water is scalding, it does nothing to burn away the disgust wallowing inside me. At Theo, at Jess for letting him crash our girl's night, at me for not being strong enough to fight off my attacker.

Submerging myself beneath the water, I will the liquid to fill my lungs. To consume my last breath, to put me out of my misery. Obviously, I'm not built for a world where those who want - take, and those who hate - prevail. No doubt Theo has got away by now while Jess tends to his wounds and laps up his lies.

Hard not to feel bitter at that thought.

I *know* it was him.

Bubbles drift from my lips as I find a moment of utter calm. Peace beneath the surface, silence amongst the noise. My lids drift half open, spotting the outline of a man hovering over the tub.

"Ahhh!" I scream, shooting out of the water and thrashing around. I'm completely alone in the room, my heart lodged in my throat. I know it's only a matter of time before he comes for me again, and next time, there won't be a shadow to save me.

Not when I'm already seeing the demons of my terror in the steam.

I feel violated, the dark energy that slithered across my skin like a snake in the water coils around my body and I shudder. Repulsion thick in my throat. I stand to step out of the bath, a sharp pain shoots through my ankle and I fall forward, tripping over the fluffy black rug that is decorated in splotches of red. My head cracks against the sink, a wide gash opens along the curve of my temple and I fall to the ground with a startled cry.

Stars dance in my gaze and just as I pass out, the outline of a stunning face twirls in my vision.

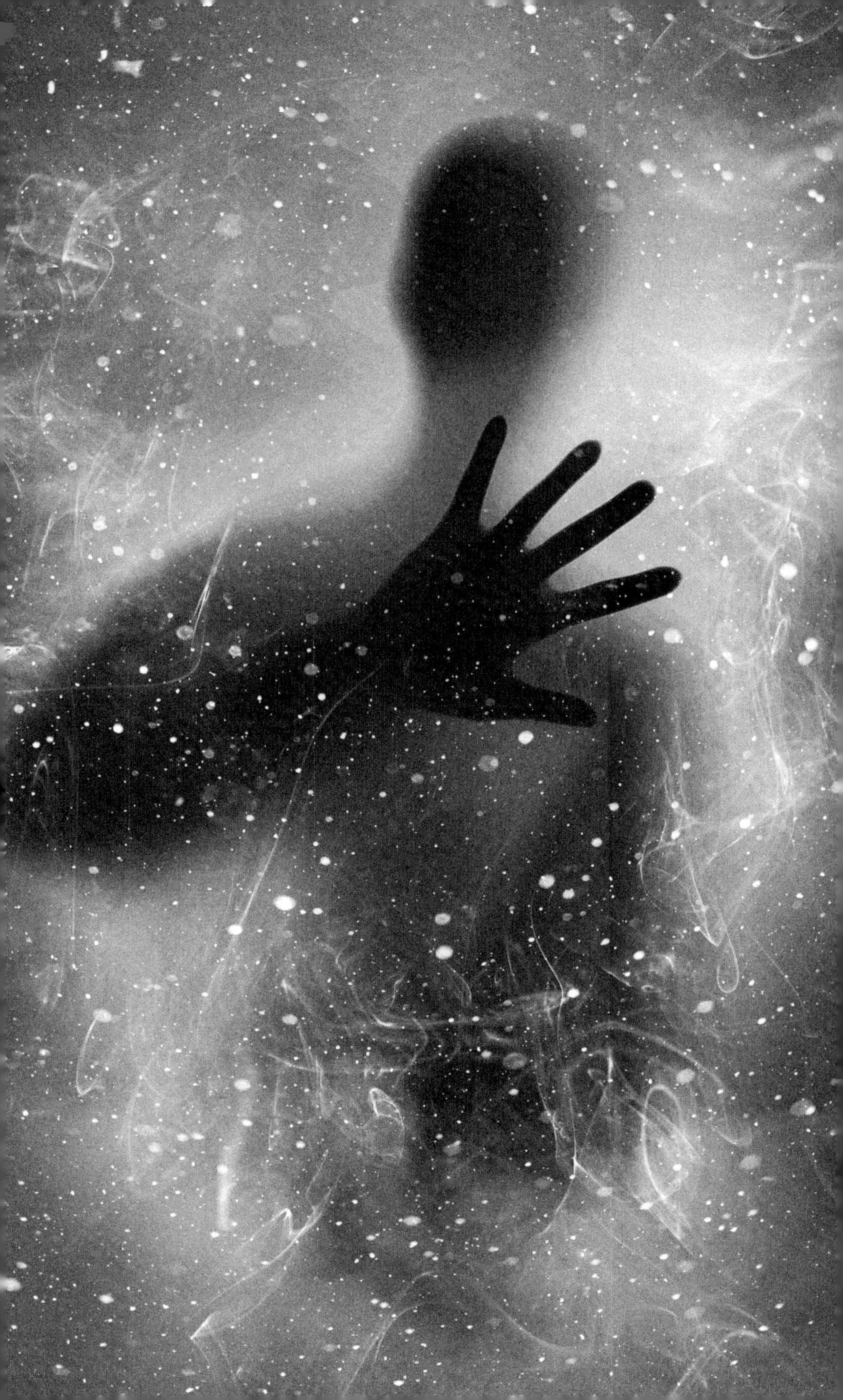

CHAPTER SEVEN

Hunter
Dancing After Death - Matt Maeson

I stare at the clock with narrowed eyes in tandem with looking back and forth between the wall and my translucent hand. The ghostly whitish-blue skin looks taut like a latex bubble with fine hints of arctic white. So much time has passed beyond the veil of life and death and at the same time, no time has passed at all.

I have absolutely no concept of it.

The minutes that would drag in any given day float by on the wings of a phoenix to me right now and I'm in awe of it. Lost to the unfamiliar sensations as to the fact that I'm actually dead, hasn't yet fully sunk in.

I can't be dead. It's *impossible*.

I mean, how could I be dead and yet here? Beside the woman I have craved ever since the moment, those ocean blues looked back into the storm that brewed within my depths and still stood before me unwavering with that intoxicating smile on her lips, unfettered by the dangers that swam there.

After I tripped over my corpse and got soul-sucked right back to Astra's side, I had a little wobble. And by wobble, I mean I had a massive freak out, running through walls and sinking through floors. I tried to find perches, to make any kind of noise to let her know that I was here and she wasn't suffering alone.

That she was safe.

To keep me from the broken shards of my mind that couldn't comprehend what the fuck was happening to me.

I am being pulled under by the current and she is my anchor pulling me toward the shore.

Then she sank beneath the surface of her bath water with such sorrow, I knew she never needed the water to feel like she was drowning but she wanted to feel it more so than the pain in her heart.

That guts me and suddenly, the thought of being dead pales in comparison to the pain of standing by as she is hurting. It tears me apart and brutalizes me more than the knife that killed me, embedded into my side.

She'll never see how I ached for her in life, but *believe* me, she'll know how much I yearn for her in death. She'll feel what dwells beneath the surface of a rough and dangerous man who is now free from the confinements of his physical shell.

Now I'm free to look at her, closer, transfixed by the light that graces her skin. I wonder if she's my heaven.

Because this certainly isn't hell.

Where is the demon that should be waiting to punish my tainted soul for its sins?

I can't deny the facts—what I saw in that alley and how I can be here inside Astra's bedroom as she sleeps restlessly within her coral sheets. I got inside this room because my translucent body walked through the damn door.

I'm a dead man.

There are no two ways about it.

She tosses and turns in her sheets, distress from the memory of her attack clearly weighing on her mind as she clenches the satin sheets in her anguish. A small cut frames her temple. When she fell from the bath, I felt as if my soul jumpstarted. I have a surge of energy and am able to get her into her bedroom. I lift her and lay her down in slumber. There is something dark that tickles against me. A chill to my soul that gives me a feeling of urgency.

Like if I don't get her out of that room, she would be even more harmed than she already has been. The second her head hits the pillow, my energy wanes and I am utterly depleted. More taxed and tired than I have ever been in my life.

I lay beside her, caressing the air that thickens between her cheek and my feathered touch. She shivers, almost like she can feel me and I push against the veil harder, hoping that she will wake and see me here.

Me beside her and she'll wake up to finally learn of the truth that is Hunter North.

She'll know she's safe and that I have always been watching her—close by and within arm's reach. That I am the one person within this entire world that truly knows all of her.

Inside and out.

There isn't a single part of her I haven't uncovered. That I don't plan to caress.

The good, the bad, and the naughtily wicked.

God, I get hard just thinking about it.

I look down and see my heavy cock grow at the thought of my Siren and a shudder runs through me at the sight.

I don't feel dead.

My dick sure as fuck doesn't *look* dead.

Maybe I'm in a coma inside some no-man's hospital somewhere?

They say that shit happens, right?

Well, if that is true, I hope they pull the damn plug because I wouldn't give up being this close to Astra for anything, not even life.

In fact, I don't feel anything at all other than riding the waves of a towering ocean. An emptiness that makes me feel afloat in the wind, swirling within the leaves of the world and within the grains of sand scattered across the earth.

I feel like I'm here and nowhere at all.

Between seeing myself lying dead on the ground and somehow teleporting back here to where my girl is, with nothing but a thought that consumes me, still seems odd, but I haven't been this close to her before knowing she couldn't wake and fear me standing over her.

I shift, moving a thick strand of hair from her face, and hum in awe when it falls from her temple.

After she arrived home, she cleaned herself up and broke down in the bathroom. I wish more than anything that I could reach for her, that I could pull her from under the surface and watch her draw air back into those beautiful lungs.

I have to see her breathe.

Watching her lying lifelessly in the tub, swaying in the depths is as tormenting as it is perfection. She looks so angelic, so at peace until she opens those storm-filled eyes and her ocean blues darken to a terrible fear that would have stolen the air from my lungs if I could still breathe.

I see her vulnerability, the one I know she never shows the world.

It's *mine*.

All mine. Just like *she's* all mine.

Even death won't steal her from me. The reaper himself cannot keep me from being at her side right now, holding her hand.

Right where I belong.

Her eyes pinch and hard lines of tension distort her once soft face as a nightmare plays across her features. There is an insistent tugging in my soul to ease those worries, to smooth the crease between her brows.

But there's nothing I can do.

I'm just a dead man.

I move closer to her, slowly bending my head so I can place a tender kiss on her parted lips. My hand's coil around her plush hips, my hold firm.

'*Settle my love, nothing will harm you here.*' The low rasp of my voice whispers through the darkness, like a tendril without mind. Free without embodiment, in search of the ears needing to hear it most. I can feel it, like a beating heart pulsating within the air enclosing me, kissing against me like a feathered caress of a lover.

The quick succession to the steady low thrum that calls me near. A compulsion to follow blindly, to the connection that bestows the promise of love.

'*How can you be so sure?*' a gentle voice replies.

It's a voice belonging to the lost.

A voice belonging to the afraid.

'*It's so cold here. So empty of life. I don't like being afraid.*' The voice is almost childlike, a raw innocence that can only bleed through vulnerability. '*Don't let him hurt me. Don't let him take it. He'll come for me. He'll come for me until he steals my fear.*'

I want to see who belongs to that voice, I want to see the face that has implanted a living thing inside of me that grows impulsive to pull the owner of that sweet, sweet musical sound into my arms. I rush through the darkness, a stark abyss the only thing I can see as I extend my hands to caress the smoothness of the nothingness around me.

Then I stop.

Not needing to search any further.

I may not see her, the beauty with the voice of a siren, but I can feel her.

My essence presses against hers, I imagine my chest, firm against her back.

I can hear the soft sound of her breathing, the sensual whisper that strokes against me. I reach forward, my hands on her hips. The darkness makes it impossible to see anything at all. Even the shades behind my closed eyes are brighter than the shroud I'm cloaked under. I clench my eyes tightly shut, forging a silken white silhouette out of the tiny specs of silver.

Who really needs to see when you can close your eyes and bask in the sensations of a delicate touch?

'You may not see me. You may not trust a lone voice in the darkness. But I know you can feel me.' I pull her closer to me, so she fits sleekly against my large frame. My delicate touch turns into a brutal hold on her slender curves. *'But you can take certainty in the fact, I will never allow another living soul to harm you again, Siren. Never. Again. Your fear? It's mine!'*

There is a loud buzz on the bedside dresser. I blink, pulled from my deepest desires as her phone lights up and dances across the flat surface and I realize I was asleep. Or something similar to it. I swipe out a frustrated arm not wanting it to wake her. She is too tormented to come back into the world of the lucid. It clatters to the ground and even though it was an instinct to throw the thing away, it shocks me to see and *feel* that I can actually do it.

My entire soul quivers in little aftershocks of electricity that pulse through me. The sound of it hitting the ground echoes throughout the cottage and Astra stirs in her sleep, jolting upright breathlessly as she stares around in panic before her gaze turns on the phone still buzzing like crazy on the floor.

She wipes her eyes before leaning over and picking it up. Clicking the screen, a shrill god-awful voice whines down the line. "Oh God, oh God! Astra, he's dead. My Theo is dead," Jess cries and I wince, the sound as annoying as it's always been.

Why is she crying over that sack of shit? He tried to rape her best friend for fuck's sake. Not that she would be smart enough to wonder why he wasn't outside the Empire but down some alley. I guess most people would have called the police, but there is no normal in a situation like this, where your control is being stolen from you. Astra went from walking the world blissfully unaware of the horrors that linger in the shadows to being a victim of it. That truth is a hard pill to swallow and she did it the only way she could, by dealing with her emotions first so she could lock them away today.

She's a smart woman, one so many people disregard and dismiss as anything less than excellent. It angers me and I get that cramp in my neck, the one that feathers into my shoulder until I crack my spine and the chilling sound gives way to the tick that has my temper brewing. I guess some things never change, even in whatever the fuck this is. Jessica didn't even call Astra to make sure she got home safely last night.

Another voicemail plays again. "Dammit, Astra! Answer the phone, I really need you right now!"

"It's me again, I'm struggling here, Astra. I need you!"

"Please, please, Astra. I don't know what to do."

"Call me when you get this, I'll be at my ma's. I can't face going back to the apartment right now. Not without him," she sobs through the line and I cringe, lip curled as I roll my eyes and lay back casually against the headboard as I stretch out my funky-looking legs with a yawn.

Hmmm, I wonder If I can still eat?

That's a thought.

Cold, I turn dangerous eyes toward the bedroom door when somebody has the nerve to thump on the front door like a S.W.A.T team. I glance at the clock and see that it's two in the morning and my temper only grows. Startled, Astra jumps before throwing her legs over the edge of the bed and standing. Picking up a throw from the end of the ornate, curved seat at the end of her bed she goes to wrap it around herself tightly. Stopping when her shirt rises and she sees the colored bruise marks of thick fingerprints on the fleshy part of her hips. She narrows her eyes, a moment of uncertainty fleeting in her gaze before there's another knock again forcing her to dismiss the odd marks.

Huh, guess when I kissed her last night I also left behind the evidence of my hold on her perfect waist.

She stumbles toward the door on slow-moving feet and hesitates before she peeks through the hole, and takes a step back. Like the veil that separates us, something dark and shadowed falls across her face and she breathes in deeply before palming the handle and opening the door.

Two police officers stand on the other side, one that is around six-foot-two and the other one that can't be more than five-foot-three. I scoff, looking at the bean and the damn stalk. What an odd fucking pair of socks.

"Miss Stone?" the stalk asks as he looks Astra up and down and I growl. The sound gathers a small wind that rushes past the three of them, making them shudder, no doubt thinking it's the wind from outside.

"Yes," she answers smoothly.

"I'm Officer Stalmyer. This is my colleague Officer Bea. May we come in?" he asks her softly with a skin-crawling leer to his appreciating gaze.

I want to pluck those eyes from his head.

I walk toward him, standing between a space full of people and I'm utterly unseen. There is something empowering about that. I'm not over here crying about it, or mourning the life I have lost.

Fuck that.

I'm doing what any sane person would be doing in my position.

Trying to poke out the eye of an asshole.

I put a little force behind it and Mr. Stalk-man blinks rapidly then quivers.

I smirk, knowing that he feels me.

Ten points for skill.

"What is this about?" Astra asks before she demands to see their badges like a good girl. She steps back once they flash them and they step inside. I huff in frustration at having any male this close to my woman and my anger seems to brew a small whirlwind strong enough to have the door slamming shut. Mr. Bean jumps in the air as he spins, hand on his gun at the abrupt thud that echoes throughout the room with the loud slamming of the door, making me grin even wider. Mr. Stalky glares at his partner before gesturing for Astra to take a seat on the couch. She stares back at the door for a moment, mutely.

Not having jumped at all.

If anything, she looks more curious than afraid.

"About Theo Nyera. His body was found in the early hours of this morning," Tall and lanky explains to her and with eyes as dead as mine. Astra just stares at him waiting for him to continue. "We found surveillance but it was positioned at an odd angle. We know that he attacked you, but beyond that, the camera doesn't tell us much else. We discovered another body with Mr. Nyera. Would you mind telling us what happened last night and why you thought it would be a good idea to not report the attempted assault?"

Slowly, her head rises as sorrow fills those emotion-filled eyes. I hate that look, the one that mourns the loss of my life. I don't even have the time to process the fact that he just confirmed my demise, enraptured by her and her every expression instead.

She inhales deeply and I become fascinated with the dip at the base of her throat that inflates and deflates with each one of her sweet, intoxicating breaths. "Someone died? Someone else was there?" she asks weakly. Like the answer may be too much. But the asshole cops just raise their brows at her waiting for her to fill in the blanks of the unfinished story for them. She scowls, eyes turning mad in her fury. "Theo attacked me. After that? I'm not sure what happened. I ran."

"Did you see him? Either of them?"

"No," she utters as she flutters her eyes trying to stay in control. "But I smelled him. Theo I mean."

"You smelled him?" Mr. Beany-no-balls asks incredulously as he quirks a brow at her.

"Yes."

"And your relationship with the victim, ma'am?" the other officer chimes in as he leans forward, inching closer to my girl.

"He was my best friend's boyfriend. He had always been a creep and I assure you is no goddamn victim. That vile, disgusting piece of shit attacked me. He attacked me while my friend naively sat inside the Empire and waited for him. The world is better off," she spits with venom. "Who was the other man? The man who saved me?"

"His name was Hunter North. A big name around these parts. He owned the Empire you claim your friend was at. But I've got to say, you don't seem all that sorry Mr. Nyera is dead."

I want to kill him.

What kind of ass victimizes a victim more than she has already been victimized?

I stand behind Officer Bea and clamp my hand around the back of his neck and play with my strength, wondering what kind of damage I can do with the right motivation. His back snaps ramrod straight and a small tremble begins to course through his body as it slowly builds into a slow shake.

"Excuse me?" Astra scoffs, the throw falling from her shoulders as she leans forward. "I'm sorry, would you have me cry for the man who would have raped me? The only life I'm sorry that was lost is Mr. North's. He never deserved whatever happened to him for saving me. But as for Theo? He can rot in hell." She sneers, eyes aflame in a vicious kind of fury. Officer Stalmyer places a hand on her knee and my anger increases, as does my grip on the back of his buddy's neck.

"Of course not, what my colleague was trying to say is, that we don't have any other witnesses other than you right now. The investigation is still underway, but we may need to question you again. Right now, you're the only one who knows what really happened." The guy offers her a squeeze as he turns his head to glare at his friend, only to narrow his eyes when he notices him shaking in his chair. "Dude, what's wrong with you?" he hisses, pissed at him for acting so unprofessional and confused as to why he is acting as if he stepped onto a jackhammer.

He can't answer, the quivering only intensifying, I purse my lips and nod in approval before letting go. He slouches forward and fights for each breath.

"I have no fucking idea," he wheezes, face ashen as he experiences the violation. "But I don't feel good. Something - something just grabbed me. *Controlled* me. "

Blinking dumbly at the pair of them, Astra shakes her head and comes back to her senses, dismissing his absurd claim and zeroing in on the last part of their conversation. "Wait, are you saying I'm a suspect?"

"What we're saying, Miss Stone, is don't leave town."

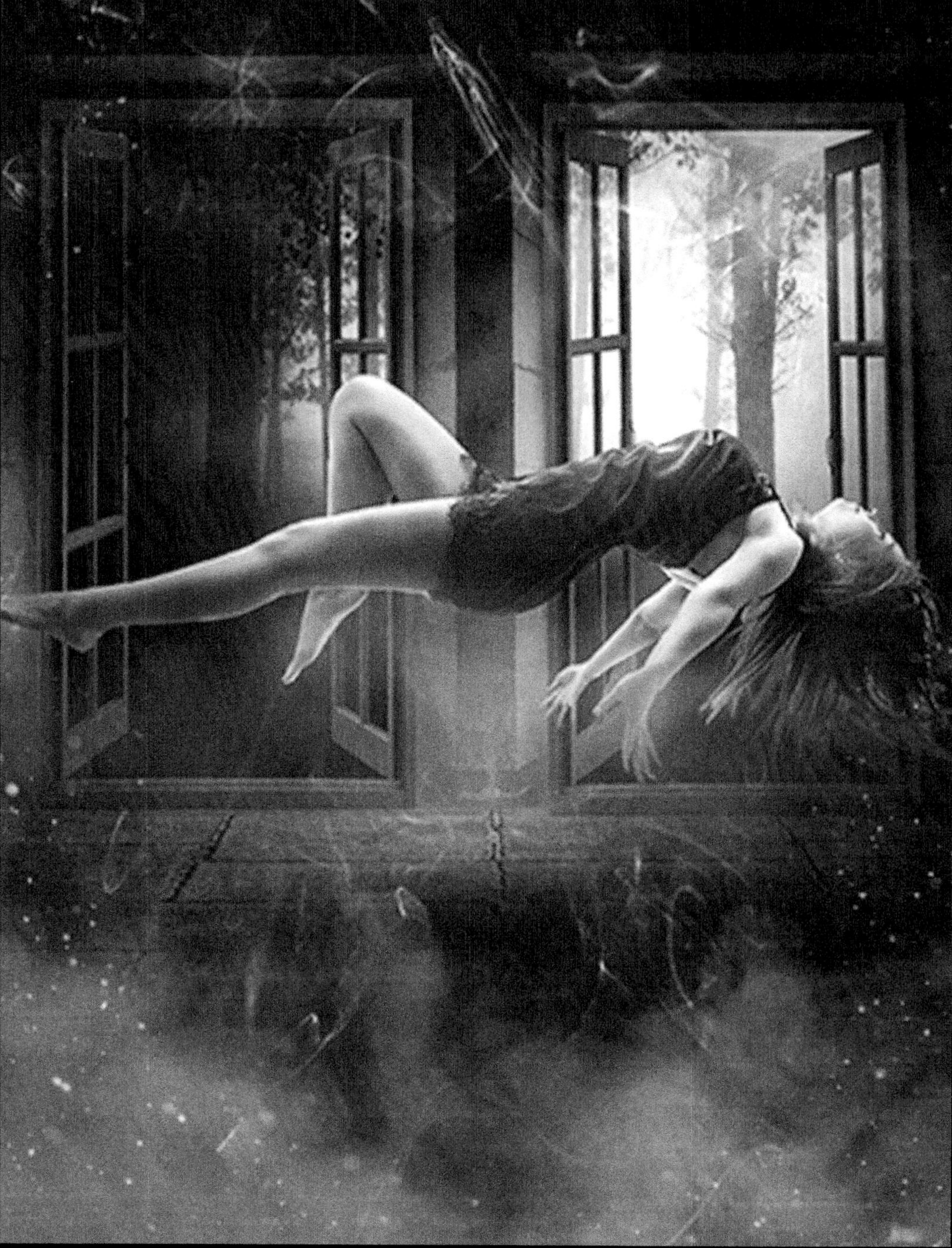

CHAPTER
EIGHT

Astra
Blood On Your Hands - Veda

Slamming the door closed, I thud my forehead against the wood and huff. I'm a fucking *suspect*, of course, I am. My phone begins vibrating again, dropping off the edge of the mattress where I left it and ricocheting across the floor. Hopefully, it's smashed by now or just gives up on whatever battery life it has left, but luck isn't in my favor right now. So instead, I stride over to pull my bedroom door closed and leave Jess to cry into my voicemail some more. As I walk back into the lounge, a photo of me and Jess falls from the wall, shattering at my feet and I startle, eyes narrowed as I stare down at our distorted faces.

A better friend might be taking more consideration of how upset her honorary sister is right now, and maybe in the morning I'll be able to locate a more caring nature inside my jaded heart. Tonight, however, as I pour myself the largest glass of wine I can without filling the entirety of my home with it, I leave that shattered frame on the ground, discarded like my emotions.

I feel like bashing Jessica across the face with a brick instead of asking if she's okay right now.

None of this would have happened if she wasn't so blind.

Sure, she didn't tell Theo to attack me in an alley - but she's still the love-struck fool who looks in all the wrong places for it. Then she decides to leave me there, in the dark with a predator while she cries wolf. I know I'm hurt and angry and right now, all of that is directed onto the only living person in my life. That is why I can't speak to her. I need to take care of myself and allow everything toxic with my rage to drain from my aching body before I can even look at her.

A man is dead because of me.

He died saving me and the only thoughts running rabid in my mind is that I'm so *not* fucking worth it. I'm alive and I hardly live at all. This man owned the Empire. It's clear that he seized every single day and could contribute to this world so much more than I care to even be bothered to. If Jess had never brought that cunt into our life, Mr. North would never have died at all. The blame burns and brews and at this moment in time, I'm not sure who I hate more.

Jess, Theo or myself. Fuck, I even hold some resentment for Mr. North. He should have kept walking. He should have left me there to find my fists and fight or fall.

Just like my daddy taught me.

What if he has a family?

Loved ones?

If anything, all I can hope is that his death has saved Jess and others a similar outcome and jars her onto the path of decent catches. Just because I never found mine doesn't mean there isn't a whole sea of respectable men out there.

Not every man thinks it's acceptable to take what isn't theirs to have. Seriously, if I don't hold onto that, I think I'll spiral into even darker territory.

Fuck.

He owns the Empire. My favorite place in this whole entire world other than my parlor and I never even met him. I don't even know what he looks like. With the sudden urge to google his name, I dig my nails into my palm until tiny specs of blood glisten.

I refrain.

Force myself to keep my hands idle and sore from my frustrations at my side.

I *can't.*

I can't look into the perfect picture of a perfect man and drown within the eyes that now lay lifeless in a morgue somewhere.

All because of *me.*

I grit my teeth and cover my face with my hands, screaming into my palms when I feel this surge of hopelessness.

Dropping back onto my couch, I pull the throw over myself and hug the wine glass that swirls back at me with a million sapphire penises that entwine with the red liquid. Jess has a matching glass, and right now I fight the urge to smash it against the wall.

I've never not seen right through her.

In every moment—through every emotion—I've been there.

But she has never had the ability to see through me.

Honestly, nobody ever has.

I put on a brave face and smile and she thinks my whole world is bright. When I tell her my feelings toward her relationships, she brushes them off like they're trivial and absolutely nothing I say holds an ounce of merit, and just like always, I'm left to deal with the fallout when it blows up in her face.

Only this time, the shards of her broken tower have left me with very real scars.

I inhale a deep breath, then blow it out, hoping some of the tension leaves me. It doesn't and my neck begins to ache with the metaphorical weight of it all. After my temporary moment of insanity in the bathtub, I dug out my most luscious bed attire to remind myself of the damn queen I am.

After I woke up passed out and naked in my bed, I guess I must have stumbled there after my fall before passing out for a few seconds.

I should probably worry about that.
Eh. It's just the trauma.

No man can dampen my spirit, or for a matter of fact take it from me. I don't hate myself for breaking down, I prize myself on getting the fuck back up.

When we become familiar with the things that go bump in the night, it restarts our heart and that's okay, as long as when it starts to beat again, it isn't with the rhythm of fear. There's a pair of police officers out there who have seen the entirety of my cleavage in my satin pajama playsuit and more thigh than my OBGYN and yet I'm still standing despite the events of the last twenty-four hours.

Even as bile fights my resolve.

Even as it burns the back of my throat and my stomach churns.

I start to feel violated all over again. The darkness begins to creep back in.

But I'll be damned if I give into that unwelcome feeling.

The longer I sit here, the louder the voices in my head become. Starting as a slow whisper of what *if's*. It forces me to wonder. Soon it bleeds into a concoction of screams inside my soul. Bellows of *'what happened to those years of self-defense classes'* and *'you should have known better'* that sound oddly like my mother.

A military brat should be nobody's victim.

It's disgraceful.

But it's also life and one of the most natural things in the world.

In this kill or be *killed* world.

The war of self-loathing and core strength coils together inside of me. Fisting the TV controller, I flick through Netflix, trying to settle on what will suit my mood best. A soppy rom-com, a big *fuck no*. A home decor show, I'd rather not have *'Here Lies Astra Stone - A Fallen Victim To The Plague Of Boredom'* carved into my headstone.

So alas, I settle for the best and most likely stupidest option—the latest horror flick everyone's been raving about at the tattoo parlor.

Love Me From Beyond.

"Yep, I'm gonna need something stronger for this," I mutter to myself. Downing my glass of wine, I hoist my ass off the couch and pad my bare feet with blood-red painted toes back into my kitchen. This cottage is my safe haven. A slice of reprieve from the outside world, and most likely the last place people would think I live. I like it that way.

I like being unexpected.

It's hard to be a human and hate every other human around you.

I get by though. Live life like a normal person.

But at the end of it all, solitude doesn't scare me.

Living in an unliving world does.

Apart from the newly installed kitchen and bathroom down the hall, I've left the building's character intact. The original beams span the length of the ceiling, adjoining the entire lower level where I prefer to be. Upstairs is used as a storage facility—the out-of-sight, out-of-mind trick working wonders for my *Feng Shui* and my art studio.

An old fireplace sits apart from the bench dining table I eat alone at, creating a perfect sketching corner looking out onto the terrace. Being the last cottage on the end, I have a clear view of the city beyond and the encroachment of green terrain and high trees that surround the perimeter. An expanse of glass forms the outer wall and whenever I curl up in my grandfather's leather armchair or the porch swing outside, I can smell the concoction of the city's toxins and sweet, savory pine that bespoke of the outdoors.

I have a little bit of everything here and I couldn't love anything more if I tried.

The cozy little house needs more renovations than I have the time to give it, but as I round the kitchen island to my father's housewarming gift, a restored Victorian sideboard that acts as my alcohol unit, the latch is ajar. I know for sure I didn't leave the door open, let alone wide open. A bottle of whiskey is nudged further forward than the array of bottles lurking further back and I swallow hard at the creepy thoughts running through my head. It's just my mind playing tricks on me, I tell myself passing a quick glance at the sliding glass doors again. To be fair, it's gone three in the morning following the night before and I would consider myself to have experienced a hefty dose of trauma, so it's more than likely I left the door open when retrieving my wine and told myself otherwise.

Making a mental note to tell my receptionist I'm not opening the shop tomorrow or for like the next *two weeks*—once Jess has stopped blowing up my phone of course—I take the whiskey and make a point of testing the hinges and latch of the door. Seems pretty secure to me. This time, I forgo a glass and return to the corner of my couch where I solidly imprint my ass cheeks. To match the mocha and cream theme I've got going on, the suede cushions are light in color and oh-so strokable in texture. My fingers flex when I think about it, but being a sado who is sitting here stoking her cushions, I do *not* want to be.

Pressing play on the movie, I tip the end of the bottle up high, guzzling the harsh amber liquid when movement catches the corner of my eye. I see it before I feel it. The fluffy faux cow-print cover I'd left crumpled in a heap, shifts, coiling its way up my body. Starting with my feet, my heart thunders in my chest as it rises higher and higher. Fuck, it's going to strangle me.

Death by blanket here I come.

Dropping the whiskey bottle, it shatters over the wooden flooring, and the blanket halts, just over my tits, and evens out perfectly. I swallow, not having been able to move in fear of tangling myself up in the throw like something out of *Final Destination*.

I'm a movie buff.

Sue me.

There's a moment of still where the world stands frozen and I hold my breath, waiting for an impending attack. As if the blanket will rear up and bite me. Before I let myself freak out, I close my eyes and try to find gravity. Scurrying to bunch it in the palm of my hand, I toss the offending throw onto the arm of the couch while I climb the back of my seat. I've cornered myself, the smashed glass all over the floor twinkling on the ground where my feet were only moments ago.

Some bimbo on the TV shrieks, making me scream along with her.

Clutching my chest, I growl at the blonde actress laying around waiting to be stabbed. Throwing her hands in the air, she does a come hither dance before finally running away.

What the fuck?

Why doesn't she get up and run first, or at least try to protect herself beyond what her stereotypical hair color would suggest?

Erm... Yet again, here I am cowering away from a fucking blanket. A *blanket*.

Let's add schedule an appointment with a therapist to the list of phone calls I need to make in the morning.

Because fuck this.

I reach for the remote to find a better horror movie, one that might be so horrific it distracts me from my own nightmares. But just as I reach for it, the thing jumps away from the brush of my fingers and skitters to the ground. With a huff, I go to stand in annoyance and pick it back up again when a torrent of wind rushes around me, forming a live tornado in the center of my lounge. It rushes me. Cool air, a feathered kiss against my heated flesh. There's a pressure, something heady pinning my curvy frame to the couch, as the aspiration of a cloudy face billows into view. But it's just a distortion, a mind manipulation that has my eyes fluttering and my mind lolling.

It's like the dusty clouds hovering above clean water. There, but almost impossible to decipher. Soft strokes tease my satin skin and I shudder, breathing deeply. My heaving chest is harsh and frantic, searching for even a slither of calm.

My mind riots as my sensitive skin pebbles and every part of my brain tells me to question this, but every inch of my soul is mewling with how right this feels.

It's a sensual caress, an anomaly that has my core warm and my clit tingling. I arch my back, half afraid of this strange force manipulating me and half elated that I've never quite felt euphoria like it.

The tendrils of a cool breeze touch me everywhere. The expanse of my body is worshiped by this unknown source of arousal and uncertainty lodges itself within the back of my throat. The stampede of stallions restarts my heart as ravens flutter in my core. My shirt lifts, smooth against my abdomen, and I see those strange bruises again and my mind begins to burn the fuck out.

I'm terrified and I'm aroused.

I'm aroused *because* I'm terrified and the only thought echoing through my mind like a megaphone is...

No more horror movies.

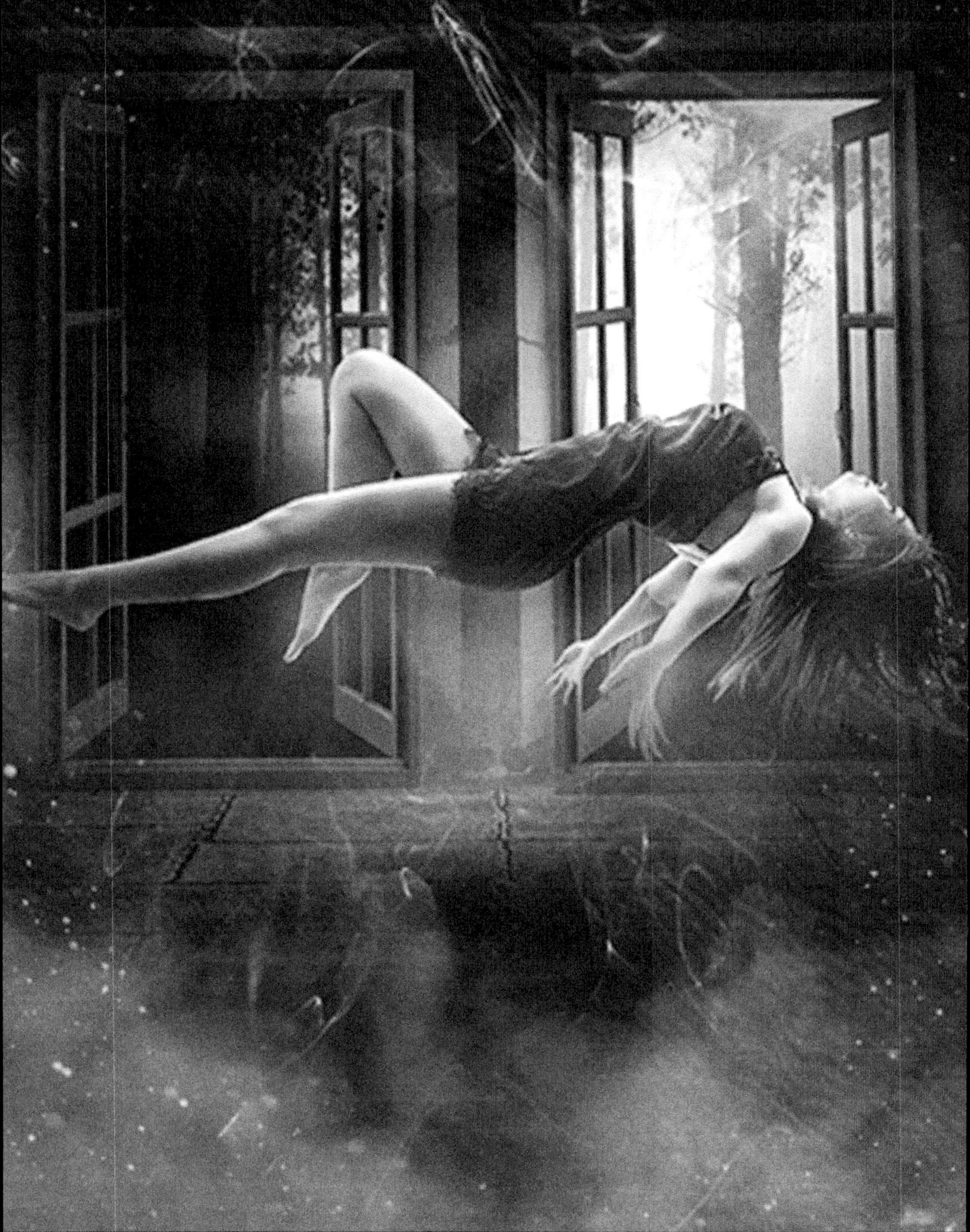

Chapter Nine

Astra
Cravin - Stileto

Sweat glistens against my skin. Slick, wet, and heaving for every breath. My back arches, my neck exposed as soft lips trail a delicate caress along the column of my throat. I'm a live wire, burning under the heat of arousal. Something lives beneath my skin. A wild, untamed, and rabid need to chase a high that was so close, yet so far out of reach, it had tears welling in my eyes. I'm somewhere without time, in a plane without burden. All I know is the sweet, wicked temptation of desire and I am relieved from the thoughts of my living nightmares.

They can't hurt me here.

Here I'm in the in-between, the side of life that is made up of naughty little dreams and I never want to return back to the land of the living.

Fuck that.

I need more of this.

I need more of him.

"God, Siren. This is all I have ever wanted. All I have ever dreamed about," a deep voice tickles against me, and I shiver. The teasing breath cool against my pebbled skin.

I'm losing my mind. The thick cloud of passion is plentiful enough to make my vision dance and my senses soar. There is a man between my thighs. A glorious creature made of sweet, sinfully wicked things that can take you to the little place called oblivion.

Fuck, I want to soar in a little place called oblivion.

"Feeling your delicate skin under the rough contrast of my palm. Kissing these fuckable lips that taste greater than the sweetest cherries. Fuck, Siren, you're everything I thought you would be. That I knew you would be. Kiss me, kiss me like you see me, love," he rasps a moment before tender lips claim mine. I press forward, my hands reaching out blindly as my deft and slender fingers entwine within the thick strands of his tousled hair. I pull at the root, my ample breasts pushing into a hard chest that chafes my sensitive nipples in all the right ways. Everything is cool, that perfect sensation when the temptation hits just right and human contact feels like a silken caress.

I'm losing myself in that feeling. Drowning under the perfect texture.

"Oh fuck, oh fuck! I'm close, so freaking close," I chant to the Adonis without a face.

He's here, but all I can see is that glorious light at the end of a very dark tunnel. Wispy breath kisses my hardened nipples as he moves down my body. The quiver that skates down my spine, a direct freefall to my clit.

I'm blind, unable to see beyond the colors bursting to life behind my very eyelids. A heavy thumb circles my clit, pressing down without mercy. The head of a hard-as-steel cock flexes against my entrance. Then I feel him, flattening me beneath his huge frame once more as wicked lips press to my ear and he husks, "I died for this."

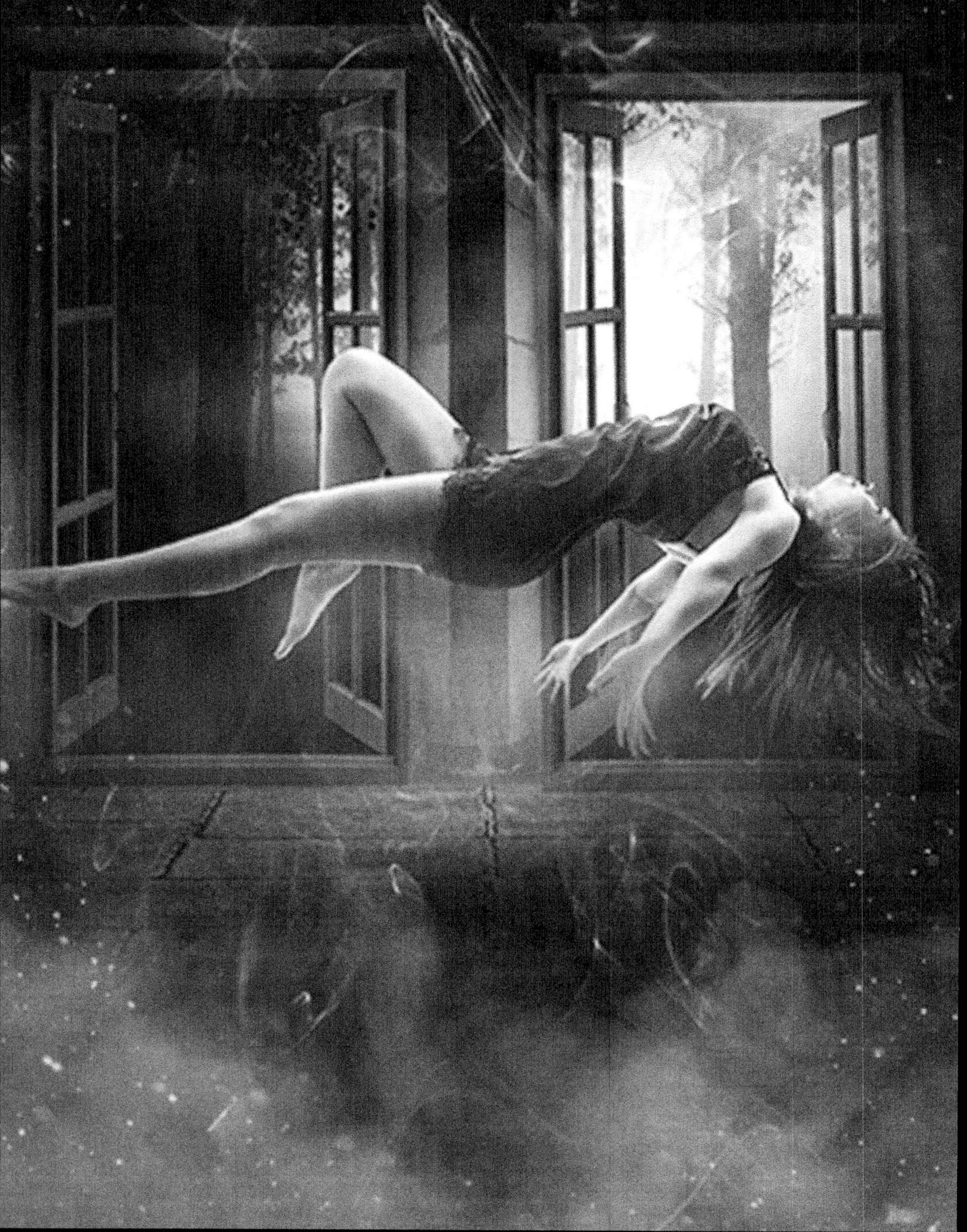

CHAPTER
TEN

Astra
Burning House - Cam

I gasp, the world around me settling back into place as my senses calm from a frantic overdrive that has me breathing heavily. I don't know at what point I fell asleep, or at what point vivid sex dreams became my escape from reality, but the crick in my neck and sun searing through my eyes tells me it wasn't by choice that I hit the deck. I stretch, then groan when every muscle within my body begins to ache like a sour bitch from high school getting her revenge because she thought I was prettier than her.

Fuck Daniella Timothy and her accidental *attack on my face with a dodgeball.*

It's been two weeks since I was attacked, two whole weeks that I've been wallowing in self-pity, and five whole nights of depraved orgasms alluding me.

I'm hot, my tits are heavy and my mood is fucking sour.

It's not enough that I'm living through hell in real life, but now my dream man wants to edge me to the point of pain? The police came back around a few days after our first interview and said that the investigation is still ongoing and that until they can determine there is no connection between me and Mr. North and they can be sure no murder conspiracy was afoot, I still need to stay in town.

After that, my only friend lived in the bottom land of Tennessee.

In a glass.

Filled with amber liquid.

I mean, there was more to me not leaving the house in a while.

It wasn't just because I was drained, mentally and physically, but because I just felt the most comfortable at home at the moment. More so than normal. Like there is something here, a shroud around the cottage that just makes my heart rest easy.

An alluring presence that makes my only burden figuring out how to stay awake And keep my glass full.

The one reprieve I'm allowed when my own dreams deny me such.

It's like every time we get to the good part, something pulls my consciousness back into a lucid state and it's the most unwelcome interruption ever. My body is sexually wired, denied of the release in my taunting dreams and even when I try to finish the job myself, I fall flat. Unable to come at all.

"Ergh!" I slap my palms against my thighs and groan in annoyance.

I need to get a grip because the *woe is me* act with a sprinkle of *nymphomania insanity - fuck me in the warped ashes of my trauma -* shade of miserable looks utterly shit on me.

Wherever the hell my mind is at, it is in a place of chaos, in a land with no orgasms. I'm tense, I'm frustrated and I want to go back to sleep and finish myself off.

Lifting a heavy hand, I peer at the living area through the slits in my fingers, regretting not installing black-out blinds in every room, instead of just my bedroom. Once again, the TV has put itself on standby and as I assess the awkward angle I'm lying at on the sofa, I notice my throw is pulled up to my shoulders and tucked in on all sides. A bubble of hysterical laughter leaks from my mouth as I drag myself upright and push the heels of my palms into my eyes.

This can't continue. The drinking, the hallucinations. I'm going to drive myself stir-crazy if I allow the darkness in, allowing it to form demonic little demons within the walls of my mind and hold me hostage.

Within the hour I've swept the floor free of glass, had a shower, washed my hair and now I'm standing on my back porch with a mug of coffee in hand. The seasons are mid-change, the summer morning mixed with a faint breeze of autumn, tugging at the surrounding trees to loosen their leaves. As such, I'm able to pull off a pair of baggy sweatpants and fluffy socks, with just a crop top dividing my torso of tattoos.

The best part about learning the trade, my curvy body has become a work of art as a group of us apprentices used to practice on each other. Detailed high under my sternum, the abstract blue orchid spirals like the legs of an octopus with drops that start as splashes and end with a black heart above the column. Inverted wings frame it from the underside up, looking like a flipped image of identical setting suns and small blue roses connecting the center to the feather-inspired wings has the heads of two beautiful skeletal, day of the dead looking women woven in. It's so intricate and one of my absolute favorite designs.

I drew it after the death of my father. He suffered through a war he had no business fighting. He fought for a country that never fought for itself and it was always a bitter pill to swallow. Only to have a house fire kill him and my brother five years after his service in the military. I was twenty when they died, my only brother, twenty-two.

I've known the loss of my father and my best friend and during the dawn of that nightmare, I died right alongside them. They left me in a dark world without any beacon of light to guide my way back to them and I feel the pain of that like a dagger in my heart to this very day. I never grieved them, I never laid them to rest and for as long as my soul screams in the agony of my turmoil, I never will.

My father Henry and my brother Lucas were the only things in this world that shone brighter than the sun and my world eclipsed when they left me here to suffer my mother alone. Lucas was always the overbearing brother, but I'd do anything to cry in his arms because I'd scraped my knee one last time. He was everything. A figure that was just there. I never had to think about it, I never had to hope. He knew me better than I knew myself and even when I wanted to suffer alone it was impossible.

Because he was always there to hold my hand and teach me to brave the storm instead of fear it.

I'd do anything to hear my father call me his little mermaid because he knew how much I loved the show *H2O Just Add Water* as a kid. I was his little Rikki, throwing fists first, asking questions never. He also always said he could imagine me putting a guy through his paces and stealing a boat or two when I got older.

If only he knew that it was the darkness that waited for me.

Not a knight in shining armor that would buy me a juice bar.

My father was the blood that pumped through my veins. You never realize just how important a role a father has in a little girl's life until they're gone. He taught me how to play the world instead of it playing me. He showed me how to fight, how to survive, but most importantly, to know my fucking worth.

Their deaths bleed a black shadow on my soul and day by day, it grows.

But as much as I refused to grieve when they left me, I have never quite felt anguish like it, I found it hard to mourn the life I dream they can be having in the afterlife. A life free from the weight of burden and pain, where the word fortitude doesn't exist. I dream that there, all they know is whatever their hearts feel for the people they love. That there, nothing other than every desire and unfulfilled wish can come true.

I hope that there, in the afterlife, ran a hell of a lot differently from real life and that everything that has the power to hurt us, is just gone—in a cloud of smoke, all that is left is utter peace.

Is it a warped way of thinking?

Yes, but it's my way of thinking. I yearn for anything to take away the pain that this life has caused me. This world isn't fair. It steals our soul piece by piece as it rips good people from this world and leaves behind only the bad.

Then when I think about it, I wonder how they became so bad in the first place.

Who have they lost?

Somebody, they love? Or themselves?

I gasp, raw tears filling my eyes as I think about my brother and father again. A searing pain pierces my chest as my eyes fly skyward. I choke, breathing raggedly as I try to stop the breakdown that's brewing.

I can't explain how much it hurts.

I'm losing again, losing the will to survive.

The tears roll down my cheeks, and the horrid sound of broken wheezing fills my ears as I fight my body for control. I refuse to cry. I'm doing everything I can to stop myself from giving in to this torment.

Sniffling, I'm about to wipe my face when a soft caress of a feather trails across my cheek. I' still, fighting my mind on the feeling of just being touched. I stare out into the woods, my mind rioting as another tear is wiped away and I shudder before a gentle pressure settles on top of my hand and my shoulders sag.

I close my eyes and let the final tear fall onto my knee, it burns the cuts still scratched across my right cheek before I blink open my eyes, lick my lips and stare back out into the woods again feeling like there is an essence here to save me.

Maybe I'm not as alone as I thought.

Jess has come by the cottage more than once. Some of those times, I'd hid in a dark corner drinking my sorrows ignoring her, and the other half of the time, I was unconscious and never heard her cry through the door at all, no doubt.

The light of my phone brightens from the low coffee table, the power bank finally doing its job. Settling into the porch swing, I exhale steadily, preparing myself to face the world—another day, another dollar. Thirty-seven voicemails from Jess and one from a cheery female officer requesting I come to the station to make a formal statement later, it's only taken them two damn weeks to get to this part of the investigation.

I curl my lip in disgust at the preppy lilt to her tone. I'm ready to curl up and block the world right back out again.

But that'll solve nothing.

Besides, I've never run from a fight, and like fuck will I start now.

As I knew it would, the fresh light of a new morning has brought with it the guilt of being a shitty friend. Regardless of her taste, Jess really loved that prick. It's evident in her voice how broken she is, and in her time of need, I ignored her in favor of my own.

Then again, she's talking about how much she is mourning the guy that tried to rape me and murder me. Not once has she asked how I'm doing.

Sipping on my coffee like a lifeline, I bring up her contact and hover my thumb over the call button. Indecision to rid myself of this bad friend wars with the fact she has been like my sister for years. She has been there through it all and right now, I'm not in the best frame of mind myself.

Might as well get this over with though.

Because I already know that I can't really disown her. She's the only connection I really have to my brother and father.

Except that the screen glitches and suddenly, as I tap my thumb against the screen, the ringtone echoes through the speaker with '*mom*' flashing back at me from it.

Wait, what - Fuck no, just *fuck the fuck no!*

"Hello?" Her voice shrills and I groan into the headset, mustering the willpower to receive her judgment and bite it back so I don't hammer in the final nail to her ever-securing coffin. There's not enough coffee in the world to deal with her. She became a different person after my pa died. After she lost her son. A person I struggled to tolerate. She's always been eccentric. Always craved power and spent years getting them into debt. But she was always my mom. All until she wasn't.

Yet as her voice rings out again, tears prickle at the backs of my eyes. "Astra? You there? Is everything okay?"

"I-I..." Come on, Astra, you can do this. She may have run off to live in Switzerland with her latest husband and left you to fend for yourself with all of the debt, but she's still your mom. She'll have compassion hidden somewhere behind the diamond necklace and Versace dress she's most likely wearing. Marrying for money is my very own mom's niche, whether he be eighteen or in this instance, eighty-three.

After Dad, she took what she thought she deserved. What she claims he never gave her during all of those years he had left her alone to fight for her freedom. She turned into a cunt made of ice and every time I hear the intrusive tone of her voice, I have the urge to tear out her vocal cords.

She tarnishes the memory of them every single fucking day with the shit she pulls. Her latest insurance policy is about to kick the bucket, but he has enough money to clear me of the debts I acquired after giving my father and brother the send-off they deserved. I was practically a teenager, just turned twenty and I fought for every last cent just to know they sailed into the afterlife in the way they deserved. Three months after the service, she was married to a man she had met by a chance encounter within the diner at three in the morning, when she was trying to eat away her supposed grief.

"What have you done this time?" she sighs in exasperation and I cut off the call as I clench my jaw so tightly that the sound of my teeth churning throughout the air makes me cringe.

But I don't recoil.

Fuck that.

When will that human part of me stop searching for the mother that I lost and just move the fuck on?

Mourn both of my parents and just have it fucking done with it.

Never mind.

Finishing my beverage, I instantly go make another one.

Why I'm so emotional is beyond me. I've been through worse than this. I've hardened my soul to the darkness that bleeds through this world. Built myself up to thrive from it. For where there is depravity, there must be those with steadfast morals and an attitude of steel to stand up and fight back.

I cannot be the only one.

I refuse to believe it.

But maybe that's the issue here. I didn't fight, I ran two weeks ago. Someone else did what sheer panic prevented me from doing.

A stranger I don't even know.

A stranger I haven't been able to stop thinking about.

A hero I can't thank, and that doesn't sit well with me…

Not in the slightest.

"Fuck it. I'm going to work," I announce to the empty house. I can't stand around with my thoughts driving me insane for a second longer. I have a client this afternoon, I've yet to cancel, so I'll take the distraction.

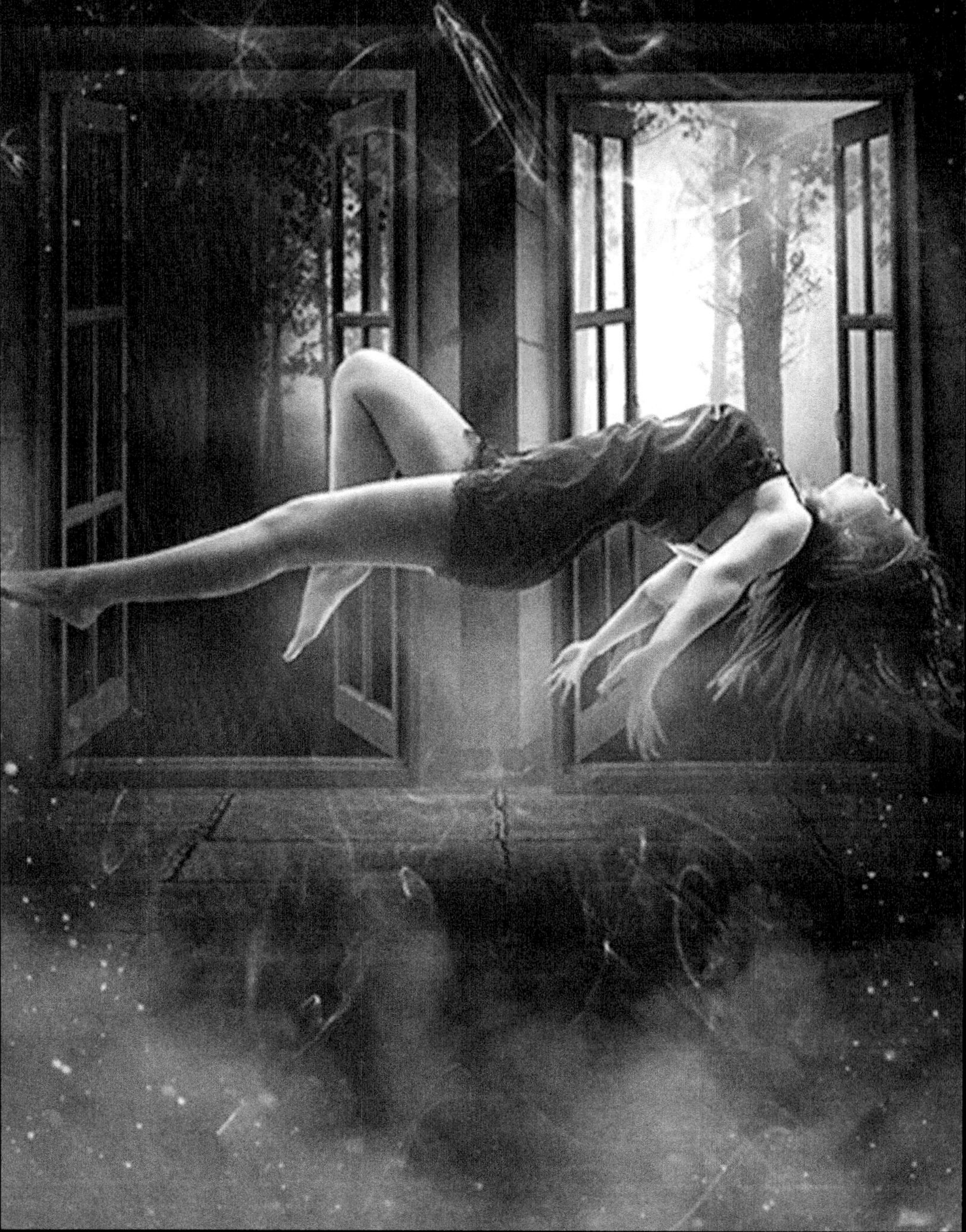

CHAPTER ELEVEN

Astra
Scars - I Prevail

Getting drunk and blacking out clearly didn't stop me from dialing Hazel at 4:00 a.m. the night the cops left and telling her I didn't know when I'd be back to the land of the living again. So I check my schedule before I leave, and everything from yesterday onward has been left the same. Yesterday was a Sunday, so the parlor was already closed.

Yanking on the matching gray sweatshirt over my crop top, I grace my fingers over the mysterious bruises I keep waking up with. They look like fingerprints. Dark and ominous and something about waking up with them makes my pussy flutter. I mean, it's probably something like an issue with my iron which I should definitely get checked. But still, the deluded air of mystery is a fun mind game.

Not sure what the docs would say about the indent of subtle bite marks around my nipples though. Honestly? I think I'm going crazy. Maybe from the shock, or from my sanity not only breaking but shattering into ashes and dust. I rub my chest, the strange marks playing on my mind in the quiet of the early morning that's dawning.

I go for full comfort and no fucks given today. My long black hair is still damp when I curl it up into a messy bun and after grabbing my sketch bag, keys and phone, I'm out just in time to catch my car before she chokes again. As I toss my bag onto the passenger seat, a bill letter falls to the floor and I huff.

I forgot all about that.

Picking it up, I fish through the contents of my bag until I pull out my phone and my little A5 binder with all of my credit details. Dialing the number, I reach my accountant quickly. "Hello?"

"Astra? Hi, I wasn't expecting to hear from you until the end of the tax year."

He knew I am supposed to be paying off some of the debt around this time of the month, so that's odd. "Okay? Listen, sorry I'm a little late. But I want to transfer you some funds and I need you to clear off a chunk of my debt. I've finally saved enough."

I put my keys in the ignition and twist, the engine turning over.

"What do you mean?"

Narrowing my eyes, I groan not in the mood for this. "Have you been drinking? What do you think I mean?"

"Astra, you have no debt. Everything has been paid in full," he tells me and my shoulders hit the back of the driver's seat like somebody has just thrown me back into it.

"What the fuck are you talking about? I haven't paid anything."

"Your friend called, nearly a year ago now. He paid everything."

"He?" I question weary, tension and anticipation ticking the back of my nape making the hairs there stand on edge.

"Yeah."

"Name?" I'm robotic now. Too stunned to have emotion in my dull and dumbfounded voice.

"Don't know. Never said. But he had all your details and funds that were legit, so I never asked questions."

I hang up and throw my phone to the floor. It bounces off the skeleton mat on the passenger side and I'm grateful when the screen lands face down and I can no longer see the light.

What the actual fuck?

My heart thunders and my palms sweat. The space beside me shimmers, glistening blue light distorting the air in line with my shoulders and I pull back in my seat. It flutters for a single moment before fading again, it almost looks like the air that warbles on a hot summer's day. Clearing my throat, grunting, and breathing deeply, I back out of my driveway and decide that my sanity will function once I have a good liter or twelve of coffee in my system.

When I get into town, I stop by the bus stop. I've isolated myself for weeks, I feel like I really need to see a familiar face right now. Daniel beams when he sees me, then frowns when he glances at my cheek. "What happened to your face, girl? Who did that to you?" I have never seen him look angry before. Never seen his aged and tanned skin turn so red from his rage. It's been two weeks, but like a true carpet burn, brick burn fares not even a tiny bit better. I have thin red lines that have cracked from the scabs that have dried and what looks like irritated, crusty little spots, reddened from the attack, still evident. But it honestly isn't as bad as it sounds. The worst is over, but anything on the face will always be obvious.

"I fell up the steps at home, caught my face on the decking. I'm fine, Dan. Have a good one okay? I just wanted to stop by and say hey," I utter, then slowly pull my arm free from his hold, from when he reached out to hold my wrist in worry, then hurry down the steps without giving him the chance to claim bullshit to my story.

I don't need to worry him.

I don't need pity either.

I just need a fucking double heart-stopper to deal with this hangover.

The double heart-stopper was probably the most basic and unsavory thing on the menu in the Empire. But they have a whole list dedicated to fixing the hangovers from the night before. So before I head to work, I head to the Empire. Finding joy in the fact that when

Theo asked for something like this, the staff told him they never offered such meals on the menu. The alley isn't too far from the restaurant, so I have to take the long way around because I can't deal with seeing the crime scene.

Not right now.

Maybe not ever.

Fuck knows how it looks after two weeks.

The sun is still rising, I got here before it even opens and then I curse myself for being so stupid. No sane person is awake at this hour on a Monday. I feel like I could weep when I get to the glass doors and see that they are closed. Resting my forehead against the door, I sigh, wanting a black hole to consume me. I'm just about to step away when a voice cracks through the air.

"Miss Stone? How good to see you. Please, stay there. I'll be down in a moment."

I jump, looking around frantically to see where the hell that masculine voice came from, and for the life of me, couldn't work it out. When the double glass doors open and the manager appears, I almost yelp in surprise but purse my pouted lips like I'm the one in control. He must see my confusion because he points up to the chunking that is sealed around the frame of the door. "Hidden cameras. This place has great surveillance. What can I get you? Are you hungry? Thirsty?" He ushers me inside and I narrow my eyes in confusion.

"I thought you weren't open until nine? It's only seven-thirty."

"Normally, yes. But we saw you outside and we couldn't leave you out there wanting now, could we?" he asks politely with a warm smile. "Now, what can I get you?"

"We?" I question again, seemingly unable to just accept they are open and I can eat until I explode.

"Yes, this building actually has five floors. One is dedicated to on-site staff. Our boss likes to be prepared as he says we'll never know when one would require to visit the Empire."

"He makes you live here and wear suits at seven-thirty in the morning?" I dip my brows and leave a question in my gaze. When he just stares at me with a soft smile, my shoulders slump and I give up. "If it isn't too much trouble, I'd love a double heart-stopper with a triple helping of dirty fries and the girl's gone wild shake. Quadruple Reese's Peanut Butter please." I cringe when I read my order out loud, it must sound like I'm some kind of a slob, but honestly? I'm very lucky. I can eat what I want and all that love fat just sits in my tits and hips. I have an ass to die for and boobs bigger than the globes of the world and I love it.

"Of course, let me show you to your regular booth. I'll get the chef to attend to you imminently." He shows me to the same booth I always seem to sit in and when I sink into the seat I groan. Tears well in my eyes at the cool and familiar sensation, and I have to take a deep breath to center myself.

Today is a new day. I won't dwell on the pain of the past.

Or in my case, the last two weeks I can barely remember living other than my sex dreams.

Tapping my index finger on the tabletop, I start scratching the wooden texture and make a tiny mark on the otherwise immaculate surface. The more the soft texture chips away, the more insistent I become until blood pools under my cuticles and something heavy lands on the back of my hand like a dead weight. But despite it being heavy, it almost feels like a gentle caress. Like somebody is holding my hand and telling me it's all going to be okay. A lone tear falls and I just sit there, staring at my idle hand willing myself to see through the veil.

Maybe it's my father? Or maybe it's Lucas?

I scoff, a small chuckle leaving my parted lips as my heavy breathing becomes that much more breathless at the unusual sensation seeping into me. Shaking my head at the absurdity of that bullshit thought, my shoulders slump and I throw my head back, resting it on the booth as I let my frustrations leave me in a deep sigh.

If my family were here, they'd take me with them.

I'd be happier dead and in their arms, than I would be here and alive.

I shudder when a trail of something cool like ice swipes across my satin cheek as a lone tear falls like the sad path of a raindrop that splatters onto the tabletop. I blink away the rest of the moisture that wells within my sad gaze, refusing to allow another tear to shatter against the wooden surface like the explosion of my life.

The anguish creeps in like the plague that slowly engulfs me in a poison of sorrow I won't be able to escape. But this time it feels different.

It doesn't feel like me.

It feels like the hand of depression is reaching into my chest and squeezing my heart. Like I'm being assaulted from the outside and I fight for the light that is warring with the shadows. Then suddenly, the suppressing heaviness is gone and I can breathe again.

Sniffling, I right myself and crack my neck. Rubbing away an ache in my shoulder, that feels like the vicious hook of cruel fingers tearing apart my flesh. I wince, the pain too physical for me to ignore as I glance behind me while the agony ripples through my left shoulder. I stay with my right arm resting on the table, unable to pull away from the warm presence I'm feeling at the moment. Something Settles within me.

Something I never knew was even unsettled like a tornado to begin with.

I'm going crazy.

"Would you like anything else, Ma'am?" a waiter asks as he approaches my table.

He lays out my high cholesterol breakfast with my dirty fries and shake to match, while I stare into the distance, lost to the mural on the far wall that stretches to the kitchen.

The entire place is understated and beautiful. The deep purples and rose gold accents are flawless. But I'm an artist, and the more I stare at the soft and subtle brush strokes of various colors along the walls that filter around the place like random splashes of color, the more I start to paint a picture of something else altogether in my mind. Have you ever seen an abstract puzzle? Where something that looks like nothing, soon turns into something as intricate and complicated as a human or an animal?

The perfected strokes I'm staring at now have hints of blues, so vivid but so scarce, you hardly see them.

But I see them...

The eyes that stare back at me.

Eyes that look as blue as mine.

"Ma'am?" the young man asks again, breaking me from my thoughts.

I clear my throat and shake my head, turning to look up at him with a soft smile. "I'm sorry?"

"I asked if you'd like anything else?" he replies gently.

"No, thank you. I'm fine."

"Just call me if you do. My name is James and I'm happy to get you absolutely anything you need."

My entire face lights up, this kind gentleman restoring a speck of my faith in humanity. Whether it is because the tips are great here or he is a genuinely nice person, he has just given me a little kindness that might just see me through the day. "Thank you, James."

He leaves me alone, and I blow out a harsh breath that takes everything that is too heavy for me to handle with it. Because fuck it, I'm the master of my fate and the world that has become a massive bitch lately—a *judgmental*, massive bitch—can utterly go fuck itself.

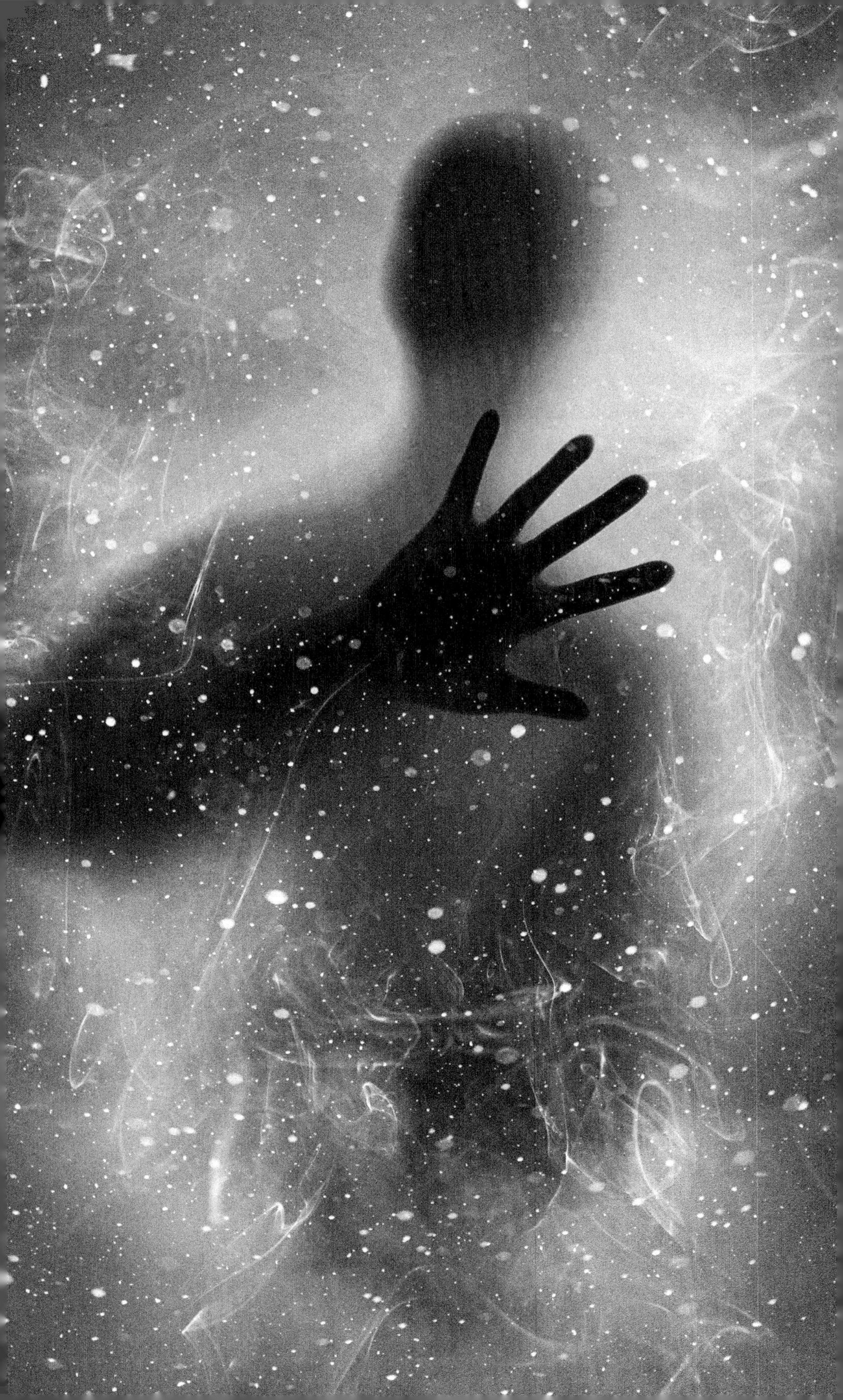

CHAPTER TWELVE

Hunter
How Villains Are Made - Madalen Duke

"Love, please don't make me kill the help. We all know those smiles are mine and mine alone," I growl, my hold on her hand tightening when her face lights up for James.

The little shit just got the first genuine smile I've seen from her in an entire year and it makes me want to throat punch him and thank him all at the same time.

His small act of kindness gave her a little strength for the rest of the day and I'm grateful for that.

Since I've never had that in my life, something inside of me settles knowing that she does. I've had to fight for absolutely everything I've ever had, from my businesses to the fortune I've earned—every ounce of strength instilled within my core came from years of fortitude. Even something as simple as a smile or a job well done, son, was elusive to me. I had a father who was manic and a mother that was invisible.

Every day consisted of hating her and plotting ways to kill him. I knew deep down he couldn't help it. Something just wasn't wired right in his head. That's probably why I never did it. Doesn't mean it hurt any less on the days I'd have to barricade myself in my room at five years old because my dad thought I was a demon sent from hell that had consumed his perfect little Hunter and dragged him into the depths of Hell.

If only he knew I was born into it. Fucked-up parents like that do a number on a kid.

I never wallow in it.

I thrive in it, and made them both fucking sorry when I built my empire and left them staring up at me from the foot of my throne.

Right now, I am torn between the same emotions when James smiles at her. I can feel Astra. I could feel her before, felt ever so connected to her, but from the other side, I mean I can *really* feel her now.

And she is so far from okay.

I can feel darkness too. Some kind of live entity that surrounds us and I don't know if that's her pain or just my own anguish at still being so far away from her.

But whatever it is, it feels fucking toxic and I have to use my strength to fight away the black shadow that is looming over her chest.

It has my mind all kinds of fucked up.

Astra is slowly giving up and I can't have that. I need her to live, I need her to enjoy the life that she has, for the both of us. I need her to have even the slightest taste of what it feels like to have everything she has ever desired even if only for a moment.

I pick up a dirty fry and bring it to my mouth, sucking the BBQ sauce clean off, the bacon and cheese with it. I groan, the taste sensational. More sensational than it ever had been when I was alive.

It's almost orgasmic. But everything over here feels ungodly visceral.

As crazy as it is, this is perfect.

Being on a date with my siren.

Even if she can't see me or anything that I'm doing at the moment.

I will the fry to become something more than satisfaction for a dead man and infuse with it the anger of a ghost so she can actually see me enjoying the food with her.

But there is a veil, a cosmic energy that is separating me from her world, even though my world looks exactly the same. When I use my energy to save her from this thing that haunts us like the plague, I have little strength left. So I'm working on building it up. I'm not going to beg for flesh and settle, on incorporeal.

I just need her to see me.

But she doesn't. Not even in her dreams.

The only place I can sink between her thighs and kiss her sensual lips.

Both of them.

It's a mind fuck, but I'll take it until I can get the strength to show myself to her as more than just a whisper on the breeze.

She winces again and I shudder, something dark pressing against my flesh and I sneer like a man who has been touched in violation. I don't know if that is the breeze on this side of life or if it is the damn Grim Reaper trying to rip my ass away from my woman and send me straight to hell. If it is, he can fuck right off.

I finally have everything I've ever wanted.

And nothing and nobody will ever take that from me.

My obsession is pure. She's perfect and she's *mine*.

Her thick lips part, wrapped around the rim of her glass as she drinks down her Reese's shake. When she pulls the glass away, thick ropes of cream line her lips and I quiver in desire as her pink tongue darts out to lap away the sweetest temptation. She nibbles her bottom lip, almost lost in thought as I lean forward and lick away the stray wisps of white from her pouty mouth. I groan, my eyes rolling back in my head as my cock throbs in wanton need. I lick her again, unable to get enough of a taste that will curb the obsession to feel her again. Finally, I kiss her. Soft, tender. I move a strand of hair behind her ear and she shivers like she can feel me, her mouth parting as she releases a sharp and sensual breath. Her eyes flutter closed.

I pull back, settling into my seat as I watch her chest rise and fall. After a moment, she gathers herself and absently tears into her burger.

Four patties, four crispy chicken breasts, salad, sinners fries, and a sauce to salivate over, stacked high. A hungover lumberjack's perfect meal.

She consumes it just as elegantly as if it was a Caesar salad, though.

"The things I want to do to this curvy body of yours, love. Your curves are as stunning as your eyes." I push her shake toward her, this time it slides across the table. I'm filled with longing, maybe that adds to my core desire to be seen by her, the strength that just gave me the ability to move this shake toward her in an offering.

She blinks, looking down at the table blankly, unsure if she had just seen her glass move or if her eyes were playing with her insanity. Numbly, she lifts it once again and finishes its contents before she slams it down and moves it away from her, pinching the bridge of her nose and shaking her head.

A feral grin lifts my lips, my ego inflating at the power I feel over something as little and as tedious as moving a simple glass. It's taxing, exhausting all of my energy, but she is worth every damn second of it.

"Your father would be proud of you, Siren. You no longer have to sing your siren's song. I'm here, baby, you lured me in. The longer you sing, love, the more you'll slowly die inside." The lines of my chiseled face pinch, my brows furrow as I'm upset and it hits me hard in the chest. "Nobody ever told me that the siren still sings for death after her other half dies. Only during that time, she sings only for herself. I don't know where your family is, love, but if they are here, I will find them."

She shudders, her eyes glaze with unshed tears and I swear, she can *feel* me, *hear* me. She *knows* that I'm here, that she'll never be alone. She has to!

One last sniffle and I can tell she is about to ready herself to stand and face the day ahead. "You're so beautiful," I whisper as I lean forward and twirl an AWOL strand of dark and silken hair around my fingers before allowing it to flutter back against her cheek. The same stubborn strand I had just tucked behind her ear, exposes her ocean blues to me. She blinks, a slight tremor in her hand that still remains under mine. Slowly, she eats the last of her fries, a faraway look in her gaze as she shoves the plate away from her. "You'll have it all. Soon, baby. Soon, you'll know just how much I loved you." A little closer, I lose myself in her eyes. A little deeper into her complexities. "How much I love you still. Soon, pretty Siren, you'll be the queen of it all."

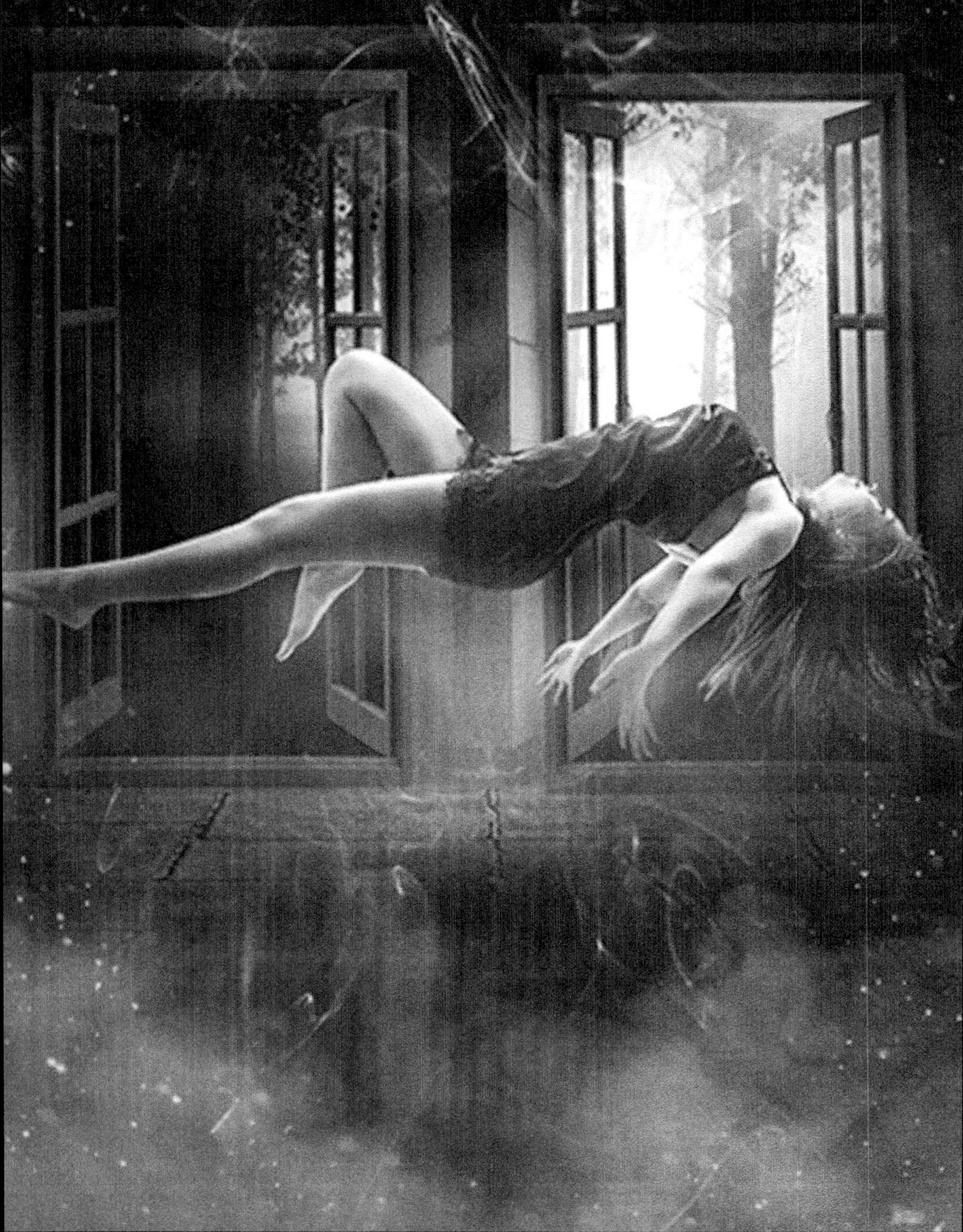

CHAPTER
THIRTEEN

Astra
Rest In Peace - Dorothy

J ust as I left it, my parlor is nestled between a hairdresser's and a nail salon on the rougher side of town. The owners on either side of me are lovely, always inviting me out for coffee although I've never accepted. Something about mixing business and pleasure unsettles me for the pure fact that if I wake up on the wrong side of the twisted sheets one day and ever feel like reporting Lana for her booming speaker system or Isabella for the unlicensed massages she gives to the male clients that enter her salon, stops me from knocking elbows with most people in the world, *especially* them.

No judgment here, but I'm also not going to be dragged down with a sinking ship. Daddy taught me better than that.

Stepping down the street, my headphones nestled in my ears, I spot the same pair of police officers that were at my home that night leaving through Siren Ink's front doors. Officer Stalmyer tips his head to me as they slide into their vehicle and glide away before I make it across the road with a fiercely narrowed glare. They must be here checking up on me, considering they were leaving the store, I guess Hazel is already here. As I approach, a gust of wind blows from nowhere to open the parlor doors for me and I stop before the threshold to see if they will push back and knock me on my ass. Weird, none of the other doors along the street were affected but I don't have time to dwell on it when Hazel waves me inside with a worried smile. That crazy feeling in my consciousness, like it is being influenced, whispers to my actual soul itself—is more settled in my chest than five minutes ago.

Those weird sensations almost remind me of that episode of *Charmed* when Rex astral projects and makes Piper feel like she needs a shrink.

Hazel's an energetic girl, still perfecting her art and getting her license before I let her touch anyone in my shop. Alongside some admin work for me part-time, she loiters around here learning everything I can teach her. Her red-tipped ponytail swishes as she rounds the desk, placing a Joy's coffee in my hand. Thank goodness for small mercies.

"Hey, are you okay?" Her widened eyes search mine like she'll find answers lingering there without any words. True to her name, her gaze is a stunning shade of brown flecked with glints of amber. "The police said you were attacked. They were asking all sorts of questions about your demeanor and those self-defense classes you took last year. Is that why you took two weeks off?" Of course, they did. I sigh, dropping my bag behind the desk, and finding a leather swivel stool to perch on. "Oh my God! Your face. It's all scratched up," she panics and I find it hard not to recoil at her concern. "And these bruises? Did they choke you?" Not one to be tender, she blurts the words out, then winces when she hears how raw they sound.

I can't tell her the bruises around my throat weren't from the attack, but from some strange-ass reason my early morning wake up calls, I can't do anything but lie. "I'm fine," is the best I can come up with, and even I can hear how weak it sounds. "Some asshole tried it on and the first chance I got, I ran. That's all there is to it. And yes, I needed the break." Although as I relay the information out loud for the first time this morning, my thoughts drift to Hunter North. On instinct, my head tips in the direction of the Empire, the top shard of his glass tower just visible over the rows of buildings separating us. I suppose it's not too unrealistic a millionaire might have been strolling the alleyways around a business of his, for some fresh air, but something's off.

I can feel it.

You'd think he'd be flanked by guards at all times, not lying dead, out of sight of surveillance with a lowlife scumbag. Especially not in this city.

I'm probably overthinking it. It's not like he's the president or anything, but it gnaws at me, this niggling feeling I have in my chest. I still haven't been able to bring myself to google his name.

This man *died* for me.

It's all I can think about.

Not a nice way to go.

Thankfully, Hazel doesn't ask any more questions, giving me a briefing on today's client. I remember him as the bearded biker that came in last week and took an interest in the stunning pinup woman with an intricate day of the dead, skeletal design on her face, bent over in a saucy little lingerie set with the Grim Reaper standing at her back. Hands on her hips and his death-inspired head thrown back in pleasure. I have it pinned to the wall. The whole piece screams dark, twisted and a real good time.

Perfect for a hairy-ass biker. He asked for something similar on his calf. I've already started the piece and spent the rest of the morning working to complete it.

Pencil in hand, music on, this is my Zen place. Hazel putters around, dusting or rearranging the artwork plastered on every wall, faintly answering calls in between songs. I have to say, I'm fortunate enough to have enough business to keep it afloat, and enough talent to charge what I like. Which then leads me to thinking about the savings in my bank account. I'm utterly stumped on who the fuck could have paid my bills.

It makes me feel sick thinking about it.

Like I now owe somebody a blood debt for helping me.

And pissed as fuck that I have been getting by on scraps thinking I never had a cent to spare. I dig my pencil in a little too deep and snarl. By the time Hazel is sliding a baguette in front of me, I've just finished the last touches of the curve of the woman's breasts and fixed the thicker strokes of her thighs I'd accidentally done in frustration.

"Seriously, are you okay? I mean, you aren't really a social person... I get that, but right now? You feel as cold as the Arctic," Hazel comments and I stop, eyes down as I stare at a single black marking on the page.

"Hazel, I appreciate it. I do. But I don't want to talk about this. Right now, I'm confused, I'm sore and my mind is tired. And all of that? It's just from the last two weeks. I just want to move on. I *need* to move on. I was attacked, I'm pissed and nothing is making sense to me right now. I just need my art, okay?"

A moment of silence falls before a gentle hand rests on my shoulder and my entire body clenches. "Okay. But I'm here if you need me, tell me that you know that." Her voice is quiet and I can't bring myself to answer, so I just nod instead. Staring back down at the page, I focus on the design I just drew.

The delicate woman is all fine lines and thick curves. She's ample in all the right places wearing a leather bodysuit, cut low around her tits leaving the rounded flesh to spill over the restriction. The color, a shade of a blooming rose, bright in luxurious red, thrives against all odds, staring back at me. The outfit is scarce, showing more skin that it's covering. Cut out in a way that screams she's ready to be wicked. Little devil horns poke out from under her thick brown hair and I'd say she's a bitch ready to be naughty. I marvel at the piece, memorizing every line as I finish off my lunch and the door opens to reveal my next victim. Dressed the same as before, in a leather jacket and high boots, he smiles handsomely and presents a box of Krispy Kreme's that he's holding in his hand before me.

"Aww." I stand and brush myself down. "And to think I was going to cancel on you." His smile widens on his youthful face, his dark brows and top knot putting him around thirty. Even in my baggy sweats, his chocolate eyes glint with appreciation.

Only a biker can pull off joggers and a cut.

"I'm glad you didn't." He dips his head. The doughnut box shoots from this hand, managing to somehow smash against the glass cabinet of artwork Hazel has just finished cleaning. The three of us stand staring at the box, slowly falling down the length of the glass door with a trail of cream painting a white smeared cloud, escaping the plastic lid following in its wake.

"Umm, yeah... there seems to be a bit of a wind today," I offer, not knowing what else to say, my eyes unable to pull away from the cabinet as if something standing beside it calls to me. The air warbles again and a pain forms along my brow bone from the concentration.

"Maybe you have a ghost, darling. Just say the word, I'll protect you," he offers with a soft wink and a deep, raw, and gravely chuckle.

I return the laugh, finding that sentence humorous. "I think they'd need protecting from me."

One of the needles, wrapped in packaging sitting on a steel tray, busts free, and stabs me in the thigh. I hiss, pulling back to look down at the thin needle sticking out of my leg and frown. I can't keep shaking off the crazy things that have been happening since the night after my attack.

It's been two whole weeks of confusion and I'm starting to fear my own mind.

Everything feels wrong. These twisted energies are entwining around me and now I have a fucking needle sticking out of my leg and a very concerned Hazel staring me down.

"Oh, shit, girl. You okay?" my burly client asks in genuine

concern. I pull it from my thigh and chuckle awkwardly, waving it off like it's nothing.

"Damn packaging. They should check these things before they send them out." Chucking the contaminated needle into the trash, I head to my seat and place my thumb over the tiny pebble of blood. The needle is tiny, I hardly have a scratch on me. Like a blood test, I stem the bleeding and forget it ever happened.

But as I settle into my seat, ominous energy settles heavily on my shoulders.

Hazel spurts into action, cleaning the unit again while I show the biker to my stabby seat. That's just what I like to call the black leather recliner that took months to pay off, and it's officially *all* mine. I run my hands down the soft leather, offering my baby a small pat of appreciation.

Sliding off his jacket and joggers, he lies on his front in a tight T-shirt and tighter boxers so I can get to work shaving his calf free of hair that's grown back since the first time we worked on this piece. His body is decent, and he's clearly put a lot of work into it, but there's a void between what I find attractive in the man laid within this chair and in real life. Like the moment I put my professional hat on, the ink is all that matters and I'm blind to who I'm actually tattooing.

They're just a lump of flesh and skin stencils for my portfolio at this point.

Checking he's happy with the stencil and giving me free rein on positioning, I set up the fresh needle and black ink, glove up, and just as I switch on the machine the door whips open again. Except for this time, it's no wind, but a furious-looking Jessica. I roll my eyes, anger the first and most primal and agitated emotion that hits me in my chest.

"You're working?!" she screams accusingly. Her brown hair is a bird's nest of knots upon her head, her cheeks permanently red from crying. The streaks of mascara have stained beneath her chocolate eyes, pooling them with a bleak contour that speaks of no sleep.

Wow, she does look like shit and it goes to prove I underestimated how much she could care for that fucker. "Theo is dead. You don't answer your phone for two freaking weeks. I can't catch you at home and now I find you here, *working*?!" she spits the last word like a curse, her usually dull eyes wide with fury.

Placing down the tattoo gun, I apologize to the biker and ask him to excuse me briefly. Then, all manners vanish as I tug Jess into the cramped bathroom.

"Have you spoken with the police?" I hiss, giving her shoulders a rough shake when a sob tears from her throat.

No more crying wasted tears.

Not a chance in hell.

Especially when my cheek begins to sting from the marks of my assault.

"I've just left the station. It's been two weeks and they wouldn't tell me anything! Decided since you won't answer my calls, I'd come looking for you!" she shouts, yanking out of my grip. She's still in the same mini dress, turquoise with dark glitter fading from the bottom up. On her feet, a pair of thin canvas shoes, that look like they are prison-issued, give her no grip as she almost slips over the toilet. "What happened?! You need to tell me right now! Theo must have been checking you were getting home safe and they say you attacked him, now he's dead! I know you didn't like him but-"

The crack of my hand connecting with her cheek must be heard from outside this tiny stall. Silence follows, both inside and out, cutting off the light chatter between Hazel and Mr. Fine and Burly When I speak again, seeing pitch fucking black for the first time ever in our friendship of sisterhood, I can feel the final thread that was holding us together snap.

It's in a low tone laced with unbridled rage that has her back straightening and her eyes widening, that I respond to her, "Get the fuck out of my shop." I want to be sympathetic, I want to care. I want to tell her to pull herself together and take a fucking shower for

Christ's sake. She must not have gone to her mom's in the end because there is no way Teresa would let her still look like this.

But most of all, I want her to ask if *I* am okay. To have known me better than to accuse me of what the police have clearly planted in her head. Every emotion passes through her delicately beautiful face.

"Astra," she whispers so brokenly I can feel the pain like it is my own.

"Get the fuck out, before I throw you out, you self-centered, stuck-up bitch. Look at my face, Jess. I didn't get this as a result of attacking that piece of fucking shit now, did I? No! I got it when he slammed me into a brick wall two weeks ago and tried to rape me!" God, saying those words out loud has something vile tasting tormenting my mouth. "Now get the fuck out!" I lose it, no longer willing to be her punching back for regretful mistakes. I reach out and snatch a handful of her matted hair and shove her toward the door.

Jess releases herself from the bathroom and storms out with fresh tears, crying uncontrollably. I catch the eye of the biker now sitting back on the stabby seat and raise one finger with the best smile I can muster.

Letting the door close again, I hang over the sink and breathe. In for three, out for five. Running home to wallow in self-pity isn't an option. Not if I want to survive the next few days when I only have myself to rely on.

Peering up in the mirror, I freeze as an outline of a transparent hand on my shoulder appears. Curled around the fabric of my sweatshirt, leaving a visible imprint of a faint caress underneath as if the hand is really there. Not just an illusion of a cheap and crappy mirror in my dingy little parlor bathroom. Something hot brews in my core, a lust for an aspiration thick in my apex as my thighs clench at the sensual feel seeping into my skin. It's like ink dropped in water. A tiny pinnacle, before it spirals and consumes you whole. It's like the wind that kisses against me is infusing me with calm and tranquility.

Reaching up, the appendage disappears and it feels as if a weight lifts from my body. The release in pressure leaves a pang of sorrow in my heart as the feeling that I was being hugged from behind disappears with it.

I didn't feel anything on my shoulder until it disappears though, only seen it, but now I'm wondering, did I really see anything at all?

It's too familiar to be such a foreign touch.

What the fuck is happening to me?

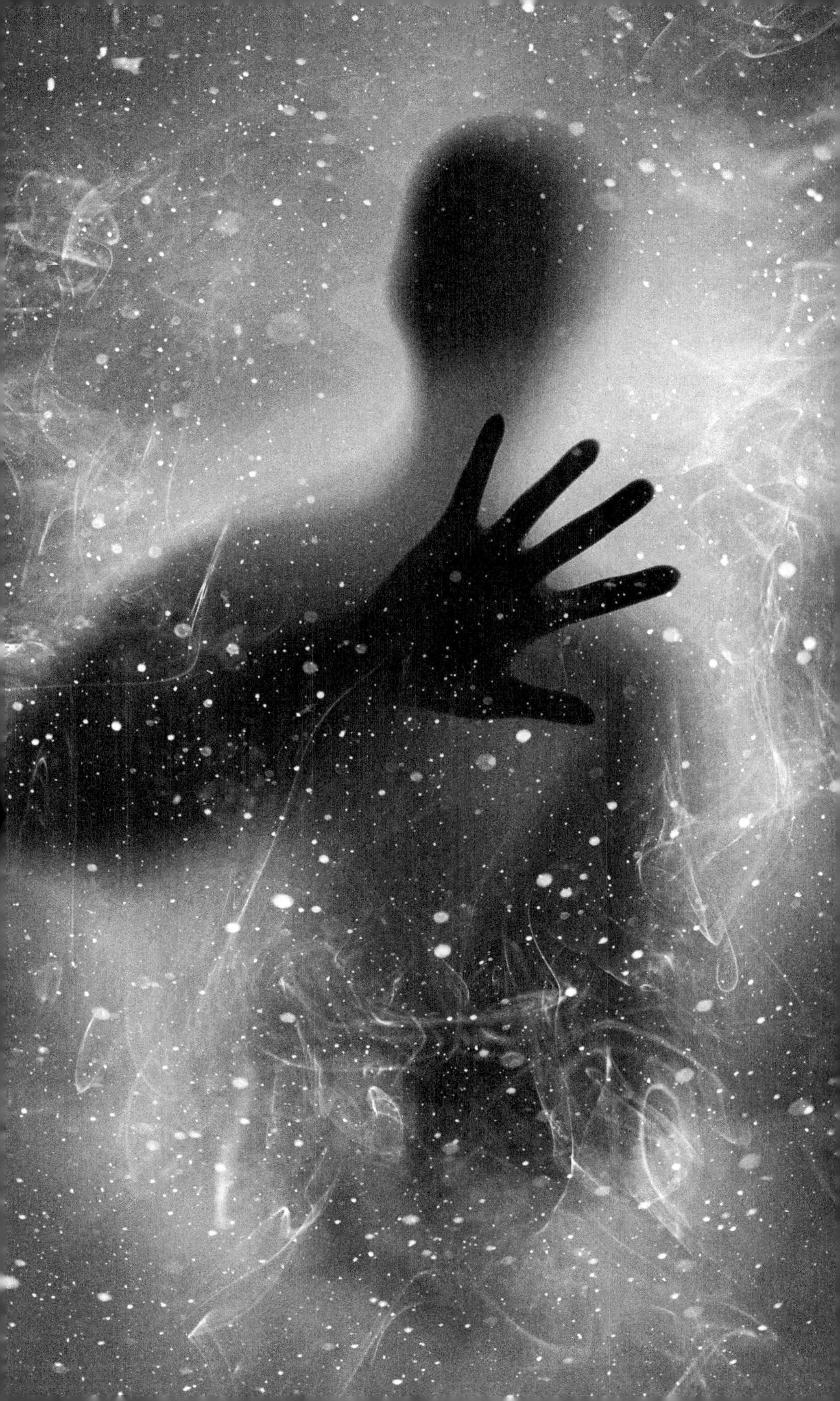

CHAPTER
FOURTEEN

Hunter
In Case You Don't Live Forever - Ben Platt

Jealousy courses through my spirit, the rage simmering beneath the surface causing Astra's tattoo gun to sputter out. She taps it on her thigh, distracting me with the ink splot on her creamy skin to get it working again. I tried locking her in the bathroom in an effort to keep her from touching this cunt's calf again, but it only worsened the situation. After her foot slips into the toilet whilst trying to gain enough height to climb out of the window, she soaks her entire leg. Then the preppy receptionist loaned her a denim mini dress to wear. Thick straps hook over her shoulders connecting to the metal buttons curved over her shoulders. The crop top separates her perfect breasts from the rough material. I'm as livid as I am ravenous, barely resisting the urge to jack my ghostly cum all over her. I can't allow myself to become too distracted while this asshole on the bench is giving her the same lustful eyes as those boring into my skull like hot coals. I might miss him leaving and my chance to follow him home and fuck up his entire life will slip from my fingers.

Killing this fucker will make perfect practice.

I don't care if I'm dead. I'll do anything to mess up that rugged face of his.

Astra won't even recognize him after I've learned to harness my energy on lifting heavy objects. Smashing doughnuts over the cabinet will seem like child's play.

I'm so caught up, my focus zeroed in on that ink splot, that I only cue into the phone ringing when the receptionist rushes through me to answer it.

Holy fuck.

A skip in the beat of your heart is nothing like the jitter of the skip in your soul's very essence.

I feel *violated*.

Disgusted.

She walked right fucking through me.

Cold fucking damn.

"Siren Ink Tattoo Parlor. You think it, Astra Inks it. Hazel speaking, how can I help you?" she quips cheerily, following her greeting with mmmm's and uh huh's before wedging the phone between her shoulder and ear to call out over the tattoo gun's vibrations.

"Hey, Astra, it's that bar you like to drink at - the Empire?" she calls and Astra tilts her dainty head, a tussle of raven curls coiled into a bun, lose strands falling in the heat of the store slipping over her bare shoulders and concealing some of the metal buckles and the unique shoulder tattoos of unnatural butterflies on her shoulders that draw my attention.

Astra straightens at this, her curiosity piqued.

As is mine.

"Um, yeah? I was literally just there this morning. Did I leave something behind?" My Siren starts to pat herself down for some invisible possessions, soon remembering she isn't even in the same outfit and I swallow thickly, my mind running away with the thought of her touching herself.

Smoother, slower.

"Not quite. There's a waiter called James on the phone and he's asking for you personally. Apparently, they're having a service for their boss that died a few weeks ago. He's extending you a special invite, forgot to mention it earlier. *Weird, right?*" She covers the receiver to whisper the last bit but if Astra finds my memorial *weird*, she doesn't show it. Half shrugging, Hazel takes down some scribbled notes and hangs up. Somehow, I doubt she has a career as a receptionist but not everyone vets their staff as strictly as I do.

Or *did*.

I'm still adjusting here.

Glancing back at the scene before me, Astra swipes the loose strands of her black hair over her shoulder, craning her neck side to side. Smoothing my thumbs over her nape, she releases a soft moan and shifts as if my touch is bringing her comfort so I continue. The two-headed snake drawn into Skully's calf is taking shape. Incredibly realistic detail has been added to the slick scales, drops of moisture cascading along their intertwined bodies. The rose in the center is currently an outline, but I can tell it'll be a sight to behold.

In that moment, with my presence soothing the tension in her posture, I can see the truth. She's a master of her craft, a rare talent in a sea of impostures. As her future, her dead man walking and her soul mate, I need to let her work. More than that, I'm here to protect and worship her, support her every decision and celebrate her success. That's the resounding thought coursing through my mind and allowing me to release my tender hold on her nape and take a step back so she can continue with her work without moaning sensually in front of the prick she is tattooing, thinking those sensual sounds are for him.

I have no idea how our relationship will be moving forward, but as I grow stronger I'm more determined to make her mine and make her *know* she's mine. My woman has an empire to build, a legacy to create. One dead man's pound of flesh at a time.

Because anyone who touches her or is touched *by* her is a dead man.

It's simple facts.

My footsteps take me to the doorway and with a strike of satisfaction when she looks back for me, I slip straight through the door. Hovering over her every move isn't healthy for either of us, even if she has become my obsession. Watching from across the street and lingering over her shoulder are completely different scopes of creepy. I mean, don't get me wrong. I have no boundaries, never have, never will.

But I need to navigate this new path in my life, find myself in the life after I guess, and I can't do that if the anger of another man under her delicate touch is blinding me with rage instead of focus.

Besides, Astra hasn't shown any interest in the many males that have passed through her tattooist's chair, so why would I be concerned now? If anything, I'm closer than ever in making her mine and she doesn't even know it yet.

She doesn't even know that I'm here at all. She feels me, but knowing it's the man who died saving her and placing a soft hand on her shoulder to comfort her is something she'll never understand until I find a way to make her understand.

Before I know it, I've drifted a few streets over, into the disregarded shadows. A stray cat hisses in my general direction, toppling over a trash can in its haste to escape my unholy energy. The officer posted at the end of the alleyway twists to cast his eyes over the crime scene at his back that is cordoned off with yellow crime scene tape. Guess now they got the witness shit out the way, they have informed my team.

That means things will be moving along smoothly, and quickly.

At my feet, a darkened patch of our blood has bled into the stone. Lacking the crimson, absent of the coppery smell, and instead becoming a patch of dirty onyx, leaking into the crack, soon to be washed away by the rain and that... is my legacy.

All that's left of Hunter North.

A stain on the earth that over time will become forgotten history.

My hand absent-mindedly rubs my side, not a shred of regret marring my sacrifice. When I look down, I notice the transparency of my dark cloudy essence has a scar across my ribs. My battle scar. My required sacrifice. My death wound haunting me from the other side.

If I hadn't saved Astra last night, I'd have slit my own throat just to revel in the pain I deserve. She's worth my life ten times over. I had fallen in love with her when she was nothing but a stranger. Every day, my stalking grew into something soul-deep, something larger than mortality can comprehend, and has also become a love that surpasses the ages and the human expectancy of life.

What I feel for her cannot be explained in words.

After all, what is love if not an obsession?

Anything else is passing the time before you find it.

If your whole world is turned on its head, fucked up, and left in the ruins of an explosion due to a result of a collision of passion, all without a reason why... you know that's love.

If you're able to explain love, twist it into words of poetry, it's nothing but an infatuation.

Because when your soul screams for its other half, all you need to know is they are yours because they aren't bellowing reason back at you. They are bellowing an urgency. An insistence to consume and devour, to claim and to conquer, and to never look away in fear of another predator stealing what's yours.

As if tugged by the pull of that very notion, I peer up to the vision of my desires striding past the end of the alleyway. The officer has disappeared, the sky having dipped into darkness, hooded by clouds promising an incoming storm. I've stood here pondering my wasted existence from afternoon to evening and as Astra halts to stare into the alley, I can feel her eyes boring into my soul. Ocean pools of turbulent blue, pondering the *'what ifs'* I ache to erase from her furrowed brows.

Pained memories are replaying over her features, her gaze dipping to the stain at my feet.

I stride forward with measured steps, more confidence thrumming through my being than I ever had when alive. I'm sure some would call me a coward, but I call myself courageous. To see what I want and commit to learning her every dream and desire. To put in the time others so easily shrug off.

Winning a woman like Astra isn't a fool's errand.

It's a hero's fucking quest.

Cupping her cheek, she subconsciously leans into me without realizing it, her eyes closing briefly. When she's ready to open them again, all traces of torment becomes a distant memory. A hardened glare faces the alleyway, filling my chest with the pride that attracted me to her in the first place.

How she combats the world with steely armor protecting the heart meant for me.

Turning on her sneaker-clad heel, looking hot as all hell in the denim mini dress with frayed threads stroking the back of her thighs, she leads the way back to the Empire.

My club. My restaurant. My home.

Her Empire now.

The sharp point to the glass building spears the storm clouds, dropping a smattering of tears for me. Catching up to Astra's side, I throw both main doors open for her, catching the attention of my entire staffing team. Every eye regards her with the appreciation of a queen, their training and NDA's still in full effect after my demise. Heads slightly bowed, they welcome her into their fold exactly as I'd expected. After all, the members of staff currently circling the bar, where an oversized framed portrait of my face hung, could be considered the only family I had in this world. It's only natural they'll accept Astra as their new hierarchy since it won't be long before the keys to my fortune are nestled in her palm, all before she can even have the chance to blink.

Just how I wanted it.

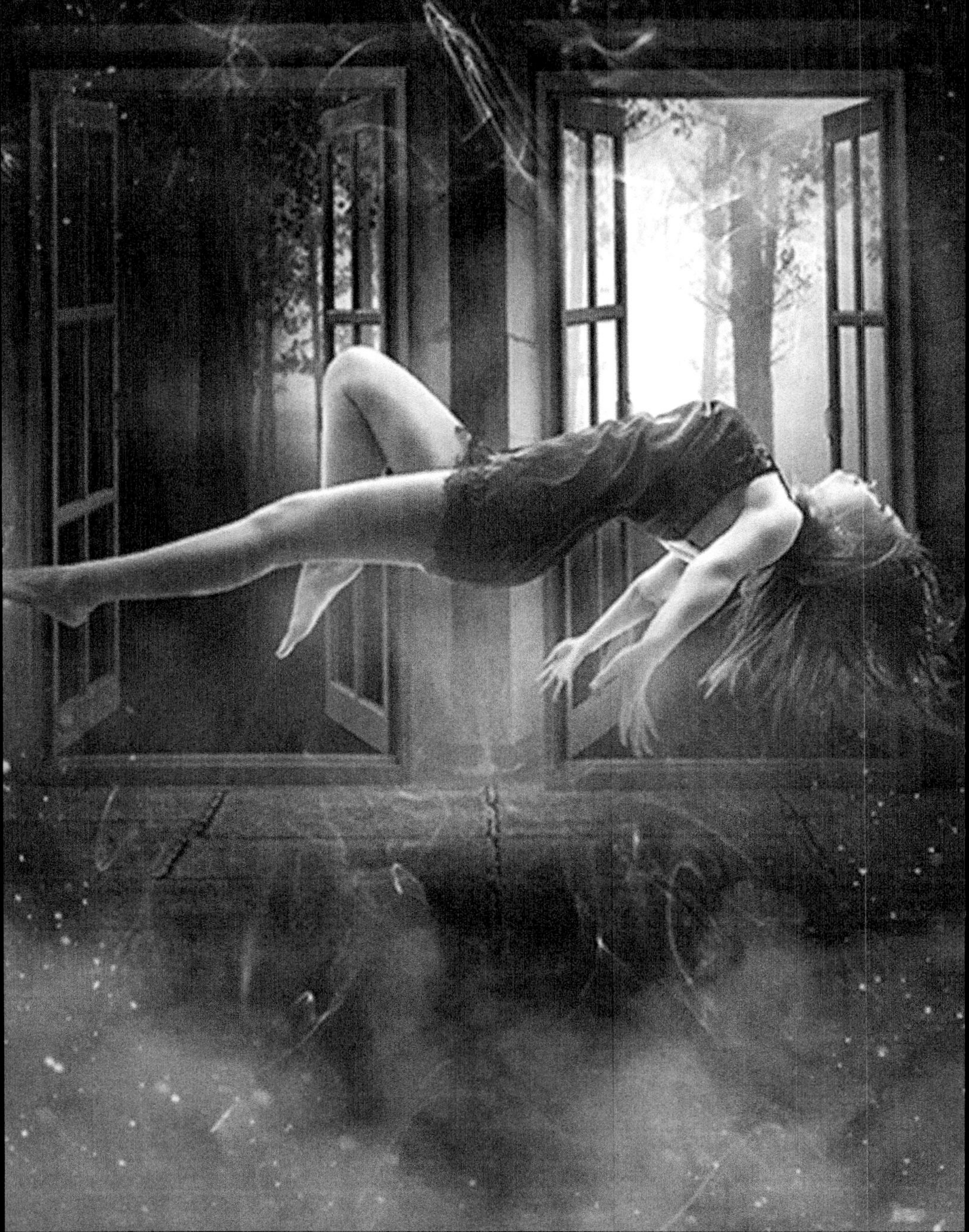

CHAPTER
FIFTEEN

Astra
Carry You - Ruelle

C onfusion like a heavy cloud surrounds me, mirroring the storm clouds in the sky. When the doors burst open like I'm royalty descending the red carpet and all of the employees turn to welcome me like I run the place, nerves swim in my core. I've always been drawn to this place and not once have I ever walked through these doors feeling regret. But that is all I'm feeling at this very moment.

Heavy regret.

Honestly, everything has happened so fast that I haven't had the time to process what I'm doing here. I was given facts and I denied them. Now I'm standing in one of my favorite places in the world to offer tribute to the man who saved my life. A man I had never even had the pleasure of saying two words to.

I never knew him and now I wished more than anything I had.

When I glance at the memorial image, shame floods me like a

tidal wave. My back buckles under the affliction, then I'm stolen by the current that pulls me under.

It all comes rushing back.

I know I can't do this—look at his face. I've kept myself from doing as such for two freaking weeks.

Now that I have, I can't unsee it.

How can I pay tribute to a man I just killed?

I ran like a coward in that alley, lost to my fear and unexpected attack. So that when I was free from the shadow of terror, I fled and just left him there like his life somehow meant nothing compared to mine. I never even turned to see who it was that saved me. I never even turned to see if Jess had followed us out.

That is my shameful truth.

Nothing.

Nothing but cowardness.

Mortification burns fiercely in my chest as I turn, swallowing thickly, and run from the building. On the sidewalk, I double over and heave deeply, trying to catch a breath that isn't filled with confusion and anguish. For the millionth time today, a hand falls on my shoulder and calmness seeps into my soul. I yelp when that soothing coolness turns into a firm grip of heat and I spin into it, finding a man behind me.

This time, I'm no damsel and I grab him by the wrist, bending it into an arch that has him turning with it, in fear of it breaking. Once I have his arm firmly against his back, I shove his face into the brick wall and almost choke at the similarity of it. "I don't know you," I hiss. "So why the fuck are you touching me?"

"I-I'm sorry!" he splutters and chokes as I let him go and step back, on guard in case he tries to attack me. There is a good chance I just overreacted and an even bigger chance I'll refuse to admit that. "I'm so sorry to startle you, Ma'am. But I am, er, *was* Hunter North's personal assistant." He clears his throat and turns to face me. Straightening out his suit, he runs a worried hand through his dark blond curls.

"And that has you touching me... why?" I question with narrowed eyes and confusion clear on my face.

A running fucking theme today apparently.

"He requested that in the event of his passing, his will shall be read at the wake. He wished for all parties to be present and that specified you, Miss Stone." I pull back like he just sucker punched me and my head spins like he just did as well.

Round and round it goes as bile rises in the back of my throat.

I turn around and give him my back. Inhaling a deep breath, I center myself and prepare to walk away from this rabbit hole I do *not* want to fall down. Glancing over my shoulder at the flabbergasted assistant I say, "I think there has been some confusion. I have never even met Mr. North."

Just as I lift one foot off the ground he adds, "Oh, but Miss Stone, he has definitely met you."

I knew that.

I knew that I tattooed him a year ago. That he came back every week for a new piece and never uttered two words to me. Just as I never uttered two words to him. Too lost in my art to find the words of the masterpieces I was etching into his skin for life.

I never mentioned it because it was irrelevant. He was genuinely a stranger in my seat, all until I saw that photo. I didn't really know him at all. I never asked his name, never saw his face outside of the moments that he came to me, and sat stoically as he watched my hands move across his satin skin.

God, his skin.

As smooth as silk, and as perfect as an artful masterpiece.

He was my favorite client.

He gave me everything I needed. Silence, patience, praise.

The energy between us was more than an idle passion for something we both loved. The ink and the art.

It was electrified. It supercharged in between our silence as words were unspoken.

I thought I was the only one who could feel it.

But him needing me at his will reading?

That's insane.

"Honestly, sir. You have the wrong person. As I said, I never knew Mr. North." Then I started my way down the sidewalk with a heavy heart of regret.

Yeah, I had a secret and it was mine to keep.

I knew the man who saved me and now, I have to live with the heavy grief of knowing that I was the one who got him killed.

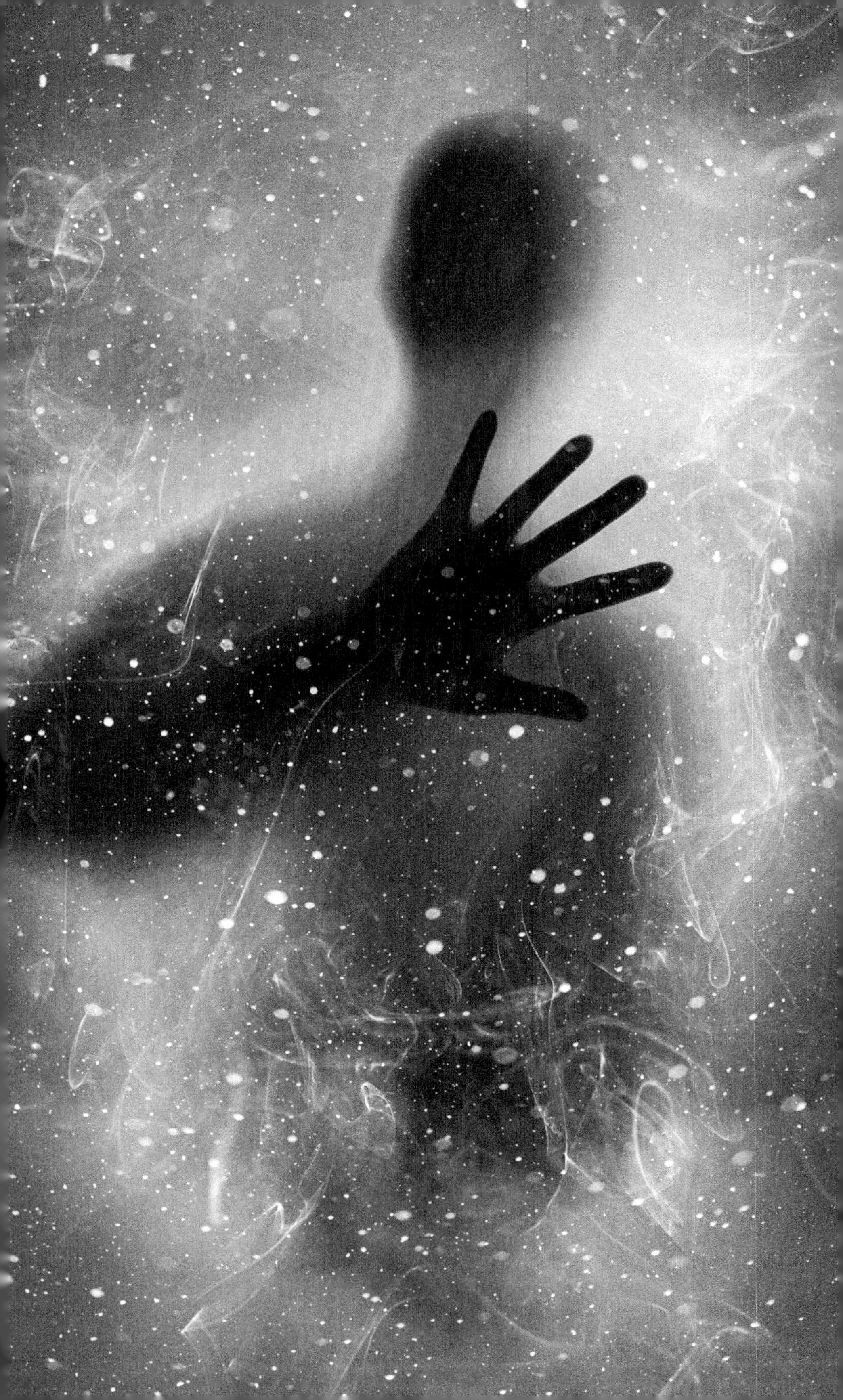

CHAPTER SIXTEEN

Hunter
Don't Forget About Me - Emphatic

The hurt in her eyes is devastating.

She walks away without even looking back and something inside of this wavering soul of mine twinges. I wish I understood her pain, wish I could feel it.

Normally I would. Normally, I am so in tune with her, I feel like we are one being, because even in the shadows I can feel her inside of me like a living entity.

But right now all I can feel is my own gut-wrenching turmoil.

My own soul-crushing pain.

It consumes me and overshadows everything she is feeling right now.

I'm drowning in regret and grief.

It isn't enough that I died for her.

Now when presented with the truth, she doesn't even *remember* me.

I thought it was cosmic. That she would see my face and just *know*.

She walked into the Empire, saw my face standing there on that stupid memorial display, and *left*.

I thought it was because she finally recognized me.

That she finally *knew* everything I have done and everything I have been for her all of this time. That the pieces I know confused her, would finally fall into place.

That since that very first moment, she has been mine.

That she has never been alone and I have always been by her side. Watching, waiting, protecting what I love most in this world. I thought it would click into place and she would finally know how much she mattered.

When I saw her standing there in the bank, just after I had left an important meeting about my finances well over a year ago, it was luck.

The first time she walked into the Empire, it was fate.

I knew our destiny was entwined.

That she is mine.

That it will all end with her.

From the start of my day to the sweet and succulent end.

Instead, she stands in front of Damien and denies ever having met me. By the time we get back to her house, I am in a rage that would scare even the dead.

You know... if there are other dead people around me that is.

I don't know how the afterlife works, but I never thought it would be so lonely.

I gave up everything for her. I gave up my life and she can't even remember my face. Something wild courses through me and as soon as she steps through the front door, I slam it closed. This time, my strength is stronger than it has been in the last few weeks. The sound echoes, ringing throughout the room as the hinges warble and the material splinters. Astra yelps, turning in a full circle with her hand on her chest as she stares at the offending front door with suspicion. Keeping her eyes trained toward the front of the house like something will jump out and say *boo*, she gingerly takes a step away, with a creased frown, then walks toward the stairs.

The hallway is immaculate, nobody would think that chaos lies behind closed doors, but every room up here bar one is used as storage and filled with absolute shit.

The stuff she has never wanted to deal with.

She wanders toward the only room that she has ever cared about and opens the door leading into her art room. The room is barren apart from a set of drawers that have been built so deep into the wall, you can't even see them. She has painted over their outward surface with various designs, so as not to take away from the feeling she was creating around her. There is a huge chest in the corner, one that looks like a treasure chest, with gold, sapphire, and blood-red crystals. The rest of the place is minimal. Murals and sketches cover every inch of the walls. A thick and plush gray carpet with the biggest bean bag chair you have ever seen in your life sits in the center.

Up on the ceiling, dark but tender strokes of wicked angel wings sprawl across the expanse of the room and twist with something darker, something warped and depraved but sinfully beautiful.

She has painted a beautiful, anguish-filled dark angel that is all fine lines and angelic beauty. There is deep sorrow in her eyes but it's mixed with something soul-deep, something that looks like love as her interruption of the devil is wrapped around her from behind, head on the dark angel's shoulder like he will forever be her sentinel soldier.

Her devoted protector.

I look down, the same image as on the ceiling, etched into my right arm with silken ink that now has a blue under light from the flicker of my tormented soul.

It's *my* tattoo.

When I first ever laid eyes on her, I knew I'd be her Devil. That I would drag her to Hell but be the sentinel that kept her safe and gave her a slice of heaven every time I touched her delicate skin. That is why I had her create this design, I asked for it at the moment that I knew this is what I'd always be...

Hers.

Her nightmare, her protector, her man.

Somebody who will save her from all that goes bang in the night.

Somebody who will save her from herself.

Only, there was never anybody to save her from *me*.

She's been in my dreams for so long, that the moment I lay claim to it all, she'll never even see me coming. I know that is in our cards.

But I never expected to matter to her before she even knows I am the shadow that follows her through the storm.

I stumble forward, stalking her every move as she pulls something from the chest and then slumps down onto the beanbag.

Flicking through a stack of pages, she looks through designs she has drawn and each and every one of them is mine.

Tears well in her eyes as she studies them, running her slender fingers over the lines she had drawn with such love and tender care. "I'm sorry," she whispers and confusion filters through me.

I fall to my knees, my hand on her thigh and as soon as I make contact she gasps, and the first tear falls. "I'm so sorry that I killed you, Hunter"

She remembers.

She remembers *me*.

The sound of my name was like sin on her thick lips. It burns through my chest like a fine shot of whisky and I groan.

The need to comfort her is overwhelming. The need to take away all of her pain is an agony in my soul. If I can't find a way to comfort her now, the afterlife will mean nothing when the bowels of Hell consume me in their flames.

"I am so, so sorry that I killed you," she sobs again and the words hit me like a spear piercing the center of an apple.

Lifting my hand, I wipe away the trail of her tears and she shudders. "Oh, love. You didn't kill me, Siren. I was always ready to die for you. That was my fate," I rasp back, wishing more than anything she could hear me.

She inhales deeply, the intake of air makes her shoulders rise and in doing so, causes her to pull a little farther away from me.

Slowly, those tear-filled eyes look upward.

Blankly for a moment.

Then they focus, meeting mine.

She tilts her head tentatively, and they widen to something so far beyond confused and awe-struck, I'm not sure there is a name for such a look.

"Hunter?" she whispers, the world stops and time stands still. The molecules around us freeze, and the low light in the room lightens up the space as if the universe had just realigned and the stars in the sky have just exploded.

She withdraws, falling backward out of her bean bag as I rush forward, leaning over her to brush the strands of tear-soaked hair from her face. Astra trembles, shaking uncontrollably as she looks me in the eye and falls shock-still.

"What I would give, Siren. For just one more moment in this life. I'd do it all right. I would make you mine the second I lay eyes on you. I'm sorry it has to be like this, I'm sorry that you'll never know. But even in death, love, you will always be mine. I will always be here and you will never, *ever* be alone." My brow furrows, my frown deepens as I caress her cheek lost in my thoughts.

She trembles, her wide eyes fluttering as she stares at an image before her I know she can't place. I know it's her fear, messing with her mind and soon, I'll lose this delicate moment.

I can't believe she kept it all. All of the artwork, all of the countless hours spent designing them to my specifications. Only to now see the biggest inspiration she has, is the one that matters most to me sprawled across her ceiling.

I am wrong.

She does remember me, she is just too warped within her emotions to admit it.

She thinks she killed me.

She has no idea that this was something neither of us could escape.

I was always supposed to die for her.

I'm snapped back to reality when she opens her mouth and utters, "B-but you're dead!"

My gaze widens at her words and I fall to my knees, making her squawk like a raven and crab crawl away from me. "You can see me?" I ask, frantic. Thinking it was just a moment in time we had both just stolen, not that I had found a way to breach the veil that parted us.

She turns and crawls away, struggling onto her feet before she flees. Artwork crushed in her hand as she runs down the stairs like a bat out of Hell.

I suddenly have this overwhelming urge to not let her escape, and before I know it, I'm blocking her retreat at the bottom of the stairs without ever having moved my feet.

"Astra, wait!"

"Satan rose the dead," she exclaims in shock and I cock my head at the strangeness of it, then smirk at the absurdity spewing from her fuckable lips and my ego inflates knowing that she never talks like that unless something has really gotten under her skin. "I'm going insane." Then she storms past me toward the front door, shaking her head like there is an escape from the madness I shroud her within.

If she can see me, it's game over.

I can up the antics.

Rushing forward, Astra's hand extends to the door handle just as a thud reverberates through the splintered wood. With a shriek, she jumps back, until the knocking continues and she has no other choice but to respond. Standing on bare tippy toes, she peeks through the tiny hole in the door and heaves a steady breath.

"Who is it?" she asks as she leans her forehead against the cool wood and I growl.

If somebody had a gun on the other side, it really would be game fucking over.

I need to teach my girl better than that.

"It's Julian Cross, Ma'am. I was Hunter North's attorney." True to the irritating sound of his voice, I can confirm it is, in fact, my attorney.

I grunt, brows furrowed at the nerve of this bloke. Nowhere did I ever state that in the event of my demise that any *man* should come to my woman's fucking house. Crowd in on her personal space and mark their disgusting scent all over her home.

If I could, I'd punch him in the face.

The door swings open and I figure I'll try it anyway.

I step in front of Astra and throw a right hook. Julian twitches, face turning ever so slightly that it looks more like a tick before he rubs his jaw and frowns, shaking it off and turning back to a horror-shocked Astra.

Her mouth hangs open as she stares at me mutely.

"Ma'am? Are you alright?" Julian asks as he steps forward and places a hand on her shoulder to steady her as if he thinks she'll faint. I jab him in the shoulder and he flexes, something akin to pain clearly shoots down his arm because he removes it from my woman and circles his shoulder before straightening his suit.

"You don't see that?" she asks in a whisper, barely a breath even spoken. "You didn't *feel* that?"

"See what?" he replies in confusion as he looks around the tiny hallway of her cottage before looking behind him, back down the long driveway.

"T-that," she stammers as she points. I lean against the door jamb, ankles crossed, arms folded with a smirk of satisfaction on my face. "I-it's like a cloud!"

"Well, yes." He nods like it's obvious and I straighten, eyes narrowed as I watch him. "There is supposed to be a storm rolling through. Clouds are natural. Nothing to worry about," he finishes skeptically like she's a mad woman who has never seen a cloud in the sky before.

I chuckle at the stupidity of him.

"Did you hear that?" she rushes, arms out wide like she's feeling the air.

"Did I hear you ask me if there are clouds in the sky? Yes." Now he's encroaching on the type of attitude that has me wanting to pull the teeth from his mouth.

She looks at him like he's the crazy one and then shakes her head in frustration. "Never mind. Why are you here?" she questions, flustered.

"Well, Ma'am-"

"- Stop with the fucking Ma'am. I'm not your granny, tell me what you want then leave," she snaps, pinching the bridge of her nose as she turns and walks through the open entryway toward her living room. She sits on the edge of the couch and waits for him to follow her.

"My apologies. I'll be brief. As I was saying, I was Mr. North's attorney. He had paid an exceptional amount of money that in the event of his death, his will shall be expedited and the recipient of that will shall be notified immediately."

She stares at him blankly, her temper slowly rising. "Listen, it's been a hell of a fucking week. Stop talking in riddles and start making sense. Why the hell would a man who I have never even spoken to put me in his will?"

"He didn't just write you in, Miss Stone. He made it so that if he should pass, you would inherit everything. His entire fortune, his businesses, including the Empire as well as many other ventures," Julian explains in a clinical tone that makes my soul crawl.

Squares make me shiver.

"Okay, so... I'm not insane, but the world around me is?" She chuckles brokenly. "Why the hell would he do that?"

"Because, Miss Stone-"

"-Astra!" she snaps.

"Astra. He did it because you were of great importance to him. If he passed unexpectedly, he wanted you to remain under his guard and fully protected. With the full extent of his resources and connections, you will be fully provided for. He cared most about your security."

Shaking her head, it falls into her hands as she groans into her palms. "Please, just leave," she asks in a tone that is so tired, that it almost puts me to sleep.

"Sure, I understand this is a lot for you. But please be aware, Astra. Hunter was always there. Through every moment of your life from the very first second he saw you. An unhealthy obsession, if you ask me. He considered it protective to watch you from a distance. Despite his skewered intentions, he only wanted what was best. I will need your signature here, just to say I have made this visit."

She scrawls her name on the contract he provides without paying any attention to what she is actually signing her name to and I smirk in victory.

Knowing full well what she just did, I lean back against the doorframe and smirk again.

"Also, in full disclosure, Astra." He clears his throat while his cheek twitches. I can see he's trying to hide his devious smirk. After all, I'd only ever have a cut-throat shark on my payroll. "This is actually a contract of you accepting your inheritance. It was specified by Mr. North we conduct business this way as he feared you wouldn't have accepted his fortune. I apologize for the cloak and dagger act, he was very specific." Then Julian pockets the papers and stalks back toward the front door.

"Wait! Are you fucking serious?" she shouts, on her feet a second later to follow his retreat. "You can't do that! I don't want his fortune. I don't deserve it and I don't fucking want it!"

"Unfortunately, Ma'am, what's done is done. All I can suggest now is that you enjoy it." Then he walks out and the door closes with a resounding thud behind him. Astra picks up an empty glass from the unit and throws it at the door, intending for it to shatter against his back, but she was too slow.

"What the fuck just happened?" she utters to the air, face slack in shock.

I step up behind her, hands on her hips as I whisper, "It's simple, Siren. I finally made you mine."

Then she shrieks and bolts for the door, out into the cold night air, leaving me to chuckle darkly in her wake.

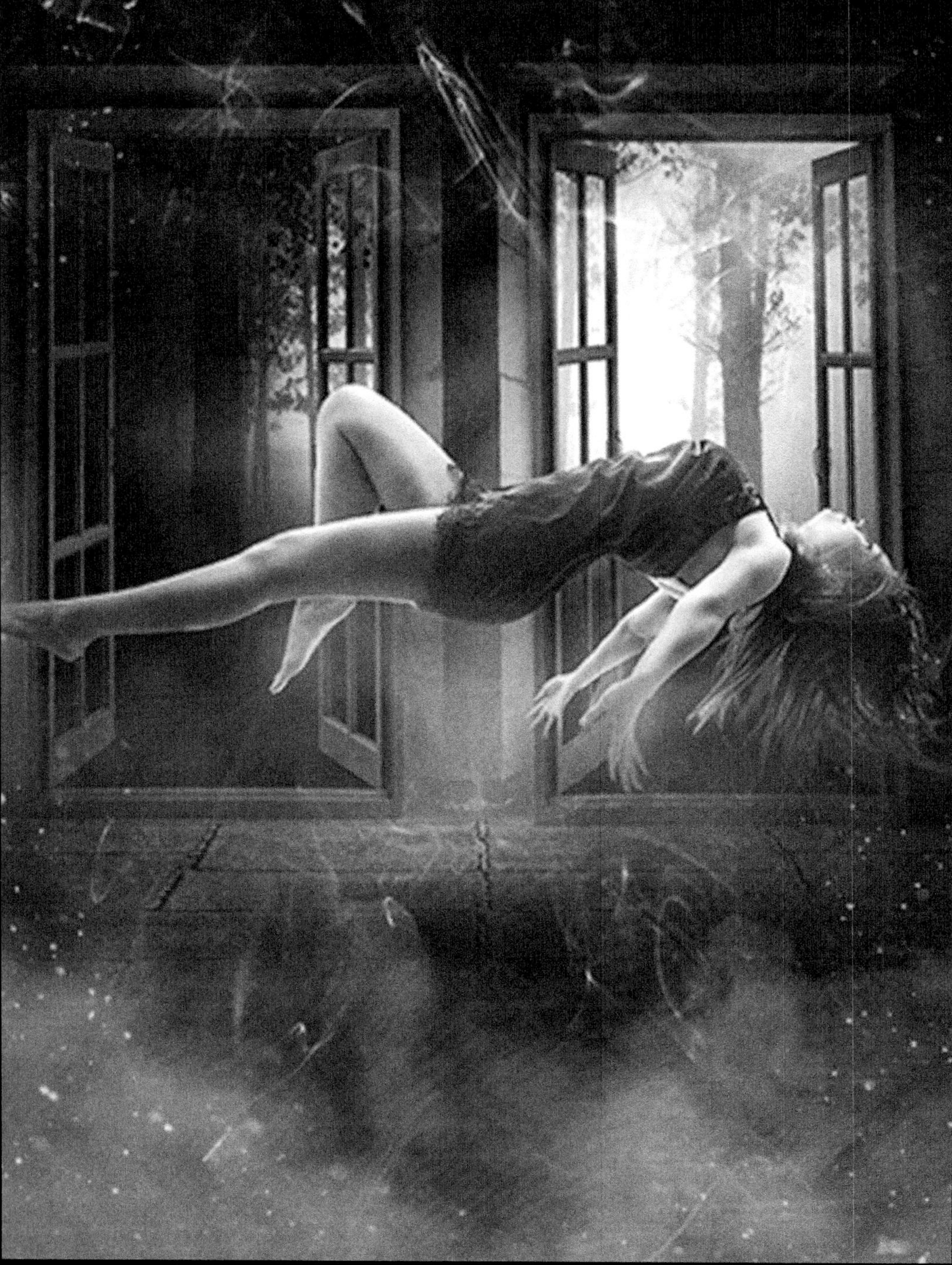

CHAPTER
SEVENTEEN

Astra
Game of Survival - Ruelle

R*un.* Because that's what I do now. Run from those who seek to harm me. Run from the figment of my imagination that's adamant he's here to save me. Or is it my own sanity that has me halfway down the street, barefoot with the scrunched sketch clutched in my fist?

The sound of my own door slamming closed is the only reassurance that I don't need to turn back, my shadow is swallowed by the orange hue of lamp posts. Each one shines in my eyes, sending me further into the spiral of confusion that's hindering all rational thought. My eyes are unfocused, my breathing erratic.

All I know is the dread following my every footstep. The rising anxiety lodged in my throat, threatening to choke me unconscious.

I finally made you mine.

That's what I heard, without a trace of doubt slithering through the fog of my mind.

I *know* that's what I heard.

I've questioned my sanity before on multiple occasions. But for things like putting dark chocolate in my carbonara, or wearing the same jeans to bed, then out the next day. Not in the deranged, I've misplaced my marbles way like I am right now. And without even thinking about it, my feet are jogging up familiar stone steps, my finger smashing against the call button of the keypad. I must be seriously losing it, but I had nowhere else to go.

"Astra?" the feminine voice sounds through the speaker system, the small lens of a camera staring at my face. "Have you come to apologize?"

I growl at Jessica, giving her my no-shit stare.

"Let me the fuck up, bitch We need to talk." I don't know what possessed me to run into the city and arrive at her apartment block, but maybe that's just it.

I've been possessed.

After all, it's a two-hour walk from the suburbs to the city.

The door buzzer sounds while I shake that thought out of my head. There's absolutely no reason that the ghost of a billionaire who rescued me would be stalking me unless it's for revenge.

Because I killed him... or am the reason he was killed at least. There is a dark energy that follows me and it implants itself in my heart. Sometimes, a sense of peace and calmness follows and that terrifies me even more.

The calm before the storm.

The storm that's only happening because of Jess's terrible choice in men.

Before I know it, the three flights of stairs are behind me and I'm standing with my fist raised, not making a move to actually knock. In all of our sixteen years of friendship—ever since Jess stumbled into the tattoo shop my dad co-owned with his best friend from the military—we have been inseparable. She was fourteen, pissed out of her head and needing her teenage heartthrob's name removed from her chest. The guy was eighteen and safe to say, once my dad found out, he covered the tattoo and beat the guy within an inch of his life. He never sniffed around Jess again.

We have been friends ever since and I've always helped to calm her down and keep her safe. Don't get me wrong, I'm a tatted, foul-mouthed chick that shoots straight whisky and I've shown her a good time or two. But I'm smart. Trained well.

Not like her.

This is ironic considering the world still tried to make me a victim.

The two of us have never fought like we did earlier today. I have to believe my friend is still in there, grieving and hurt. Maybe I should be more sympathetic. Even though her affections were being wasted on a sleazeball-prick, the love she felt was real, and that's what she's really mourning.

The twisted notion that he was the one.

When in reality he's just *another* one.

"Are you going to come in?" Her voice sounds from right behind the door and just like that, all my defenses come crashing down. Bursting into her apartment, we collide with each other, a mess of sobbing limbs that pools onto the floor. Our tears free fall all for different reasons, yet there's no judgment here. She can cry for some asshole while I fret over losing my damn mind.

"I'm so sorry, Astra!" she cries.

I can't manage to address any of that right now. Can I crash here tonight?" I ask in a whiney voice that makes my own ears cringe. "I can't go back to my place alone." I swear there's a distant growl across the hallway and I flinch, looking around through the sheen of my tears. I can't see anything or anyone, but that doesn't mean I don't feel it. Feel *him*. Apparently, my sorrowful desperation for a decent man dying has stretched as far and wide enough that seeing one death portrait of him is enough to conjure him up in my mind.

"You don't even have to ask," Jess replies, drawing my attention back to her. We pick ourselves up from the ground, still locked in a tight hug. "I'm sorry for how I acted. The police called me back to the station, showed me some surveillance of... well you know. I tried to call but your voicemail is full." Her lip twitched as if she wants to smirk through her sadness,

"Yeah, some doe-eyed moron kept grief-dialing me about some asshole who didn't deserve her." Even in my frantic state, I still can't let her down gently. It's in my nature to call a brick a brick, or in this case, a foolish sap and foolish fucking sap.

Jess manages to find a chuckle from somewhere deep in her misery, drawing me into her kitchen where she's already drowned herself in two-thirds of a bottle of red wine.

"I just can't believe he left me to go after you like that. And then me showing up at your parlor? Fuck, how are you even still talking to me right now?" she rasped on the verge of another breakdown.

"I was pissed, sure. But it's been a rough couple of weeks." Just saying that sentence has me reaching for the wine bottle and chugging the rest of the contents. How has so much happened in just the space of a few weeks? Last month's problems of paying the rent seem like a whole other world away. Not that I have rent. The cottage and the parlor are the only things I own. "It was hard enough for me to admit that I was a victim, let alone share the humiliation with you as to why I was a victim. I should have seen that snake coming." That is the reality of my rage, my shame. Her not believing me was only half of it. "Holy shit. I'm a... billionairess," I choke and Jessica snatches away the empty wine bottle.

"Wow, that went to your head quickly."

"No, like seriously. Grab more wine and the Chunky Monkey we were saving for your next breakup. We need to catch up, *pronto*. I think I had a stalker." I head for the living area with her hiking a shocked brow at me. Dropping onto the couch that will be my bed for tonight, I breathe out softly. A charcoal gray pull-out sofa bed with a mattress that is more comfortable than my real one squishes under my ass. USB slots in the side of the arm allow me to charge my phone and a small fold-out table is always primed for the coffee Jess will make me in the morning.

Damn early risers.

Jess's place is a brand spanking new development. The wallpaper is barely dry and all paid for by mommy and daddy. I'm not bitter, *much*, because whatever she's handed so easily, she pays back to the community in kindness.

Volunteering to help victims of domestic abuse and never considering herself to be one, serving dinner at the soup kitchen on Christmas Day before making her way to mine. She's my bail-out excuse to never fly out and spend the holidays with my mom. That in itself would have been enough but Jess had insisted on putting the deposit down on my beloved tattoo parlor for my thirtieth and has never once let me repay her.

Sinking into the cushions, I hear her cluttering around for a pair of spoons and a set of glasses.

The exhaustion of running for three hours and all of the tears of my insanity has left my eyes heavy. Through the thick fog of my mind, it's the slow-settling weight resting on my lap that has my fleeting attention. My eyelids have already drifted closed, my hand lifting to shift over the silky head of hair resting on my thigh. Threading my fingers through the satin strands like a mad woman stroking a cat, I hum lightly to myself.

A hot, rich... stalker-ish... cat...

What the fuck is wrong with me?

"I let you down, Siren. I'll never do that again." Those are the whispered words I hear, right before I pass out on Jess's couch, without even having a mouthful of Chunky Monkey.

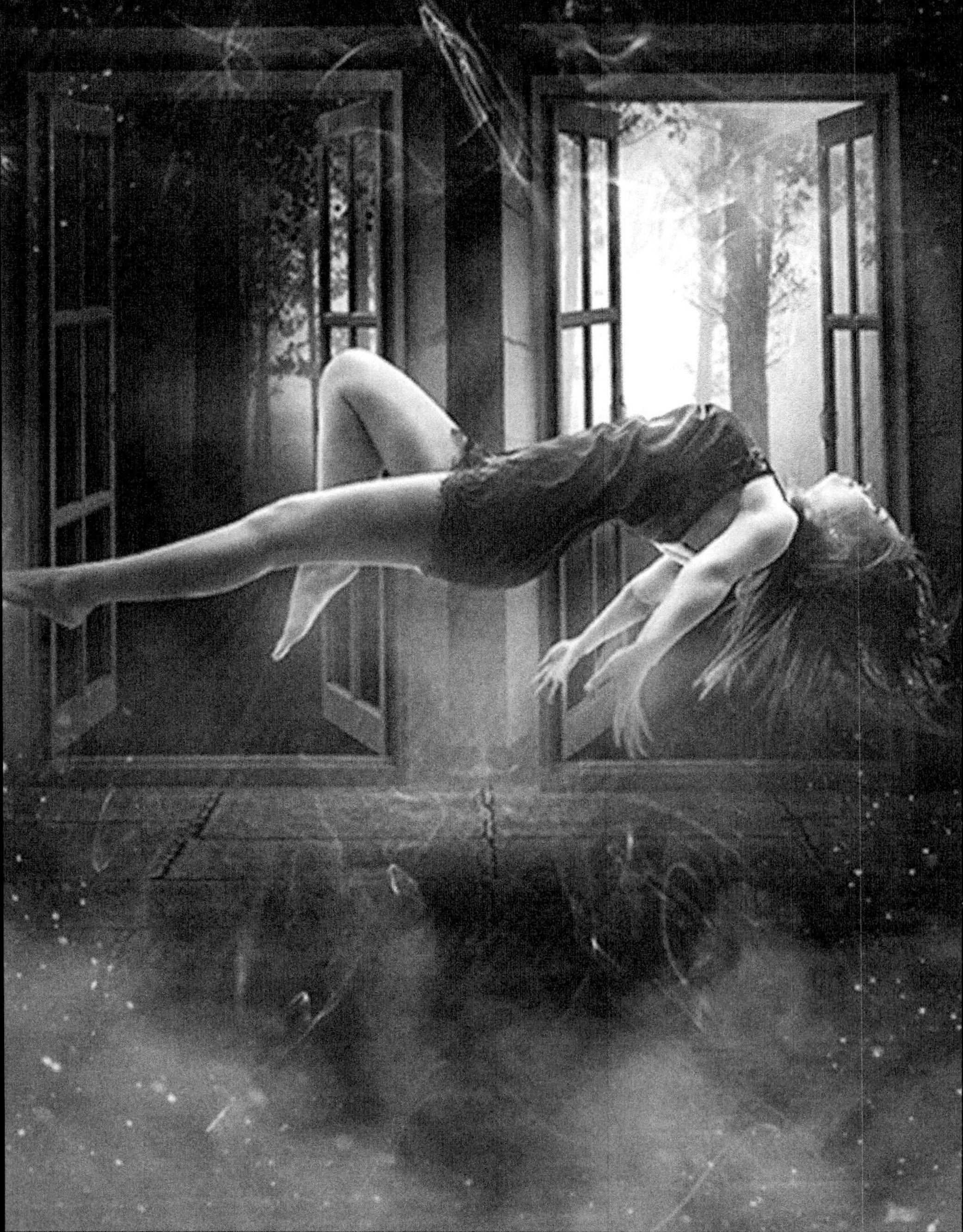

CHAPTER
EIGHTEEN

Astra
Crazy in Love - Eden Project

I mewl, back arching as I tussle within the silken sheets and shudder. The feather of desire is a glorious, overwhelming necessity that pulls from me the most wicked of sounds. Firm hands spread apart my thighs, a wicked assault on my sensitive core. Oh God, it's happening again. The cool, wet thing that teases my pussy is playing with my mind. I clench and flutter, needing so much more than what he's giving me. I'm delusional, seeing nothing but the hand of ecstasy calling me near, but it feels like an ocean between us. Cool waters trying to douse the elicit flames that burn me alive in the thralls of inferno-lit passion. As if feeling my frustration, as if just knowing what I need, those firm hands land on my hips, and I'm flipped over. Pulled to my knees, ass high in the air, I gasp with a sensual quiver.

My ample breasts push into the mattress, but not before he coils a long and rough arm around my waist, deft fingers pinching my nipples. I cry out, shocked when his mouth once again finds my core. I'm weeping, desperate. Needy. I feel as though the world will end if I am not able to soar amongst the galaxies of my release. "Please, please don't make me wait!" I plead, the first of my tears soaking the silken sheets.

"That's it, Siren. Fuck, that's it. Give me your tears, cry for me, love! Show me how much you can feel this is real, how much you can feel me."

"I feel you, by the devil, do I feel you!" I have no idea who I'm feeling, but fuck me if I didn't feel him everywhere, all at once, without a moment of mercy.

My dream man is hitting all of the right spots and soon, my soft purring becomes a desperate cry, "Please!"

"I love it when you beg for me, Siren. When you cry out in desperation for the things my mouth can do to you." I thrust forward, one of my hands darting out to clench the heavy headboard as two thick fingers drive inside of me. My mind short circuits, shutting down, so all that I know is heady dizziness that has me seeing the stars of my arousal. "Feel me, Astra. Who am I?"

"You're the God of my pleasure! Fuck you're my benediction and my damnation. Please, please destroy me! I can't take it anymore, I need to come, fuck I need to come!"

"Only good girls get to come, love, and for as long as you can't see my face, Siren, even here in your dreams, you will remain a very, very bad girl."

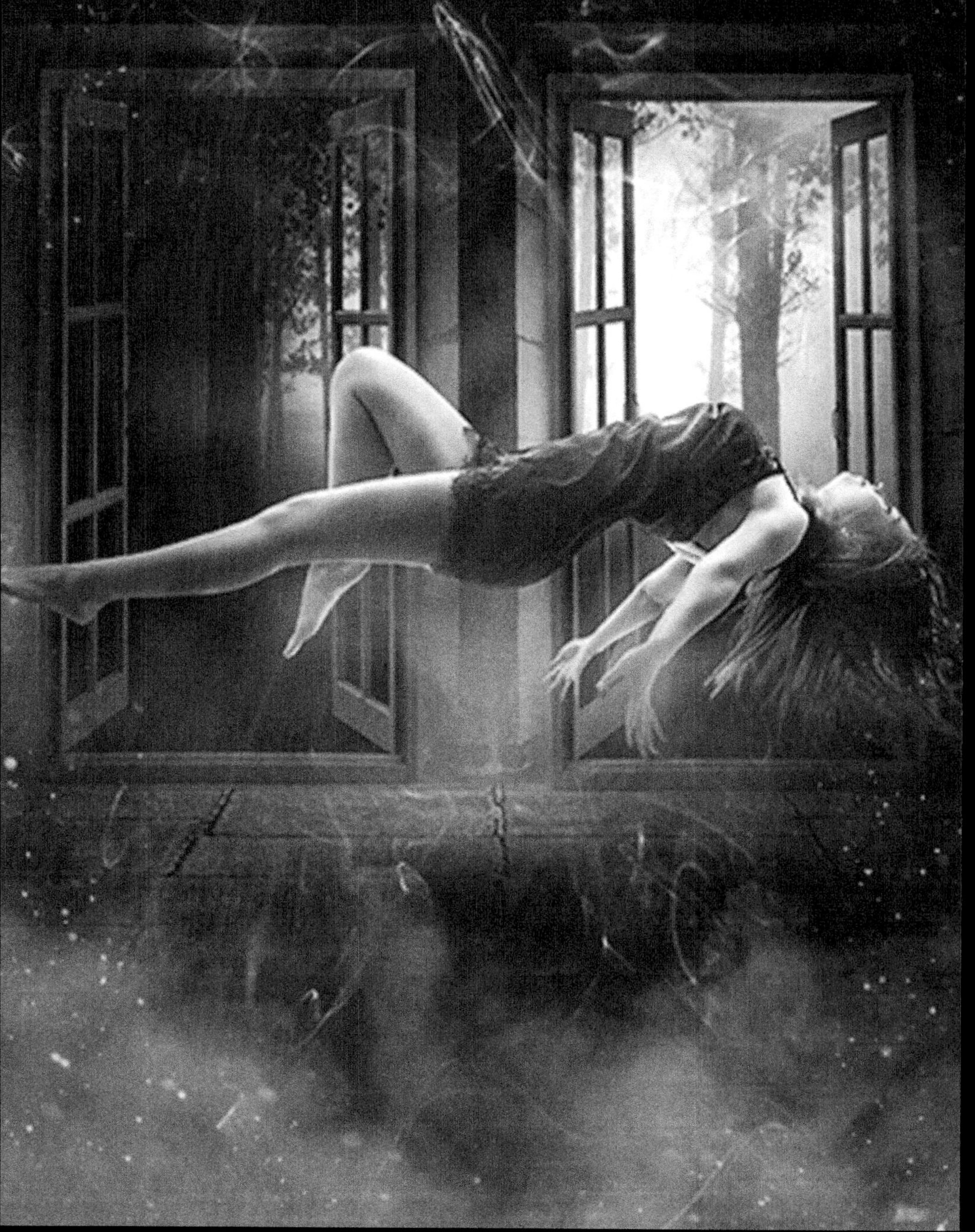

CHAPTER NINETEEN

Astra
The Hunted - The Rigs

"Rise and shine," Jess shouts and I jolt upright on the sofa bed. A blanket covers my body, rubbing me in all the wrong ways for being at my bestie's house.

"You stripped my clothes off?" I ask, spying the steaming mug of coffee on the table. Jess is sitting on the couch adjacent, her own mug raised to her lips and eyes glued to a rerun of Dr. Phil we've watched together a hundred times before.

"You wish." Jess chuckles. "You stripped yourself before passing out. I went to fetch you a cover and by the time I got back, you'd pulled out the bed and had gone full fetal. I've seen enough of you to last me a lifetime, but am curious to know who did your nipple piercings." She smirked and the cheeriness of her tone made my head thump.

Her eyes slide to me, mirth clouding their murky depths below a cocked eyebrow. I blush red, my cheeks burning. I've never been known to sleepwalk before, but there's a first time for everything right? Last night was just a delusion of overworking myself and an overactive imagination. I knew I should have taken the day off. A gust of wind flies through the apartment, the large windows overlooking the city fly open with a thunderous bang and I shiver, tears immediately filling my eyes at how wrong and repulsed I feel at the breeze that just brushed against me.

"Jesus fucking Christ," Jess wails, jumping from her seat and rushing to close the window. "There isn't even a storm cloud in the sky. I feel like somebody just walked over my damn grave."

"Maybe you should stop calling Jesus's name then and start swearing off the devil. Where the fuck is your sage?" I hiss, suffering a horrid shudder.

"In the shop with the rest of my witchy supplies. Where the fuck do you think?"

The feeling in the room fades, passing as quick as a shadow over the moon and I settle back into my chair as she does the same.

"Mmmm, well anyways. What's the plan for today? Because fuck knows I need distracting." Reaching for my coffee, I slide back under the cover, hunting for my clothes. I spot them, draped neatly over the dining table—denim dress, crop top, panties, and all. Interesting choice for me, usually I just chuck them in a heap at my feet. I eye them with suspicion. Doubt creeping into my mind. How long can I convince myself the sensations that are thick in the air around me are all in my head? How long can I make excuses for the things that don't make sense to me?

Last night, I was losing my mind. Jess was my only escape, my place of solitude, but even here I feel like I'm not alone. Like there is something around me trying to get my attention any way that it can.

So I did something.

Something when I was alone on the streets last night, moments before my bare feet brought me here...

I stood outside the Empire.

"Don't judge, but I have an appointment with a clairvoyant this morning," she utters quietly, so quietly it was like a part of her was hoping that I wouldn't hear. "Originally, I'd wanted answers. Answers as to why he attacked you. Now I just want to give that prick a piece of my mind," Jess adds with more venom than I knew she had in her.

I smirk at this, finally seeing the slither of a mean steak I've been waiting all these years for. Who knew it'd only take an almost rape and double death for it to happen? "You're welcome to join me, if you like?" She smirks and my eyes widen inside my skull.

Fuck no.

"Me?" I sit upright, almost spilling my coffee. "What-why would you suggest that? I'm fine. All good here." The longer I talk, the less I convince myself whilst looking around with aching eyes for the figure that appeared to me last night.

I know it wasn't a dream.

It couldn't have been.

"Mmhmm, and you muttering '*oh Hunter, Hunter save me*' in your sleep was just a coincidence?" Jess bobs her eyebrows. "I know who died the other night too. Maybe you could do with some answers of your own. We never did discuss the delusion of you being a billionairess." Rolling my eyes, trying to play off the fact she's just panicked me even more about my own sanity, I look at her properly for the first time.

Her tousled chocolate curls fall around her shoulders in purposeful waves, the sheen of a recent condition shining in the morning light. Her bare legs are tucked beneath her, unhindered by a yellow summer dress patterned with small daisies. She's going to catch her death outside, the gales of autumn approaching in full force, but I appreciate the initiative.

Dress for the desired mindset.

"Okay firstly, how long did you hang around while I was asleep? And second, why do you look so... okay?"

"Wow, thanks for the compliment." Jess downs the rest of her drink and hops up to cross the living area. Taking a pile of folded clothing from atop her desk, Jess pops her charitable donation to my naked cause on the edge of the mattress with an easy smile on her pale-painted lips.

"Here, get dressed. And to answer your first question, I slept next to you all night. Didn't want to be alone." She shrugs one shoulder and disappears out of view. Weird, but I can't say I'm anything less than grateful.

Within the hour, we're exiting Jess's purple mini and striding down the sidewalk in the posh part of town. The streets are cleaner, the air fresher and the buildings triple in size. Each one attempts to outgrow the last, like glass children standing on their tiptoes for bragging rights. White clouds lazily roll across a blue sky, betraying the imminent season and giving the feel of another relaxed summer's day. Like my own parlor, many shops along this stretch are closed on Sunday, but today is Monday and I'm pissed.

"I really don't think there's any clar-"

"Here we are." My best friend beams, pointing her thumb at a single door among two high-end retailers. I stare at it, noting the lack of anything worth mentioning but an intercom system Jess is already speaking into. Granted entry, I merely stand here until she hisses at me to move it.

Am I really doing this? Talking to a clairvoyant about the man I saw in my home last night? The man whispering in my ear?

Beats a psych evaluation I suppose, I sigh and follow Jess inside.

A thin staircase leads directly up to the second level with little other option. Up or out, as the helpful sign over the railing suggests. My expectations are low until we step through a beaded curtain at the top and find ourselves in a room of equal size to a wedding venue. Never mind the woman in a smart pantsuit at the far end beside a deluxe coffee machine. This place is more like a museum than the stuffy room with crystal balls that I was imagining.

"She's a spiritualist to celebrities. I managed to get Uma Thurman's cancellation," Jess whispers before starting the long walk across the room with her hand already raised.

"Of course you did," I mutter. Taking my time, I prefer to

meander slowly and examine the range of artwork lining the walls. A mandala tapestry sways gently beside an open window, the blue and green repetitive pattern appearing like a peacock's tail feathers fanned out proudly for all to see. Incense burns on the window ledge, tingling my nose pleasantly. Not the typical tiny, overbearing room I'd imagined would give me a sensory headache. The noticeable scent of vanilla intertwines with many others I can't distinguish, but all in all, fills me with a sense of calm.

A marble statue of a Buddhist god sits on a plinth across the other side of the window, his arm extended in greeting. A robe covers his straight frame, the drapery carved into the stone incredibly lifelike. Throwing a quick glance to the clairvoyant who's engrossed in a conversation, I gently place my hand on the statue and exhale with my eyes closed. Maybe I'm being a silly twat, or maybe I'll find some clarity.

"Are you hoping to tune me in or drown me out, Siren?" That husky voice sounds by my ear and I flinch at the same time my traitorous pussy clenches at how sensual it sounds.

Silly twat it is.

Rushing over to the couch, I hastily plant myself down to hear Jess being told Venus is in her star chart and love will present itself within the next sixty-day cycle.

Here we fucking go, I think to myself. Whatever it takes to keep the client happily dipping their hand into their purse and coming back when the advice doesn't hold up I guess.

"Oh wow," the woman opposite gasps and I finally gaze up into her eerily blue eyes. I thought mine were enticing, but hers are endless. So pale, they could be made of ice. Boundless glaciers that spear my soul, unearthing every dark corner I'd spent years learning to cover. She continues to stare through her circular glasses, with a frizz of honey-brown curls blocking out the rest of her mousey face.

"Care to share with the rest of the class?" I snap when the silence stretches on too long. Jess elbows me and we share a psychic argument while the woman shifts her open palms into my personal space.

"You have such a strong energy around you," she breathes. I catch sight of an ornament on a shelf past her head, the white lettering all linked together to spell the word 'Opal'. Okay, we'll go with that.

Opal is fucking nuts.

"It's not bad per se, but dangerous. Toxic, perhaps. You need to be careful how you approach the next few days. Your future is unclear." Withdrawing her hands back into her space with her arms crossed pharaoh-style over her chest in a feeble effort to protect herself from my bad juju, a deep rumbling chuckle sounds by my left ear.

"Seems like Opal is full of shit," he grumbles, humor filling his voice. "The only danger you're in with me is losing your heart. I promise to protect it though, in exchange for you holding my own." This time, it's me who inhales sharply.

"Everything okay?" Jess whispers over to me. Concern swirls in her brown eyes, her mouth making the perfect 'O'. "Is it him? Can you sense Hunter North?"

"Ahh!" Opal shrills, jumping up from her seat. "That name resonates with the blue and gold entity I see. His energy is looming over you like a shadow you'll struggle to escape if you so wish."

"What do you mean if I so wish? Do I have a choice? Why does it sound like I don't have a choice?" I ask, seriously questioning my sanity now we're openly discussing ghosts and colored energies. "Because I was beginning to think he was my stalker in real life and I'm really, *really* not sure I want him to be my stalker in death!"

"There's always a choice. If you allow yourself to accept this other presence in your life, the stronger your connection will become. However, if you wish to rid yourself of him, I can give you remedies and the number of an exorcist that can cleanse your home." She begins riffling through her purse for a business card and just then, a wave of nausea rolls through me. Like a gust of wind that sweeps through my body, making my limbs as heavy as lead yet my mind sway with dizziness.

"That won't be necessary." My voice sounds, but I didn't say it. Neither did I raise my hand or cross my ankle over my knee to make room for the girthy dick I don't have either.

The fuck?

Opal pins me with her blue eyes, slowly lowering me back into my seat.

"Very well. You know where to find me if you happen to change your mind. Maybe we should return to the conversation we were having, Jessica? You wanted to know if Theo had made any contact."

My eyes roll in my head, my back slouching further into the cushions without my permission. "That dude was a catch." That wasn't my voice either. Jess chuckles, like that was a dig and I was being sarcastic but I genuinely never fucking uttered those words even though they whispered past my lips.

Opal lifts a thread of crystals from the small table separating us, humming as she draws her fingertips over each one carefully.

"I'm afraid I can't sense him, or he doesn't want to speak. Either way, I'm afraid I'm unable to procure the answers you seek." Jess's shoulders sag, but not in grief. A blaze of anger contorts her features beneath the curtain of her hair and as much as I want to reach out and comfort her, my hand refuses to move.

"Suppose he's having way too much fun as a soul wandering around the afterlife, haunting stuck-up bitches," I say instead in a throaty chortle that sounds nothing like me. Even Jess forgets her grudge to throw a curious glance my way. "Well, with all due respect," I slap my thighs and stand, "this hasn't been enlightening at all. Sorry to have wasted your time, Opal-who's-full-of-shit."

My legs are moving then, my psyche curling up to die inside the shell of my body I no longer possess. Nearing the door, I hear Jess apologizing for my behavior, stating I'm still dealing with my recent trauma. She doesn't realize just how correct she is. The beaded curtain sweeps over my face as I make no move to shield myself, my movements jerky like a robot is in control of me. Or a billionaire with a stick up his a-

Easy. I can hear your every thought in here, the grumble reverberates around my head. *Why are you jerking around?* Coming to a halt inside the door, the reflection of the glass pane is split down the center by white paneling. On one side, my reflection shows the sweep of black hair against a pink cheek and vibrant blue eye. On the other, a man whose face has been cut from stone. Stubble lines his hard jaw, dark hair falling forward to trickle over his intense stare. He stands right beside me, almost as if he is fused with me. Then slowly, the more he bleeds into my skin, the more I feel like the darkness is being drained from my chest.

We both freeze, our souls merging into one being. That darkness inside of me fading, the wrongness of whatever just had control of my body dwindling.

I'm still freaked the fuck out and not sure why I haven't rammed my head through the glass yet, but I'm running out of reasons to scream over in my head. I'm just stuck, cold and confused.

The side of his mouth tilts upwards, the ferocity of his tone escaping, his lips flooring me with its resounding honesty.

"We don't need her bullshit, Siren. We don't need anyone."

Then I run again, leaving Jessica with the freaky lady, who is so shitty at her job she didn't notice I just got fucking possessed.

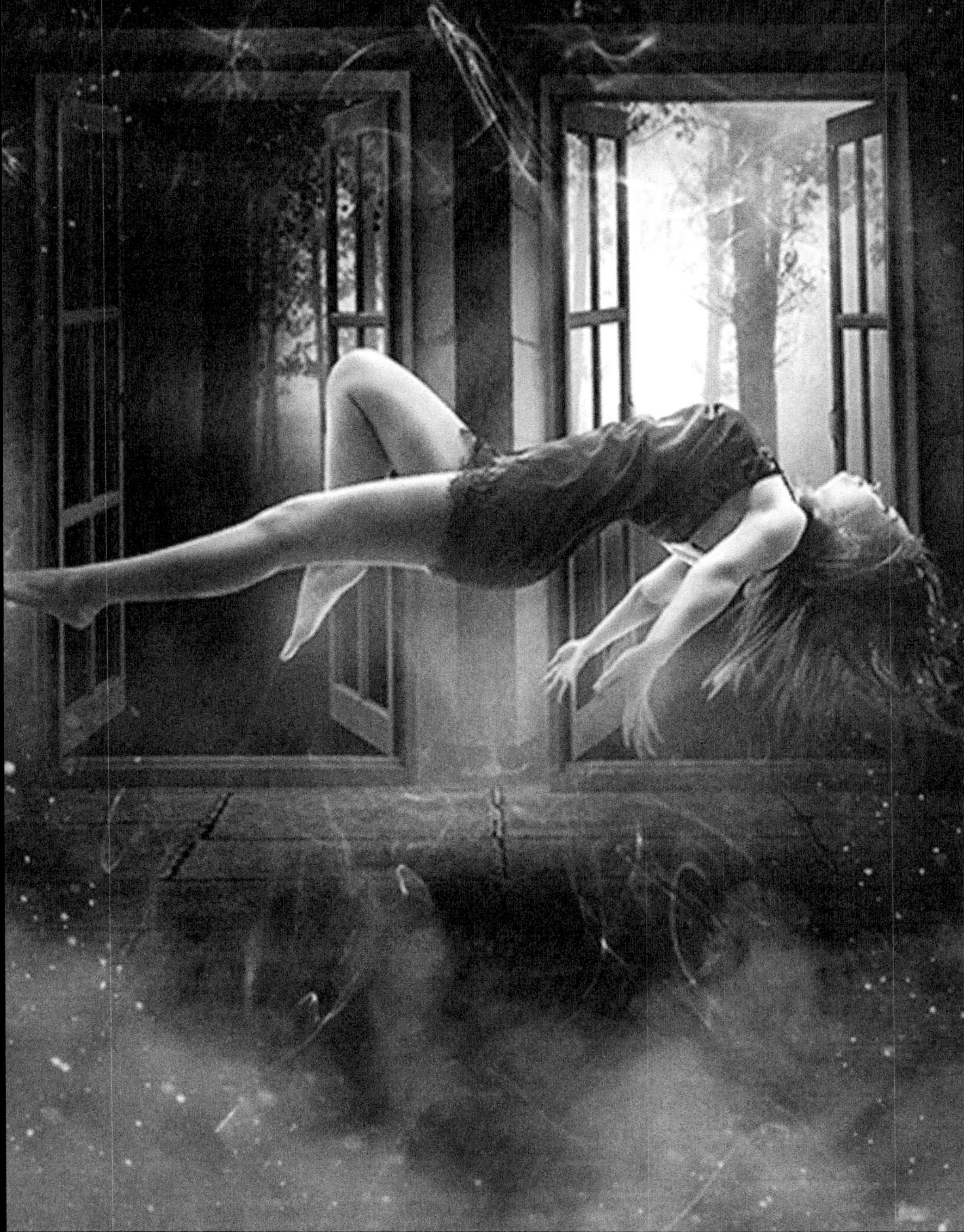

CHAPTER
TWENTY

Astra
Middle of the Night - Elley Duhé

My front door closes with a click behind my back, a sigh shuddering through my heaving chest. Pressing the heels of my palms into my eyes, I rub out the soreness that's resided there after the half squint I held up all the way home, avoiding the reflective glare of each shop window and every passing vehicle. Tension headaches are a fucking cunt and now that I have the weight of an elephant putting pressure on my skull, so is my temperament.

A burst water main gushing across the street from the clairvoyant gave me pause for long enough to spot a silhouette lingering over my shoulder and that was all the incentive I needed to send me sprinting the rest of the way home. That silhouette was so different from the bluish ghost that strangely brings me comfort. This one was toxic, vile and all fucking wrong, it made my soul shiver.

My mind fractured and that was all that I needed to outrun what I could never understand. The survival instincts inside of me are greater than this unexplainable occurrence currently happening in my life. Which was a funny thing, because surviving was seemingly a lot harder as each day went on.

Now, here I am.

Faced with the silence, presented with the eerie darkness of my cottage I loved only a few days ago. I don't need to see him, in order to know that he's here.

Lurking, watching.

My mind spirals with questions. With the burning need to find answers.

"Come on then, get it over with!" I call out bravely, flinching at the volume of my own voice. It's a shock to my senses and I shiver, my limbs dancing as I feel something sinister skate down my spine. But other than that, nothing stirs, nothing moves.

Awareness prickles at the edge of my consciousness as I shift away from the door, keeping my back to the wall all the way into my dining room.

Once there, I reach back to unlock the glass door and slide it open, giving myself an easy out via the porch. Sure, I'd have to jump the fence, but it's better than fleeing down the street for the second time in the last two days, like some maniac running for her life from a Michael Myers wannabe.

At least my poltergeist hasn't tried stabbing me yet.

After a while, after deeming myself as a complete pussy, I slip into one of the unnecessary six chairs at my dining table and place my hands on the wooden surface. Have I truly gone crazy?

After a moment of silence, I slump forward, arms sprawling across the surface as my head thumps against the wood while I let out a heavy soul-burdened sigh.

Did I let Opal, the bullshit clairvoyant, get into my head?

But even as the thought crosses my mind, I know it couldn't have been faked.

I know what I felt. It was too real. Too physical. I can still feel the repulsion of it under my skin. Something was there, wrong and sinister as it slithered inside of me, chased away by the cooling feeling of comfort and protection.

Like the sun chasing away the darkness of the moon.

My body submitted to a force much greater than my own. An entity took over my limbs, claimed my voice, and walked my ass away from an outstretched exorcist's business card. Yet he's not possessing me now, nor is he appearing from the darkened corners to take whatever he wants from me.

Did he even possess me at all? This is the bigger question I'm terrified to ask.

What does he want from me?

Revenge?

An unresolved vendetta maybe?

Am I about to become a tormented toy for an assassin from beyond the grave?

"Your eyebrows crinkle when you overthink," a cocky yet smooth tone rolls through from the kitchen. My back snaps ramrod straight, ridding myself of the hunch I'd slowly inclined into, just as the lights overhead flash on to reveal the person owning the voice. And there he is, in all his chiseled and gorgeous glory.

Hunter Fucking North.

Postured against the sideboard, whiskey glass in hand.

I knew I wasn't crazy - unless this is only proving the fact further, that I most *definitely* fucking am.

Unlike the glimpses I've caught before, he's shiny and new, in full technicolor. Not a mere memory I barely paid attention to, or a framed portrait on top of a bar.

Hunter North, the man that died saving my life and gifting me his fortune, is standing in my kitchen like some transparent form of an ungodly beautiful man.

Drinking whisky.

My whisky.

On numb legs, I stumble towards him, take the glass from his translucent hand and knock back the burn of amber liquid, hissing when it drips all too smoothly down my throat. I stare at him with a gaping mouth, eyes wide, and a heart that beat an uncertain pattern into my ribcage.

"Why did you possess me?" I whisper tentatively. The first words to slip free after *Satan fucked up the grave.*

He narrows his eyes. "I never."

Brown hair falls free of his styled pushback and curls at his temples. A raw ruggedness to the five o'clock shadow fixed to his sharp jawline looks like the shine of white pearls glossing over his bluish skin. He definitely looked like a man, but he looked like a man built from nothing but the fibers of a dark, angelic soul. Dark slacks hug his thick thighs, his loafers still glossy and uncreased. I imagine he wore a new pair every day. The crisp white shirt clinging to his broad chest, unbuttoned, pristine, and rolled up to his elbows. Other than the strip of red tucked into his side, beneath his forearm, he was flawless and perfect.

He is what nightmares are made of. Nightmares that were dreams for the dark hearts that walk this earth. I've felt like I was drowning before but never have I felt like somebody was holding me under until the wiring in my brain short circuits and reprograms itself. I blink rapidly, my pulse flickering against the taut skin at the column of my throat.

Yet none of what spirals around me in confusion compares to the stunning, breathtaking beauty of his eyes. Endless stones of pewter gray draw me, like a thread to my soul and a threat to my sanity. I stumble closer to him. Each time he sat in my tattoo chair, he was just another client. The perfect client. The broody man that gave me everything my antisocial heart desired.

How could I have been so oblivious as to not look up and become ensnared in his quick-silver freckled depths?

"How are... I thought... you were dead, Hunter. You died."

"I am dead, Siren, but not gone. Not even the fiery clutches of Hell can drag me away from you." Despite myself, I reach out a hand and rest it against his chest. No warmth meets my palm, no firmness stopping me from reaching right through his translucent cavities. His smirk doesn't falter but I withdraw my hand, feeling like I've violated him somehow. Invaded his personal space and touched the sacred parts of him that belong solely to a wicked lover under the veil of darkness, coiled within the satin sheets.

"I don't understand," I whisper, not sure I even want to. Unsure if I ever could.

"You've already accepted my presence, Siren. Imagine the fun we could get up to when you start believing in our connection. In that twinge in your hammering heart." Downing more of the whiskey, he takes it back from me, finishes it off, then sets the glass down on the counter at his back. It instantly disappears. Gone, as in fucking *vanished*. My eyes are still searching for a ring mark when his fingers brush my cheek and a squeal leaves my lips. Yet he doesn't let up, rolling his thumb across my cheekbone in such a delicate caress, my body shivers at his gentle touch.

Even worse, I stand there and let him. Unable to move, unable to blink, to break this frail connection between me and the thing standing on the other side of the frightful thing called life.

"I don't understand any of this. I don't understand what's happening," I breathe, my eyes fluttering closed at the feel of him gliding across my senses.

"I imagine you don't. It's not exactly a normal occurrence is it, sweet girl?"

I can't open my eyes. I can't break this tender moment between us that's drawing me in.

What if I lose this sensation?

"Why?"

His hand stops, a fraction of a second passing by before he begins his caress one more time. The question was vague, but he knew exactly what I was asking. "I still remember the moment we met, your touch on my skin. The way the needle broke into my flesh, leaving behind such a glorious piece of art. The awe I felt in that moment never wavered. It never waned either. I had realized I was merely existing before I felt that thing within my chest beat again and with each pulsating thud, I noticed it no longer hurt. The first time I ever *saw* you though, was in the bank. It never happened like it does in the movies. Time didn't slow down." He smirked, watching the way his finger moved along my skin like the memory was a sweet one for him to relive. "In fact, it was the loud noise that caught my attention. You cussing out one of the staff for messing around with your paperwork. You were fire, sweet girl. Your voice? A Siren's song that consumed me in that very instance. It wasn't me who possessed you, love, it was you who engulfed me."

"I made you feel all of that?" I whispered, unable to open my eyes and stare at him. Unable to give my mind to this moment, lest it breaks before my very eyes.

"You made me feel all of that, Siren. You made me feel everything. Confusion, awe, a soul-deep passion I never knew how to handle. That I never knew I could *feel*."

"Why did you leave me everything? Why did you never talk to me?"

"Because those tender moments I would have spent on meager words, meant nothing without you *feeling* me first. I wanted to be the hand of comfort you longed for. Not the man you feared."

"Y-you stalked me?"

"I watched you. I protected you and when you needed something to rely on, I was the firm wall of support that kept you standing."

"How long? How long were you there and I never even knew it? When did your obsession become an infatuation?"

"I felt both the very moment I saw you, love. But how long have I protected you? For over a year." A cool breeze whispered against my parted lips. I shuddered, shivering from the prospect of that being the cool air from this ghostly man.

"I believe in us, Siren. Do you?"

"I don't even know you," I breathe, my basic instincts screaming at me to run away and never return to this side of the country again. But the ferocity in his gray eyes, that I can feel boring into me, the way his silvery flecks flare as they dip to my lips when he forces me to open mine, tells me it's no use.

I've got myself a poltergeist. A ghostly stalker who will never let me go.

Shifting my head aside, I watch his hand curl into a loose fist and outstretch again. The thinnest translucent layer coats his skin, barring his spirit from physically coming into contact with me. The air between his palm and my skin thickens, a deep pressure the only thing telling me he's reached for me at all. This time when his fingers slide around the back of my neck, I notice the difference I couldn't tell from the last time.

A trail of protection tingles against my nape, and in this instant, I'm not sure if I'm happy or annoyed because of it. Uncertain about what I should let in and what I should fight with everything that I have. Because I feel his light, but I also feel ominous darkness too.

"Your eyebrows are crinkled again." He smirks, the most striking smile I've ever seen lighting up his bright face.

Magazine worthy, that smile of his. Swoon-worthy too.

In fact, I believe I've seen his image plastered on the front cover of Hot Bark before and an unreasonable flare of jealousy urges me to hunt down every last issue and burn them. Instinctually, I know this smirk is one that is meant for only me, but doesn't stop me from being pissed that other women have seen it. The fact that other women have been the recipient of one similar. Makes my throat tighten with anger thick in the back of my airways, then my anger becomes angry at the fact that I'm even *angry* at all.

"How about you have a shower, wash your hair with that coconut shampoo you like so much, and put on your checked flannel pajamas? The ones with the hole on your outer right thigh, right where that cute dimple in your flesh is. I'll wait right here. Then you can finally relax."

Blinking a few times, I take a tentative step backward as if he'd be automatically pulled wherever I go. He isn't and now I look like a suspicious twatmuffin. My throat thickens, my tummy dips, and I wonder, how would I feel if this unusual being before me faded away, never to be seen again.

How many people can say they have spoken to a ghost?

How many people can lose themselves in the eyes of one as well?

"You'll stay here? You won't follow me for... a sneak peek?" Internally I groan.

A sneak peek? If that isn't suggestive in itself. "Wait, have you ever taken a sneak peek? Isn't that what stalkers do? Are you a serial killer? Were you going to kill me?" I gasp with a moment of uncertainty, then my eyes round at the look glaring back at me.

"I'm a stalker, Astra." Hunter cocks his eyebrow with a strange amount of confidence under the dark gleam in his gray eyes. Stalkers are normally acne-ridden weirdos that hide in bushes and basements. Not billionaire playboys. And I'm ignoring how my insides flutter at the sound of my name on his lips because that is sin personified in itself. My tummy swirls, my thighs clench, all until he finishes his sentence. "*Not* a rapist."

The lights flicker at that moment, hinting at the darkness mirrored in Hunter's eyes. There's a dropped decibel as we share the same sickening thought.

Not like *Theo Nyera,* he means.

This time when Hunter steps toward me, I don't cower away.

I freeze.

Embracing the hug of comfort he envelopes me in, surrounding me tightly with warmth and security. He chases away the harrowing grief in my core from the flashbacks of that night. The blanket of protection he vows to uphold at that moment, was an evident vow and something tells me it's not the first time he's held me together. That he's been protecting me for longer than I have even realized.

It's not the love story I imagined, but who can deny the appeal of a sexy, ghostly bodyguard? One who speaks of connections and destiny like they are his second love language?

Obsessive stalking is clearly the first, I note.

Reaching around the expanse of his back, my hands slip into his form, literally inside of his back instead of caressing my hands against his soft skin and my mood dampens.

It's a pretty fantasy, but not one I fully believed would ever come true.

I've always been a fan of dark romance and spooky shit, the dark and the depraved men that bleed from the shadows and consume you so wholly, that you don't even know where they begin and you end.

What if this is about some unresolved shit, and I wake up one day to find him gone?

What if his punishment for me being the reason he died is to lure me in with the sweet promise of oblivion? The one place burdens are forever banished?

What if this is a crack in my psyche and it's all a result of some hefty trauma that I've blocked from my mind?

A chuckle rolls through Hunter and I can tell he's laughing at me again, sensing my disappointment. Picking up on my inner turmoil of whirlwind emotions.

"More specifically," he moves back so I can stare up into his beautiful face. "I'm *your* devoted stalker and now I've been revealed, I'm going to show you all the reasons you can't let me go."

His hands circle my face, tilting my chin upward, using manipulation of the air. The more I look into those eyes, the more I can't help but open to him so he's at a better angle to see me. That smirk, the cold fire blazing in his gaze. He drinks me in from our closeness as if seeing me for the first time and I can't help but feel completely overwhelmed at his undivided attention. It's flattering, it warms my heart. That look? It is unmatched, it's poetry from straight out of a novel.

It's *everything*.

He's so comfortable having me exposed beneath him. I can't help but sink into those intense eyes that see every part of me.

Fluttering my eyes closed, I brace myself for the press of a kiss when he removes himself from my space completely. There's no difference in warmth, yet I feel his absence, deeply rooted in my core. A brutal ache that deepens with each step I numbly take away from him at the strange sting of rejection. A little voice in the back of my head that grows louder, drowns out everything else as I ascend the staircase alone.

Don't use your heart as a chess piece to stop the pain, Astra. Or you'll always find yourself as the pawn.

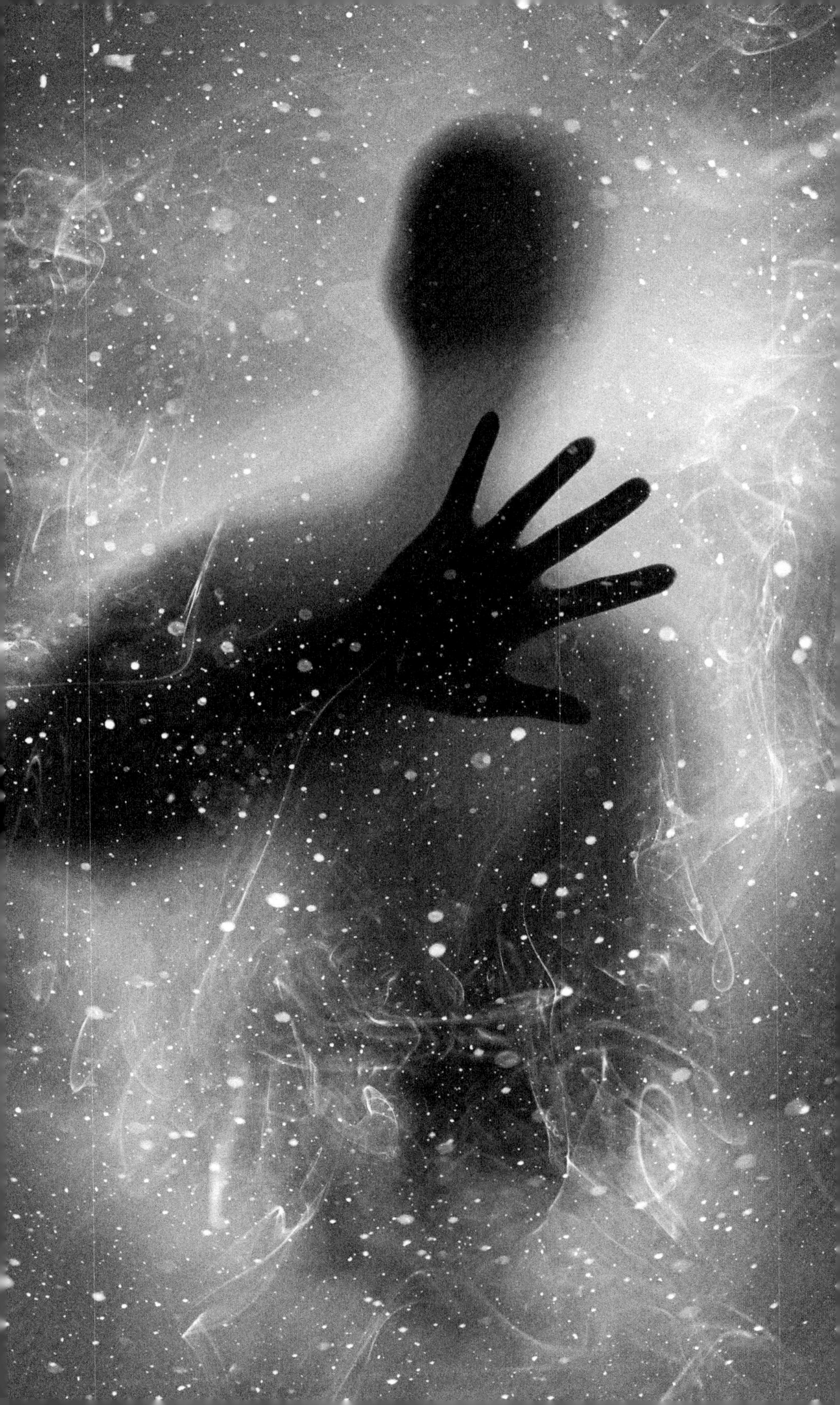

CHAPTER
TWENTY-ONE

Hunter
Another Life - Motionless In White

She's running again and even though it's toward me, I won't be another regret for her to flee from. She's afraid, afraid of what she's seen, what she's been through, of what she feels, and right now, she's afraid for her sanity. Something the shitty clairvoyant unhelpfully spooked her on. So much so, it's enough for Astra to pick me as the lesser evil over the thing that attacked her. I haven't been able to figure out what it was yet and maybe that's another reason I'm pulling back. Feeling like I'm failing her all over again. I could see it in her eyes. There was something there, a pain that was different from the rest. It was soul deep, almost a longing and it had nothing to do with me.

There is loneliness here, a desolate isolation that gives you everything you could ever desire, while not allowing you to have absolutely any of it.

I pace back and forth, the frustration of being this close to her yet still so far away a brutal resentment I can no longer hide from and pretend doesn't exist.

I thought this would be easy, that I would stalk her every waking moment and be the face of every single one of her dreams—that she would accept me as openly as I accepted her the very first time I ever laid eyes on her.

To an extent, it's true. To a further extent, it couldn't be further from the truth.

I want to kiss her, by Satan himself I want to fucking kiss her, but I know the anger will brew from the veil that keeps us apart the moment that I try.

I know that come morning, she will have played with her insanity enough and decide that she once again will need to become sane.

My pacing persists, tearing through the small attic of her cottage. Large bay windows curve on the far side of the wall, rounded in an ominous arch that draws you deeper into the darkness of the small space, just by the promise of the scarce light once you reach the windows looking out into the even more sinister-looking forest that flickers throughout the darkness like moving shadows. Stomping toward it, I lean forward, dropping my head on the stained glass, and sigh at the coolness that seeps into my forehead.

I can feel the cold, I can feel the glass, I can feel everything as if I was still alive...

Everything but *her*.

I thought being dead would mean that I would no longer have to be careful.

I was wrong.

If I don't watch her closely, I fear she'll join me on the other side a hell of a lot sooner than her destined time. There is a well of darkness in her, it fills every dip and every crevice and it aches for a reawakening into something deeper. I had never known how strong it was before the moment she leaned into my touch. Her reaction to death is a far cry from somebody who fears it as a normal person should.

I hate that I missed it.

I hate that she is becoming a casualty of life.

I growl, throwing my fist through the window as it shatters like shards of a gothic rainbow that clatter to the soiled ground. The array of colors from the moon, the skies, and even the trees turn it into various shades of doom and gloom that twinkle in the night. The heaven thunders, rain pouring down in unrelenting torrents that make thought almost impossible in comparison to the downpour roaring around this small, tiny, and almost forgotten cottage. Dim golden lights flicker in the distance, the small orbs of an empire I had built winking at me from the city lines.

A flash of lighting cuts through the skies, my face lighting up a bright purple in the wake of my turmoil. Everything is dark tonight, dark like the chaos of my emotions. Tall and withered trees sway back and forth, the large moon hidden behind the valley of a forest so vast, it makes you wonder what dwells down there in the shadows. The lights in the attic are off. Nothing but fluttering shapes creeping up around me, dragging me deeper into the pits of my awaiting Hell.

A small sob cuts through the rumbling of the angry night. The sound of something shattering echoes in my ears. My head snaps towards the staircase, the very one that would carry me down and deeper into the cottage, back to *her*. One tentative step at a time, I move toward the Siren that sings my name to the void. Beckoning me closer on unsteady legs. I move through the otherwise silent house, a blue sphere drifting through the bleak abyss.

There... another sob.

Another small cry of anguish, hidden in the thunderstorm.

I grow closer still, unable to ignore the thread that maps my way to the sorrowful seductress in this still night. The shadows paint patterns by my feet, a daunting path to the one that I seek.

Rounding the corner, the lone figure billows, and sways around the open floor plan under the arch of a glass globe, lit up by an array of nightly colors. The flashing of blue and purple eerily lights up the shadowed features of Astra as she cries to the moon while she dances to a sad song, a whisky glass in hand, more than half consumed.

I can't help but feel the pain of her grief in my heart.

The notion of her so broken overcoming me with deep grief of my own.

I stumble forward, my presence the only light in the shadows as I cut them down with savage devotion as I stride toward her. I manipulate the air, my open hand coiling around her wrist as I spin her into me. She gasps, the moment of shock breaks into a sob of devastation when she sees me standing behind her. "Astra," I whisper, her name a gentle caress fluttering past my lips. "Astra." Her name is my benediction. My voice equal parts her salvation and damnation. "Don't be sad, pretty girl. I promise I'm not all that bad." It's a knife to my cold dead heart. A ghost shouldn't know pain. They shouldn't know anguish. Yet here I am with the notion of it in my mind and a barrier of the afterlife concealing it from my chest.

A brutal frustration of the forced peace I was supposed to feel and the devastation I would be feeling had I truly been alive and standing before her hurting so damn much.

She shakes her head, her words caught in the back of her throat as she tries to respond, "H-he, he isn't here. They never came back for me." The suffering in her voice is a chokehold, a noose around my neck ready to kick me from my stool. "My father. My brother. They never came back for me."

Everything shatters, all of the cutting and lethal jaded pieces falling into the place of every deep crevice cutting me deep. All the sick and twisted parts of me find comfort in her validation that her misery doesn't stem from me. Then as that moment of reprieve lifts, her torment barbs me greater than any other affliction.

"Sweet Siren. If they could, they'd be here," I whisper, my essence feathering across her lips.

"H-how do you know that?"

"Because I know how impossible the thought of never seeing you again can be, Astra. I can still feel the terror in my soul, fearing something greater than death could part us."

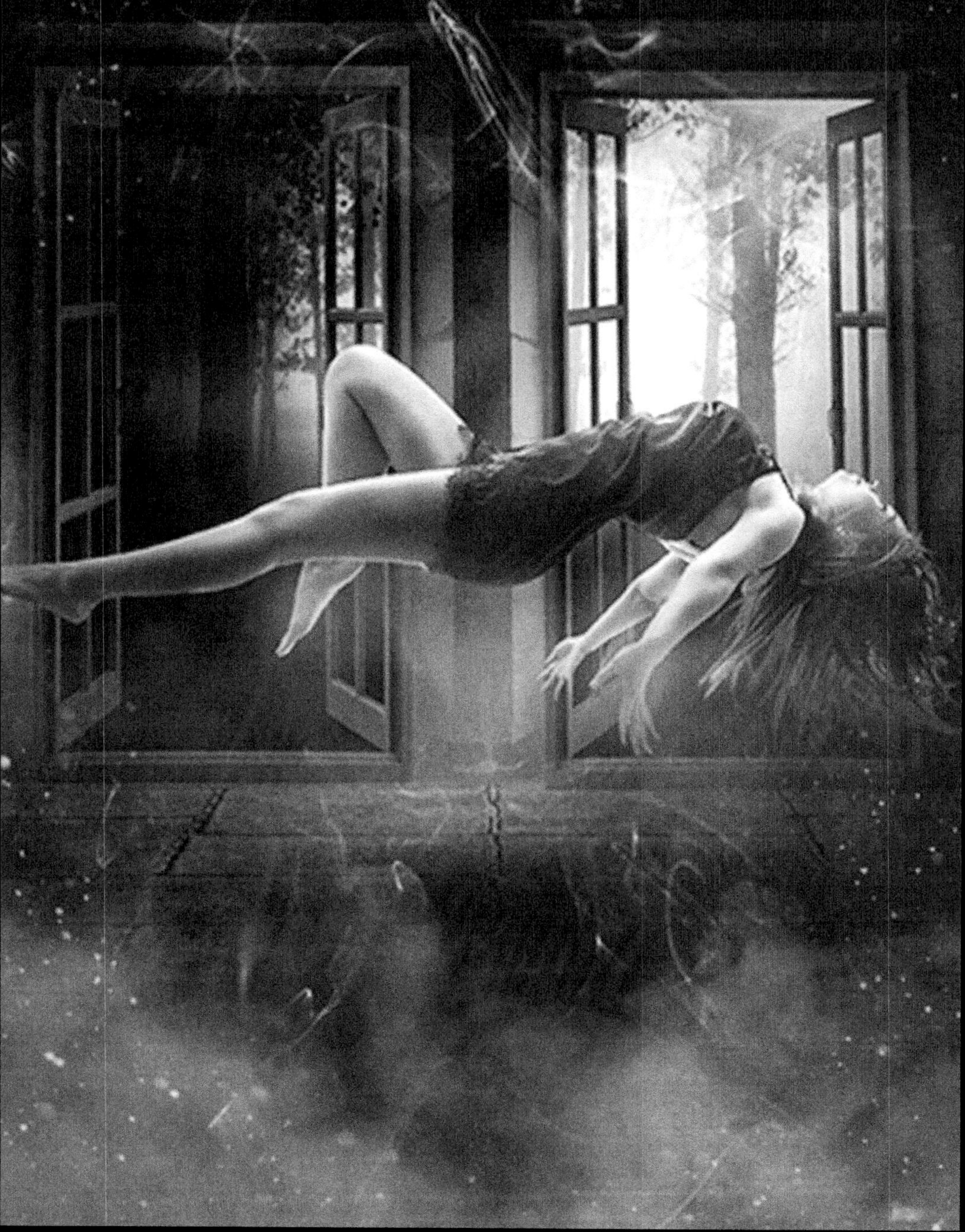

CHAPTER
TWENTY-TWO

Astra
I Found - Amber Run

I want to run into the arms of a ghost, in order to hide my heartache at the fact the ones I love most have abandoned me here, leaving me to the rotten roots of this cruel, cruel world.

My father and my brother are the only comforts I'd ever known.

I had never felt safer and more shrouded in eternal protection as fiercely as I had when they were around me. I wasn't alone in this world and when they left, the void of their absence consumed me. But now... now the possibility of Hunter means the possibility of *them*.

I fear it isn't as simple as that, though.

Hunter pulls me closer, a hefty pressure surrounds my core being as his presence engulfs me and calm settles. "Why are you here and they aren't?" I sob, my cheeks wet from my tears, my lips salty from the kiss of my pain.

"Because I'm a different kind of man, Siren. I may be dead, but my love for you is alive and death itself can't keep your stalker away."

"I-I still don't understand." I hang my head, too wrapped up in the fresh wash of grief I'd been shielding myself from. The faint flutter of a finger grazes my chin, lifting my face to peer into the endless gray eyes that consume me and spit me back out a broken woman. Until the harsh line of his jaw is graced with an easy smirk, and those fractures suddenly mend back together again, making me whole.

"Love is too easy to overcome, too easy to fake. What I have for you goes into something more potent. *Obsession* is a love beyond the ages, Astra. It's a physical compulsion that drives your every waking moment and what I imagine is the hardest thing to overcome. Basic love simply isn't enough." His finger gently rises to swipe beneath my eye and I shudder, falling into him in a last-ditch effort to feel anything other than bereavement.

"I feel like I'm losing my mind. Am I crazy, Hunter?"

"Yeah, baby, you are. The best kind of crazy. The kind that allows you to see and hear me, that lets me touch you." Hunter's hands roam the expense of my shoulders, skating down the back of my arms and I shiver. The intimacy of the moment intensifies, and suddenly, the warmth of our connection blooms in my chest and wraps itself around my heart.

In an instant, the truth I haven't wanted to acknowledge is bare for all to see. I'm not alone. I haven't been alone for as long as this man has known me. With this new reality, I should be running for the hills. Not standing idle, taking comfort in his soothing embrace wanting him more than anything to consume me.

"What's it like?" I pull back, my doe eyes seeking his cold ones for answers of life beyond the veil of comprehension. "Being dead? Is it without anguish? Are you at peace?"

So many questions, and not enough time.

Time?

What the fuck is that anyway.

"It's everything, Siren." He smiles again. "It's like a cool ocean carrying you to paradise, but I feel like I'm missing something. And I can't truly be at peace until I get it."

I panic, thinking of my family and how they may be alone out there, wandering about the world, confused and afraid, not knowing how to settle their unfinished business. A visceral concern that is either plastered all over my face or bleeding into our newfound connection has Hunter seizing my upper body in a tight embrace again.

"The fact they aren't here, love, is a better sign than if they were. I know everything about you, Astra. *Everything*." The way he drawls the word everything is like a vice around my heart. Images assault my mind, a fog horn in my ears that has me stumbling away. A figure in the shadows, movement on the edge of my subconscious. Gray eyes staring through my windows. Skilled fingers reading through case files as easily as they shift through my mail.

He's been stalking me. *Investigating* me. Somehow in my desperation to not be alone, I've overlooked the obvious. This sinfully gorgeous and equally dangerous man has had me in his sights for longer than even I could bear the thought.

What has he learned? What deep and dark secrets of mine has he uncovered?

Suddenly, I can't breathe. A heavy weight sits on my chest as I double over, gasping for air. I'm ripped in half, torn between life and limbo where the air no longer survives. Horror-filled eyes meet Hunters and I see how wild his are, how untamed and furious.

What the hell was I thinking?

All those sweet words of obsession don't mean he doesn't still want to kill me!

Of course, he does.

After all, I'm the reason he's dead. I'm the reason he lost everything.

He was my stalker, not my friend. Not a tender man who I should be allowing to hold me within his arms. How many times does a girl need to watch *Beauty and the Beast* before she understands the concept of Stockholm syndrome? Or how beasts can turn into beautiful men and lure you in. Hunter's my beast. A monster that lurked in the shadows and now he was trying to kill me, dead.

He looms over me now, cold and detached as those hard lines of his face turn sharp and lethal. And as those endless gray eyes darken into wells of inky blackness, the pressure on my throat increases.

I withdraw further, fighting against his ghostly clutches as I claw at my throat, begging for air. My heart squeezes, and my ribs groan in protest as everything inside of me shuts down in complete agony. Darkness encroaches on my vision, the pain spreads across my chest and all sound dissipates from the world around me. My panic mingles with dread and slowly, ever so slowly, the lights dim until all I see is black.

Then, suddenly, just as the world riots and lightning strikes against the earth, the lightbulbs in the dual dragon lamps shatter on my side tables. The windows around me in the sunroom burst like raindrops of tiny spears and I fall to the ground, slumped in the ruins of broken glass. Through the bleak abyss, I stumble to my feet and flee straight out into the night. I run for my life, not even sure if I wanted to save it. But I knew if I was to meet my end, it would be on my own terms and not at the hands of a monster.

Fright consumes me, my breath still leaking in and out in tiny pants, as my bare feet pound against the sodden ground and further into the forest. Rain falls, dousing me in the cold rush as my legs carry me as far as I can go before exhaustion wins. The low droning of the world around me whizzes to life, and even the critters of the night, fall silent from the storm.

The only sound was an insistent buzzing that rang in annoyance within my ears.

Something calls to me through the wood impairing my hearing, and my mind distorts as everything around me spins in rotation. "Astra!"

My name is bellowed and I spin trying to find the source. It seems to be coming from everywhere and nowhere at all, a megaphone from the universe calling my name and beckoning me to heel. But I can't. I have to keep going, true terror the vicious hand that shoves me forward.

"Astra!" I stagger, falling over a broken stump, hidden behind the brittle leaves. I scream, my hands coiled in my hair as I shout my frustrations out into the universe like that is the only defense I have against the aspiration that wants to kill me. I roll over, my breath as cold as ice as I fight the urge to move more quickly than my body allows, but it's too late.

As soon as I'm on my back, looking for the moon to guide me, he's there, towering above me. I shriek, realizing that for the first time in lengthy minutes, I'm able to breathe properly again. "G-get away from me. Get the fuck away from me!" I cry, my voice cutthroat and scratchy. "You tried to kill me!" I accuse and then my hearing is back, but once again the world falls quiet, almost in disbelief.

Stopping short, he leans back and stands to his full height, no longer offering me a hand of aid, but staring down at me in fierce accusation instead. The silver in his eyes burns like hot liquid, the silver specs dance and entwine with the brooding gray and the coldness there has me shuddering. He's shut down, and that look, it's one of hurt and anguish.

"I've spent every waking moment since I've known you, protecting you, Astra. Why the fuck would I try and kill you?" The growl rumbles like a low murmur of a lion and I'm suddenly very aware that we're outside, lost to mother nature.

The rain falls heavier and I struggle to see through the thick stream of it. "Because I killed you first! Because I'm the reason you died! It's revenge, you want me dead for revenge!" I scurry back, my silken legs being torn and cut by the vines of nature as my lounge shorts snag on a piece of bark. I hurry to my feet, a small slice of my fabric tearing, left behind on the ground as I back away quickly and wrap my arms across my chest.

He scoffs a small chuckle of derision and my eyes narrow at him in confusion. "Astra, love. I died saving you, I'd die for you again. The only person I am mad at is *myself*. I should have been prepared for anything, but I was too angry. So consumed in the thought of him touching you, of him *hurting* you, I didn't see the knife until it was too late. Until I was standing above my corpse, right before my soul brought me here, back to you."

He steps forward, and I shuffle back. My shoulders dug into the rough bark of the tree as he corners me, my back pressed firmly against it.

"My only rage, my only regret is the fact that I left you here unprotected." He leans down, forehead touching mine as his lips hover close to where mine part with shallow breaths.

The aspiration of his feathers down my ribs, the icy sensation has me shuddering, my back arching to squirm away from the overwhelming tickle that has my leg lifting involuntarily. I capture a purr in my throat, my mind at war with my heart as arousal and terror mingle in my core.

Hunter trails his hand down my throat, his intense eyes watching every movement with something feral in his gray eyes and his mood darkens. "I gave it all up for you," he rasps, almost like he's in a trance, as he moves those deft fingers of a caress across my shoulder and down my arm. "I lost control and lost you in the process," he murmurs as those eyes of his intensify and something chilling passes through them. Something darker than an abyss.

"I lost the chance to ever touch you like this for real, lost the opportunity to feel you as you come undone beneath me." Circling my core, those cool fingers travel down my abdomen until a large hand is cupping my apex. I shudder, my terror the breath that leaves my burning lungs in a gasp. My arousal, the mewl that whispers past my lips as he circles my clit, stroking my pussy over the fabric of my clothing.

"I lost so much, love, but I gained so much more. Do you know what it's like when my soul touches your silken skin? It's a sensation rawer than even the greatest orgasm you could ever have. A soul is a divine gift, it allows me to feel your every waking moment. Every tender second that passes. I get to feel you in ways I've never felt anyone. The connection my heart had with you in life, is nothing compared to the connection my soul has to you in death. You're still singing your siren's song, Siren, and I'm a man going down with his sinking ship. I wouldn't stop it, I wouldn't change it, because you're finally mine and the feeling of that? It is indescribable."

I'm breathing a little heavily, torn between his words and my greatest fears. I felt it, whatever *it* was. The thing was a demonic presence inside of me, one that wanted one thing and one thing only... It wanted me *dead*. I open my mouth, ready to tell him how I felt in the daunting moments that lead us here until a twig breaks in the distance and a dark shadow steps from behind the trees. I scream, to the devil himself, do I fucking scream. My hands thread through my hair, I slump down the tree. The warm pressure of my aching pussy fades. Hunter steps away from me and I cower.

I pull at the roots of my hair as I spin in a wild circle hoping that my broken insanity will act like a barrier against whatever has come to kill me next. Because I ran out of time, whatever it was that stalked me is here, and I have to bide my time until I can fly into action and put them on their ass.

"Miss Stone? Miss Stone, are you okay?"

"No, no, no, no, no!" I chant, the night as my witness as I become frantic in my confusion of terror.

"Miss Stone? Miss Stone what happened, is there a threat?"

My eyes crack open and I see the sheen of a gun, twinkling under the scarce moonlight as it breaks through the trees.

"No, no, no! Satan, go back to Hell!" I bellow as I fly into action. I disarm him, snapping his arm at an odd ankle so he'll release his grip on the gun before I throw it deeper into the thicket of trees. I spin, throwing him over my shoulder until he lands with a heavy thud and I have a chance to take off, trying to run to safety.

The look in his confused eyes is the last thing I see before I try to flee, but all I end up doing is falling down into a ditch. My ankle twists and the thin layer of my cami rides up my flesh until the soft skin of my torso is chafed by the dirt and rubble. I'm red, raw, cut up with a million tiny little inflictions that hurt a hell of a lot more than if I had just stabbed a fork through my hand.

"Fuck, if he wasn't already dead, he'd kill me!" I hear whispered behind me, but that's the thing about the wind, it tells you everything if only you just listen.

But I'm not listening, I am screaming. I am screaming like a woman possessed and to be near me would mean contamination. But this fucker doesn't seem to care he is about to get his ass consumed by sugar cane candy with a pension for screaming like a dolphin as she stabs you to death.

"Astra, Astra. love, calm down!" Hunter soothes, rushing to my side as he throws himself down into the ditch like a pro. The ruble kicks up behind him, a sputtering of dirt arching in his wake. "It's Damien, he works for me. Breathe, darling, just breathe through those beautiful full lips for me."

"Who the fuck is Damien? And why the fuck is he stalking me into the woods?" I shriek, panting heavily. Being haunted by Hunter the ghost is harder than it looks.

I don't know if I'm coming or going.

If I can believe him or if this is all one big trick to drive me into insanity.

He said he never tried to hurt me, but I know what I felt. The disgusting, vile toxins that slithered against my soul, killing me slowly. It's impossible to forget. I shudder, still feeling the residue of such insidious things inside of me.

"Good question," he growls, turning to look at Damien over his shoulder. The gun he's holding is pointed out into the darkness around us, clearly having found it again.

"Good question? What do you mean, good question?" I ask dumbly, blinking at this cloudy man who seems to darken in rage. "You think *he* wants to kill me?"

"Who the heck are you talking to?" Damien barks, the shadows concealing half of his features. "Ma'am, I need you to calm down. I need to know if there's a threat. Are you being attacked?"

"From all sides," I mutter stiflingly another scream of wild frustration.

"I was outside watching the house from my car when I heard something that sounded like a bomb exploding. When I got inside, the sunroom was shattered and you were gone. We need to get inside and find cover, now!"

I stumble-crawl backward, getting to my feet and readying myself and my sore skin to flee for the second time tonight. The effects of the whiskey are slowly subsiding, but I still feel intoxicated. Dizzy and like I'm a moment away from passing out which I do not want to do in either of these asshole's company.

"You were watching me?" I ask cautiously, taking another small step backward. "Hunter, why was he stalking me?" Thunder cracks across the skies and I'm sure my last question was lost to the wilderness, but Hunter hears me.

"What's mine is yours, love. Say hello to your new bodyguard."

That's it.

That's about all I can take before my body gives out and that vile energy inside of me takes hold. I fall to the ground, the world slows down and moves in slow motion as everything spins and the last thing I see is a furious purple claiming the sky.

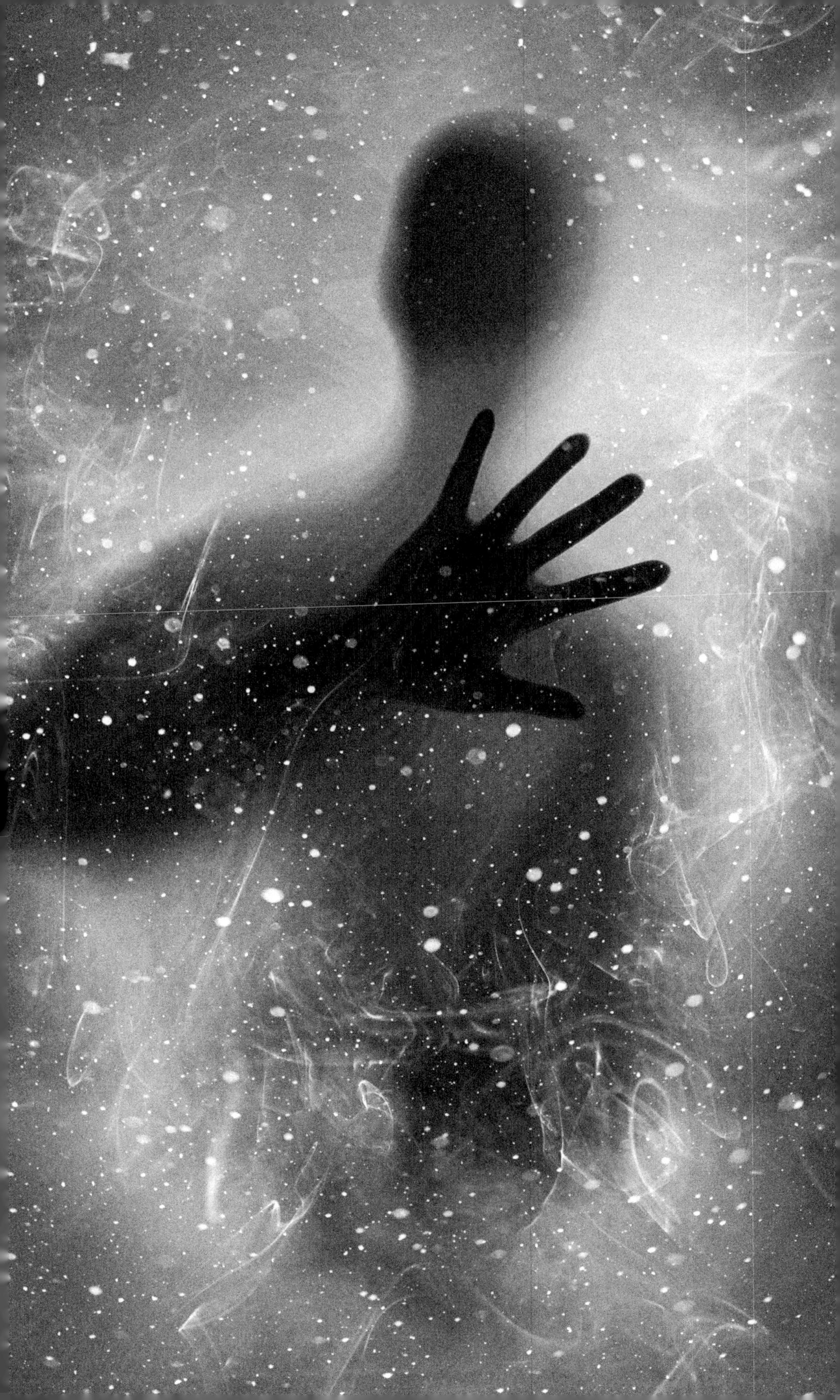

CHAPTER
TWENTY-THREE

Hunter
Parachute - Kyndal Inskeep

'It's okay, Love. Stay with me a little while longer,' I rasp, my gentle touch caressing her hairline. The dark strands of her hair part like a veil and her angelic face is revealed to me.

Siren looks back up at me, a tender calmness in her ocean gaze, wider than the world that sucks me in.

Here, she never asks questions.

Here, I am her world and she knows nothing but peace. We're cocooned in such tenderness, that I never want our fragile bubble to burst. I can keep her safe here, shielded from the burdens of the world. From human emotion that sits heavy on her shoulders. I don't know what to tell her, how to take away the pain she seems to be drowning within in regards to the loss of her father and her brother.

The secret of the night she lost them is like a snake in my throat, coiling tighter and tighter until I can't breathe at all, which is ironic considering I breathed my last breath down that alley, with a knife embedded into my ribs.

I died with her name on my lips and took her biggest secret to my grave.

The truth will either set her free, or it will destroy her. Call me a selfish man, but I want to heal her before I threaten to break her even more than she already is.

"Just accept it, Siren. Don't fight it. I can feel you, baby, I can feel how much pain you're in." I know she can't see me. That here, I'm a voice without a face because that is usually how dreams work, but this is the only place I can give her everything I know she needs. "I can't stand it, Astra. I can't stand the pain in your eyes. Please, love. Just a little while longer. Stay with me a little while longer and let me save you. All I've ever wanted to do was save you."

A lone tear falls from her glassy eyes. She's crying even though she's in a sedative state. Because her mind might be at rest, but her soul is in utter turmoil. Everything is becoming too much. Everything that has happened from the losses she bears to the attack she suffered. Let's not even start with my death, the man who stalked her for nearly two years and then died saving her. The man who has done everything humanly possible to stack the odds in her favor. From buying out the other tattoo parlors to having live-in staff at the restaurant. Now she's faced with inheriting everything from my demise, plus a six-foot-two, ex-military bodyguard, which now that I think about it, was probably the dumbest move I could have made.

If he tries it on with my woman, I'll hang him with his own fucking tie.

Damien carried her home and once he assessed there was no threat, laid her down to rest in her room and cleaned up downstairs, making sure the ground is glass-free before she woke again in the morning. He's been watching her for weeks now, but he knew to keep his distance until the dust settled. It was a part of the contract and NDA I made him sign.

I may have been a possessive man with little foresight beyond the woman that I wanted, but I am most definitely a conscious man too. I will never leave a stone unturned when it comes to her.

Not in this life or any other.

I've never wanted to cause my love any heartache, but she's mourning.

She's mourning the life she feels I never deserved to lose. If only she knew, my life has begun and ended with her in the very first moments I ever laid my storm-brewed eyes on her.

I want to own, dominate and control, for sure. I wanted her and there would have been nothing to stop me from having her. Not even her own refusal. I would have made her mine one way or another, even through her avid protest.

Luckily for both of us, it never got that far.

Lucky for me, she's receptive, even if it's through sweet dream manipulation and gentle caresses. My soul aches, longing for its other half. My nights and days are growing more daunting, darkening around me as I feel my resolve waver in grief and fear. I want to comfort her, I need to comfort her, but there is only so much that I can do. As much as I indulge her, I also have to accept the fact that I terrify her too. But it isn't because I'm dead, or because I'm some kind of horny Casper, but because she found comfort in her version of the afterlife, and I've ruined that for her.

She thinks that she's ruined me, stealing my life and now my afterlife too.

If only she knew how fucking worth it all of this was, just to be able to lay here as I am now, staring down into her tear-filled ocean blues.

I don't know what's worse - dying for the one you love or her never truly being able to grasp just how deep that love ran before the last breath in your soul whispered past your lips.

"I love you, Astra. I always have and I'll love you still, even through the pain. Lean on me, Siren. Just lean on me. I promise I won't let you fall, baby. I got you. Just stay with me a little while longer."

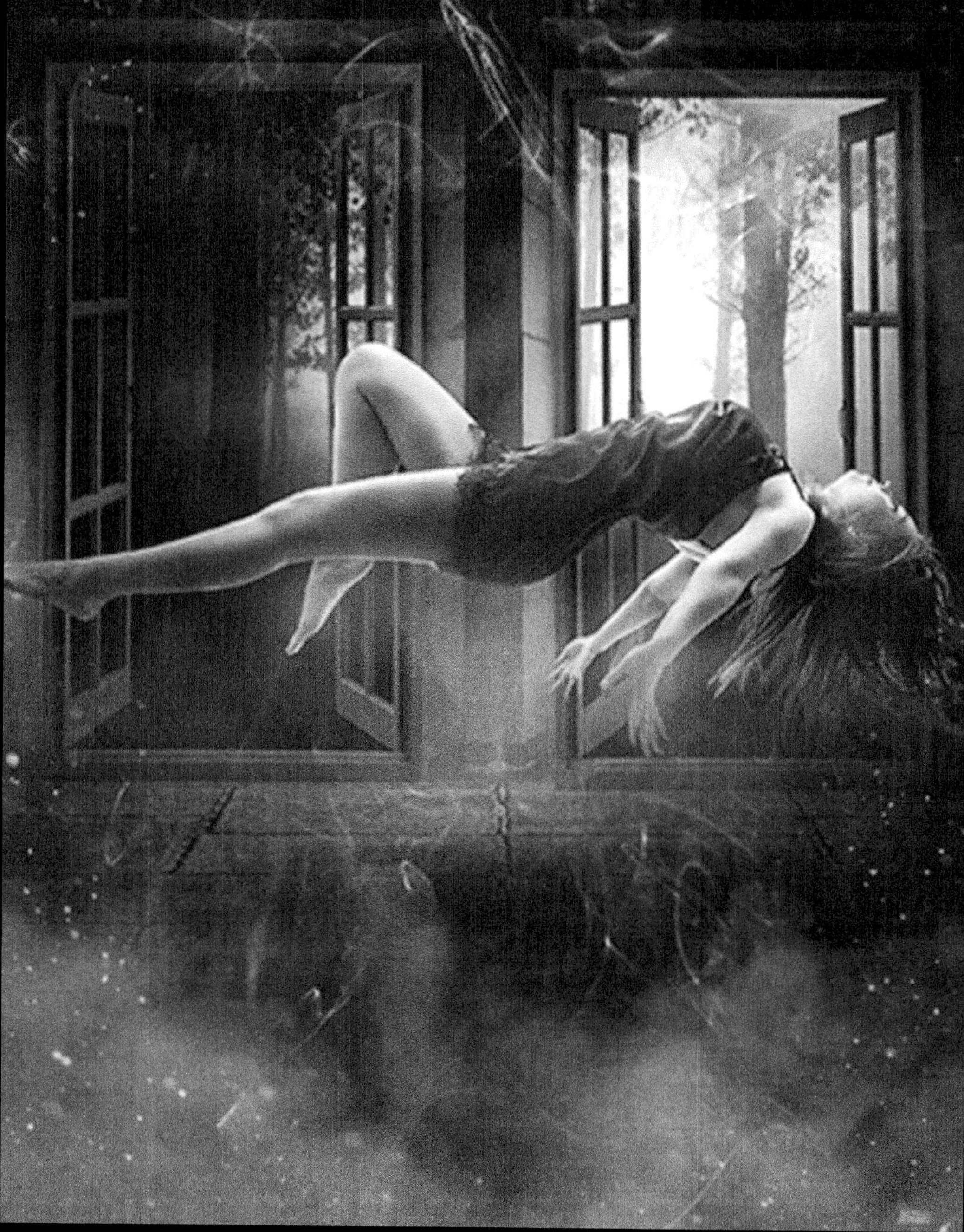

CHAPTER
TWENTY-FOUR

Astra
Bury - Unions

I'm lost in the darkness but as I stare out into the abyss, the fleeting shadows of feathers even darker and more silken create the shape of wings fluttering toward me.

I know this isn't real, that it can't be.

It's purely a figment of my conscience that is coming to life in my time of need, and this bleak man is a comfort I didn't know I needed.

He is longing to hold me. I can feel it.

Like a tendril of his essence, it strokes me from the inside out.

A warning. An experimental touch.

This creature doesn't want me to fear him. He wants me to accept him and the more I fall into the warmth of his embrace, the more all of my terror fades on the subtle breeze of my darkness.

The harder I stare though, the more the shape comes into view. Soon, I'm a small orchid, in the arms of a wild beast keeping me safe. A delicate light, swaddled in an empire of darkness. I lean into him, my slender head resting on his broad shoulder.

He's hunched, a giant folded for the woman who called to him.

He holds me in a silent embrace, tears of anguish pool in my eyes, and then, at the feel of his touch, it all dissipates and I feel nothing.

I am nothing, nothing other than his.

I'm his beauty and this harrowing shadow? Is most definitely, my beast.

The further I fall, the faster I find that I no longer want to leave my dream world. That I'd rather lie in the darkness than walk through the murky gray color of life.

I pull myself to my knees and crawl closer to him. He leans back, moving with my unspoken intentions. Slowly, with my hands, I climb the length of his golden body. This creature is my escape. I coil my fingers into his tousled hair and pull, his neck cranes back, and with unhurried movements, my eyes appreciating him wholly, I move a little closer still. My lips ghost across his defined abs, all the way up to his hardened pecs. He moans a raw and primal sound that fuels me with his own carnal need. His eyes, unfocused within my own, flutter closed before suddenly snapping open. He lunges forward, hands on my ass as he lifts me, bringing my core to rest against his very erect and naked cock. It's harder than steel, feels as cool and silken as steel too as it glides against me.

Large and heavy, it nestles between my thighs, pushing between my folds. Slowly, ever so fucking slowly I sink down, allowing him to fill me so wholly I feel it within the brewing ache of my core. I moan, my head rolling back before I strike, throwing my head down and sinking my teeth into this throat. "Fuck, I need this," I gasp, as I hum around a mouthful of his sweet, sweet skin. Pushing myself further down in favor of depth. The deeper he is, the more I burn. "I need to feel you, I need to feel you!" I chant, desperate. Needing this release, begging for my escape. "Please, please! Don't let me go!" I'm begging for comfort. For solidarity. The longer I'm here, the more I begin to feel whole. "It only makes sense here," I whisper, more for myself than the aspiration of my dream.

"What does, Siren?" he husks, head bent low. He breathes against my neck, and I shudder, leisurely rocking his hips as my clit grinds against the core of his shaft.

"My life," I whisper. "I don't want to go back, don't make me go back," I plea, my nails digging into his flesh, drawing diagonally down his shoulder blades as I dig for perches.

He hisses, rocking into me harder, more brutal. With deadly intent, his left hand collars my throat, squeezing tightly. "You play dangerous games, Siren," he growls, the restraint in his voice wavering. "You don't know what you're asking for. You belong there, in the life of the living."

Unfelt tears well within my eyes as I'm overcome with the thought of emotion. Here, I'm unburdened but like a psychopath without the knowledge as to why tears leak from his eyes, I rock against him harder, my human body knowing that it's lying in sorrow, my soul fighting for the bliss of ecstasy only this life can bring.

"I belong with you," I declare, his massive wings wrapping around me and concealing me in darkness. I'm lost in an abyss, the feathers ghosting sensually across my back. Right before the ground opens wide and my soul is sucked back through the void and I'm left clawing for his outstretched arms once more, my eyes snapping back open into a life that is becoming more of a hassle than it's worth.

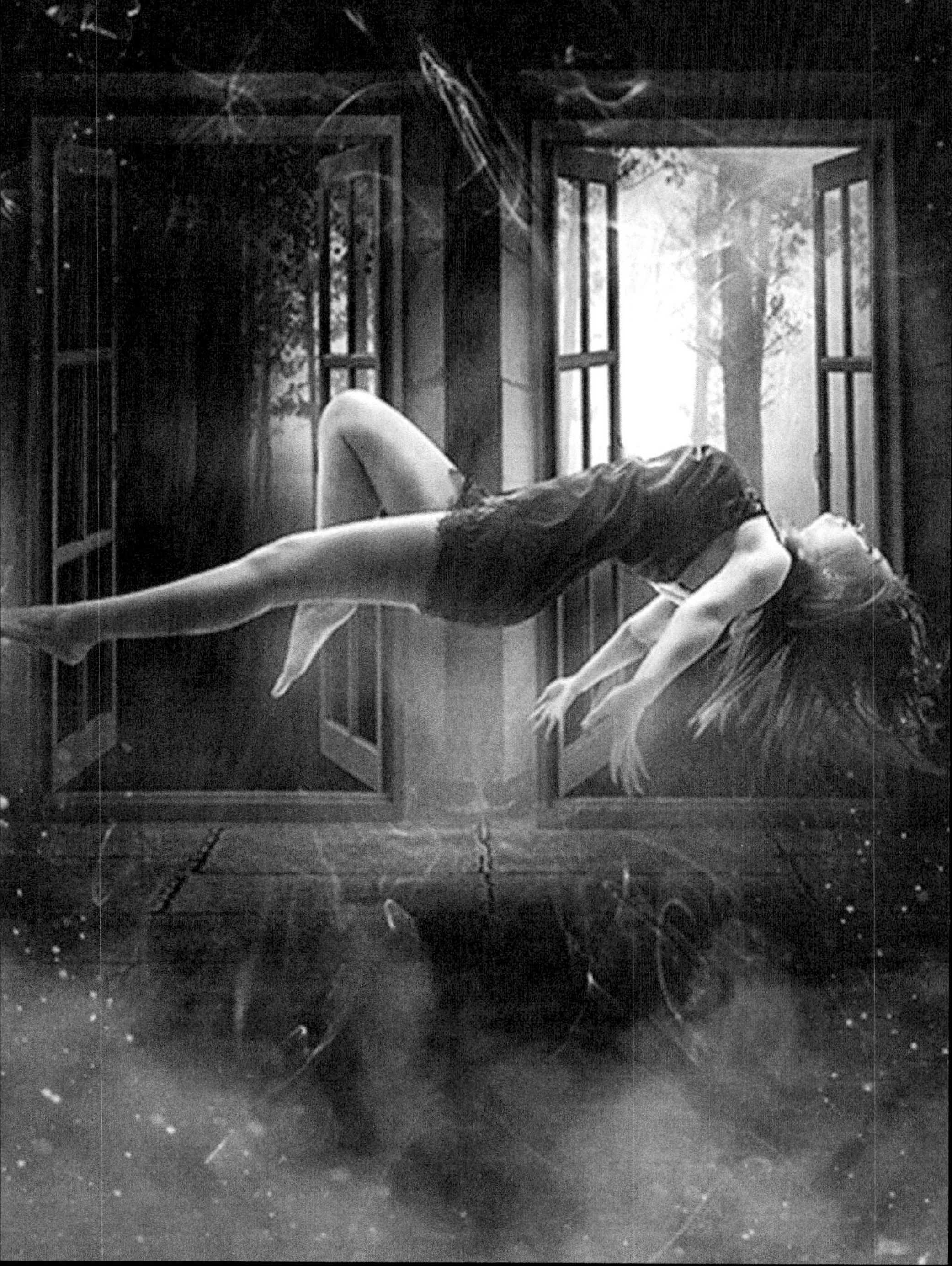

CHAPTER
TWENTY-FIVE

Astra
Kill the Lights - Set It Off

I groan, a small huff whispering past my lips as I rub away the ache that is forming along my brow bone. I don't remember much of last night other than sinking to the endless depths of liquid bliss. I can still feel the burn in my chest. My lungs warm, and my head throbs like a bitch. I somehow feel like the jackhammer in my skull has nothing to do with the sweet temptation of Tennessee Whiskey though, and everything to do with the overload of fucking crazy that made my brain fry like the ass of a bacon strip on a hot grill. I'm sour I've woken up, back into the life of real issues instead of getting some hot dick back in my dreams.

I sigh, my hand trickling down my stomach until I reach the waistline of my shorts. I hiss, the sting from the cuts on my body painful, but I use that to my advantage. As I dip between the waist-line of my panties and begin to tease my clit. I'm already wet, soaking in fact from the dream that refused to let me finish. Reaching into my bedside drawer, I retrieve my vibrator and my dildo. My legs fall open. Into the shape of a triangle and my back arches and I shift into position. First I tease my opening, the taunt of the penetration over half of the arousal that seeps from my cunt. Circling my hand, I play my clit like a musical instrument. Carnal sounds whisper past my lips and burn the back of my throat as I become frenzied. Insistent on that high that has eluded me for almost a month. Quickly and just as brutally, I jerk my arm and fuck myself with the dildo. The black ribbed cock slips inside of me with ease, pushing past that barrier of my folds and hitting me right where I need it most. My arm holding the vibrator to my clit vibrates, my entire body seized and locked up as I chase that rabbit running down that hole.

"Fuck, fuck, fuck. Please! Oh, fuck please!" I plead, back arched, sweat beading on my brow. My fever rises, my skin hot and slick as I writhe within the sheet.

I fuck myself harder, circle my clit savagely. My pussy burns, turning numb under the assault. The precipice is there, I'm standing on the edge, the rubble falling into the cool oceans below and just as I take the dive, a gust of wind sends my ass back over the cliff to land on my back, not an orgasm in sight.

It's just gone.

Sucked away from my beckoning cunt.

I'm hung out to dry, sore and frustrated as I toss my vibrator across the room so it smacks against the bedroom door. I fall slack, my energy depleted. The dildo still deep in my pussy. A cool gust of wind tickles against my thigh and then the dildo is pushed inside of me that much further and a dark voice whispers, "Even your orgasm is mine, Siren. But nice try." Then it's pulled from my fluttering cunt and I gasp, my chest pulling up from the bed as if guided by a string and I heave. Sitting upright, I frantically gasp for every painful breath that leaves my mouth dryer than the Sahara. The dildo thrown to the ground. I narrow my eyes, flopping back to the bed as my mind works to calm itself down from this crazy shit.

"Fuck you," I hiss and a dark chuckle is my only reply. I narrow my eyes and start to wonder...

When I wake, my dreams are always evasive. They elude me as much as my happy endings. I begin to wonder if it's my spiritual stalker that I dream about.

Because it was most definitely him on my mind when I was just trying to come a moment ago. And it was most definitely him that stopped me from coming altogether.

Something cocoons around me, the firm length of a thickly coiled man. I fit into his curve, perfectly. A soothing presence that is like a balm to my soul. But I know I'm crazy and when my eyes flutter open again from my frustrations and I turn to the side and see nothing but the right side of my bed crumpled and empty, I know I'm losing it. My brows crease as I think about the chaos of last night, the man who stepped from the shadows and gave my heart a jump start.

Hunter North.

Fuck, I don't fear that ghostly man. I crave him. Because when he had me pinned against that tree, the wild fury brewed from his own frustration in restraining himself, I felt more alive than I ever had. Even if it was tethering on the vines of uncertain fear. As soon as he touched me, that dark presence that tried to snuff me out was chased away by the refreshing sensation of his essence that engulfed me like the flames of a raging fire. I burned alive under his aspiration. It was cutthroat. A compulsion.

Fuck that, this is odd and I've most definitely cracked.

I *need* more of him. I need to be *consumed* by Hunter North so I never feel that darkness that came before him again.

I wish he was here now because as much as it most certainly forces me to question my sanity, I still can't deny that I crave that feeling of eternal tranquility that I was swaddled in when he was beside me. The heel of my palm pressed firm against my eye socket, I roll to the end of the bed and throw my tender legs over the side. The first pinpricks of pins and needles pulsate in my muscles and I wince, no other feeling worse than the tedious fingers of the kind of pain that is nothing more than an annoyance. I'd rather deal with a broken bone than the ache of weak ass muscles.

"What the fuck is happening to me?" I utter under my breath as I pad my way toward the bathroom. Standing in front of the mirror, I recoil at the bird's nest on the top of my once dark and delicate curls. Then I gasp, my hand flying to my throat at the bruising I see there. Perfect marks of identical fingerprints wrap around my slender neck, and I shudder, kind of turned on by the sight. I lift my shirt, finding bite marks and more bruises along my hips and down my thighs. I quiver, a saucy smirk on my lips as a war between fuck yes and hell no, screams their justified arguments within my head.

I decide to shut them out. The voice of reason fights the war for doubt as I notice the cuts and scrapes from my tussle with mother nature.

Black smears under my eyes and the draining of my soul are seen in how vivid my ocean blues look at the moment in contrast to my pale and sickly-looking skin. I shake my head, wash my face and follow my normal morning routine of two face washes, a scrub, two different oils, rolling my face, then washing with a cleanser and some moisturizer. By the time I'm done, I have my healthy-looking glow back. Then I tackle my curls with my detangler hair brush before I end up throwing it into a messy bun anyway. My mind drifts to the dreams I keep having, the world that seems perfect of my own making keeps calling to me and I fight my heavy eyes just to stay away and not slink off back there. Last night's dream was an odd one, I had seen myself as some kind of nimble and delicate angel, shrouded within the arms of a beast.

Then I *fucked* that beast.

Wings and all.

Most would think that could be a nightmare, but honestly? I think it's the best dream I've ever had. It's a moment of reprieve on the soul that has to wear a million faces. I never had to be strong at that moment, just there, existing in peace knowing that he was keeping me safe. With a racing mind, I try to find the thing that grounds my turmoil as I waddle into the kitchen.

I stop short when I see a suited man sitting at my kitchen island.

His shoulders are huge, the expanse stretching the material of such finery under the muscles I can see rippling from the arch of the doorway. A clean-shaven neck feathers into thicker, more tousled hair on top of his head. Dark blond curls coil around one another and I gulp, wondering if I'm still drunk from last night. Then I remember that after I was fondled by Hunter, I ran away from a mad man with a gun after putting him on his ass first.

"Good morning, Miss Stone. I have your two-liter coffee from Joy's and your breakfast in the oven. Mr. Hunter was very specific in making sure you had a healthy diet, so this morning consists of poached egg and salmon with asparagus." He beams proudly as he slowly stands from his seat, giving me a rigid bow.

A gust of wind flutters through from the back door being slightly ajar, and ruffles the newspaper the man, Damien I remind myself, was reading on the countertop, upheaving all of the pages and sending them fluttering to the ground. After a moment of staring down at the floor in disbelief, he blinks and turns to face me like nothing out of the ordinary just happened.

"Did the flooring you took last night slip your mind? If that wasn't clear enough, it was a nice warning for you to leave. I don't need a bodyguard, or an assistant."

He narrows his eyes in question at me already knowing why he's here, but as true to the professional he thinks he is, he inhales a deep breath and carries on like I said nothing, getting right under my skin, "The coffee - he would have liked to change out for water but he had also noted you may have tried to drown me within it. No matter how small the bottle."

I mean... he wasn't *wrong*.

Everything about the last two nights comes rushing back to me. Returning home, seeing Hunter, spiraling over my family, to then almost being killed. It plays like a slide show, some memories welcome, some horrifying.

Something tried to *kill* me.

I can almost feel the vise around my throat again, my breathing turning shallow as I try not to panic. I can never forget the feeling, the one that felt like the claws of death.

I had never felt so cold, so afraid and when I fled for my life, the apparition in my mind had sworn to me he hadn't been the one trying to take me out from this world.

I stare at Damien blankly, my mind trying to process what the fuck is happening but despite all of the things I should pull from that sentence to start a riot over, only one thing pops out the most. I walk around my counter, not taking my eyes from his glowing greens as I reach for my phone by the oven. I dial without looking and place the receiver to my ear.

"Hey, yeah, it's me again. Same order, double the grease. Delivered to the shop in twenty? You're a gem, Benny. Thank you." Then I hang up, open the oven and pull from it my still hot plate of smoked salmon. My foot hits the pedal to open the trash can. My hand hovers over the rim with the heated plate, then I narrow my eyes. After a moment of deliberation, I shrug,

"Hmm, I guess I could eat this too. Y'know, get all of those calories in." Pulling cutlery from the drawer, I take a seat at the island, cut a huge helping of salmon, and point it to the new intruder. "He wasn't wrong. But you also just tried taking away BBQ from a hot-blooded American, so whether you live or not is still undecided. Now start talking, Simon."

He clears his throat and furrows his brows looking at me like I'm a puzzle. "My name is Damien, Miss Stone."

"Yeah, well. You sound like a man who will follow what Simon says." I shrug with my fork before shoving the hot salmon into my mouth. It falls apart into brittle little tender pieces and I groan, rolling my eyes.

"The kid's song? Simon is the one giving orders. Not the one following them," he notes with a tilt to his lips.

"Well, then. Start talking 'man who does what Simon says'." Cutting another piece of salmon, I smother it in the yolk from the egg. The golden essence drips like the nectar of God and my mouth waters, craving for me to stuff it full.

"I tried to explain last night, Ma'am, right before you passed out."

"Ew. Shut the fuck up and never call me Ma'am again. My name is Astra. Use it or lose it, pal."

"Lose what?"

"The ability to speak. It has been a rough few weeks and there is only so much more I can take before I freak the fuck out."

"Right, okay then. Once again I must apologize for jumping out at you like that. I have been watching you since Mr. North died. When I heard what sounded like an explosion, I had to come and make sure you were okay. It was Mr. North's strict instructions that I do not tell you my role until I deemed it necessary and that the dust had settled." He pulls at his lapels and sniffs, clearing his throat once more.

"I can't say I disagreed with him. This will be a lot to handle for anybody. Well, for anyone *sane*," he comments under his breath and I hike a brow at the stiff who might actually be alright after all. If I can crack that square posture of his, I might just keep him.

I've always wanted a puppy. I just hope he's potty trained.

I startle when he rushes forward and draws his gun, index finger pressed firmly against his lips as he mimes for me to hush. My face crinkles as my brows hit my hairline in shock and confusion. What the fuck itched his balls? I shake my head, in a way of telling him to fucking explain his random as fuck outburst. He lowers, his head close to mine as his eyes dart around every corner of the room, the gun pointed towards the only door out into the hall.

Leaning a little closer he whispers, "Is there an intruder, or are you just into really kinky sex?"

"Excuse me," I exclaim, drawing back and making him hiss at me in warning to keep my voice down. "What the fuck are you talking about."

He points to my throat and I chew on my plump lips. A tinge of scarlet turns my hot cheeks rosy as I look at the ceiling in avoidance.

Right. The bruises.

"This house was on lock down. I was keeping an eye on you all night. There is no way somebody got in without me knowing about it, but you also sure as fuck never had those bruises when I laid you down last night after you passed out."

"Yeah, erm. Self-inflicted. Kinky sex. Let's go with that. There's no intruder so you can put away the gun," I utter, stuffing another mouthful of salmon in my mouth.

He looks at me wearily, like he can't work out how it's possible for me to be covered in bruises or how I managed to choke myself during the sinful act of finger fucking.

So, I'll leave him to his conclusions.

"Listen, I've only recently discovered that I had a stalker billionaire, hot on my heels, for over a year. His untrustworthy sleaze of a lawyer tricked me into accepting his inheritance. So I appreciate the position you're in but whatever role you *think* it is that you have, will no longer be required. Not after I donate everything to charity."

He inhales deeply, brows hitting his hairline but not in a shocked gesture, but more of in a pitying manner. I lean forward, eyes pinched as I wait for the words sitting on the tip of his tongue. "Spill it, Simon."

"There isn't a charity out there that will accept your donation, Miss Stone. Hunter saw to that. And don't think to do it anonymously either. I don't know how he did it, but he had his ways and he has made damn sure you have no way out of this."

I sit up straighter, a fine red hot rage starts to trickle into my veins. "Why would he do that?"

"Easy. He wanted to protect you. He wanted to make sure you were always provided for and safe should anything ever happen to him. It was practically what the man lived for," he states as if this explanation was some kind of fact that made perfect sense. "What he died for even."

I gulp, a knot stuck in the back of my throat I can't seem to swallow down. Sweaty palms make the silver fork in my hand slick and it clatters to the plate with a resounding clatter when I accidentally drop it. I grunt, clearing my throat and fluttering my eyes and I wipe my hands down my jean-clad thighs and stare down at the plate.

"He wouldn't have wanted to die any other way. I know that much, Miss Stone," he soothes, my eyes full of anger snap to him and he pulls back, gaze wide. "Astra," he adds belatedly. "I was his personal assistant and bodyguard. Now I'm yours. It's with great honor that I now serve you like I once served him."

He lumbers over to me, placing a hand on my shoulder. The second his palm makes contact, the fork flies from the plate and stabs itself within the back of his hand, deep into the flesh. He hisses, pulling away sharply, and looks down at me with frantic, accusatory eyes.

"Hey, don't scowl at me. You saw that my hands were in my lap. Blame your psycho boss. After all, it's you who clearly knew how fucked in the head he was." Berating him, only had him looking at me like I was more insane than he already thought I was. "I'm being haunted!" I exclaim a little hysterically. " Like really haunted. Bad boss man has come back from the dead and he's stalking me from the afterlife!" Damn, I never meant for that to burst free from my chest. As soon as it does, I feel instant relief. All until I looked back at Damien who had a 'are you serious?' face on. I huff, realizing nobody was ever going to believe me. "Look, dude, I'm being haunted. Take it or leave it. I don't have time to hold your hand. So thanks for the offer, but no thank you. I don't need a stalker/ babysitter anymore. I still have one thank you very much."

Damien plucks the fork from his hand, spots of shiny crimson fall from the ends as thick pools of it bloom from the small wounds. "I don't know what you're talking about, but it will take a lot more than that to keep me from doing my job. You can make up elaborate lies all you want. You're stuck with me and there is not a court alive that will grant you a restraining order without a clear threat to your life. Which I am not, nor ever will be."

Freaky PA prick can read my mind. What the *fuck*?

"Not your mind, Siren. Just your file," A husky voice whispered into my ear and I shuddered, my back snapping ramrod straight. *"The file that stated absolutely* everything *there could have ever been to know about you. I'm obsessed, love. Did you really think even your thoughts were safe from me?"*

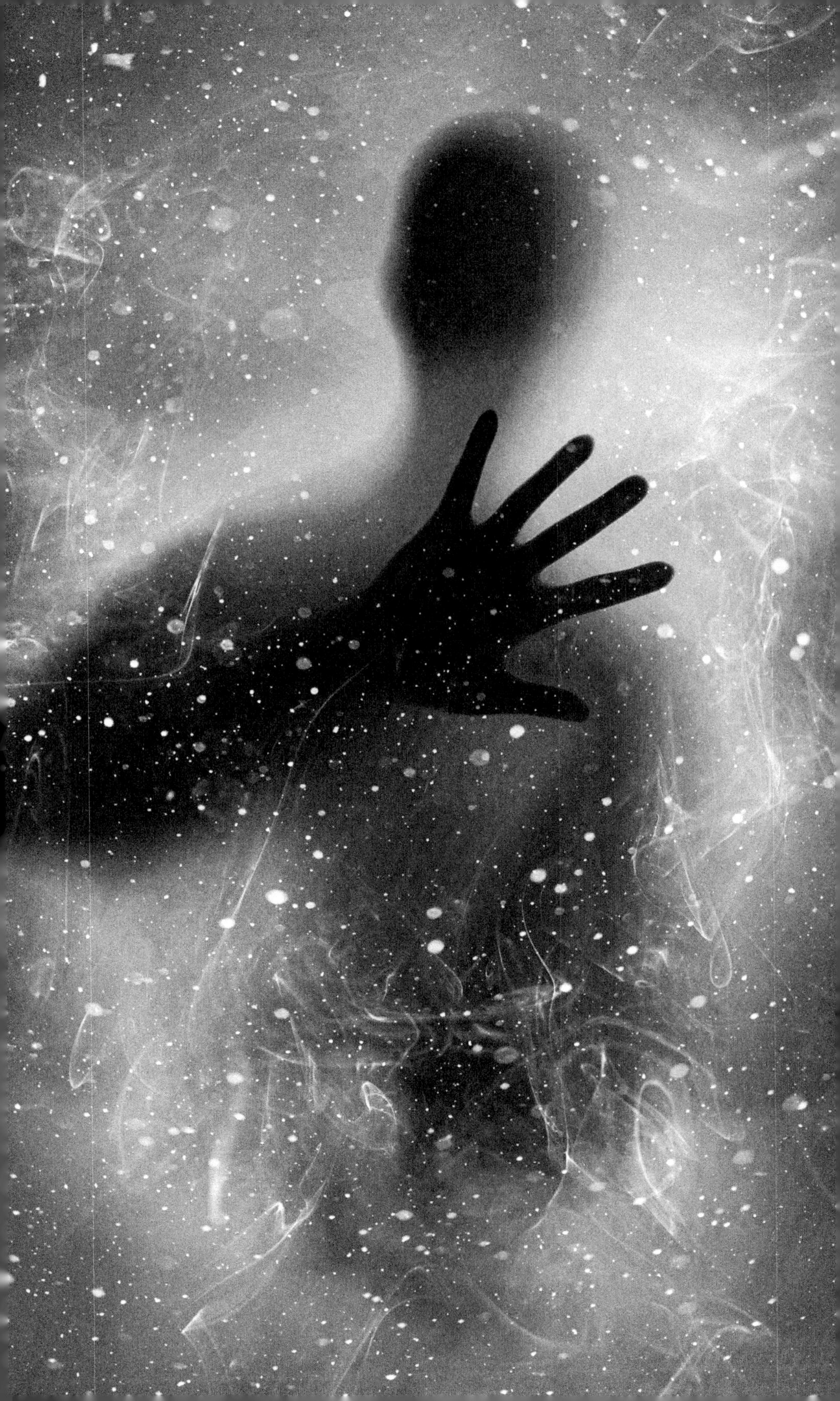

CHAPTER
TWENTY-SIX

Hunter
Addicted to You - Picture This

If he touches her again, I'll have to string him up by his ankles for a few hours and hope that all of the blood that rushes to his head will knock some sense back into him.

What a moron.

Nobody touches what's mine.

Not even him.

I've kept myself hidden from her this morning, wanting to give her some time to process the new changes before I made her think she was crazy again. Although, I don't think there has ever been a time in her life when she hasn't called herself such. Not to mention she woke up in a *much* better mood than I anticipated.

I heave a deep sigh, watching from a distance. Back within the mouth of my favorite alley. I'm back to stalking again. But this time, I'm hunting the darkness that's hunting her.

My woman is being a rebel, sitting in her store devouring a massive order from Benny's. I chuckle, knowing that it would never have been that easy for her to just one day decide to take care of herself. The fact she ate her breakfast this morning at all and didn't throw it at Damien's head though is most definitely an improvement. She sucks her succulent fingers clean and I find myself itching to get closer to her again. To pull her into another dream so I can do all the sweet, twisted things I have dreamed about doing to her for as long as I can remember.

The night before is on replay in my mind. She made her move.

She initiated the contact and burned me in the tendrils of her hot passion.

She wanted me and this morning, she wanted me still.

Something tried to *kill* her, though. Last night, something tried to steal her from me and that overshadows everything else.

After I followed her out into the woods, the sky rioting against the earth, my only thought or concern was her. Keeping her in her dreamscape so I could erase some of her panic, a persistent urge to fulfill. Because that's what I do there, every night, every time she closes those ocean blues, I'm there, chipping away at her burdens so she wakes with a little less weight on her shoulders. I blow out a harsh breath and run my hands roughly over my face.

The other side has me all fucked up.

I mean, I feel nothing but peace here. But I know that I *should* be feeling something. I know what I *would* be feeling, had I still been alive. So it's a war on my waking consciousness. I'm fighting that layer that has thickened inside of me that has made me disassociate from the human part of myself that would be in turmoil right now. On one hand, I'm elated that her idealism on the other side has merit, on the other, I'm feeling like I want to be pissed at the fact that it's a little too much like she envisioned it.

I have no room for the toxic feelings I've felt my entire life. The emotions I grew up with. When I died, all those dark parts of me fled and became an urge to find again instead of a burden I had to fight to keep in check. I guess you could say there was a numbness inside of me and it became a moot point the second she was in my arms again.

I have everything I could ever want. Slowly, day by day, I'm creeping inside of her waking mind and taking root there. I'm becoming less of a daunting ache and more of a deeply seeded reassurance.

I felt whatever it was that tried to steal her from me. It was like a haunting that plagued my peaceful afterlife. I couldn't see it. There is nobody else here apart from me. But I could feel it. Like a snake slithering beneath the skin, nibbling your insides and leaving little bites of poison in its wake.

How do I combat that? How do I find who or what this thing is?
I've only just died.

I'm not even fully aware of how all this shit works myself at the moment, let alone being able to play the hero and stop that horrible thing from happening to her again.

When it was choking her, my beautiful Siren falling to her knees in anguish, there was dark energy around us. It felt frenzied but weak. Like the electrical waves were wavering with the amount of strength it was taking in order to try and commit murder. It seemed like it was too much for the sinister essence to handle.

When I lost my shit, wild and furious desperation coiled in my gut and exploded through my chest with a soul-rippling roar that brewed deep within my core. I was able to snap whatever connection that had seemed to sink its vicious talons into the throat of my siren.

The collision of our energies caused the explosion. I could only be grateful that she wasn't harmed when the shards fell down upon her like tiny pistols of death.

Now I'm standing here, frustrated that I can't truly feel frustrated. Nothing and I mean nothing gets to threaten my love and make her fear her very own existence. I need to find out what the fuck it was and how the fuck I can kill it.

I've killed for her more than once in all of the time that I've known her, this dark entity could be a number of them. Why I couldn't see them though was still a mystery. I think in the afterlife, we have our own sides. Like little pockets of the world I guess, that belong solely to us. It's isolating as fuck and I can only hope that when your other half is laid to rest one day, they join you in your little bubble of the undead.

Fuck it, even if that wasn't how it worked, I'd shred this fucking veil just to be with her.

Either way, I need to figure it out. I need to protect her because I'll be damned if I ever see her that terrified again.

As I walk across the street, I notice Hazel wandering down the sidewalk toward the parlor. By the time she reaches the doors, I'm entering just behind her. Astra drops a rib back onto her dish, finished with her gigantic order and looks back at me with wide, storm-brewing eyes. She doesn't say anything at first, she just stares mouth agape even with Hazel relaying a triad of nonsense in her direction. Then she mutters, "Would have been your regular monthly slot if you only had skin."

Hazel turns narrowed eyes of confusion onto Astra. "What?"

"She does weird shit like that," Damien sighs, "I was hoping you'd shed some light on her random ramblings." Sparing Hazel a lazy glance, he returns to the phone clutched in his hand, standing sentinel in the corner of the store. He's trained well enough to put himself in a position that keeps him hidden from view but also so he has the vantage point of seeing every angle, always ready for a threat.

"Fuck me in the fairy and shatter me to dust," Hazel squeaks and even I widen my eyes, my brow hitting my hairline with a smirk on my face at her strange outburst. "Astra, there is a gigantic man in the corner. Why the fuck is there a gigantic man in the corner?"

"I'm her new bodyguard and assistant," Damien deadpans with a stoic face as his eyes peer out of the windows and along the sidewalk.

"Like fuck you are. I'm her assistant. And a bodyguard? You never even batted an eye when I walked in. What if I had been a ninja assassin?"

"You're in the file - Hazel May Sutton. Parents divorced, one sister. Born October thirtieth, you're a Scorpio and love all things spooky so the fact you just jumped at my presence is presenting to me as strange."

Her shoulders slump and her entire body sags as she stares at him incredulously. "How do you know all of that isn't just a cover story, hey? That it's not all a ploy and I'm just waiting until the right moment to strike?"

"It's in the file," he states blandly.

"T-the file? The fucking file? Astra, are you hearing this?" Hazel gasps and I turn, knowing Astra is still staring at me. Her eyes like beams of fire layered into my soul.

I smirk at her, loving how riled she gets when she sees me. "Told you, baby, I'm here to stay." She just blinks at me, refusing to address me in public and I chuckle darkly moving closer to her side. "When have you ever been sane, Siren? Go ahead, tell them that I'm here."

"You're an asshole, you know that? Why am I the only one who can see you?" she whispers. Hazel is back to arguing with Damien, her hush whisper lost to them.

"Because I'm yours. Not theirs." She turns her head pointedly ignoring me so I slide onto the leather recliner behind her. "I know the other night was a shock for you. Seeing me how you did. I know your first thought was your brother and father. But I want you to know, beautiful, that grief you hold so tightly? I won't let you drown in it alone anymore. That's my burden to bear now. You have too much to live for."

She turns her head to stare at me, her eyes turn glassy and emotion that I can't decipher fleets across her gaze. The blue in her eyes sparkles with specs of something crystallized and she suddenly seems so far away as her lashes flutter. "What if I don't want to live?" she breathes, so shallowly, so lowly, that I almost miss it.

I shift through her body so quickly Astra gasps with the sensation of it. I fall to one knee, my hand on her thigh as I lean closer, eyes narrowed and nostrils flared. "Say that again?" I dare.

But she doesn't. She doesn't say anything. Instead, her thighs open slowly so I can better fit myself between them. I narrow my eyes, moving closer to her as I gradually move my hand up her thigh until I reach her hip. Her thick lips part and her breathing grows depthless as she pants, trembling to restrain her impending quiver. "Oh, naughty girl, what sinner have I awoken?" I rasp, my hand stroking back and forth across the crease of her groin. "What dirty things do you crave?"

Still, she says nothing as she flexes her core, her eyes firm on mine as she pushes herself against my taunting touch.

"Astra!" Hazel snaps and those emotion-filled eyes swirl like the water swirling down the drain. She shuts it all down, blinks, and plasters a smile on her face while my hand still explores her sweet apex.

"Now, now children. Quit bickering. I have a new puppy. Play nice and don't pull his tail! I feel like he might bite!" She chuckles softly, her eyes flicker back to mine once more and her soft smile turns sultry as she knocks away my hand, and throws away her trash. "You want a challenge, bad boy? Do it when I have a needle in my hand."

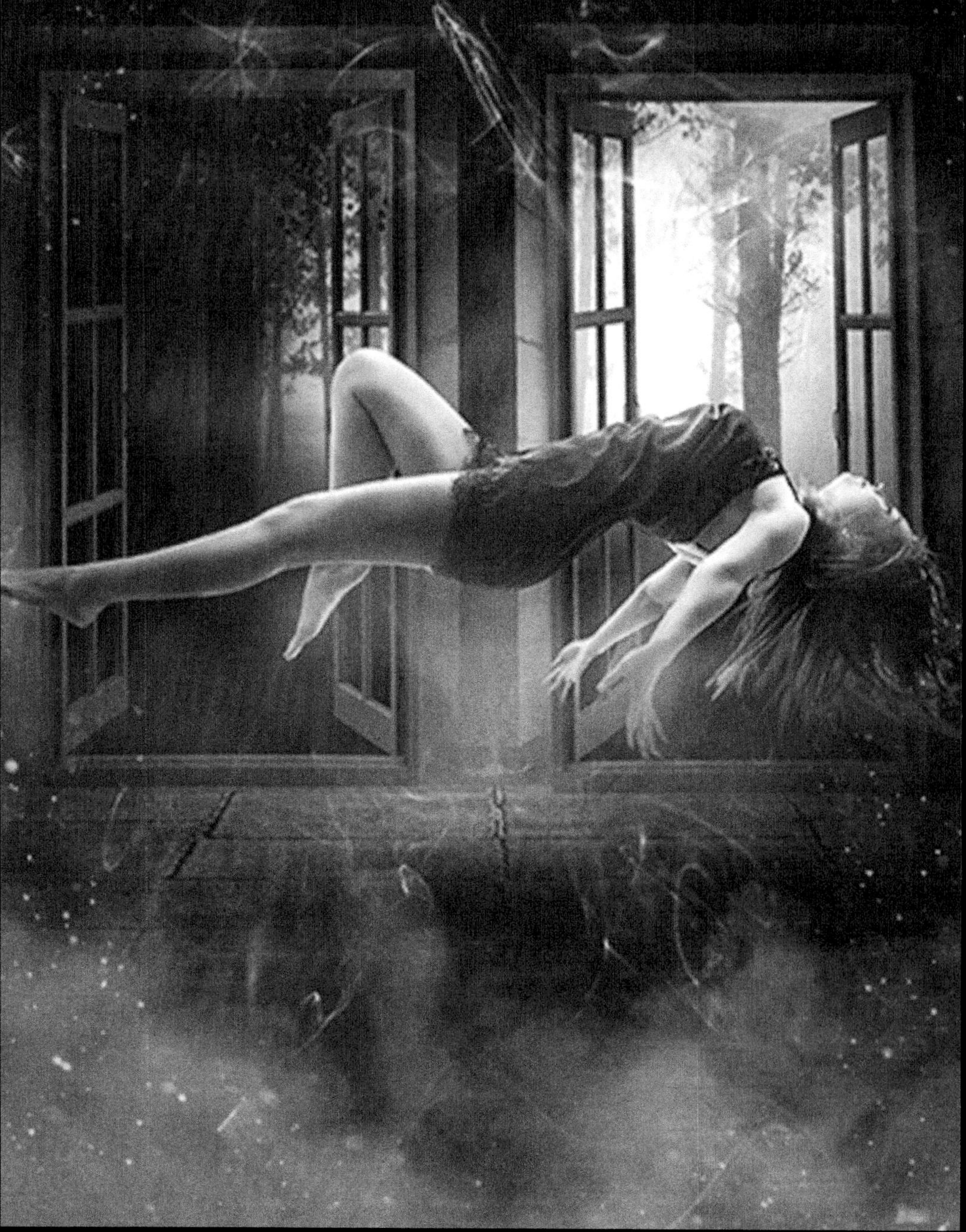

CHAPTER
TWENTY-SEVEN

Astra
Ghost of You - Mimi Webb

"Do you think you could fit a wolf in the gap maybe?" a woman asks as she stands at the desk and flips through my designs. "A really small one. Just to join in with the band? I mean, the last artist totally fucked it up. Wouldn't even trust her to graffiti a dive estate after what she did to me."

I stare down at her tattoo, the poorly done bracelet missing a part on the back of her wrist. The fine swirls are shaky, with poor execution of an unsteady hand, where the delicate swirls were supposed to connect in the middle but don't. She expects me to fit an intricate design in such a small space and I roll my eyes, not in the mood for the entitled preppy bitch act today. She smacks her lips when she talks and pops her words and I have this urge to poke her in those mocking eyes.

"Can I fill in that tiny little gap with an intricate design such as a wolf head that details eyes and each and every single strand of fur?" I question, hoping she can see her mistake before I most definitely and rudely point it out to her.

"*Be nice*," Hunter whispers into my ear and this time, my eyes disappear into the back of my skull. My mind still lingers on my devious challenge. I don't know what comes over me, but when he's near me, all I crave is his touch.

"She's annoying," I mumble, and the woman licks her lips and tilts her head as she looks at me with befuddled curiosity.

"I'm sorry, what was that?"

"No, I cannot fit a wolf in something so small," I drawl, sighing heavily as I rip the book from her hands a little harshly. She gasps, eyes flying wide but I just offer her a fake smile to appease her and flip to the page of artwork that would be doable for what she needs. "The piece will be semi-large, it will fill the space perfectly and I'll even throw in some touch-ups to fix the rest."

"You think the rest is bad?" she asks in a low squeaky voice and brings a hand to her chest like she literally didn't just tell me the whole tattoo was shit.

"Well, it isn't good." Shifting in my seat, I add "Pick one."

"I'm sorry, I'm not following. So, Hunter North. The most eligible bachelor in the whole of the states, worth more than the equivalent of the world itself not only stalked you, but left you his bodyguard and everything within the will?" Hazel spirals out loud, like she just can't figure it out.

"That's exactly what happened," Damien responds. He might a G.I Joe Robot but the man has a big mouth.

"Do we have to go over this?" I sigh, already over it.

"Bitch, you just inherited a fortune and now have some asshole attached to you who thinks he can take my job... which you can't by the way," she rattles on, enunciating the last part to Damien directly.

"He might not be able to take your job, but I can," I threaten, then look over at Damien, no longer willing to entertain any of this bullshit today. "I don't want to hear another word on the matter.

Simon, I'm out of my Coffee, be a darling and go to Joy's to replace it."

"Sorry, can't. Hazel can though. I, on the other hand, cannot let you out of my sight in a public place."

"What kind of bullshit is that?" Hazel exclaims from behind the reception desk. I swear the sound of Damien's voice alone riles her. Instead of arguing with him in front of a customer, Hazel turns her brown eyes on me. "Seriously, why is he still here? You hate people. You barely tolerate me."

"Hunter North certified," I grumble, moving over to set up my stencil equipment for when the deluded woman finally picks a reasonable image from my binder. Hazel slinks over to my side, leans her ass on the desk and crosses her arms.

"Okay, since you're not going to give me a straight answer, how about this one—why do you call him Simon?"

"Because he clearly doesn't know how to play Simon Says." I roll my eyes. With Hazel's confusion hitting me on one side and Hunter's amusement at my attitude on the other, it's hard not to feel boxed in from all sides. You know what they say about caging a wild animal, she's going to strike out claws-first.

"*No one says that,*" Hunter whispers and I scowl at him with a get-the-fuck-out-of-my-head glare.

"Okay, I get it. That's sort of funny," Hazel sniggers at Damien and I catch him flipping her off. "And it figures the bodyguard of a rumored madman is also unhinged. Not to make rash judgment but he doesn't seem to have much going on upstairs."

"I can hear you," Damien calls, stomping his way past my client to square up to Hazel. To her credit, she stands tall and doesn't even blink, whilst his nose comes close enough to hers that his breath shifts the tendrils left free from her ponytail to frame her face.

"She's not wrong," I scoff, moving around the pair to grab my thermal mug covered in the trees of a graveyard and skulls. It's coming up to Halloween, and I freaking love this time of year. "Hunter is most definitely certifiably insane."

"Is?" Both pairs of heads whip my way to question at the same time, catching me off-guard. Hunter chuckles and I scowl in irritation.

"Hey, Hazel?"

"Yeah?"

"Halloween is in like two weeks. Don't you think it's time we decorate?"

The squeal that suddenly escapes her has Damien jumping out of his skin reaching for his gun. Pursing her lips, she knocks his hand away with a light slap. "Oh sheath it, pal. Nobody likes a show off and we have a customer present." Said customer is desperately trying to concentrate on the designs in her hand, and can't risk looking up to watch our tense dynamics like a living soap opera.

"Okay, give two hours, max. I'll head to Joy's to grab the fuel, and then I'll get everything out of storage." My receptionist is halfway skipping to the door when my voice halts her.

"Great. Damien will come with you." The heat of two glares slam into me with the intensity of the sun but it's the low growl from Damien's chest I decide to address first. "As your boss, with a contract *signed* and all to prove it, you will do as I say. Or so help me Satan's thick dick, I will throw you to the wolves which are Hunter's bloodthirsty lawyers. Yes, I also obtained them in this contract of demise."

"Ew, so creepy," Hazel utters, not waiting around and leaves the store. I raise a finger, pointing Damien in the same direction to follow.

"You wouldn't," he questions, eyes narrowed trying to look fierce but I can see the first sheen of trepidation bead along his brow. If only he knew of Hunter's existence, he'd know there's a lot more to fear than the slap on a wrist from some attorney. He'd have himself a personal poltergeist for leaving me unprotected, but I need my space. All else be damned.

So I continue to goad him, face hard as stone with eyes unrelenting making him growl. His thick lips formed an endearing pout on his pretty boy face.

"Fine," he huffs. "But that reminds me after we finish here, you are needed at the Empire. The business manager wants to show you the ropes of how it all runs."

My mouth falls open and suddenly, all my humor is gone. Firm hands fall to my hips and I inhale a quick and cold breath as Hunter pushes his chest against my back. His apparition sends goosebumps to pebble along my skin and makes my tortured heart race. "Don't fight it, Siren. *Please*. Just for once, see what it's like when the world is for you instead of *against* you."

"Why have you done this?" I ask, emotion thick in my throat as I ask the biggest question of all. Why me? What did somebody as unimportant as me do to attract the obsession of a man who sat upon an empire?

Damien squints as he stares at me dumbfounded. "I'm just passing on the agenda, Ma'am." I'm going to drill that mechanical voice out of him if it's the last thing I do.

Obviously, I wasn't talking to him, I was talking to the beast of a man standing at my back. Ghostly breath feathering across my nape.

"I never lied when I told you I wanted to give you the world, Astra. I only lied when I told you, you'd have a choice in the matter. I'm dead, Siren. But never gone. Never withered, even from the other side, I will give you everything even if it's the last thing I do. Buying out all the other parlors, shutting them down. Paying off all of your debt, buying the Empire just because I knew you loved it. Heck, I even took the first booth you ever planted your ass in up to my apartment. Those were the least of the lengths I would have gone to in order to make you happy. My word is my bond, love.

"Considering my soul is eternal, love, I will hold myself to that promise until the day that you die too."

My entire world crashes to a halt, the broken pieces of the last year finally settle into place and my perspective of the past twelve months of my life change in an instant. Everything that never made sense before finally does. All of the little things that have made my life easier... bearable. All of the little things that have taken away the pain ...

Was *him*.

Tears fill my eyes and sadness consumes my soul. The profoundness of the man behind the shadows startles me. Solemn, detached, I swallow. "Okay," I utter with numb lips. "You can go help Hazel now." It's automatic. Unfeeling as my mind drifts.

Damien stares at me quizzically for a moment, then turns to leave. "Are you sure you're okay, Astra? You look like you've seen a ghost."

Blinking through the daze, I burst out laughing at his statement, shaking my head at the fact that if only he was living with my broken sanity, he'd understand the severity of what he just said to me. "Yeah, I'm fine. If Barbie doll ink over here has found a design, I'll lock the store until you get back, deal?"

He looks over at the ditzy blonde who at that very moment shouts, "Like, oh my God, this tattoo is so like *wretched* but this one is so *gorge*!"

"You finally picked one then?" I drawl. Not insulted that she thinks any of my designs are wretched. I mean, with a face as filled with plastic as hers, it would be impossible for her to know what actually looks good.

"*Totally*!" she gushes.

I don't have time to process the fact that Hunter has had a hand in every part of my existence. If I start to think about it, that rabbit hole will grow teeth and devour me.

Damien scowls, lips turning up in disgust. "Deal. Lock it now," he orders and I follow him to the door. Hunter chortles, and I turn to look over my shoulder at him with a pout.

"Like, I would have let him leave it open," he mocks Barbie's voice, flicking his hand and popping his hip. So unlike the stoic man in a suit I'm quickly growing accustomed to.

"How are you this annoying, even when you're dead?" I query and realize I said that a little too loudly.

"Are you sure you're okay, Miss Astra?" Damien hesitates to ask just outside of the threshold, concern thick in his bright emeralds.

"Yes, but you won't be if you ask me that again."

"Okay, okay, *Miss not Ma'am but definitely psycho*. I get it." He sighs with both hands extended adding in a mocking huff before he closes the door behind him and I pout in his general direction as I turn the lock.

"Bad puppy!" I snap after him.

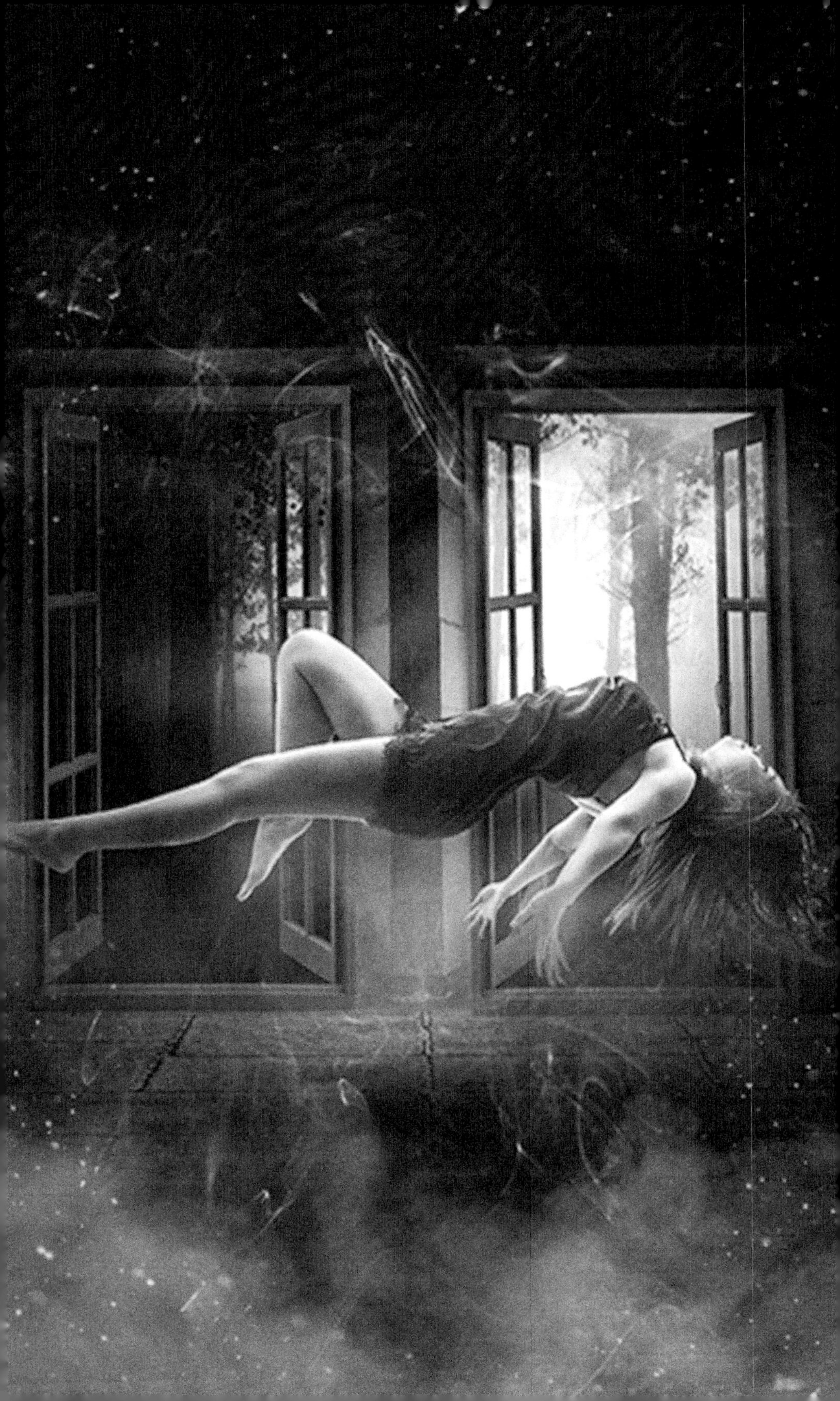

CHAPTER
TWENTY-EIGHT

Astra
@ My Worst - Blackbear

I zone out, the humming sound of my gun a hypnotic lullaby. Hunter is still here, lingering in the shadows but I don't need to see him in order to know that he's here, right beside me as a silent sentinel. He potters around, doing things like a normal man would and it took me a while to be able to turn off my focus that was so acutely aware of him when all I wanted to do was freak the fuck out.

How did I not know that he was there?

Watching me, learning me, and saving me when I never knew I was being saved.

I had always been my own savior, and finding out about everything he has done for me in the past year has shattered the walls of my confined mind that were convincing me that I have always been alone.

When he refilled the coffee filter earlier, I just stared in shock expecting the woman whining on my table to have seen the glass jug hovering in the air. She never did, so I can only conclude that not only am I the only one who can see him but that when he does his ghostly shit, I'm the only one who can see that too.

It's chilling, eerily frightful but as much as the programmed part of my mind tells me that I should fear this, the conscious part is telling me to shut the fuck up and get some ghost-dick. It's a fucked up contradiction and when those sexy and very sinfully wrong thoughts pop into my mind I start wondering who else is dead and can see us but we can't see them? Who else is watching us from beyond the veil that we call life and how much of our most wicked sins have actually been witnessed by a higher power?

It's blowing my mind and giving me a damn tension headache so the second the low thrumming buzz of my needle and gun steals my senses, I'm grateful.

I've had time to think about everything while the slim needle etches coarse and harsh strokes of silken ink into the woman's flesh. She squirms and hisses beneath my firm hand, but I don't even notice as I draw the delicate lines of the dream catcher compass I'm working on. The long feathers entwine up her wrists, the band connecting into the petals of vine-like flowers

Here, lost to the quiet, my mind starts to spiral.

Then before I know it, my mind drifts altogether, becoming disembodied. Stolen from time and space when Hunter ends up behind me, taking me up on my challenge.

The one I had forgotten all about after the revelation that changed my damn life as I once saw it. The entire world around me fades when all I can feel is him surrounding me. His hand strokes down my chest, playing with my nipples through the fabric of my bra. My eyes roll, and my pussy flutters. My nipples have always been a direct line to my clit and just as the apparition whispers against the tweaked buds has me squirming, I feel it. The heat that consumes my pussy. It gets me wild from the promise of what's to come more than it does anything else.

Hunter was a stalker that dwelled in the night, the moving

shadow that I never noticed. He has learned everything there is to know about me, and put things in place so that if I ever lost him—this daunting man who I never even knew was so attached to me—that I would still be okay and provided for. It isn't enough that I have to mourn my innocence in never having been a victim before, I am also forced to mourn my savior. A human life that never would have been taken from this world if it wasn't for me.

Truth is, I still feel guilty that he's dead. Even though I now know his depraved little stalker secret. I am more clear-headed, at this moment. I have so many questions I need him to answer. So many broken pieces of my sanity that I need to weld back into place. There is so much anguish that has crept up on me, I don't know how to handle it. I thought I had handled the death of my family, as well as any daughter or sister ever could, but when I am actually faced with death, the silken man in blue that haunts me—*stalks* me—even from the other side, I find that my grief has redoubled its efforts to bury me in the ruins of my shattered heart.

I obviously can't run from this. Not when I'm sitting in my tattoo parlor with an oblivious and obnoxious twit under my needle who can't see the reactions of the aroused woman sitting right in front of her.

I obviously can't shout it from the rooftops either, so what other choice do I have other than to give into this?

What I need is a damn exorcist, that may solve my problem, although right now it's presenting as anything but. As soon as the thought enters my one-track mind, a growl wraps around me like a roar on the breeze and I know he doesn't like that idea either.

That the only hope I have is to learn about the man who is refusing to rest until he gets whatever it is he sought from me.

My head rolls on my shoulders. Everything slows down to something drowsy and tender. The molecules of the earth move from around me, giving me the feeling that I'm floating as the sheen of sweat glistens along my tanned flesh. My heaving breasts are slick, heavy, and sensitive as a moan slips free but my mind is too comatose to notice.

Neither does the self-indulged woman I'm currently not paying a lick of attention to. She swipes through her phone, not evening noticing I've stopped tattooing her.

"That's it, baby, control it. Hide it. Nobody gets to see what I do to this sweet, sweet body," Hunter husks, and the graveled sound is like a boost to my core as arousal spikes through me and my clit throbs, my cunt clenches, and my body begins to quiver.

I can't.

Fuck me I can't.

The tranquility is like a lake disturbed by the toss of a pebble. The ripples of arousal tear through me and my eyes shoot wide and blown as I skid back, pushing away from my seat and skittering away from his ghostly fingers that have just dipped inside of my aching and torturous pussy. "I'm taking a break," I tell the bimbo on my table, placing the tattoo gun down on the sterile tray.

His dark chuckle follows me to the back room like a daunting torment. "Who knew you'd be so scared to come?"

Something he *hopefully* doesn't know about me yet, I'm a fucking screamer and if I did come, right here, right now in the middle of tattooing a client, I'd blow her eardrums and shatter the windows.

Just. Like. A. Siren. If only he'd let me.

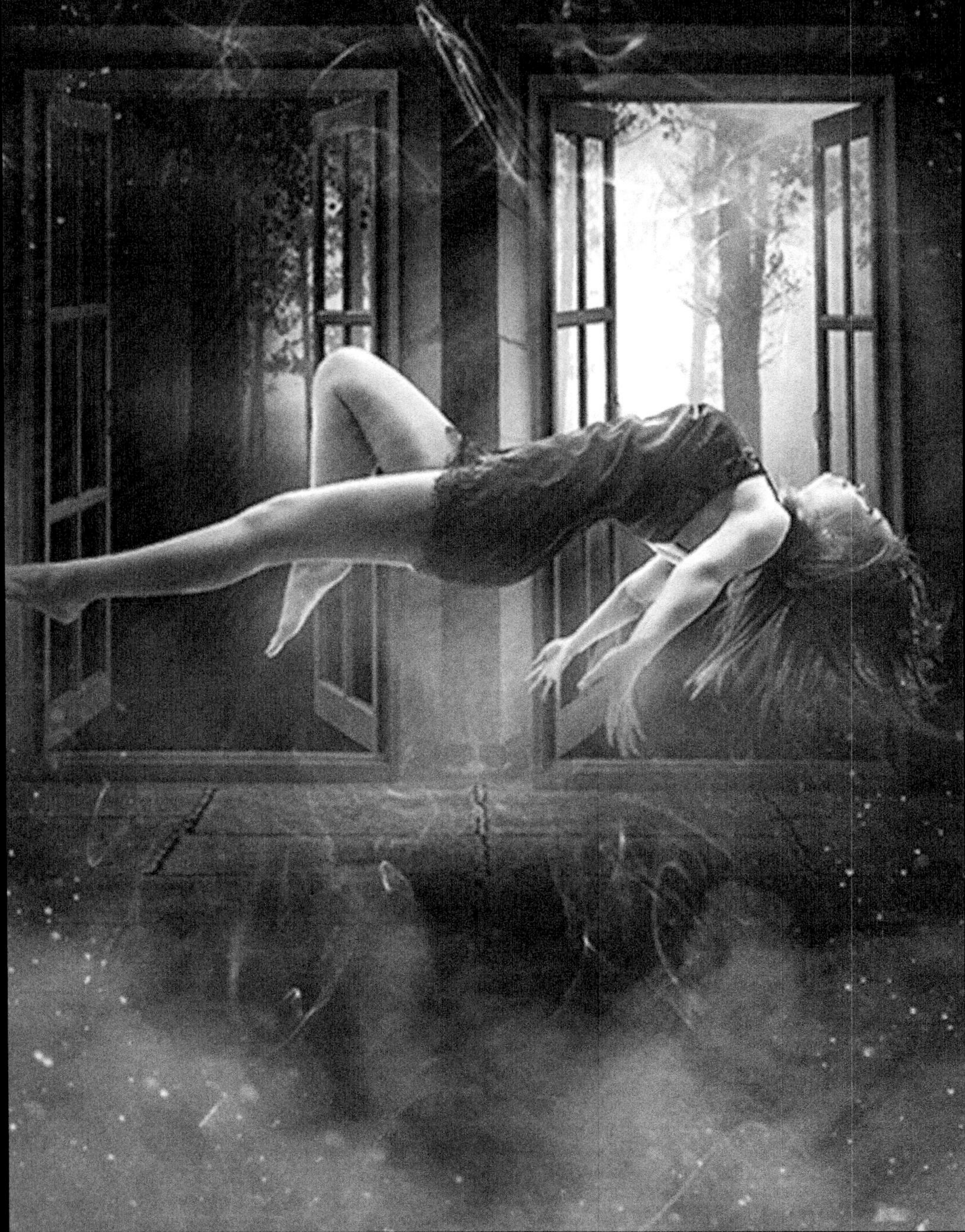

CHAPTER
TWENTY-NINE

Astra
Now We're Alone - The People's Thieves

Water bottle clutched in my hand, I sit down more frustrated than when I took my break, if that's even possible. I've never been so desperate as to ride the rigid stitch line on my jeans against my palm just to ease the burning friction of my clit. I'm soaked through, but when I came close to an actual release—on the verge of spiraling over the hauntingly beautiful man I've come to crave more than my next breath—it drifted away again. Because a quick orgasm in my shop's bathroom isn't the same as being brought to climax by his hand. His body pressing into mine, his pants coating my skin. Even with him watching, it's not the fucking same.

My eyes fall heavy, and not long after I've begun, I have to place the gun back down on the side. This piece is taking a lot longer than I wanted it to as I have to suffer through Barbie's theatrics. One moment she's oblivious, scrolling through her porn on twitter, which she plays without shame.

She's into fucked up stuff by the way...

Or she's screaming bloody murder that it hurts too much and can't sit fucking still.

Not to mention that I'm pissed as fuck that *I* issued a challenge I ended up walking away from.

Hazel and Damien haven't come back yet and I'm anxious for the peace and quiet to stick for a little while longer. I roll my head on my shoulders, watching with disdain as the woman Facetimes her best friend with fake tears in her eyes talking about how much her new ink hurts but how *bitchin'* it will look when it's done. The back of my skull comes into view when I roll my eyes so hard they literally spin in the back of my head. "Gonna crack a window, if that's good with you?"

"Sure, sure." She waves me off, literally with a wave of her obnoxious hand and I have to stifle a very unfeminine growl at how much that gets under my skin.

Without needing to open said window, a cool breeze whispers against my nape and I find myself closing my eyes and leaning into it instead of against it. You just never know how hot the world around you is until you have the soft wind that cools you like the refreshing kiss of ice.

"Damien has you pegged already. You're really not a people person," Hunter husks into my ear, tiny pinpricks scatter across my skin and I fight to contain my shudder.

"Humanity is overrated. Everyone's an asshole," I relay my mantra back absently, walking to the back room to wash my hands and hope the cold water puts some feeling back into my aching extremities.

"It's intriguing, Siren. So utterly intriguing," he rasps as he leans against the arch of the doorway to the back room. The shudder I'm fighting becomes harder to ignore and I have to bite down on my bottom lip to smother the moan he elicits from the purr tickling the back of my throat.

"What is?"

"How someone with such a big heart can despise people so much."

"It's not them I despise. It's being in their company. I prefer it alone, in the quiet. Here, all I have is the silent beats of my heart and the eternal thoughts of my worry." Silence falls between us and it takes me a moment to utter the question that is burning a hole into my brain. "Why me?"

"Why not you?" he replies with severity. The look in his brewing gray eyes was one so serious, I feel the shiver it sends into the world as it doubles back to skitter down my spine.

I don't need to clarify what I mean. This exasperating ghost of a man already knows where my mind is at. I'm not sure what I was expecting. Some profound explanation as to why he has become so infatuated with me, maybe?

Then when I think about it, I wonder what can really be more profound than that?

It defies the laws of physics.

It's an attraction that lasts through the ages.

What more of an explanation can it require than just saying, why *not* you?

As if fate itself has chosen me for him. Out of the billions that surround us, this is a question he has never *once* asked himself because he has been more than happy with what he got.

Me.

An anti-social pariah that has the ability to bite the annoying hands of humanity when they get too close to her. I hide behind my tattoos and my cozy home. I hide from the world because it's the only time my aching soul finds peace.

"I'm sorry," he mumbles and I blink, looking over my shoulder to meet his storm-brewed eyes. When he sees the question in my gaze, he adds, "I'm sorry that this brought up so many old wounds for you.

You have to believe me, Astra, I've never wanted to hurt you. I never intended to die either, but I sure as fuck will never regret that I did."

The devastation in his complexities makes me gasp. So raw, so filled with pain that I can almost feel it in my chest. A brutal ache that churns the bones of my ribs. The anguish was a blade to my heart, barbing and piercing me with a focused strike that is designed to fucking hurt. I choke up, needing to clear my throat to find some stable ground again. We stay like this, lost in each other's soulful embrace for such tender moments, that I forget the world around me exists.

"You're apologizing for saving me?" I whisper.

"I'm apologizing that my dying has hurt you. I know that it feels rotten now, that the seed of darkness in your heart is only going to grow, but when it gets too much, Siren, I'll be right here, to help put you back together."

"I don't know how to handle this, how to accept it," I admit as he pushes from the door and stalks toward me. I step backward, my back hitting the wall as he traps me, both of his ghostly arms extended beside my head, palms flat on the wall as he leans down until his dark and harrowing eyes meet mine.

"You don't have to, love. Because it's already a done deal. There is nothing to learn, nothing to accept because you *are* mine. I'm not going anywhere and I sure as *fuck*, don't share. Remember it, because the next time you flash this pretty smile at a waiter, I'm going to kill him."

I'm lost for words, stuck mute by his declaration. This is the darker side of him, the side that he has kept hidden, concealed within the shadows. It is possessive and raw, it is dominating and designed to put me in my place and relieve me of my burdens.

I hate to admit that it works, that my pussy flutters, my chest heats, and my nipples turn into hard buds that poke through my shirt at how wrong this is.

Hot and unnatural.

His lips are a fraction away from mine, a smoking gun that I find my neck lolling back, chin tilting up, just to feel them whisper against mine.

I don't care how wrong this is. How bad those words are.

I fucking want him and all of these feelings of worth he punches through my chest that came with him.

"You saved me, Siren. Not killed me." Then he kisses me, his essences filling my lungs and when I breathe in deeply, I know that it's his soul I inhale. I take a part of him into me, holding it captive and keeping it safe as those thick lips ghost against mine and I shudder, a wild tickle that I'm unable to resist with just how good it feels.

I'm Wendy floating on the clouds of Neverland, soaring through the skies.

When the bimbo sitting on my chair whines that I'm taking too long, her annoying voice carrying through the parlor, I'm about ready to kick her ass out. This is the first time he's kissed me, and something about that makes me feel like I do in my dreams.

A sensual dreamscape that removes me from my body so that my soul can take full control and *everything* I feel from that moment on is out of this world, a delicate touch that has no words, no explanation, just an illusion that the world triples and you're gliding through the layers of reality, time, space and the divinity of the universe.

In other words, it was the best kiss I've ever had and when he pulls back, it leaves me furious and bereft.

"Calm down, pretty girl. Get her finished up, then kick her ass out. I don't think you could survive another second in her kind of company." He chuckles and I scowl, eyes of lust searing into the plump outline of the lips that took me to space.

Kissing a ghost is like kissing the wind.

A drug I'm left to crave in a *very* unhealthy way.

Yeah, I'd rather just kick her ass out.

I stalk back to my seat, placing the water bottle beside me before I pick up my gun again. I may dig the needle in a little deeper than necessary, rejoicing in her painful hiss, but that is as far as I'll take my frustration. After all, I am an artist and I'll be damned if I let anybody—even an artificial brat like this—walk around with a bad piece of my art on their flesh.

I quiver in my seat with a furrow on my brow when the energy in the room darkens and I feel like somebody just walked over my grave. The high lighting above us begins to flicker and waver, stuttering from white light to a dim yellow. "Just the power," I utter, placing a quick flicker of my eyes to seek out Hunter.

He's sitting behind the desk, back ramrod straight, hand coiled into a fist on the tabletop as he stares venomously into the corner. A dark shadow passes over the store, blocking out the rays of the daylight from the outside and I allow the skeptical gleam in my eyes to shine. The woman in my seat is too oblivious to notice anything different.

But I do.

I notice it straight away as a dark mentality begins to take control. That same slimy essence of evil glides against my flesh and I quiver in repulsion, ready to put down the gun and flee from the store.

But I can't.

My hand tightens around the gun, my grip brutal and my knuckles turn a stark white, the tips a burning hot kind of red as I lose all control of my body. My left hand reaches out, gripping the woman's wrist and holding her in place as I stab the needle so far into her arm, rivers of blood begin to flow from the hidden wound and I pray, like a religious woman praying for forgiveness after she lets her husband fuck her ass doggy style while she's dressed like a dominatrix, that I never hit a vein.

"Ow," she cries. "Stop, stop! What the fuck are you doing? That's hurting me!" The shriek in her voice is nothing compared to the scream in my mind. The things in the store uplift, taking flight and swarming around the open space like a tornado and I cry out, getting hit in the shoulder with a heavy box of supplies that jars me forward and the needle deeper into her arm.

"I can't stop, I don't know how!" I'm frantic, fighting the pull in my arm that pushes down as I try endlessly to pull back. I feel like somebody is standing above me, holding me down, and that I'm the puppet to their strings.

"Hunter!" I scream, crying for salvation. Crying for this vile, insidious violation of my body, and my senses to end. I need him, I'm *begging* for him. Only Hunter can take this sick and twisted feeling away from me, the one that seems to be slithering within my veins, coiling around my bones, and taking hold like a darkness that has black veins actually appearing on my arms. "Hunter, help me!" The veins crawl from the tips of my extremities and down my wrist, circling my forearms. Tiny speckles of ashy marks start off the solid and dark coiled band, before feathering out into thin strands and working their way through me like tribal marks.

The lights cut out, and the shadow over the window darkens until we're swallowed whole in a bleak abyss. "Astra!" Hunter roars and I try to find him in the darkness, my gut telling me I'm looking right at him but I can't see anything other than moving shadows dancing around me like harrowing silhouettes of death and dread, and I suddenly no longer feel like I'm in my world. I've been sucked into a pocket within the universe, a plane not made for the living. I turn cold, my focus on fighting this possession wavering as my eyes grow hooded.

I'm falling.

I'm falling deep, into a deep slumber I just can't seem to fight...

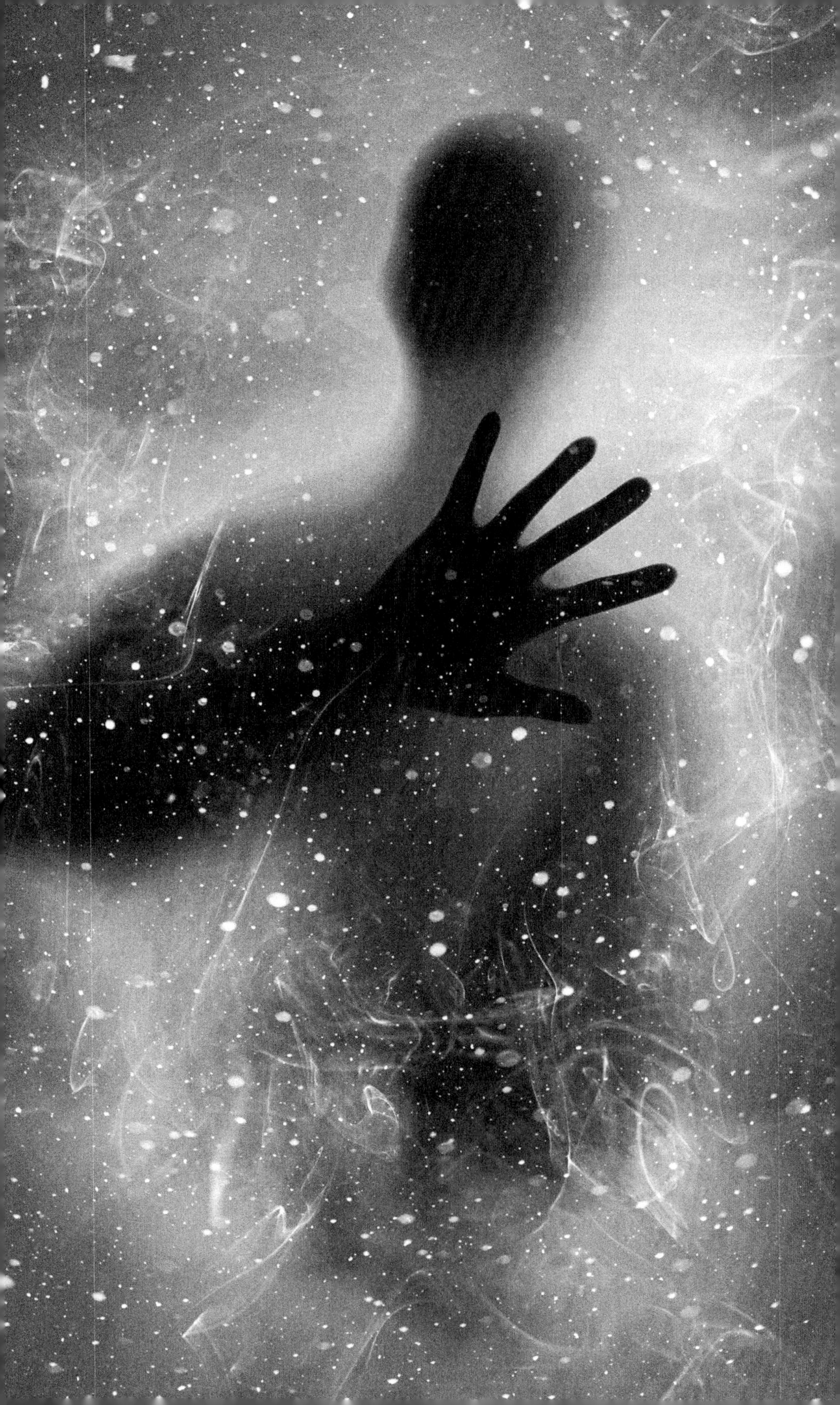

CHAPTER
THIRTY

Hunter
Desire - Meg Myers

Fight it, Siren. Come to me.
      That's it, sweet girl. Close your eyes.
      Come to me, Siren. Close your eyes and come to me!
I call her to me, and use all of my strength, every ghostly entity at my disposure, to lure her from her nightmare. I don't know what's happening, but I know the force around us is weak.

Weaker than my capabilities, but I'm sure right now she feels otherwise.

I have something of divinity to drive me.

Her.

But this plague? It's driven by anger. It can do some things, some I can't, even though I have a stronger connection to Astra than anything.

Dead or alive.

When I first truly understood that I was dead, I became obsessed with a new path. The one in making her mine was set in stone, but the one where I had an obstacle in my path had been new. I had to find a loophole, and work harder than I had ever had in my life before I ghosted myself into her bathroom, watching as she drowned herself under the heated bathwater in agony and grief.

I did everything I could to become a potency she could not ignore.

I persisted almost violently, searching for a hole in her resolve that I could wiggle through.

Slither beyond the walls of her armor and settle under her skin. Live there, and grew until she was forced to accept that there was something out of the ordinary that had shifted around her. Until I forced her to open her eyes and truly *see* me for the first time.

Something tries to steal my woman and terrorize her with the plague of horror that will paralyze her.

They have another thing coming.

I settle her mind, calling her close with the lull of my voice.

I can protect her here, in her dreams. I can save her from the darkness wishing to consume her, to hurt her and everyone around her. I don't know what it is, who it is.

I can't seem to breach that barrier. It's living on its own side of the veil.

But this woman lives inside of my soul like the very fiber constructed to hold it together.

Nothing and I mean nothing, will keep me from her.

From saving her.

Stalking her.

Loving her.

She screams for nobody but me.

"I'm here, Astra. I'm here," I coo when I can finally feel her drift into my arms.

"Oh God, oh God. What was that? I can't breathe! It's slime, there's slime in my throat!" The panic in her voice is devastating. I hold her tighter, cocooning her in my firm embrace of protection as she tries to claw at her throat. After a moment, her breathing lulls.

"Just breathe, pretty girl. You're here, you're safe."

"I don't understand, I don't understand why my mind is playing tricks on me," she seethes, the tears of her pain and confusion long gone in the veil of tranquility.

Standing in the place of uncertainty is the angry face of venom and it looks damn good on my girl. Even if she's experiencing it differently here. In the realm of no anguish.

"I'm sick of this, I'm so sick of feeling like I'm crazy! Where am I?" Unlike any other time before, she is more lucid here, pulling away from my arms in search of answers.

"There's no other woman like you, Siren. I hope there's no other man like me. When you're ready for me, for this, the apparition of your dreams will finally have a face," I tell her softly, my tender finger caressing the apple of her cheek as I step into her space once again.

A moment of silence falls, and it takes a split second for her gentle gasp to filter around me like a soft twirl of wind that makes even a dead man shudder. "Hunter?" she breathes.

"It's me, baby girl."

"Oh my God, we have been having sex dreams? You've been edging me?" Her astounding voice filters off into a word enunciated in outrage.

"No, love. I think you'll find that's the other way round. Something was stopping you from accepting me and for as long as I was a faceless man to you, your pussy stayed unsatisfied."

"This is insane," she huffs with a flare of irritation. She sits forward, pulling free from my arms once again. "I was just at the parlor, what the fuck is happening?"

"I don't know, but this is the only way I can save you. I think you've attracted yourself some kind of poltergeist, Little Siren."

"A dead man stalker wasn't enough?"

"Not nearly, but don't worry. I'll keep getting stronger and when I do, I'll obliterate whatever the fuck it is that chases you." My venomous sneer matches my tone perfectly. She turns, squinting her eyes as if she is finally seeing me for the first time and something carnal and primal settles in my core at the thought.

"The woman? Fuck, I was hurting her. I was actually hurting her. If I hit a vein, Hunter, I could have killed her! This is bad, this is so, so fucking bad." Astra fists her dark locks, pulling barbarically at the roots as she spins around in a manic circle.

"Enough!" I bellow, gripping her shoulders and turning her into me. I stare into her eyes, a clear warning in the stone gray to settle the fuck down. "Don't let it in, Siren. Do not give them your fear. If you do, you'll never escape. I'm going to let you out, you'll go back, but you'll have to fight whatever entity it is that wants you as if your life depends on it because it just might."

"I'm afraid," she whispers and I pull her into me, my forehead resting against hers. "I'm afraid of what I don't understand. Of the dangers, I can't see. I don't want to be a victim again. I just want this feeling. The one I have with you."

"I know, love. But we're all victims. Whether it be victims of life or an enemy, we're all victims. Own it, do not let it consume you." I kiss her, stealing the air from her lungs as I savor those sweet, delectable lips of hers. I pull back, finding the resolve in her wild ocean blues as she breathes against me. "Now let's go pick a fight with a poltergeist."

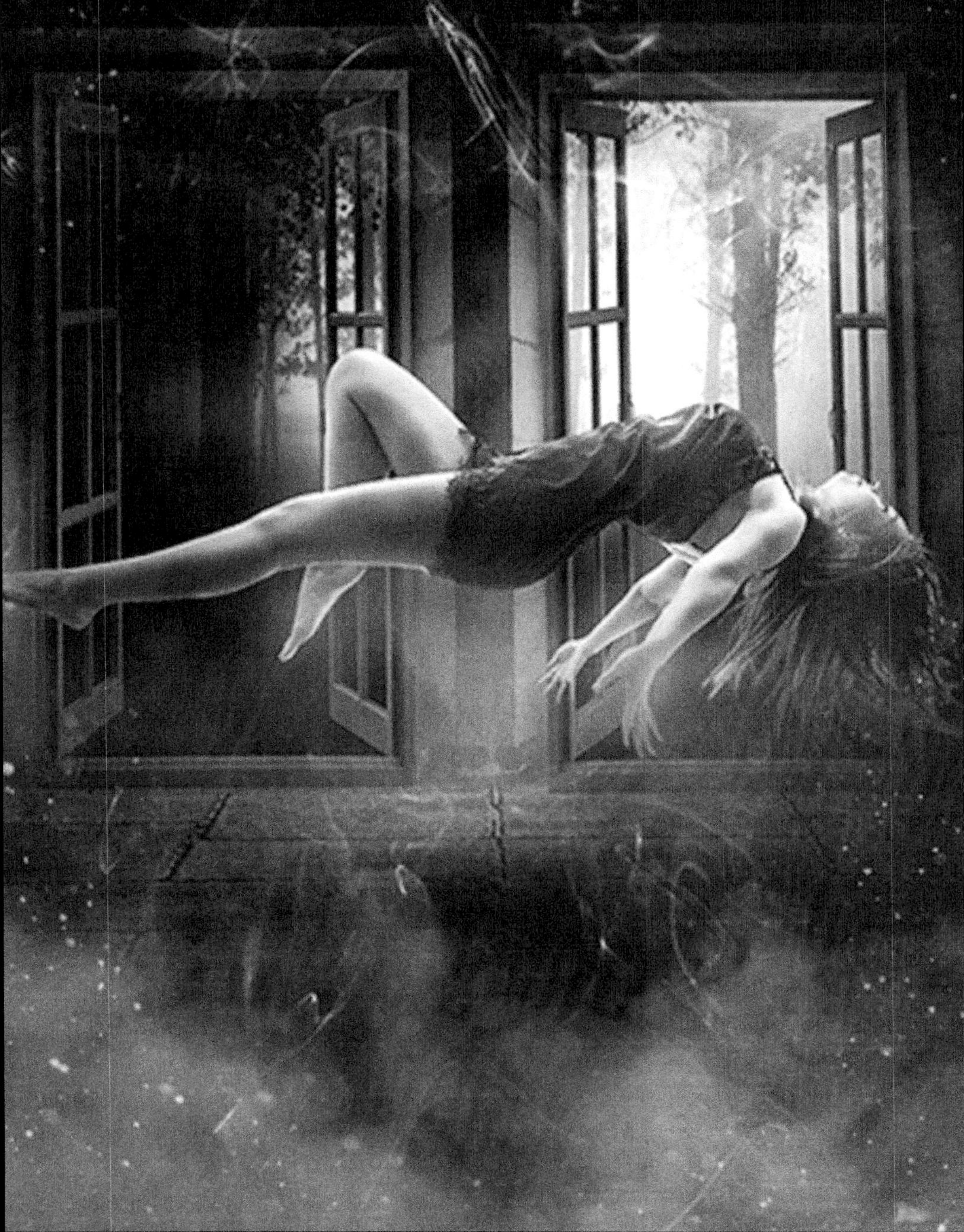

CHAPTER
THIRTY-ONE

Astra
Stitch Me Up - Set It Off

My entire body hurts and my chest burns as I roll to my side. I'm on the floor, laying beneath the ruins of my store. Everything has been upheaved and tossed around the place like a bull had been let loose in a China shop. But I hardly notice the shit that has been broken or the things that have been displaced. All I notice is the ache behind my eyes, sensitive to the dim light after darkness encroached on us. My hand slips, and something wet and silken glides between my fingers. Blinking open my eyes with a little more persistence, I try to pay attention. Slipping again, I grunt, struggling for stability when I notice the tips of my fingers are dark, saturated in blood.

The woman I was tattooing or my own? At this point, I had no fucking idea.

"Hunter," I call, needing his voice to guide me from the darkness. "Hunter I can't see." The door bursts open, shards of glass covering my curvy frame like an unwelcome shroud of needles. A shout tears from my throat and before my brain catches up to my galloping heart, I'm kicking and screaming as somebody coils a hefty hand around my ankle.

"No!" My voice is raw, so fucking raw it doesn't even sound like me, but instead some dark and manly version of myself. But I know that this time, the voice is all mine. "Get the fuck off me! Hunter, Hunter!" My bellow echoes around me and when I don't hear him call me back, I somehow panic even more than I already am.

Like his voice and presence will be my benediction in my terror.

"Astra!" another voice shouts and it takes me a moment to place it. "Stop, Miss Stone, stop! It's me! It's Damien."

Fighting the painful breath that rips apart my chest, I'm still lost, seeking a comforting hand to hold me. Like a broken record, I chant Hunter's name and when I see his baby blue frame bleed from the shadows I sigh, breathing a little easier knowing that he's by my side.

"It's okay, Siren. I'm here. I'm here, love."

"What the fuck was that?" I demand and I shake off Damien's hold as I stumble to my feet. I wipe the fragments of glass from my chest and send them clattering to the ground. My question was directed at Hunter, but it is Damien who answers.

"Good fucking question. I left you for two fucking minutes! What the hell happened?"

I blink at his uneven outburst. The informal and mechanical tone he uses is replaced with a younger, inhibition-free voice at the state he's just found me in without a good explanation.

How the fuck did I explain this?

I'm torn between the truth and a lie. I'm so overwhelmed in dealing with this alone, but at the same time, if I confide my hauntings to anybody, they will only be used against me. He already thought I was crazy the first time I told him.

Like he literally shrugged off being stabbed in the hand.

Especially if my fucked up mother got word of what the heck I'm going through, she'd destroy me not help me.

I clear my throat and look at Damien sheepishly. Hazel hurries in next and her face is ashen, pure white when she takes in the scene before her. "Holy fucking shit, Astra!" she exclaims in disgust as she stares at something over my shoulder. "I know you didn't like her, but did you really have to try and kill her?"

"What?" I mutter, spinning on my heel to find the woman I was working on slumped against the wall, arm extended on her lap, blood gushing from her shredded skin. I hadn't just pierced her flesh, I'd mutilated it with the tip of my needle.

"Oh fuck." Disgust, shame, and regret collide within me. I take a step forward, trying to rush to her aid when Damien yanks me back by the scruff of my shirt.

"Don't fucking touch her," he orders.

"The fuck is wrong with you? She needs help!" I explode, stepping into his space until my hostile nose, which is flaring wide, touches his.

"Not from you she doesn't." Pulling his phone from his pocket, he thumbs the screen before putting it to his ear. "Code One-Nine-Nine, be there in ten," he snaps into the receiver before he thumbs the screen one last time.

"Nine-One-One, what's your emergency?" a feminine voice rings out before he even has a chance to bring it back to his ear.

"There's been a break-in, my boss and her client have been attacked. The woman is hurt pretty bad, send somebody quickly," he issues, while he grabs the crook of my elbow and steers me toward the door. When we get there, he grabs Hazel's arm too, right after he pockets his phone again.

"What the fuck are you doing? D, she's hurt. We need to help her!" I hiss, my brain too fried to even say his full name out loud. My mind is spinning and the quicker it twists on its axis, the more my eyes start to blur and all sounds begin to echo, resounding back to me in a droning kind of thudding that has a pain searing into the back of my skull.

"Following protocol. Once we get back to the Empire, you tell me the truth so I can lie for you. Then we get the lawyers in to clean up this mess. Hunter would kill me if I allow you to get banged up my first day on the job."

My head shrinks back on my shoulders as I stare at the back of his head while he pulls me along. "I was passed out when you came in. How did you know that the story you just told the cops wasn't true?"

"You were still holding the gun and your hands are covered in blood," he deadpans and when I stare down, I notice he's right. I snatch in a quick breath which makes my knuckles burn.

I'm about to throw the gun white-knuckled in my hand, ripped from its cord, when he stops me. "Stop. They will most likely canvas the area. We need to get rid of it. I'll have our cleaners head to the store and set up a new one."

My eyes narrow and fly wide all at the same time. I rip my arm from his unrelenting hold and spin on the ghost that follows me. "What the fuck is wrong with you? How many times did you need to call in the cleaners, to cover up something like this?" Hissing through the confusion, it doesn't even occur to me that right now, I'm standing in the middle of a street arguing with an invisible man.

"Like this?" he asks.

"Yes, like this!" I shout, the anger clear in my voice.

"Never. When I attack someone, I make sure they stay dead," he deadpans and I stumble back, straight into Damien's arms and Hunter growls prowling forward.

"H-how many times did you kill somebody?" I whisper, wondering how my soul could have had it so wrong in finding comfort within a murderer's gentle touch.

It's the shock. Because that quiet voice in the back of my mind is more intrigued with this information than it is afraid of it.

He killed for love.

He killed for devotion.

Obsession.

That's kind of fucking hot.

"As many times as I needed to. I never made a habit out of it, Siren. But every time somebody hurt you, I'd take care of it."

"Oh my God, she's lost her mind," Hazel sobs, but at this moment in time it's all background noise.

What the fuck did that mean?

"Now start walking, love. Do not make me carry you. Damien is right. This needs sorting quietly and quickly."

"Astra? Who are you talking to? Are you okay?" Damien asks tentatively as I feel him enclosing in behind me. I stand staring for a moment, my breathing hard and sore as my chest aches with the brutality of it.

I am so fucking far from okay, but I have nobody I can trust to tell that to.

I am alone in this world and I am now only realizing how much that sucks.

"You're not alone, Siren. The point is, you never have been. Now go to the Empire and let my team fix this." Hunter nods his head down the street, expecting me to follow, and numbly... I do.

Because what else am I supposed to do?

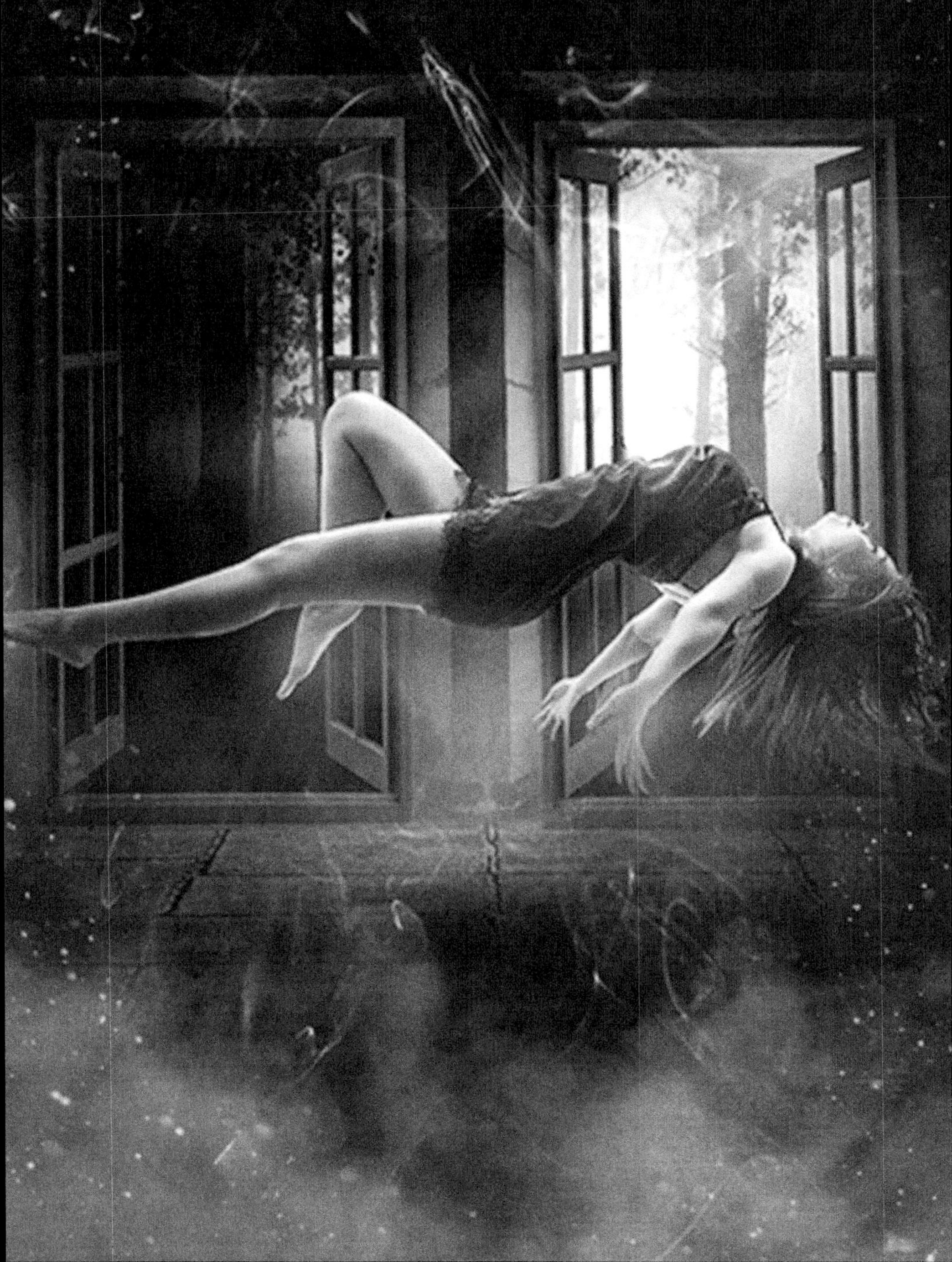

CHAPTER
THIRTY-TWO

Astra
Catch Me If You Can - Set It Off

Lost in a daze, people rush around me. Figures that blur into muted colors, whispers that hover on the edge of my consciousness, if I cared enough to listen. But I couldn't give any less of shit. Not when I'm sitting on the longest curving couch I've ever seen, in cream leather to match the furnishings in a penthouse Damien announced as mine. 'Welcome home, Miss Astra,' were his exact words and that above everything else this afternoon has sent me spiraling.

My penthouse. My club. My Empire. All because Hunter North saw something in me I can't even find in myself. Especially now, with the 'clean-up crew' pottering around and the police banging at the door.

A wet cloth scrapes over my cheek, taking care of the blood splatter I hadn't realized was there until the white material comes away stained. A woman in a purple jacket that hooks from one shoulder to the other, much like I imagine a masseuse would wear, kneels by my feet and takes my hand in hers. Mild fascination stirs in me as she cleans out the crimson from beneath my nails as if this is a usual job for her. No judgment or questions. To be fair, she doesn't look at me once and soon enough strides away.

An outfit is produced on a hanger, no doubt in my size if the chilled aspiration at my side had anything to do with it. Hunter's arms are behind his head, like an evil genius watching his minions at work. I reckon he gets some satisfaction from witnessing his well-oiled machine, still in perfect working order, long enough after his demise. What kind of power and wealth must he have processed to make sure of that?

"Leave it in the master bathroom for her," Damien tells the woman holding my outfit. A loose-fitting white pinstripe jumpsuit that will either make me look like a chic housewife or a busty carpenter—I haven't decided yet. In the flurry of people exiting through a white wood door, Damien has given me a quick pep talk and welcomed the dual officers inside.

"Miss Stone." A young officer tips his head, taking a seat on the far end of the couch. A sweep of dark blond hair is pushed back from his forehead and an easy smile greets me. He's handsome in a fresh-out-of-the-academy kind of way, unlike his partner. An older man due to retire, if he doesn't keel over and smash through the glass coffee table dividing us first.

"My name is Officer Stolworthy, and this is Officer Williams," he continues. His gray-mustached and doughnut-bellied partner takes a slow walk, peering out of the fully glassed exterior of the penthouse into the streets far below. "Strangely, we were preparing to pay you a visit when the call came in about a disturbance."

Silence. Damien hovers in the background, Hunter slowly sits upright to tug on his shirt cuffs and I just stare at the body cam strapped to Office Stolworthy's chest. The red light flashes, capturing me in full detail while I wonder if Hunter's presence will cause any disruption to the feed. Does it work that way or have I seen too many movies? The young officer clears his throat, pulling a notepad and pen from his pocket to take notes.

"Why don't you tell me, in your own words, what happened in your parlor, Miss Stone?" he asks politely but my head snaps to Damien.

"Wait, did you say *master* bathroom? What does that mean - there's multiple bathrooms in one penthouse? How many bathrooms does one man need?" Damien's eyebrows touch his hairline, his mouth dropping open but no words come out. Then my mind starts to fill the silence with just why Hunter *would* need so many bathrooms and I can only come up with one solution.

Swinger party gangbangs.

"Behave yourself." Hunter chuckles and shakes his head. "The only fucking I've had in the past year and a half is with my right hand."

"Well that's your own fault!" I half-shout back, holding my hands up in a what-the-fuck motion. "It's the least you could suffer for the predicament we are in now. And do not get me started on my sexual frustration!" As soon as the words leave my mouth, I remember I'm arguing with a ghost who literally gave his life for mine, but Hunter doesn't seem annoyed. If anything, the stupidly large smile spreading across his face shows the opposite. The fucker is amused.

Laughing at me.

Taunting me.

Fuck me, why is that so hot?

"You said '*we*'." He beams like a schoolboy and I tut at him. This is not the time to be going soft on me. Not when Damien looks like he's going to shit himself and throw up at the same time... And I've gained the attention of Doughnut-Belly who didn't seem to want to be here. Now he's intrigued as fuck and I throw myself back into the cushions in exasperation.

"Maybe we should come back a little later, if that suits you better, Miss Stone?" Officer Stolworthy asks gently, tucking his notepad away. Standing to his lanky height, he passes Damien a business card and has a quiet word with him by the kitchen island. Doesn't stop me from hearing 'psychiatric' and 'wellness check' though.

I grunt, narrowing my eyes.

I am not crazy.

Much.

"Why were you coming to visit me?" I call out, interrupting their hushed conversation. Both men turn to stare at me, from my blood splattered jeans and tee, to the ugly double chin I get from lying back like this. "You said you were already preparing to pay me a visit. What for?" Strangely, it's Doughnut-Belly that paces over and addresses me with a forced kindness in his expression.

"The previous case, involving your attack by Theo Nyera, has been closed. There's no more evidence to go on and Mr. North's death has been ruled as an accident. A tragic accident and a devastating loss to the community."

I frown at the weirdly scripted response. The impression I've had on Hunter is that, despite his money, the man was basically a recluse. A law unto himself that stalked the shadows. A billionaire with only his bodyguard for company. Peering to Hunter, he sits rigidly now, almost sensing my next thought before it's even rolled around my skull. How could someone so wealthy be so lonely?

Maybe that's what he saw in me. Maybe that's our true connection. From either end of society's spectrum, we are two lost, lonely souls who truly need one another. I just wish I'd known that before...

"So all that's left is the matter of Mr. North's body," Mustache finishes. All four sets of eyes are facing my way now, Hunter's included, searching for a reaction.

"His what now?"

"His body." Officer Stolworthy steps forward. I'm glad because he's the gentler of the two. His voice is melodic, smooth and easy to accept, but his words are not. "The morgue can't store him much longer and being his next of kin, we need to return his body to you for the funeral preparations."

The breath sweeps from my chest in a rush that leaves me cold. Damien notes the shift in my mood instantly, just a beat after Hunter does, and quickly sees the officers from the room with a vague, 'I'll be in touch.' From my reclined position, it's not difficult for me to slump over on my side and curl up into a tiny ball.

"Funeral..." I heave out in ragged pants. "I can't... I can't bury you. I just met you. I've only just come to need you." The words tumble from me, my brain short circuiting. Two men kneel before me, coming to my aid in practiced unison. Damien takes my wrist in his large hand, holding two fingers over my pulse while Hunter soothes me with words of love. Damien wills me to count backwards with him from ten and with Hunter's coaxing, I do. Until my breathing has settled, my pulse eased and the numbness of staring into the abyss has returned.

"She's calm now, dickhead. Get your fucking hand off her," Hunter growls, sending a gust of energy barreling into Damien. The bodyguard topples onto his back, kicking and punching the air as Hunter smirks. He dives on top of him, scraping around for the enjoyment of a tussle that clearly isn't happening for the first time. Shifting closer to the edge of the couch, I watch the pair throw synchronized swings at each other. Damien's eyes can't find a spot to focus on, but he manages to block Hunter's elbow and knock him aside. Locking an arm around Hunter's throat, Damien jumps to his feet, his eyes wide and fixed on mine.

"What the fuck is in my arm right now?" he asks, but we both know the answer to that question. I noticed it earlier, when the officers were here and Damien looked half horrified, half stunned. He saw something.

"You're currently picking a fight with your *real* boss, and since you can't kill him twice, I'd suggest you release him." I push myself upright to shrug. At least this is mildly more entertaining than the other prospect of burying a man I just fell in love with.

How the fuck did that happen?

Damien doesn't heed my warning and next thing I know, a flower vase of wilted blue orchids flies from the dining table and smashes into Damien's broad back. Hunter smiles to himself, passing through Damien's locked arm to stand before him. Only when his bodyguard has shaken off the shards of glass from his back and straightens, does Damien's face fully drain of color.

"Boo." Hunter nods. And to his credit, Damien doesn't faint like I expected him to. Just stares like he's been turned into stone until a single word passes his open lips.

"How?"

"Fuck knows." Hunter shrugs, his back straight and arms folded. An employer addressing his hired help, but there's more to it than that. The way the pair look at each other with complete understanding. Absolute trust, like brothers. "Once you start believing I'm really here, it's easier I guess."

Slowly, I get to my feet and move to Hunter's side. How I wish I could lean on him, to give him my stress and collapse in his arms the way he promised I could. But by the time I get there, the moment for comfort has passed as a lop-sided grin grows on Damien's usually stoic face.

"What are you, Tinkerbell or something?" He bursts out laughing, throwing a punch through Hunter's arm. Even Hunter cracks a smile, winding his hand around my waist to watch Damien prance around feigning butterfly wings with his meaty arms while singing, 'I do believe in fairies! I do, I do!' As if my day couldn't get any fucking stranger, but I've given up keeping count of things I never thought I'd see now.

"Last room down the hall on the left, Siren," Hunter whispers huskily into the shell of my ear. "The clean-up crew should have a bath waiting for you. Once this..." He waves a hand over the bodyguard who's now fallen to his knees to laugh hysterically. Or maybe he's crying. Either way, it looks like a full-on mental breakdown and

I can relate. "Whatever the fuck this is, is over, I think Damien and I need a debriefing on the past few weeks."

Nudging me toward the hallway, I sigh heavily. This is the real Hunter North. Business as always. Until a hand spanks my ass for that thought and I stroll away biting back a small smile. Possessive asshole reading my thoughts.

The hallway beyond the kitchen area blends in seamlessly, with the same white wallpaper patterned with gold swirls wrapping the walls like a shiny new show home. This place doesn't even look lived in, but that's not surprising. I just had blood cleaned from my fingernails without even moving. I imagine this place has cleaners for each individual duty. One to vacuum, one to polish, one to dust the light switches - and that was probably just for the hallway.

Naturally, on my journey, I take a peek behind each closed door. Multiple unused spare bedrooms, a gym, a music room, and every hermit's wet dream - a library. I don't know why I'm surprised yet I make a mental note to continue my investigation after a soak in what I imagine is a huge, jacuzzi tub.

Not a person is present, the cleaners seeming to have vanished into thin air as I step into Hunter's master bedroom and flick on the light. Blinking a few times, I turn off the light, take a step out and then do it again, expecting my eyes to be deceiving me. But no, this room isn't what I was expecting at all.

Where the penthouse is open, light, and inviting, Hunter's room is a cave. Shrouded in polished mahogany, encased with a rough black wallpaper akin to crocodile skin. Heavy drapes block out every inch of light failing to shine through the floor-to-ceiling window, leaving only the hanging caged bulb to highlight the unmade bed sheets. Papers cover the expanse of a thick desk, in the same dark walnut as the raised bed frame.

I can already guess what's on those pieces of paper before I've crossed the room, ignoring the glint of candles burning through the next open doorway. The scent of marshmallows and vanilla from my favorite bubble bath seeps into the room, but I can't leave just yet.

Not when I pick up a sheet and peer at the documents on my brother's and father's death.

Detailed reports of every second of their demise from when the fire first started to when it ended after emergency services showed up just a little too late.

One paragraph stands out to me above all else though, my eyes flicker back and forth rereading over the words which define a true haunting.

The paragraph that detailed how the fire was *caused* in the first place.

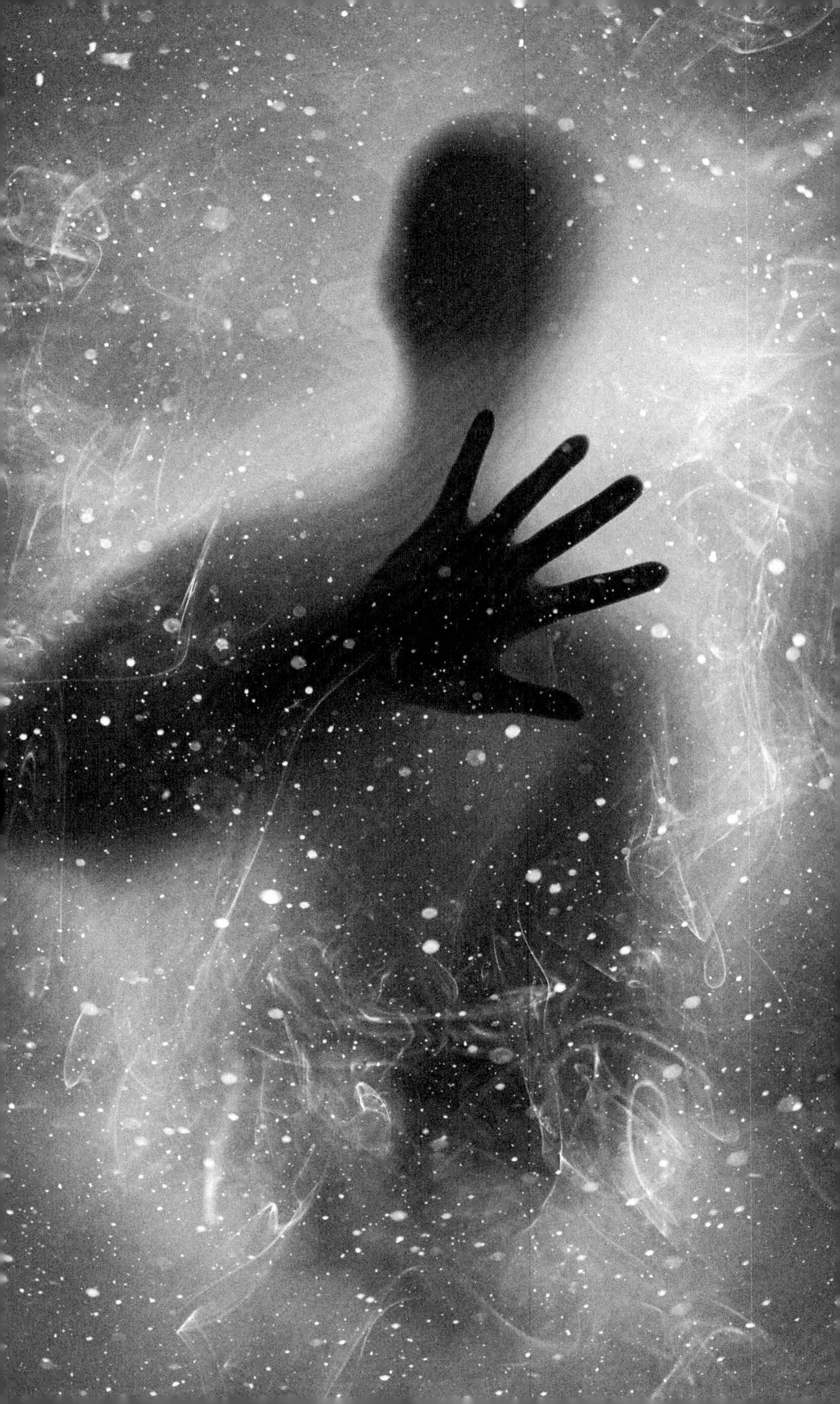

CHAPTER THIRTY-THREE

Hunter
The Lines Begin To Blur - Nine Inch Nails

Leaning back on my heels, I wait for the soft click of my bedroom door closing before sending a spiritual slap across Damien's face. The blubbering wreck on the floor snaps out of it in an instant, shooting up to his feet.

"Enough," I bark sharply. "We don't have time for this. Something happened back at the tattoo shop and we need to find out what. Flank me." Without waiting for an answer, I turn to the astral plane I'm trapped in.

The layout of my penthouse is the same. A huge flatscreen is mounted above an electric fireplace with a plush rug I had imported from Scandinavia, because I had nothing else to focus on back then. When life was a rush of cars and women, premieres and ceremonies that seem as bland to me now as my surroundings. Don't get me wrong, life before Astra was still an act. Just the best-played performance of my life. I was emotionless in relationships, probably sensing they weren't the one. Even back then, such a thing was scarce though. My money? Went into charities and doing good. But life with money comes with expectations and those were the parts I hated most.

Given the choice, I would have stayed alone.

All until her. My Siren.

There's no color here. Only shades of gray, from the murkiest pools to the softest pebble. Once my favorite color, but now it's depressingly claustrophobic. I may have put on a false pretense to Astra that it's all sunshine and daisies on this side, when in actual fact the only color I see is her. Her oceanic blue eyes, the glossy sheen of her hair, those full red lips spearing the veil of my monochrome realm. My dress shoes trample through my old apartment as if seeing it for the first time.

Not a single photo frame hanging on the walls. An ornament, a souvenir.

A memory.

Nothing.

In fact, all I own of any interest to me is currently spread across the desk in my bedroom. I can imagine Astra sitting on the floor, shifting through it all with tears pricking the backs of her eyes. But I wouldn't hide it from her.

It's not my job to reassure Astra. It's my duty to be honest with her. To give her the truth she deserves and stand by her however she intends to deal with it. Especially when she's already so confused and trying to ignore the underlying anger simmering beneath her skin. She's hiding it, mostly from herself, and fuck knows what'll happen when it's finally unleashed.

Does it take a murderer to love a murderer?

I don't want this to be the thing that really destroys her, but I know my woman.

She can handle this truth. She has too.

I don't blame her for the fury—there's so much to be angry about and most of it is my fault. Our missed opportunities, the lack of presence of her family on her father's side, the entity that is trying to haunt her.

Clearly one of the fuckers I sent to hell hasn't gotten the memo. Astra is my damsel to hunt and haunt. My perfect little Siren I'll get to break and bend to love me in return for this passion burning like an inferno within the cage of my chest.

It's time she understood the lengths I went to, to know her, to understand her. It's all I cared about, but I see it was also my downfall. I understand now what I sacrificed to hide behind those documents, all out of fear she wouldn't want me back.

Somehow, becoming a ghost and not giving her a choice seemed like the easier option. For me at least. Now, I'm not so sure.

The missed photo opportunities. The pieces of crap I could have collected for sentimental sake. What's the worth of a life which can be so easily packed up into a single box of files? And that box isn't even my life. It's Astra's which makes it mine, but still, not in a way that would matter years down the line. I've robbed her of everything a woman should have in a relationship, forcing her to settle for whatever I can offer as a dead man.

"What do you see, boss?" Damien asks, his voice drawing me back from the depths of what was too close to self-pity for my liking. I grunt, turning my eyes away from what's blaringly obvious about my wasted existence and lack of future prospects with my love and focusing on the matter at hand.

"Nothing of significance here. Whatever it is, we're searching in the wrong place."

"Let's head back to the tattoo parlor then." Damien nods. "I might not be able to waltz through the police tape like you can, but-"

"No," I cut in and he obediently meets my eye. "You stay here, watch over Astra. Collect Hazel from the bar and put in a call to Jess. My girl won't want to be alone tonight, no matter what she says. And a dozen blue orchids, you know the drill."

I leave Damien to fish out his cell and follow my demands without argument. I'd been so focused on winning over Astra up to this point, I hadn't paid any thought to how much I missed the partnership Damien and I had. He may be on my payroll, but he's the only friend I had. I feel like an ass for how I just treated him, but honestly, there is only so much a dead man can take. He can see me now, I have emotions in my mind that I can remember from being alive and it makes me awkward knowing the afterlife is numbing what I should feel for being able to speak to him again.

With one last longing look at my closed bedroom door, envisioning my Siren soaking in the bathtub where I always pictured her, I leave. It takes barely any focus to picture my destination and feel the pull of my body being thrust through space and time. Into the hallway, down to the lobby, and out into the street.

Civilians pass by, unaware I'm lurking on the other side of the veil. Grayed figures are too invested in their own issues to sense me stalking there. Silently watching, openly judging. The woman dressed in a pantsuit on the street corner with a latte in her hand, turning her nose up at the people who walk past her. The man who is so lost in his phone, he knocks a child out of his way without even realizing it. Even the mother fighting her haggle of crotch goblins into the back of a minivan. It was like watching a covert mission. Not one of the little ankle biters would sit down and shut up.

Yet on this side, I'm utterly alone. Not a single un-reaped soul wandering around this vast expanse of forgotten space that seems to be all for me. I've pondered on there being multiple astral planes, possibly one for each unavenged spirit.

Or maybe this is my personal hell, to finally confess my love to Astra from a place she can never be. Sure, all I care about is her happiness, her contentment, her sexual pleasure, but it'll never be the same as holding her in my arms. To feel her warmth seep into me without the invisible veil barring it. To feel her lips skate across my skin and her teeth to sink into my flesh on a pleasured scream.

My thoughts tumble down a dark rabbit hole, building in intensity as anger licks at my being. A shudder rolls along the length of my spine, and in an outburst of fury, I throw a gust of energy at an oncoming child. The box of churros in his hand slams to the ground, causing his bottom lip to wobble and eyes to water.

Ah, shit.

I drop to my knee, racked with guilt until he looks up at the petite woman at his side.

Too young to be his mother. Maybe a nanny.

"That's your fault!" the brat screams, stomping his foot. His expression scrunches up like a piece of paper being crushed into a ball, creased with lines that will never iron out again. "You pushed me! I want another box, right now!" The nanny nods like a bobblehead, scrambling up to fetch her purse and I scoff.

Fuck that.

Rearing my arm back to blast that little shit right into the oncoming traffic, a shiver of malice skates through my body. Coiled with hatred, bathed in deceit. I clamp my free hand down on my wrist and force myself to move away from the child.

I would *never* hurt a child like that, no matter how big of an asshole they were being.

I've felt that bitterness before, back when Astra accused me of trying to kill her. And then again today at the tattoo parlor. It's practically on top of me, yet nowhere to be seen and on the move.

That's the bastard I'm hunting.

All thoughts of ridding the world of another unentitled brat vanish as I take chase. Heading in the opposite direction from the tattoo parlor, I push my being to travel in a flurry of rushed jumps. Every time my foot touches the ground, it's on a new street. When I take the wrong turn, the trail goes cold and I have to retrace my steps, latching onto the bitterness I'd rather never feel again, but I refuse to lose the scent.

This is about protecting my girl, and nothing will keep me from succeeding.

Breaching the worst part of downtown, my frown deepens. Sure, scum would feel at home here, but when you're a spirit, you can go anywhere. Why choose somewhere the shadows loom darker? Even the astral plane knows this is a shithole. Thick layers of ash coat the streets and the pale light beyond a constant layer of thick clouds doesn't shine here.

Soon enough, I find myself standing before an apartment block. Not a soul in sight, except a rogue stray with yellow eyes and its back raised. Not at me though, but at whatever is seeping through the communal front door. The cat hisses and I take its cue, following its eyeline into a stone staircase. Testing each level, I come to a halt outside a door broken from its hinges and I know I'm in the right place.

The aura swarming from this front door reeks of acid. Venomous and scorned, a feeling of pure hatred bubbles all around as I force myself to enter. Peeling wallpaper, rusted hinges. The floor is a mess of newspapers, scattered in all directions. The sort of place rats come to commit suicide from the sheer depravity of it all.

With the sense of resentment so raw in the air, it's impossible to tell where the apparition is or has gone. Instead, I investigate for clues as to who it could be and why we're here. After all the men I've killed for Astra, the list is long, and if I think about my personal enemies... it's endless. Any one of them could have a vendetta to go after the one I love, and it's my job to make sure that shit ends now.

Stepping through the hallway with what feels like slime dragging on my every step, I breach the bedroom. A stained mattress on the floor covered in piles of clothes, each one presenting frayed hems and holes torn into the cheap fabrics. A smashed TV has been tossed aside, beside an array of crockery all coated in mold. At least the bongs have a tiny shelf to themselves. The smeared glass displaying the fire escape beyond shows a vast amount of half-smoked cigarette butts along the windowsill.

Reaching out to pick one up, inspecting the Marlboro branding, the ground rumbles beneath me. I drop the butt, spinning just in time to see a coffee table hurtling toward me. It ricochets off the doorway, splintering into hundreds of pieces that scatter toward my feet, but the point has been made.

My presence has been detected.

The building shakes again, causing a clatter to sound from a distant kitchen. The precious bongs stumble like dominos, smashing to the ground. Thick cracks ripple through the ceiling, dislodging the lightbulb above me. I duck, despite being immune to the efforts, but a scream from the above apartment rings through my ears. This apartment block isn't as deserted as I previously thought.

Dragging my feet into the hallway, I hunt for the bastard who thinks he can intimidate me. Who thinks I'm going to run scared at his pitiful attempt to harm me.

To *scare* me.

"Sir! Are you in here, Sir?!" a shout calls from the doorway behind me, a heavy boot connecting with the wood. Damien stands in the threshold, his eyes settling on mine just before he's ripped from his feet. Sailing through the air, I lurch forward to catch my trusty brother and find myself rooted to the spot. That slime I felt is visible now, thick and impenetrable as it encases my shoes and climbs the length of my shins.

Bending to tear it off, Damien's strangled yell splits through the continued cracking of the plasterboard. Being held several inches from the floor, his back slams into the wall, and his eyes bulge. Around Damien's neck, the indents of fingers press into his flesh, cutting off his air supply.

"*Leave,*" the voice growls, so low I briefly confused it with the rumbling of the building threatening to collapse. Still clawing at the slime that has now banded around my knees and claws at my thighs, I summon all the potent energy I can muster and hurl it down the hallway. A ball of swirling black with veins of blue, cackling with lightning, sweeps the bastard off my bodyguard and Damien slumps to the ground.

All at once, the rumbles stop. The cracks vanish as if never really there and the slime retracts back into the floor of my black and white world. I rush to Damien's side, checking him over before throwing a forceful punch into his shoulder.

"What the fuck are you doing here? I specifically told you to stay with Astra," I growl, coming nose to nose with him. Never mind the fact Damien is gasping for breath, reviving his body from a near-death experience. He ducks his gaze obediently.

"I-I...know. But I thought I would be more help here. With you."

"I don't pay you to *think*, I trusted that you would never disobey me. I'm already dead, Damien. It's Astra we need to protect." Fisting the collar of his black fatigues in my hands, I release him with a frustrated groan.

"Yes, Sir, as always. Astra's all that matters." My eyebrows pinch at the twinge of resentment in his tone but as quick as it was present, it's gone and he's dusting himself off. Rising back to our feet, we both search the rest of the apartment for a hint of the fucker that I blasted into the living area but there's no sign.

Whatever it is, or should I say whoever it is, they've gone for now.

So why can't I rid myself of the feeling that I've just utterly pissed it off?

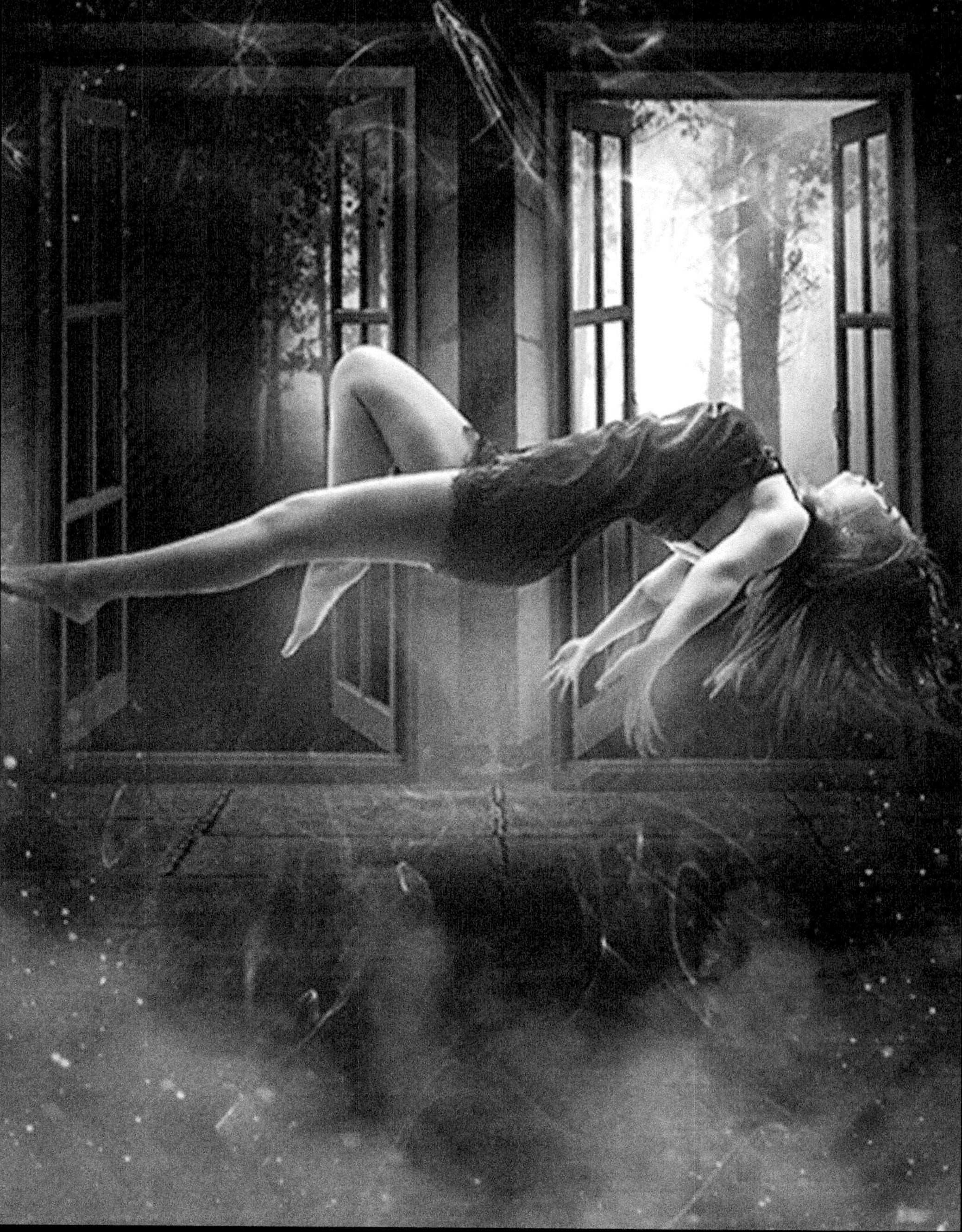

CHAPTER
THIRTY-FOUR

Astra
Ghost - Justin Bieber

The pop of a cork is my only salvation, anchoring me to the booth, despite my nails digging into the red leather. It's not lost on me how Hunter has converted this mini side room into a replica of the Empire bar on the lowest level, complete with the curved seat and wooden table with a polished finish. A bar lines the inner wall with room for two attendants to fit behind, although they'd have to be pretty tall to reach the glass shelves of bottles stretching up to the ceiling.

Candelabras either side flicker, casting a warm glow that doesn't hinder the sprawling views beyond the glass exterior opposite. A star-filled night stares back at me, the eyes of fate watching for which way mine will venture. Tucked away in a hidden room behind the living area inside the penthouse, it's the perfect place for a quiet drink or meal alone.

Alone, being the operative word.

"Do you think they'll serve us food up here? Like tapas, or maybe a cheese board? Oooh, I could definitely go for a big cheesy garlic bread all to myself." Hazel drops down beside me heavily. I take my glass from her hand before she spills it, her own sploshing over the rim.

When the security guard escorted her up, they advised me Hazel had been drinking since we arrived. I hadn't spared much thought on where she'd gone, presuming Damien would have sorted her transport home, so I was surprised to find out she'd never left.

"You know the ones like Benny's does, with the caramelized onions on top? Fuck yeah, I could *devour* one of those."

"Well, considering the house help guided me to '*Miss Stone*'s' penthouse..." Jess scoots into my other side. "I'm sure they'd send a private jet to get you garlic bread from Italy itself if you asked them too." She tries to hide the bitterness lashing at her tone and fails.

I peer shyly at my best friend, still in the dog house from the verbal thrashing she gave me upon arrival. I hadn't even considered calling her after visiting the clairvoyant. After all, I did run off, speeding through the streets, leaving her behind. Being thrust into the world of paranormal lusting, seeing the shapes of ghostly men, fucked me up more than I care to admit. Now I realize how worried she must have been, and am willing to *socialize* to make it up to her. That's pure torture for me and she knows it.

Boxed in with no chance of escape, I sink down into the silken pajama set that was laid out for me and nurse my wine glass like a lifeline.

"Wait!" Hazel gasps, shaking my arm. "Why don't we *go* to Italy?! We can go tonight!" I groan and shove her off, wondering if a little ditching and a few missed phone calls really deserves this.

Don't get me wrong, these girls are the only friends I have, but I'd happily tell them to fuck off for some peace and quiet. They both mean more to me than I've ever cared to admit. I may be a cold faced bitch, but these women are the only family I have left.

In fact, I did just that, but turns out Damien and Hunter have been scheming and reckoned some forced socializing is what I need.

"Don't think we're dressed right, and I'm sure there are laws somewhere about boarding flights drunk out the other side of your face." Jess side eyes her. She's right on both counts and I take in their pajamas with a loaded sigh. Hazel was given matching navy ones to mine with a button down long-sleeve top and silken pants.

Jess, however, turned up in a full unicorn onesie without giving a shit about the looks security gave her. From their post outside the main door, they could barely contain their bubbling laughter at the rainbow, woolen horse's tail that swished as she bounced inside, her arms filled with champagne from downstairs. Nice to see how easily my friends are adjusting to my new inheritance.

"Maybe tomorrow then," Hazel pouts and downs her drink as easily as water. "And I'm not *that* pissed, by the way." She swishes her reddish brown hair into my face and then falls over laughing, babbling on about garlic bread.

"Maybe I should call Damien, he can give you a lift home." I try to wiggle my eyebrows at Hazel. Either she's too drunk, or just ignoring me, but no one can ignore the sexual tension when it comes to those two. They're a hate-fuck waiting to happen and I'd rather it wasn't on the kitchen of my new apartment when he returns with Hunter. Wherever the fuck they'd run off to.

Jess finds a remote in a holder on her side of the booth and uses it for the high-tech stereo system to tune me out. "Ghost" by Justin Bieber comes on, and just like that the ice between me and Jess melts. The three of us burst out in hysterics at the thought of Hunter being a Belieber until we settle down and the words seep into my soul.

'If I can't get close to you, I'll settle for the ghost of you.' Fitting when it comes to us. A soft smile graces my lips.

Now the girls have settled into star gazing, I sink into my imagination. The warm press of a body by my side, a glass of the finest champagne I've ever tasted in my hand. The rest of the Bieber playlist crooning through the air as easily as the love of a man I longed to know wraps around me.

I could have had this.

This could have been my life.

"What's wrong with your face?" Jess queries and I quickly scowl at her. "Oh, that's more like it," she jests and bumps my shoulder. Her pale lips blow me a cheeky kiss, her brown eyes glazed over with mirth from the alcohol. She always was a lightweight.

"No, seriously, who's got you smiling like that? Not this Damien you're referring to? His voice certainly sounded swoon worthy and I can't imagine anyone around here being any less than ruggedly beautiful."

At this, Hazel chokes on a slurp of her drink and blushes bright red. It doesn't take more than a jerk of my eyebrows in her direction to bring Jess up to speed.

"Ohhh, it's you who's digging a slice of the Damien pie. Hmmm, Hazel?"

"Now you listen to me." Hazel throws herself over me as if she's in the mood to beat Jess unconscious but settles for a pointy finger in the face. "That asshole can go sit on a rusty nail for all I care. He's rude and bossy and... and... smells like a high-class ogre!" From beneath her, I give up on trying to drink my sorrows away and set the flute on the table.

"So you've been smelling him then?" I add to the mischief, quirking an eyebrow. Hazel's honey-tinted eyes shift to mine, so close she could shove her tongue in my mouth if she so wanted, but bursts out laughing instead. Dropping into my lap, I mouth to Jess it's time we found this one a bed. It's been a confusing day all round and I'm not sure what Hazel is trying to suppress by getting shit-faced, but I'm not one to judge.

Slipping out of the booth, Jess and I take one ankle each and slide her easily along the leather, thanks to the silk covering her body. Hoisting one arm over each of our shoulders, we half-drag Hazel through the penthouse, almost falling over twice when her legs give out. Only once she's tucked up in a bed do we return to the main living area, where Jess promptly flicks on the coffee machine.

"I need to sober up before I sleep or I'll have nightmares." She shrugs, as if I don't already know that about her. We've had many nights of us curled up together after a recent heartbreak and me resisting the urge to chastise her for never listening.

After finding the switch for the electric fireplace, we both settle in on the couch and sigh in unison. Heads together, staring at the orange flames, licking and dancing around the expanse of their glass confines. Content, at last.

These are the moments I relish. Utterly at peace in silent company. Even amidst the drama, we ease into our bubble of calm as if nothing else matters. As if nothing is drawing closer, threatening to tear my life and sanity apart at the seams.

Reaching for her coffee on the low table, Jess briefly shifts my position and my eyeline falls to the fingers clutching her mug. Deep scores line her nails, leaving raw wounds where her cuticles should be. Some are smeared and fresh, linking with the blood beneath her thumb on the opposite hand. I sit quietly, waiting for her to settle whilst hunting for the right words to say.

"Hey, Jess." Her head turns my way, her easy smile at the ready. But I see the truth now. The cracks behind her facade. The sadness locked in her brown eyes, the darkened circles concealed beneath her foundation.

Fuck, I'm the worst friend ever.

"I've been so caught up lately, I wasn't there for you when you needed me. The circumstances weren't... desirable, but you lost someone you put your heart and faith into. How are you holding up? Be honest, there's no judgment here." And just like that, with the slip of a single tear, the water damn bursts. I retrieve Jess's mug before it slips onto the plush, patterned rug at our feet, allowing her to go full fetus in my lap.

"I know it's stupid," she sobs, her words slightly slurred from earlier. "But it's like I'm mourning the man I wished he was. I thought I could fix him up, break his bad habits and make him... worthy of the better life he claimed he wanted."

"That doesn't sound stupid at all." I soothe her, stroking her brown waves through my fingers. I'm hardly in a position to be judging her for mourning someone she shouldn't. I'm over here falling for an apparition. "You have such a big heart, Jess, but not everyone can be saved. People will better themselves if they truly want to. You need to find someone who's worthy of *you*. Who wants to *better* themselves *because* they love you."

"It doesn't matter now. I'm done. There's no one out there for me." Somehow, these damn pajamas have me slipping down to spoon her on the wide couch, our fingers interlinking as Jess sobs.

"Come on, Jess, there are so many men that could be Mr. Right. You just have to forget about whatever 'kennels for assholes' charity scheme you're trying to open up and pick one that's already got his shit together." A rumble of laughter leaks through her sadness, vibrating through her back and into my cheek.

"It's not just that. I feel so fucking shitty about what happened to you, Astra." There's a pause between us, the memory of that fateful night plunging to the forefront of my mind.

I can't tell her it's okay because it's not - but was it worth it? An attack for the reveal of a ghost who's hellbent on protecting and loving me. But even as I think that, I know nothing could be worth the loss of Hunter's life. I'd rather have never known him if it meant he'd be alive. He'd be free and maybe with more time, he'd have plucked up the courage to speak to me.

But even that brings me shame. Because I know deep down, I've fallen for whatever limbo we're in. I've had a taste for him and I'm not sure I can wish that away.

Even if that makes me a bad person.

Shit, I feel awful even thinking that like.

A deep inhale crackles through Jess's chest before she speaks again, this time in a rush of words she can't contain. "The police told me Theo had an apartment on Dale Street. He'd told me he lived in his mom's basement... so I went to check it out."

"On your own?!" I shoot upright, sending Jess flying. She scrambles across the floor and upon sitting upright, I see the expression she was trying to hide from me. I'm not going to like what she's about to say.

"Yeah, I went on my own, and I'm glad I did. The lock was busted and it was... disgusting. But there were... photos."

"Ew, I don't think I want to know. What was it - OnlyFans, a foot fetish? Worse?"

"It was *you*." Jess blinks her large brown eyes up at me, as panic swirls deep within me. "You plastered everywhere. Pictures pinned to the wall with darts and knives. Some were burned, some with the eyes missing. It was awful. God forgive me but I'm glad he's dead. He's out of our lives for good, but I can't open myself up to a mistake like that again. I won't do it."

I drop to the floor to cradle my best friend, oblivious that she'd been carrying that around. I listen to her cry, feel the weight of grief and guilt thunder through her shudders. All the while ignoring the pounding of my own heart. The icy cold tendrils of dread skating into my bloodstream at her confession. Pictures of me, *everywhere*.

I know that he hated me. That I hated him, but that was just because he was an egotistical asshole I called bullshit on. He had this way, this slimy air to him that managed to manipulate everyone in his presence. Everyone other than me. He had to be perfect all the time but whenever I saw him, I ripped apart his life. Now I think about it, the prick had all the makings of a damn serial killer. No wonder he was a rapist too.

He's *dead*. Out of our lives *forever*...

We remain there so long, my legs have pins and needles that try to keep me weighed down. The steam rising from Jess's coffee mug has dwindled while the liquid goes cold, although I don't think she'll be needing it to sober up anymore. She's cried herself into dehydration. Pressing a kiss to her forehead, I draw Jess up to her feet and brush off her unicorn onesie of invisible dust.

"Come on, let's get you to bed." But Jess doesn't move, her hand clutched around mine.

"What did you mean 'too'?" She tilts her head and I frown.

"Hmmm?"

"You said 'I'd lost someone, too.' Have I missed something?" I hold my friend's gaze, a lie quick to burn at the end of my tongue. I could pretend I was referring to the family I'd lost, but something in the purity of her expression beckons the truth from me. And maybe, a tiny part of me wants to say it out loud. To voice the words that question my sanity. Jess is into her crystals and clairvoyants—if anyone was to believe me, it'd be her.

"It's... Hunter. Hunter North. I've been, sort of, seeing his ghost and falling head over heels in love with him. I didn't mean to... I mean I really fought against it. But he's always been there, and I think he's... all I've ever wanted. Getting over the fact he stalked me, bought out all the other tattoo parlors, paid off my debt, and left me his fortune. He only bought the Empire because he knew it was my favorite. He's always protected me without me even knowing it." Jess doesn't blink, doesn't falter, as she slowly pulls me back down to sit on the couch facing her.

"Okay..." She nods her head slowly, picking apart all of my words. "I'm sure there's a thing somewhere about people falling for the idea of their hero. You've probably built him up in your head and now you've fooled yourself into seeing him. You know what a vivid imagination you have. It's natural after suffering a trauma."

"No, I actually *see* him, Jess," I protest. Tightening my grasp on her hands, I implore her to believe me. To look me in the eye and see that I'm trying to bare my soul here. "Look, I'll show you. Just trust me."

Looking around the apartment, I call out Hunter's name, asking him to return from wherever he's gone. To show us a sign of his existence. Jess looks completely freaked out now, so I release her and stand. Taking her coffee mug, I stride to the kitchen sink, pour the contents away and perch it on the edge of the central island. "Hunter! I need you to knock this mug off for me. It's important."

The mug sits there in all its ceramic glory. Larger than the standard size, featuring a zebra print and unmoving. Huffing through my nostrils, I hold up a hand when Jess tries to walk over to me. I can't handle the concern etched into her face, can't bear the pity when I know I'm not crazy. "Come on, Hunter. Please."

A tense moment passes. Then I give up and lower my hand, slapping it against my thigh. Why am I surprised I've been let down? It's a usual state for me when I let people in—alive, ghost or otherwise. Jess slowly walks closer, crossing from the plush carpet to the tiled flooring of the open kitchen when the mug flies off the counter and smashes onto her foot. She screams in shock and pain, a shard of ceramic piercing her skin like a spear. I stand frozen in shock.

"Astra! What the fuck?!" Jess howls and I spurt into action, my hands shifting back and forth like a broken machine. I should grab a tea towel for the blood, but I can't pull the shard out, but I should call an ambulance... holy shit! I'm panicking.

The front doors burst open, Jess's screams calling the security guards posted outside into action. I take a step toward them, an explanation rushing to my lips but no words come out. A blow slams into my chest, knocking me onto my ass heavily. I wince, but it's nothing compared to the pain exploding in my chest. Like a clamp, the agony closes in on my heart, a vice tightening around my most vital organ.

I can't breathe, can't move. And all at once, an invisible weight straddles my hips. Spots prickle at my vision. Somewhere between my eyes un-focusing and my lungs screaming for air, a darkness looms over my body and that's when I smell it. Thick as tar, suffocating and toxic. Cigarette smoke.

There's no escape, a graveled voice drifts through my skull. Not bypassing my ears, but inside my fucking head as if it's stuck there. *He's* stuck there. I shudder under the weight, my body immobile as a guard drops down by my side and starts performing CPR. In the midst of all the figures and a cloud of black all around me, a lone, wet sensation drags up my cheek.

It feels like a tongue.

The disgusting realization has bile rising in my throat, threatening to finish the job quicker and my only thought is if Hunter will be waiting for me. If leaving this world is anything other than a blessing that relieves me from my mortal form.

As quickly as it began, the hand clamped around my heart pulls back, taking the stench of thick cigarette smoke with it. He's gone, and as I lie there spluttering in the guard's arms, a name batters around my mind like a wrecking ball.

I know what's haunting me. I know who *he* is.

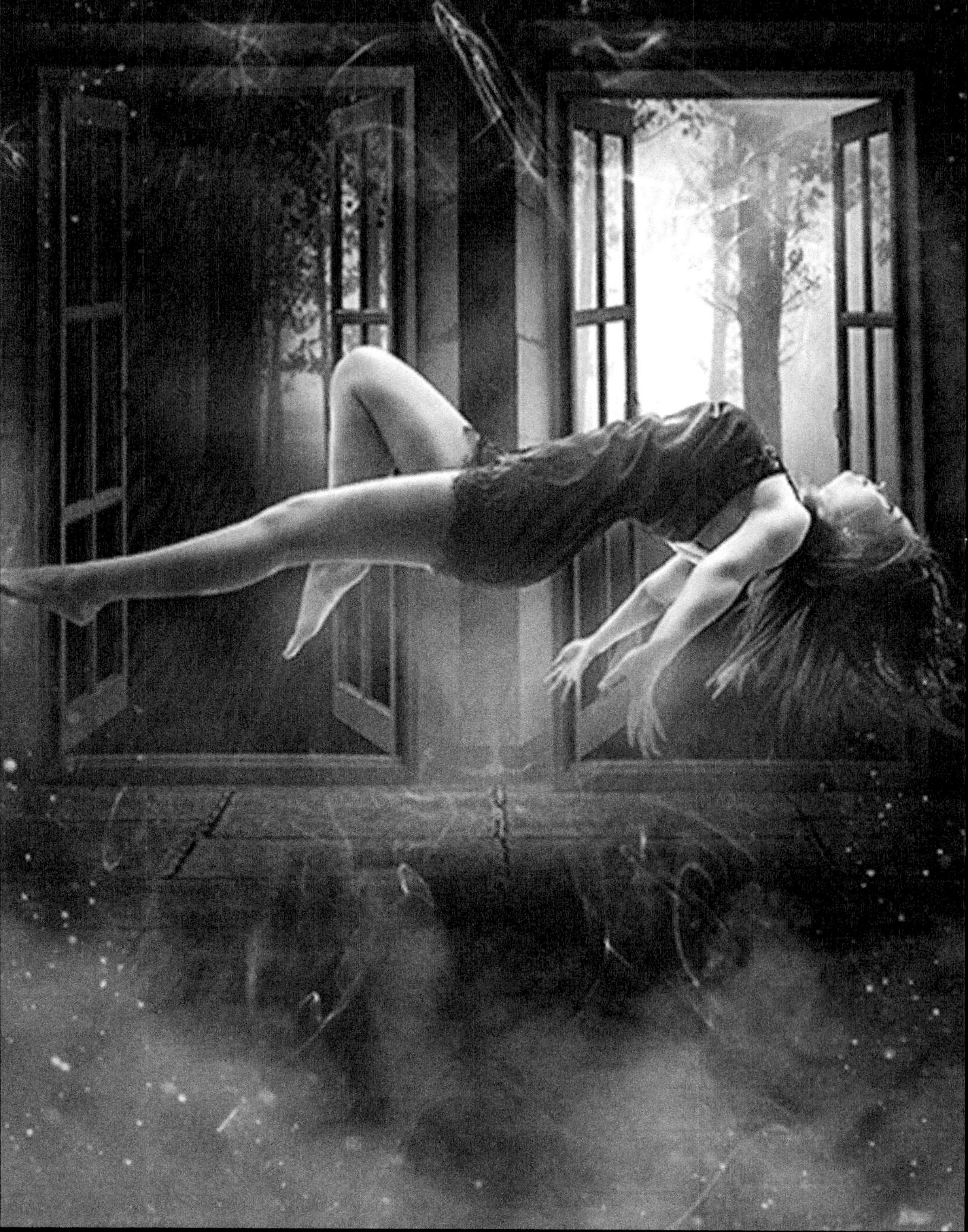

CHAPTER
THIRTY-FIVE

Astra
Monster Made of Memories - Citizen Soldier

The royal blue bed sheets tucked too tightly into my sides do nothing to quell my anger. In fact, it only serves to heighten the rage churning inside of me. Damien returned not long after the medics had finished checking me over. The security guards gave him a full rundown from the surveillance cams hidden around the penthouse. Funny how they left that part out when introducing me to *my* new living quarters. Still no sign of Hunter though, and good fucking riddance. I'm done with near-death experiences, no matter that when he is around me, it seems to be the only time I can ever truly feel alive.

Ironic, that.

Tossing the covers back, I roll over and become cocooned in a dip on the right side of the memory foam mattress. Pausing, I stretch out my limbs, trying to fill the gap Hunter left.

My body fits perfectly, like a Russian doll as my small frame becomes engulfed within the shape of his huge one.

This is impossible in all senses because he's over six feet tall.

But apparently, the bed was made for a giant, and his legacy—the very same pillows that captured all of his dreams and all of his nightmares—is already swarming around me like a nest of bees coveting the sacred honey.

I can't escape.

I'll never be able to wrap my head around the hole he's left in the world, or the expectations of me to continue it.

Right now, all I can think about is how this was his preferred side of the bed. The opposite side to mine. Did he know that or is it a coincidence?

Did he favor this side of the bed because it's directly in front of a huge bay window that has massive bookshelves built around the frame, filled with what happens to be all of my favorite books and even a few I've never seen before? Or because the sun rises on this side of the building and he needed to be awake when the first rays broke through the darkness just so he was up and out on time, ready to stalk me?

Pah, I should know by now, nothing about Hunter North is left to coincidence.

Throwing myself out of the bed, I stride into Hunter's walk-in closet with an itch to burn. I can't lie around here a second longer, stewing and waiting for the ghostly fucker to have his way with me. I need to *do* something. The light in the closet flicks on automatically, sensing my movement, and presenting me with more clothes than a local high-street retailer.

Organized by occasion, suits line one side, into casual wear and then sports. Below the heightened rails, the matching footwear and accessories from belts to fabric face masks are displayed in open glass units. Through the racks of clothes, there's the hint of another corner, delving deeper into the closet but I don't need to venture that far.

On a heightened shelf above it all, clear boxes are stacked with fabrics I imagine aren't for Hunter at all. Shimmering diamonds on sheer mesh, silks and satins in all shades of the rainbow. It might be pretentious to presume he was preparing for me, because they could either be leftovers from an ex, or he could have moonlighted as a drag act called Honey Compass. Who am I to judge?

Shrugging it off and reaching up on my tiptoes, I lift a hanger free from its home, nodding in approval at the activewear. Charcoal gray lycra with an electric blue stripe that travels down the side of the T-shirt and seamlessly blends into the matching sweatpants. A little baggy, just the way I like it. Beneath, a pair of Air Jordans have been tucked back from the rest, strangely in my size and waiting to be broken in. Sportswear can only mean one thing—there's a gym nearby, and I intend to find it.

Dressing quickly, I pause just inside the doorway to glance over a white shirt hidden from my first glance. Tucked back from view, the collar has begun to twinge with yellow. A lone, black hair is knotted around one of the buttons, a smattering of ink and blood dots dried over the pec area in the shape of a teardrop. Stepping closer, the rich cologne douses my senses and I'm temporarily pulled back in time.

Leaning over the broad chest, trying to ignore the scent that flows through me on each inhale. Sweet like berries, with a raw woodsy underlayer. A scent that could easily distract me from my work, just as equally as tattooing a drool-worthy man. I don't look him in the eye, for fear my heart will stutter out and I'll stab him too deeply with my tattoo gun. A smell as enriched as this one comes from money - the type of money that could close down my shop and sue me with the snap of his long fingers.

Fingers, which I'm also, totally not *looking at.*

"Oh, Hunter, you cowardly bastard," I huff and pull the shirt from its hanger. Burying my face into the cotton, I breathe in that scent now. I hinge my thoughts on it, torn between wanting to delve into fantasy and continuing with my new and unbearable reality.

Alone, how I've always liked it. Or at least I used to. With a frustrated groan, I fist it into a scrunched ball and chuck it across the closet.

Tiptoeing out of the master bedroom, I can hear Damien

puttering around in the main living area. The doors either side the hallway are closed, one of them containing a passed-out Hazel and the other with a sleeping Jess, her foot wrapped in a bulky dressing. Just the thought of her being hurt because I called forth a spirit has the length of the hallway closing in on me, darkening around the edges of my vision and I spurt forward on silent feet.

Due to the main area being open plan, there's nowhere to hide. Luckily, Damien is currently removing every glass from the cupboards and bubble wrapping them for storage with his back to me. Essentially, he's baby-proofing the penthouse. The foam protectors now pressed onto the coffee table corners almost makes me snort out loud and give me away. I hold it in, along with these Air Jordans concealing my footsteps perfectly until I make it to the main doors. My hand touches the handle when I realize there are probably guards posted outside again, and the faint red flash of a camera is staring at me from the corner.

"I'm going for a walk. Don't fucking follow me!" I announce, throwing the door open and strolling out with the attitude of a top bitch. "That's an order!" The two men jolt, their hands on their firearms but to their credit, they don't move. They don't look happy about it, by any means, but obedience is a trait they can put straight on their resumes. "Good boys." I wink and keep walking to the elevator shaft at the far end.

"I wouldn't antagonize the help, if I were you," a familiar voice breathes beside me, whispering into my ear. I roll my eyes at Hunter's timing, holding back the bite of an accusation. I don't want to be that needy bitch, but seriously - where the fuck has he been? Ignoring him instead, the elevator opens and I enter, reaching for the keypad inside. "Allow me." Hunter smirks, and the button for floor three lights up.

"You're so... overbearing, you know that?!" I growl, keeping all the other adjectives to myself. Frustrating, annoying, fuckable. Argh. Pursing my lips and tapping my foot, I reserve any further judgment until the doors reopen and his presence exits with me. Silent, but smug all the same.

Music hits me first, loud enough to force me back a step. Then comes the stench of sweat, potent enough to slap me across the face before I can take in the glorious sights. Sweat glistens beneath a spotlight, the pounding of knuckles against bruised flesh flashing before the crowd roars with excitement. Caged inside a hexagon of wire, two men, equal in size, struggle for the upper hand as a clock on the wall counts down to zero. A buzzer releases the door and their brawl tumbles out into their dotting audience, both seemingly unable to leave the fight in the ring.

"It's a fucking fight club," I breathe in awe. Probably the last thing I was expecting with the city's finest restaurant and the state's most popular nightclub on the two levels below. A stuffy room of pervy men hunched over poker tables with a young waitress being tipped with smacks to the ass maybe, but not this.

I thought this was a gentlemen's club and in money talk, I guess gentle means violent.

The men are pulled away from each other by security when their fighting endangers too many others. The one with a red mohawk and chest filled with tattoos spits a wad of blood onto the ground, grunting at me as he passes and disappears into a locker room.

It's dirty. It's gritty, and it's perfect.

"You wanted to vent, beautiful, have your fill." Hunter's spirit begins to stride away, the jerk of his chin beckoning me to follow but I'm enraptured. The ding of a bell rings out between songs, followed by the tannoy asking for the next round of fighters to enter the ring. A female steps forward, her long blonde braid whipping against her spine as she warms up with small jumps. The crowd crane their necks, hunting for an opponent who doesn't come forward.

Show time.

"Hey, wait a minute," Hunter suddenly appears at my side when I jog over to the man with a clipboard in one hand and mic in the other. "When I said vent, I meant there's a practice sparring room around the back. All the latest equipment, you can work up a sweat and tire yourself out until…" My heart is pounding, I'm done listening.

"I'll fight," I announce confidently. The man, in his fifties with an impressive amount of chestnut hair reaching his broad shoulders, looks me up and down. He, himself, is wearing his workout gear, alluding to him being both the organizer and a participant, but I don't accept his judgmental glances all the same.

"Sorry, Miss, this club is for experienced fighters only. Health and safety and all that. You're welcome to watch, but the most violence you'll be reaping tonight will be through a video game." A couple of the guys hovering around him chuckle and bump into others to draw their scrutiny my way.

My cheeks flame, bursting with a flush of scarlet. I know the spotlights won't do me any favors, I resent that.

Hard.

But still, I'm too pent up to back down. I have hatred to burn, and I'll be doing it in that cage.

"Don't you know who I am? I'm Astra fucking Stone, and apparently, I own this club. So, get the fuck out of my way and let me fight." I grit my teeth and challenge him to disagree. I hate doing this, throwing around my name which is unimportant and my fortune which I never wanted. But I also hate the past couple of months, so sue me.

My name is echoed then, below the pounding of the music, muttered between the crowd as they all shift their attention my way. I suppose I'm more popular than I thought.

Not another word is spoken as the organizer jots my name down on the clipboard and twists it my way long enough for me to sign a waiver about my safety. All the way, Hunter is in my ear, begging me to head out back for a one-on-one training session. The only kind of one-on-one session I want with Hunter involves his head trapped between my thighs, and since the fates aren't aligning on that front, this is my back up plan.

Heading into the cage, a mix of weak cheers and gossiping whispers reach my ears. Craning my neck side to side, I mimic the blonde's warm-up routine until the organizer steps into my view once more. Without his clipboard in sight, he and a friend bind my hands with black wraps and shove a protective guard into my mouth. It's slimy and I balk, wondering who's worn this before me but there's no time to spit it out now.

Everyone else steps out of the ring, the door slams shut and the bell dings overhead. I've watched enough MMA matches on TV to know how this goes. Stepping forward, I raise my fist to bump with my opponent out of respect. Reaching out, she dodges my knuckles at the last moment and jabs my jaw. Due to its lack of proper fit, the mouth guard ricochets against my gums, slicing into my flesh. The audience roars in support of her and I seethe through my nostrils.

Fuck this bitch.

Keeping my hands up to guard my face this time, Whipper and I dance around one another, neither wanting to be first to make a move. She's equal height to me, although about half my size in the waist. Her well-defined set of abs mock me from between a neon pink crop top and spandex shorts.

Jolting forward, her leg lashes out, catching my side. I knock her shin away with my forearm, giving her the opening she was hoping for to punch me straight on this time. A thousand pinpricks flare across my eyebrow, the warmth of blood seeping free of the cut. Clearly guarding my face isn't working, so I rely on what I know I'm a master of doing.

Going utterly psycho.

Running forward, I throw my fists in quick succession at any glimpse of skin I can see. My breasts shove her back into the cage, pinning her scrawny frame in place. A whistle blows from somewhere, the music quieting for a ref to shout words I'm not listening to. All I can hear is the rush of adrenaline and blood in my ears, and of course, Hunter.

"Step back, love. Give her a moment to compose herself. I'll coach you." I do as he says, only because the element of my surprise attack has faded. When the bell dings again, I'm ready.

"Duck left. Swing at her ribs. Front kick her back a step, keep that distance, Siren. That's it! Don't let her get any closer," Hunter encourages me, pushing me on and for a brief moment, I feel like I've got this. Blood splutters across my fists, a cocky smile graces my lips and the man who causes me to feel emotions I came here to escape is spurring me on.

I want him to see I can defend myself. I want his support, his pride.

I want to roar my rage to the wild and declare I'm their queen.

Until Whipper's foot slams into my gut, knocking me off kilter. She gains the upper hand, swinging elbow after fist. Knee after shin. Each part of her connects with my torso, drawing grunts from my lips as I crumple to the ground. Yet the bell doesn't sound for her. The ref doesn't call out and it becomes all too apparent who the house favorite is.

Not its new heiress, that's for sure.

Lost to the pounding of the bass and throbbing of my skull, my cries are lost into the crowd's cheers. I can't even hear Hunter now. Her assault doesn't falter, a foot connecting with my ribs hard enough I'm sure one of them cracks.

As the first tear leaks from my eye, an explosion of sparks bursts from the lock at the cage door. The bell over our heads begins to ding ferociously, the spotlights spluttering out for the rest of the club to be cast under one glow. Whipper is thrown backwards and then he's there. Hunter's hands aid me to my feet, his concern making me feel nauseous. I didn't come here to be cared for like a little princess.

Jerking out of his hold, I wrap my arms around my body. Suddenly self-conscious of what I'm doing here. A curvy girl with a point to prove. A traumatized being with a grudge to dispel. I may have gotten my ass kicked, but I just wanted to feel something real for a change.

"What we have is real," Hunter jerks back, offended by my

thoughts. If that's the case, maybe he should stay the fuck out of my head.

"Well, you aren't!" I scream, whipping around to stun the whole arena into a confused state of quiet. Even the music cuts out, the in-house DJ unsure of what to play for my reputation's demise. Eyebrows pinch beyond a sea of camera phones, all pointed at me to witness the exact moment Astra Stone lost her damn shit for the entire world to see. Might as well give the people what they want.

Lashing out, I catch Whipper off guard. My fist slams into her temple just as my leg sweeps out and she slams onto her back.

I was raised for this. Born for this. My daddy made sure of it. I seem to have forgotten who the fuck I am and where I came from. But that's the thing about fear, it wins for as long as it drowns out the scream of strength burning in your core.

I'm not afraid anymore and I'm burning a-fucking-live.

True to her own strength, she tries to fight back. She struggles, like a woman fighting for survival but still, she's hopeless under my rage. I see flashes from my past, second after second of heartache and abuse. From my childhood, the loss of my family, my mother. The attack, losing hunter, being haunted still by a man who took enough from me.

When she throws a sloppy punch, I break her wrist. If there's no rules for the fury, there are definitely no rules for the fucking wicked. I lick my teeth, thriving off the blood and she slumps close to becoming unconscious.

All of the air rushes from her lungs, aided by me stamping my sneaker on her stomach while throwing my head back and screaming every ounce of my pent-up frustration at the sky. The anguish, the fear, the shame. It all burns like lava as it pours from my throat in agony. Take that, tabloids.

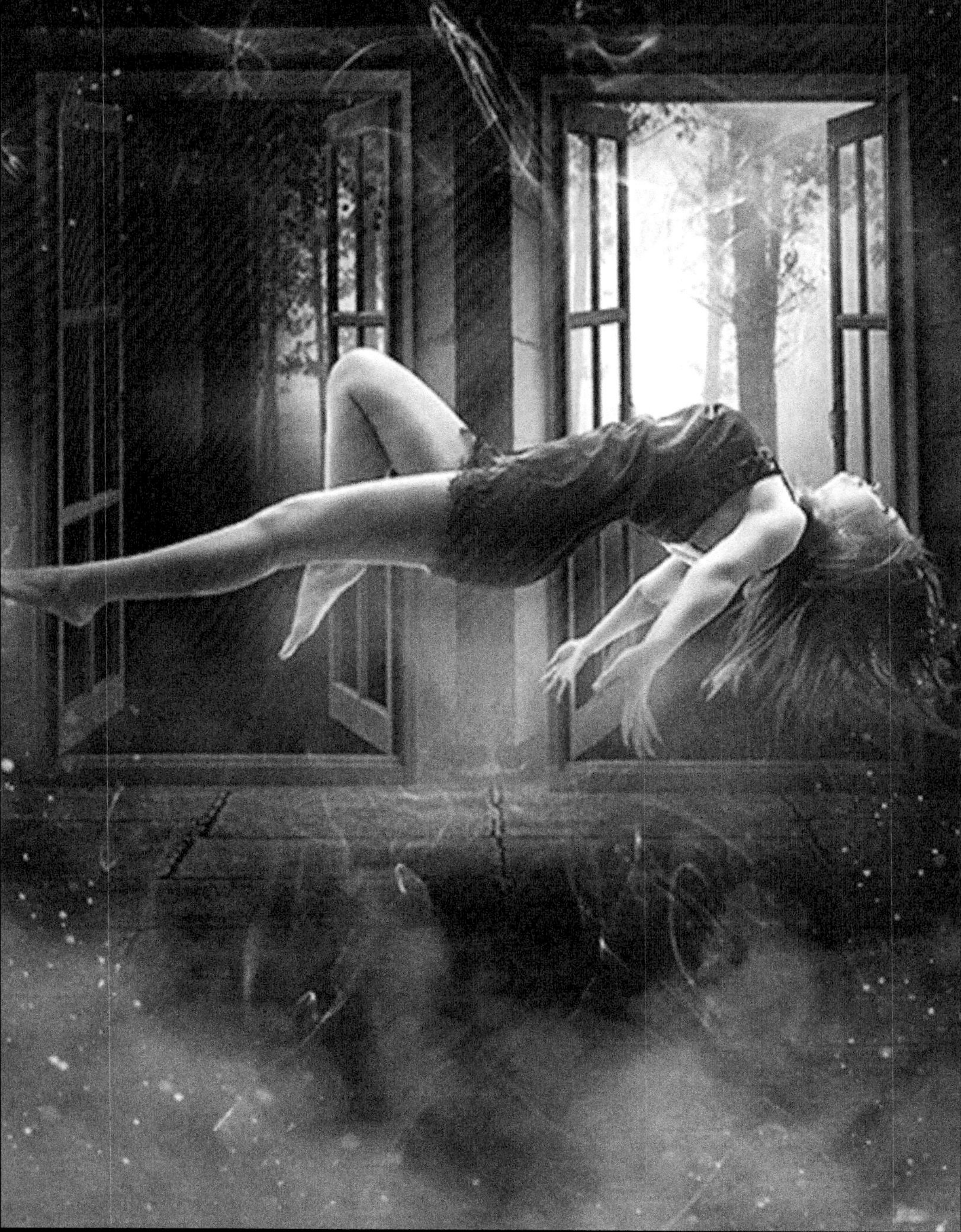

CHAPTER THIRTY-SIX

Astra -
I Found - Amber Run

It shouldn't feel this good, to be this battered and bruised. But last night was life changing. I've always been a chick that liked to roughhouse. Always been a take-no-shit, get-down-and-dirty type of girl. But as morality would have it, you can't exactly go around and beat the fuck out of people for shits and giggles. Had I known hunter had an underground fighting cage here, I would have met him way before he got shanked doing something stupid like saving my life.

But to him, I was worth it, and for me?

He was worth so much more.

I'm already craving another fight. Another opportunity to scream my turmoil to the rafters and have the audience bellow out my frustrations with me while all of the rage and grief, the confusion, and the heartache leaves me in a brutal rush that might leave me depleted, but blissfully content too.

This building is more than an empire and last night taught me that every floor of this structure is crafted perfectly with me in mind.

It's been a refreshing twenty-four hours.

I finally admit to myself that my stalker is now my truest love and I have absolutely no freaking idea, don't know how he did it.

If it's Ghostholm syndrome or because I'm genuinely a weak-ass human being that every time someone gently caresses my cheek and you know? Saves me from being murdered, I become a puddle of gushy shit on the floor.

Three times now.

He's saved my life three times and all I've done is bitch and complain.

But it's true. His quirky apparition has filtered under my skin and made me his. Although I now have the feeling I have always been his. I was just too naïve to notice it.

I'm not going to sit around feeling sorry for myself anymore. This man has given up his life for mine. I won't sit here and cry until I've killed myself over some trivial shit like being haunted by something evil.

I have to get my shit together. Find out what the fuck is going on with my family's death, give Hunter the best funeral that a man could ever have, and kick some poltergeist ass.

But first, I have to swing by the hospital and apologize profusely to the woman I almost butchered. By some miracle, when she came around to being conscious again, her story was the same as mine. And even though it wasn't my mind orchestrating the attack, it was my hands that delivered it. So, I do have to say sorry even if she was an annoying bitch. The others are still asleep and I don't want to wake them. I plan on being back by the time they are awake anyway with some good food and even better coffee.

God, food.

Who can ever live without it?

Blinking open my surprisingly refreshed eyes, I crack my neck and roll my shoulders. The aches of last night doing something wicked to the sensitive areas of my womanly body. Crowns and jewels don't get a real woman aroused. Power, strength, and fortitude do and now I've had my ass handed to me and I gave theirs back to them in smithereens, I definitely feel empowered and ready to take on the day.

But first, I have an itch to scratch with a real urge for a cold shower.

Turning my head, I squint toward the red flashing light on the nightstand telling me it's six in the morning and I purse my lips in satisfaction. Unless I have to be at the parlor which doesn't open until ten anyway, I won't wake up for a nuke.

I love my sleep too much

Lifting Jessica's arm from across my chest and Hazel's face from between my thighs I shimmy free and crawl from the bed. How I'm the only one who can sleep normally without doing a full three-sixty throughout the night or fighting a damn gorilla in my sleep is beyond me. Escaping free from my wriggling friends, I stumble toward the master bathroom, stripping my clothes as I go. The bath last night was spectacular. I've never submerged myself in a bath that felt like a warm ocean before. My muscles were well equipped to deal with my fighter chick moment and even now the ache is more of an annoyance than it is an issue. This morning I want to be quick, I have too much to do.

Walking toward the shower, I pull open the door and step inside. The huge flat shower overhead has my mouth falling open. There is a fancy dial on the sleek tile wall, and multiple different buttons and I wonder which one I have to pick in order to get water to come out of the damn thing. Don't get me wrong, when you have the money the things around you can be beautiful and I appreciate that, and if Hunter was here, right beside me, I might even find a way to truly learn how to live with it.

But he isn't and I can't.

I'm just not this girl.

To be honest, I'm not sure what kind of girl I am. Everything that should be considered easy in life is so damn hard for me and every day I'm fighting a new battle just to stay alive. It's got to the point when I begin to wonder why. I look around the opulent bathroom, no emotion thick in my chest as I take everything in numbly.

It's a strange thing being raised to believe that your life matters in a world of billions of people. Truth is, more than half of the human race will be forgotten.

We won't have our names in history books for snotty nose teenagers to turn up their noses and come lunch, not even remember our names at all in years to come. When we die, we're just dead. Easily forgotten, painfully remembered like a blemish on our loved one's memories. Just another soul left to wander this earth with no place to call home.

I remember my family and fuck me does it hurt.

But my pain and the remembrance of their life will die with me.

"Huh," I utter, for the first time in a long time feeling anything other than agony.

I feel nothing, like that realization has just lifted a huge weight from my chest but threw it onto my shoulders instead.

Soft hands coil around my waist as firm palms spread across my abdomen. My head lolls, falling back and this time, he feels a little firmer behind me. I close my eyes, feeling myself changing as I sink into the feeling he exudes from me. I should be careful, protect my heart and ward away the sinful touch of a dead man.

But I can't.

This is the feeling that I've begun to live for. The feeling of him wrapped around me and holding me close. Engulfing me in a warmth that has the vein of a deep refreshing coolness that makes me feel like I'm soaring through the skies.

I turn into his hold, my eyes still closed as I reach out a soft hand to caress the apparition of his cheek. I swear I can almost feel a shudder. When I give myself over to my senses and forgo my mind, I feel like I'm high on NOS and that this man is my dreamscape. I wasn't sure how I felt learning that it was him. that he was the man between my thighs and every dream I had featured his beautiful, darkly chiseled face that I was too ignorant to see.

I know the cost and I know what I want.

I want him.

To feel him, to lose myself in him. I need him to know that even in death, he is enough. That I see him and appreciate him for everything he has done for me.

I step closer, and my ample breast pushes against him as I begin to caress the apple of his cheek, along his throat, and down his chest. I can feel every dip and crevice under my deft fingertips as I trace the lines of his abs. I'm lost to my senses when a low beep sounds in the distance and the first rays of water from the shower head fall down upon us. The water is like silk as it glides down my tender flesh. I'm lifted into the air, my legs wrapping around nothing but a strong force of air that nestles between my tights. A rough hand coils within my wet strands, bringing my head backward as soft lips press against my pulse point that thunders under his attention.

"Open your eyes, Siren," he whispers into my ear as I shudder. "Open your beautiful eyes and look at me, sweetheart. Really look at me." The rasp in his thick tone is like a horse feather brushing against my sensitive skin. "Now, love." His gentle voice turns into a firm demand and when a sharp sting assaults my right nipple, my eyes snap open until I'm consumed within the depth of a murky gray that steals all other colors from my sight. I gasp, back arching into the opening of his mouth as his wicked tongue swirls around my hardened bud.

I quiver, overcome with every sensation that a person can feel all at once. My heart beats faster as my mind slows down, the air around me shifts as if it's moving around me and I'm standing still, watching the world pass me by. I need this, I need him. Sliding my fingers through his hair, I tug, pulling him away from me and up to where I needed him most.

My lips.

I have to feel him against me, that excitement to perceive the wind that whispers across my parted lips is a funny thing to explain. All I know is that I need it.

I crave it and when his lips touch mine, I let go.

Under the spray of warm water, I give myself to him.

Mind and body as the feel of him against me is enough to sate the monster raging in my chest for more than I'm able to give in this very moment. His tongue duals for dominance and mine relents to its alpha. I moan into his mouth, rocking against the whisper of cool air that tickles me in all the right places.

He owns me, one hand around my throat cutting off my airway, the other clawing into the rounded globes of my ass. I can feel the slashes from his nails. All of the bruises, all the bite marks finally make sense and I desire more of it.

Need more of it.

"Hunter," I mewl.

"Oh, how sweet my name tastes on your lips, Little Siren."

I'm lifted higher until my legs wrap around his broad shoulders and his mouth is lapping at my core, diving between my folds and searching for a hidden cave in order to uncover the gold.

I'm hot, my breasts heavy as I pant like a bitch in heat. Everything is raw, almost painfully so and I'm consumed with all of my senses burning hot at once. I feel like my nerves have been stripped back layer by layer, exposed, and tormented until I'm on the verge of tears. The feel of him burrows under my skin and caresses my very soul. I tremble, quivering from those thick lips that kiss my cunt, all while that devious tongue of his strokes against my clit like a man skilled in pleasing his woman.

The thought is toxic as I narrow my eyes, the stream of water beading along my fluttering lashes as the stream of it has my vision blurred, and the world around me distorted. Anger stings, chasing away the high before his hand is back around my throat and I suddenly can't breathe at all.

All the horrid thoughts about his past vanish and all I know is this sweet, sweet moment of contentment. My head swims, my hips rock and I push myself closer into his face, deeper into his mouth. His nose and tongue work in tandem to get me to my release and it's so close, I can almost taste it in the air.

He pulls back, staring up at me through those dark eyes and my heart skips a thousand beats. "You're so fucking beautiful, do you know that?" he rasps and I just stare at him numbly. "You're more than this. More than your body and these honeyed moans you please me with. It's you, Siren. It's just you!" And then he places his hand over my heart.

Just then, a dark shadow looms behind him growing larger and larger until I gasp, clutching the thick and tousled strands of Hunter's hair tighter, refusing to let him go, "No!" I shout, startling him, and as soon as the word leaves my mouth, he is ripped from my arms and consumed by the darkness while I fall to the ground crying out, no longer held up by his solid strength.

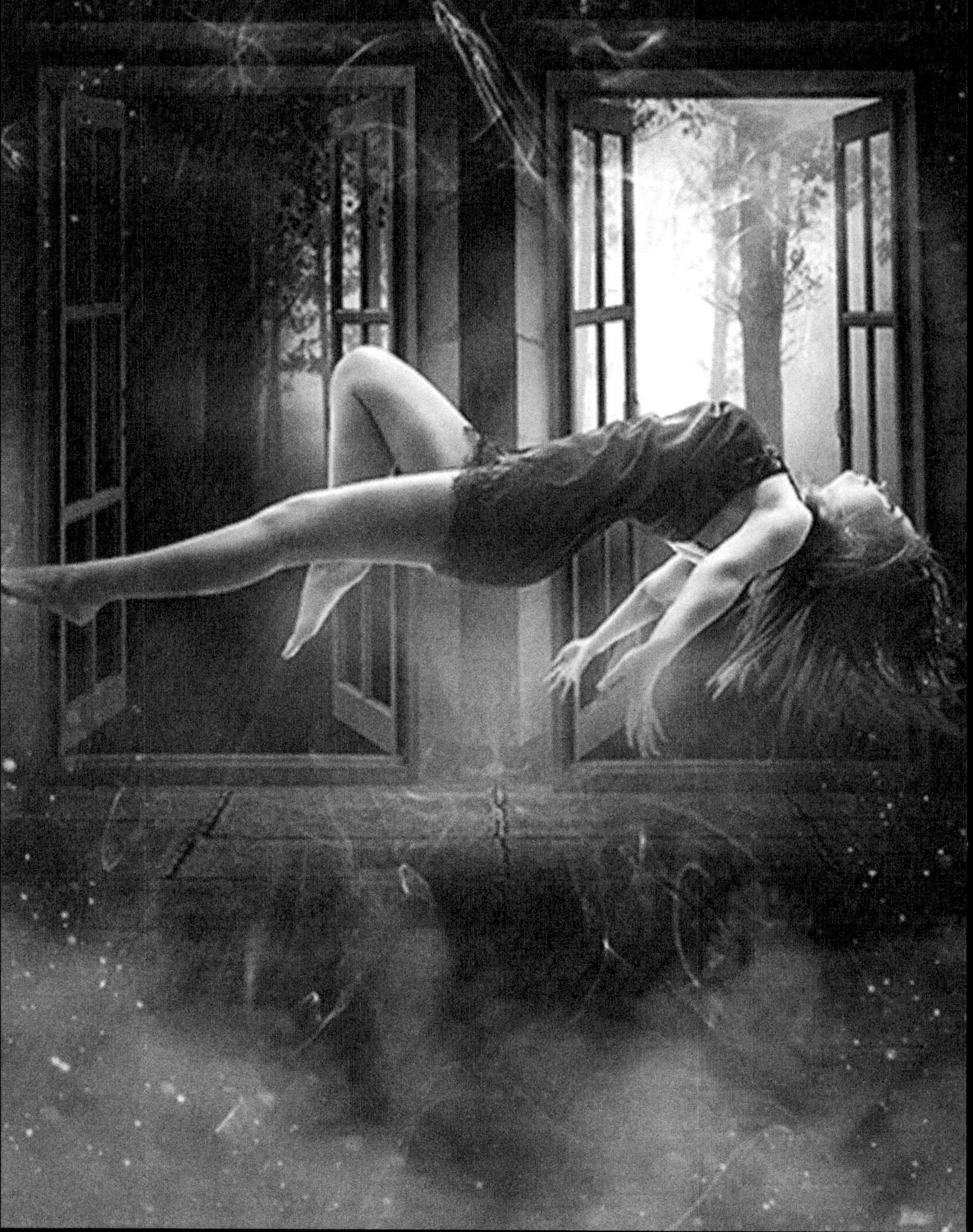

CHAPTER
THIRTY-SEVEN

Astra
Moonlit - Rivals

Wrapped in a towel, I hurry from the bathroom, my tailbone already bruising from my abrupt fall. "Damien!" I bellow, insistently. Terror pushes me to run through the penthouse screaming his name in desperation.

I don't know what to do, or how to process any of this. Hunter was ripped from my arms and I couldn't do anything but watch him go.

Does this mean his time on the other side is waning?

Did death finally come for him?

My mind spirals as my heart twists painfully in my chest. I stop, doubling over by the door to the great lounge. My hand presses firmly against the door frame, my palm flat and this action the only thing keeping me up as I heave for every breath. It hurts, pain that is cold as ice claws through me and I suddenly can't breathe at all and I panic.

Damien comes frantically rushing around the corner, he pulls to a stop as he takes in my appearance.

Fuck, the towel.

I'm sure he's seen it all before.

The first thing his dark emeralds are drawn to is the bruises that cover my skin. He looks up at me, helplessness in his harrowing gaze. If I wasn't already choking, that look of failure and pity in his eyes would be enough to steal all of the air from my lungs. "Astra," he says my name in sadness, like the word, was the definition of sorrow. "What did you do?" He rushes to my side, trying to help me stand but it doesn't work.

I can't straighten, I'm too lost in grief and worry.

What the hell am I going to do?

"I-it took him," I wheeze, breaths brittle. "It took Hunter."

"What did? What took him?" he asked in concern.

"I-I don't know. It just stole him, ripped him right out of my arms. What are we going to do? How do we find him? He needs us, Damien. He needs us and I don't know how to help him!" I hadn't realized just how dependent I had become on his presence.

I hadn't even noticed that he was the air around me, which made breathing even possible. He made it easier, always there with a comforting hand that landed on my shoulder and showed me true peace, and now he's suffering and I don't know how to pull him from the abyss that has eaten him whole.

"Astra, stop! Look at me. Just look at me and focus on breathing!" he demands, but it falls on deaf ears. I'm panting, ragged, and broken as I try to find my own way out of the darkness that is encroaching around me.

A firm hand on my shoulder, almost bruising as he shakes me, insistent on getting me to listen. Reluctantly I bring my ocean eyes up to his. Staring back at me in the deep pools of his swimming emeralds are the depths of my own eyes.

The ones consumed by agonizing despair.

"This is Hunter we're talking about. The man that defied death itself just to come back to you. He loves you, Astra. He loves you so much that his peace, his final place to rest, wasn't in some white light, but right here." There is such sincerity in his voice, it implores me to truly listen. "Right by your side. I don't care what you say took him, he won't stay gone. Nothing in this world or the next could rip him away from you forever."

I want to believe him.

I have to believe him.

But I can't deny the fear in my heart telling me that there is something greater than us out there. Something demonically malevolent and twisted that wants to hurt us. "Okay," I stutter, trying to calm my breathing. "Okay, you're right. He'll come back. I have to trust that he'll come back."

He looks at me and offers me a sweet, mischievous boyish smile. "What's it feel like loving a dead man?" he asks as he winks at me.

"Like his love is alive," I respond and something profound and content flickers in his gaze.

"It must be nice."

"Undecided," I mumble as I finally straighten and pull the towel tighter around me. A tense moment passes. Damien's eyes drag across my bruises again and I clear my throat, looking for a reason to stall. "You... handling this ghost stuff exceptionally well. Didn't even need any convincing, huh?" His green eyes sparkle, not fooled for a moment but Damien humors me anyway.

"When you've seen the shit I have, it's naive to think something as simple as an afterlife doesn't exist. The real nightmares are right here, in the real world. Now, are we going to speak about why you're black and blue? How did you get these, Astra? I checked with security and you didn't leave the building." The disappointment is clear in his facial expression. Furrowed brows, narrowed eyes, and a soft frown on his plush lips.

"Hunter took me to the fight club downstairs. I just needed the release, let's not make a big deal about it, okay? I just needed to breathe."

"And getting beaten to shit helps you breathe?" he asks skeptically.

"Yep. It did actually. It took away all of the turmoil and I screamed it into the crowd with the rest of the audience. It worked. So let's just leave it there, okay?"

He purses his lips, looking at me like he is contemplating wringing my neck or shaking my hand. "Fine," he concedes. "But you have to promise not to sneak off and I promise to let you do you. I just have to make sure you're safe, okay? That's all that I ask."

It is a fair request and as long as he sticks to his part, I can stick to mine.

"Deal."

"Deal." He smirks.

"What did you and Hunter do last night?" I ask, brow hiked in curiosity.

"What we normally do." He shrugs. "Cause a shit ton of havoc."

I shake my head, fully believing that. "Did he tell you?" I ask and he gulps but otherwise keeps his face stoic. "Did he tell you that it was my mother that killed my brother and father?"

Saying that out loud for the first time has a knot forming in the back of my throat and it's suddenly impossible to breathe again. After a moment, I gasp, the air leaving me in a rush and entering me just as quickly when I inhale deeply again.

"He told me. He wanted you to know. Felt like he owed it to you," Damien offers and his somber expression cracks for just a moment. I'm grateful that he's trying to hide his sorrow and pity for my benefit. I can't deal with that right now.

"How long did he know?"

"He didn't. Not until after he died. The PI took a while to uncover the truth. The papers were delivered here and I left them on the desk in his room."

I nod, not wanting to continue this conversation anymore. The rage burns like a wildfire in my core and if my mother was in front of me right now, I would rip her head from her shoulders just to beat her with her own stupid face. "I better get dressed. I'll meet you in the living room in ten," I offer, turning to walk back down the hallway and into the master suite.

Damien calls out after me, "The closet on the right, Astra, is yours."

I stop for a brief moment listening to his words. Anticipation coils in my stomach as I enter the bedroom. Hazel and Jessica are now spooning one another, both with drool pooling on the silk pillows due to their open mouths.

I walk toward the right-side closet. The door is built into the wall, opening up into another room full of clothes. I gulp, unease in my lower belly as I look around at all of the clothes he has picked for me. You would assume that a man of his class would expect his woman in fine satin and pantsuits. Tears well in my eyes with a little bit of pride as I look at the closet that is anything but elegant. Hunter has picked an entire wardrobe of chic and no-fucks-given causal. Cut-off boy shorts, ripped jeggings that look like jeans and so many shit-kicker Doc Martins. I think I count at least twenty pairs.

There is an entire section dedicated to my sweats and drawer after drawer filled with sleepwear. He catered this entire room perfectly to me and my heart swells at the thought of him knowing me so well. I walk through the closet, eyes scanning the expanse of the square room. The plush couch in the center of the room is calling my name, the obsidian gems twinkle at me nestled into the divots of the light gray couch.

Instead, I pull from the rail a pair of stressed-looking leggings with tears in the thighs and a nice red cami that has a satin texture and lay them on the couch before I grab some underwear from the drawer. Wiggling my ass into a pair of lacy blues and a matching bra, I get dressed. But instead of the Doc Martins, I opt for a pair of black pumps with gold chains across the top and a floor-length gray cardigan. Ruffling my wet tousled hair, I wipe my under eyes with chilly fingers and try to put on my brave face, but the worry for Hunter is still a dead weight in my chest. My body almost feels infused with lead, sluggish and withdrawn from the world around me. But I have to carry on, he'll be back. I have to believe that and right now, I have shit to do.

I leave my towel over the couch and head back into the bedroom. The girls are still asleep and by this time it's still only six-thirty in the morning. I want to walk around a little before I head into any stores. I need time to think about what I need to do next. Loosen up my stiff and achy muscles from last night. Leaving them to Hunter's cozy bed, with a little envy, I stalk back into the lounge and find Damien pacing the length of the floor-to-ceiling windows. He stops when I walk in and turns to face me with a sweet but apprehensive smile on his handsome face.

"Are you sure you don't want to go back to bed?" he asks and I sigh, shaking my head.

"No, I have things to do. It's okay, I need a good morning. It's been a while since I've been up this early."

"Do you need something for that black eye? It looks sore," he fusses, coming closer to me.

I roll my eyes, wondering if I could flip him onto his ass again. "Honestly, I don't even feel any of the marks. I feel good, actually," I admit, the twisted truth of my pain.

"So what do you need to do today?" he asks, eyes narrowed like he wants me to sit and wallow in my bruises until they heel and he deems that I'm actually okay.

Before I get a chance to answer, the elevator doors open and some men in suits walk in. In a flurry of hurried but elegant steps that swarm the place, Damien is instantly on guard at the intrusion and that has my back snapping ramrod straight. His hand flies to the gun sitting on his hip, tucked away neatly by the drape of his sleek black suit jacket. Where his is fitted to the hard lines of his sculpted body and stretched taut across slender muscles, these men don't have the same finery. Their suits are loose fitting, the white shirts somehow whiter than white, and their faces more daunting than the mind can comprehend. They have an air to them, and I couldn't place it until one of them started to address me.

"Miss Stone, I presume?" the front guy asks. His gray hair darkened under the low lights of the early morning and the custom settings of the penthouse.

"Who the hell are you?" With narrowed eyes, I keep my eyes trained on his friends who stand at his back.

"Funeral directors, Ma'am. The best in the city and we'd love to take on Mr. North's funeral. He deserves the best after all." I pout, eyes wide at the nerve of this fucker. He clicks his fingers and the men he came in with—all three of them—circle me and open satin brochures, bordered by thick binders. Images of coffins, urns, and flowers surround me and I have the sudden urge to throw myself from the window.

Better yet, I have the urge to throw this arrogant bastard out of the window instead. "I assure you, Mr. North will have the extravagant send-off he deserves. We have worked with the families of celebrities, politicians. Our clientele is very selective and given Mr. North's fortune, we have deemed it only right to allow you our services," he whittles on mechanically, and my heart rate rises as I stare at him utterly dumbfounded with a slack mouth.

"Since you're his beneficiary we'll just need you to sign off and pick one of our selected services which you'd like for Mr. North."

Oh, I'm triggered. Slowly, calculated, I raise my eyes slowly to meet his. Utter fury and contempt stared back at him. He winces, drawing back as he catches my glare.

"Clientele?" I ask with a lilt of menace in my tone. Damien's eyes widen as he latches onto my anger. "Who the fuck let you in here?" I hiss, eyes furious as I gulp past my urge to throat punch him. "Hunter North was more than a celebrity or a politician. He was more than some fancy name you can add to your stupid-ass brochures." A madness brews under the surface when I see that one of the brochures actually lists the names of people they have helped bury.

"He was a human being and he deserves a fuck ton more than your shitty little funeral parlor could give him. Fuck, I might just even use all that hard-earned money of his and buy it right out from under you just so I can demolish it." I step closer, getting right up into his face and when Damien steps forward, ready to intervene, I lift a stern finger and keep him in place.

"Now get the fuck out of his home and don't you ever come back. We will not be obtaining your services because it is quite evident you do not give a fuck about Mr. North or what he would have wanted and he deserves someone who actually cares to plan his send-off. Now get out before I throw you out."

Quicker than a rat scurrying from the gutters, they head straight back to the elevators and descend back down into the restaurant.

I'm furious. Beyond furious that somebody so entitled thinks he'll be worth the fame that will come from wielding around Hunter's name like some gold trophy.

I'm breathing heavily again, spiraling into a darkness that is urging me to go find that prick and smack him in the head for his disrespectful behavior.

"Well, you handled that excellently. I'll have a word with downstairs, and make sure nobody else gets passed." He relaxes, breathing easier and when I turn cold eyes onto him, he bulks.

"Don't bother. I think it's time they finally met me. Let's go," I state as we walk toward the elevator.

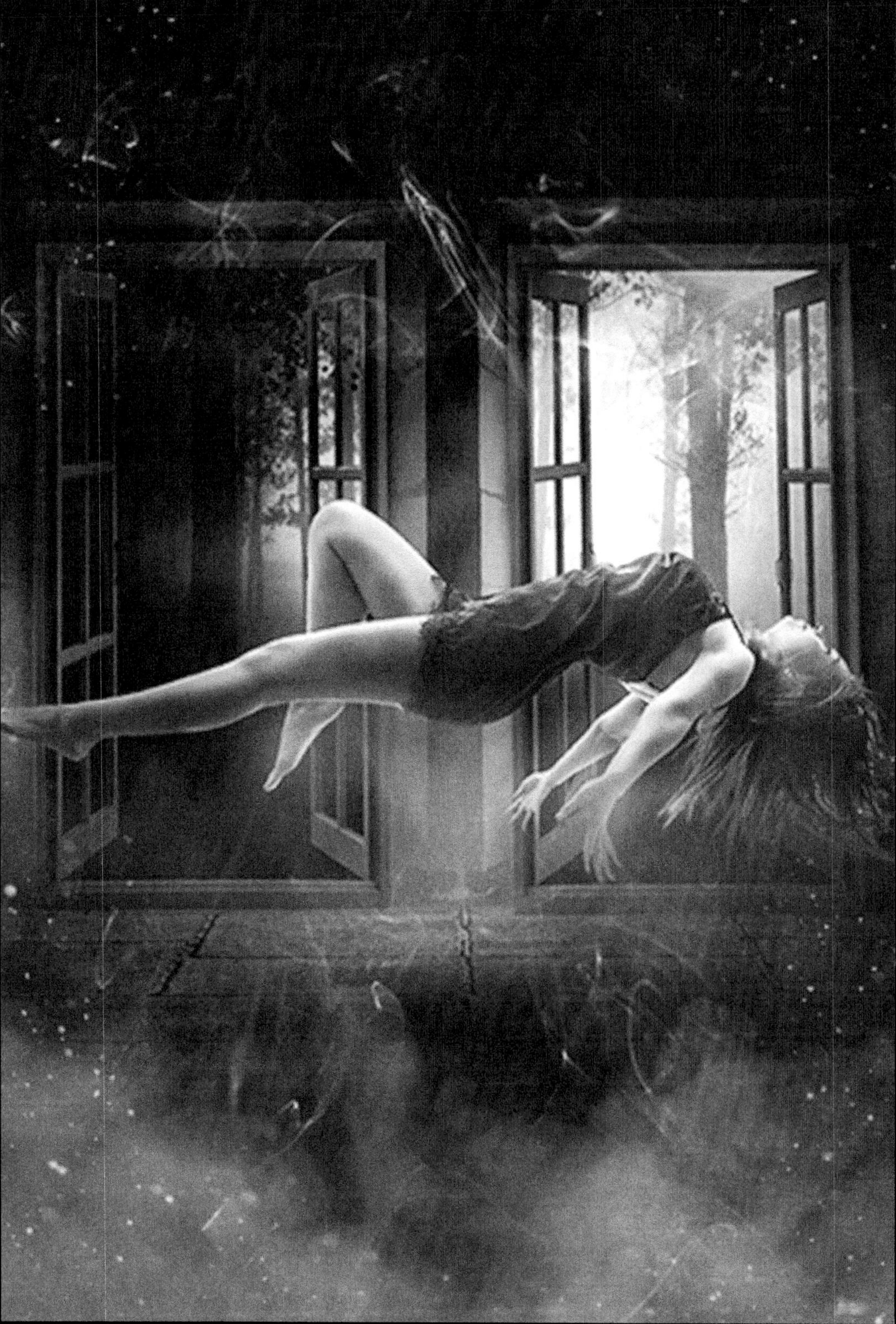

CHAPTER
THIRTY-EIGHT

Astra
I Don't Deserve It - Lisa Cimorelli

The ride down is quiet, there is still so much tension tight in my shoulders and I'm really in no mood to be pushed today.

I'm trying. Fuck me, I'm trying to evolve and handle everything that has happened, but I'm only human. Breathing through it helps, but hardly. I just want to riot at the world for the injustice and agony that thrives within it. Is wanting peace really so much to ask for?

When the elevator dings, the doors slide open and I step out into the restaurant. It's six-thirty so it's not open yet, but there are three staff members pottering around. They all seem to be busy, making sure things are set up before the doors open. All of them, except the woman sitting at the front. Her feet are kicked up onto the table as she scrolls through her phone. Marching over to her, she lifts dull blue eyes up to meet mine and tilts her head like she can't work out who I am.

"I'm sure it's common sense that one should never just permit strangers into somebody else's home without checking first, right?"

Reality dawns and she finally notices who I am. "Miss Stone! I'm so sorry, they said they had an appointment," she explains and I can see it in her eyes. The appointment part is true, but so is the lack of shits she gives.

"You're fired. If Mr. North had been alive and those men had been anyone other than funeral directors, you would have risked Hunter's life. I can't have that. So collect your things, and be gone by the time I get back."

Not that I had any intention of coming back. Unless I had the sudden urge to lie on the floor of Hunter's closet and become engulfed in his smell again. I need to figure out where I want to stay. I know the Empire is technically mine, and I will feel closer to Hunter there. But my entire life has been my cottage.

My safe haven and place of solitude. Except when Jess visits.

"Ahh shit, I've done it again!" I wheel around on Damien, pounding my fist against his chest in frustration. He doesn't respond, his green eyes cooling watching my meltdown take place.

"The girls upstairs," I sigh and he interjects.

"Will be safely escorted home when they wake, North gift hampers in hand." I chuckle to myself and roll my eyes at the extravagance of it all.

"They'd better be sorry-for-being-a-shitty-friend worth to assuage Jess from dragging my intestines out of my throat." Damien drops his head to hide his smirk and I thank him for knowing what I needed without having to be asked. Something tells me I'm not as opposed to a full-time assistant as I thought I would be.

Turning, I find the red-haired, blush cheeked, spluttering woman still in her seat and click my fingers to jerk her into action before heading toward the door. James is there with a warm smile as he opens it, holding it open for me. That sweet smile of his instantly fades when the flashing of bright lights blinks into view and begins to blind us. I recoil, eyes clenched tight when I become dazed. I can't work out what's happening until the broken words and full sentences break through the silence and filter around me.

"There she is!"

"Looks, it's Astra Stone! Miss Stone, how did you do it? How did you convince Forest City's most eligible bachelor to sign over his inheritance?"

"Was there a child? Did you trick him?"

"Are you a long lost sister? Another family member perhaps."

"How does it feel to be handed an empire when you're a nobody? What plans do you have for his fortune?"

My brain hurts, my eyes sting and as they fill with water, I wipe them away and squint through the stark white lights.

The sidewalk is swarming with paparazzi. All of them asking harmful and insulting questions while shoving cameras in my face. Damien conceals me, his huge body blocking mine from view as he lifts an arm and tries to make a path for us to escape. My mind catches up, more questions assaulting my ears, all of which overlook the magnificence of the man himself and the legacy he left behind.

This is what I was talking about. Beyond the politics of life, nobody gives a shit about the lives that are lost as long as they make for a good article header. Damien wraps an arm around my waist, dragging me toward the town car that pulls up.

"Why has nobody ever heard of you before? Did you scam Mr. North? How did you manage it? How will you swindle away his fortune?"

I pull up short, heaving each and every breath. Damien tugs my arms, whispering, "Don't," as he tries to coerce me into the vehicle. I tug my arm free and spin on my heel, snatching one of the offending cameras out of a stubby man's hands.

"What the hell is wrong with you people? Hunter North built an empire. He owned multiple businesses and donated more than half of their profits to charity. He's been to third-world countries and offered aid and shelter. Food and clothing. He was a human being who lived and then died. He died saving my life from an attack that may have killed me and you stand here, shoving cameras in my face asking questions about his fortune which I couldn't give less of a shit about instead of speaking about the life he lived. The good that he's done. You should all be ashamed of yourself."

I berate as I smash the camera into the sidewalk, it shatters against the concrete and before the man has time to blink, I'm turning to the town car, ready to get inside.

Officer Stalmyer is there, holding open my door with a vein of unhinged malice in his gaze. Only today, he's in normal clothing. Dark jeans and a light green polo. Slowly, I take my final steps toward the car, and just as I'm about to step inside, he grabs my arms and bends low to my ear. "I don't know how you did it, bitch, but you need to watch your back. Not all of us believe the story Hunter's men cooked up about his death. Not every cop in this town can be brought." He then lets me go, helps me inside and before I have the chance to allow the words *'excuse me'* to leave my lips, we're driving downtown, Damien at my side.

"Damn, remind me to never mess with you." Damien chuckles, but I'm all dried up on humor. "He'll be okay, Astra."

It would astound me that he knew why I was so upset if I still wasn't thinking about Hunter and him being okay. It's driving me insane not knowing, not being able to feel him close to me.

We get into the quietest part of town and Damien accompanies me to the smallest flower-shop I've ever seen. Christiana was the lady who handled the arrangements for my brother and father and they were beautiful. It's bittersweet coming back here. She's old, quirky and has the kindest soul. She has more than enough money to open her own store but has said that she finds it more soothing to work in such a small space. It's about the love and care she puts into her work. Not the floor plan. I always knew she was right about that one.

She smiles up at me through aged eyes and white hair when we approach. I thought I wouldn't know what I wanted when I came here, but I'm wrong. The second I see the small blue hut and smell the plethora of the mixed flowers that drift around me I instantly know.

I remember seeing collages in the penthouse. The dark and broody images of orchids taken by various photographers. My favorite flower had become Hunter's, for the pure fact that he knew I loved them. I order more than what's probably necessary for a funeral, but I want him to have some around his home as well. With a special request that each one gets sprayed in a mixture of his cologne and my rose scented perfume, so they exude the smell of us both entwined.

I know he would have loved that too.

When we get to another funeral directors, ones we once again used for my family, I order a sleet gray coffin. All dark and sleek, exactly how he liked it. I also added a request that the coffin be lined with his bedding from the penthouse so that he'll feel at home when he's laid to rest. I also asked that on the bottom, directly under his back, that it be made out of my bedding too. I want him to know he'll never be alone and if he finds peace with him, he can take what I find peace in with him to the ground.

I fight back tears for the entire day, not so unfamiliar emotions thick in the back of my throat as I plan his funeral. I hadn't intended to do it all at once, but once I started, I just couldn't stop. If anything, this is for me. A way to ease my guilt. The guilt I've carried since that very night. Not to mention this is for him too. In a world that constantly took from him, he deserves to know somebody actually cares about him.

Even under these circumstances.

There was so much more to do, but after picking out his song, the one I discovered was on his speaker system and I know reminded him of me, I had finally squared it all away. Now I'm in the hospital, taking another damn elevator to the top to apologize to the woman I hurt.

A bunch of bleeding hearts in my hand. They're pretty flowers in their own right, they just have nothing on orchids. I asked Damien to wait in the lobby, told him I'd only be two minutes and I planned to be. After today, I just want to crawl into a ball and consume myself within my art.

Walking down the corridor, I find her room. Angela Holland. Huh, it only now occurs to me I didn't even know the name of the woman I almost killed. I knock once, then open the door, wanting to get this over with.

As I step inside, I instantly chill. She looks small and fragile in her huge hospital bed. The gown does nothing for her pale complexion. Her wrist is wrapped tight in bandages. Blood splotches the taut white material and I shudder. After a moment, her head turns toward me as she draws her eyes away from the large window showing her the dreary day.

"Angela?" I ask, tentatively taking another step forward. Fear enters her wide gaze and I gulp, my throat thick at knowing I'm responsible for that look. I hate it and wish there was something I could do to take that look away. "I'm so sorry about what happened. I've been thinking on the ride over here what I would say to you, but nothing seemed quite right. I mean, there is nothing I can say after what happened."

I walk toward the bed and lay the flowers down on the side, taking a small step back because of how uncomfortable she is.

"It's okay," she answers meekly. Nothing like the woman in my parlor last night. "It was an accident. I know that."

"Do you?" I ask with narrowed eyes, watching as sweat beads along her brow. Her dull blue eyes flicker back and forth between mine like she can see darkness there and she's cautious it may bleed from my gaze just to consume her soul. I turn my head, looking over my shoulder wondering if she's looking at me or through me.

"No, yeah. I mean-yeah, no. I know it was an accident. I know," she stumbles, muttering her words like they just don't make sense in her brain.

I step closer again, taking her hand softly in mine. "Honestly, Angela. I would never hurt anyone on purpose," I implore, hating that she's so afraid, she's turned into this strange docile creature that looks like she's scared of her own shadow.

"It was the thing inside of you." She gulps as she brings her arms up, covering her chest and cowering in on herself like she's terrified. With unease, I walk away, moving toward the door to give her some space as I frown, looking back at her through furrowed brows. "I felt it. It's gone now."

I'm going to raise Theo from the dead, just so I can fucking kill him again.

I know it's him. The vile insidious feeling that slithers inside me, the same strand of wrong I felt when I was around him in real life. The stuff Jess told me yesterday, there is no way it's not him that's haunting and trying to kill me. It wasn't enough that he hurt me that night, or that he killed Hunter, now he wants to torment us still.

Rage and upset war with one another as I hang my head, looking back at her one last time. "Honestly, I'm really sorry. I hope you'll be okay."

I have a feeling a psych ward might be on the cards for that girl. She felt what I did, felt the unnatural air as it ominously stirred. You don't come back from that and if I never had Hunter there to combat the darkness, I would probably have fallen into insanity too.

Pushing the button for the lobby a little too hard, I cross my arms over my chest as I breathe out when the doors close and the elevator begins to descend slowly.

10, 9, 8, 7, 6

The floors flick on by, and I can't help but try and reach out to Hunter. "Hunter? I don't know if you can hear me, but I really don't like this. I need to know you're okay, please tell me if you're okay!" I ask the empty space around me and my skin remains normal, it doesn't fill with electricity as the static energy of my man consumes me. I feel nothing and I know I'm alone. "Hunter, please!" I beg.

5, 4, 3

Then a chill skates down my spine and a black vise encircles my heart. The air leaves me in a rush as the elevator begins to free fall, the suspension of the small cart gone as I drop through the air, screaming bloody murder expecting my end to come when my brains are splattered all over the damn metal floor. I'll be damned if he kills me without me giving him a piece of my mind.

"Ah fuck! Fuck, fuck, fuck you, Theo! Fuck you!" I scream with the urge to shake my head and stamp my feet, but I can't. My entire body weight is gravity's bitch as I'm pulled back down to the center of the freaking earth.

"You puny, small-dicked fuck face! What? Couldn't scare me in real life so now you have to play the dead man's game? You don't scare me, you piece of shit! You're nothing but an egotistical narcissist that couldn't get out from under his mommy's tit!" I'm not ashamed to say the profanity spewing from my mouth was a hot mess or that my anger and fear hadn't collided into a ball of an unladylike explosion, but fuck him.

"I hate you! I hate you! I fucking hate you!" I chant the words like they'll save me. My arms are spread wide, lodged wall to wall, in some vain attempt to stop me from flying around. In hindsight, not the best idea because if I survived this, my arms wouldn't.

But then I feel it.

The white light in my soul that takes away all of the fear. The white noise, that takes away all of the sounds. The essence that has me drifting through time and space.

Hunter is back.

The cart crashes to a stop, suspended just before hitting the ground with a fierce thud. The doors slide open. I'm sprawled across the middle with knees bent and arms wide, and a shrill voice drawls, "Sweetheart, just what are you doing? And who are you shouting at?"

The shriek penetrates my ears, my arms falling slack and I fall to the ground, slumped to my knees. Right before Damien knocks my mother out of the way and hurries inside to see if I'm okay.

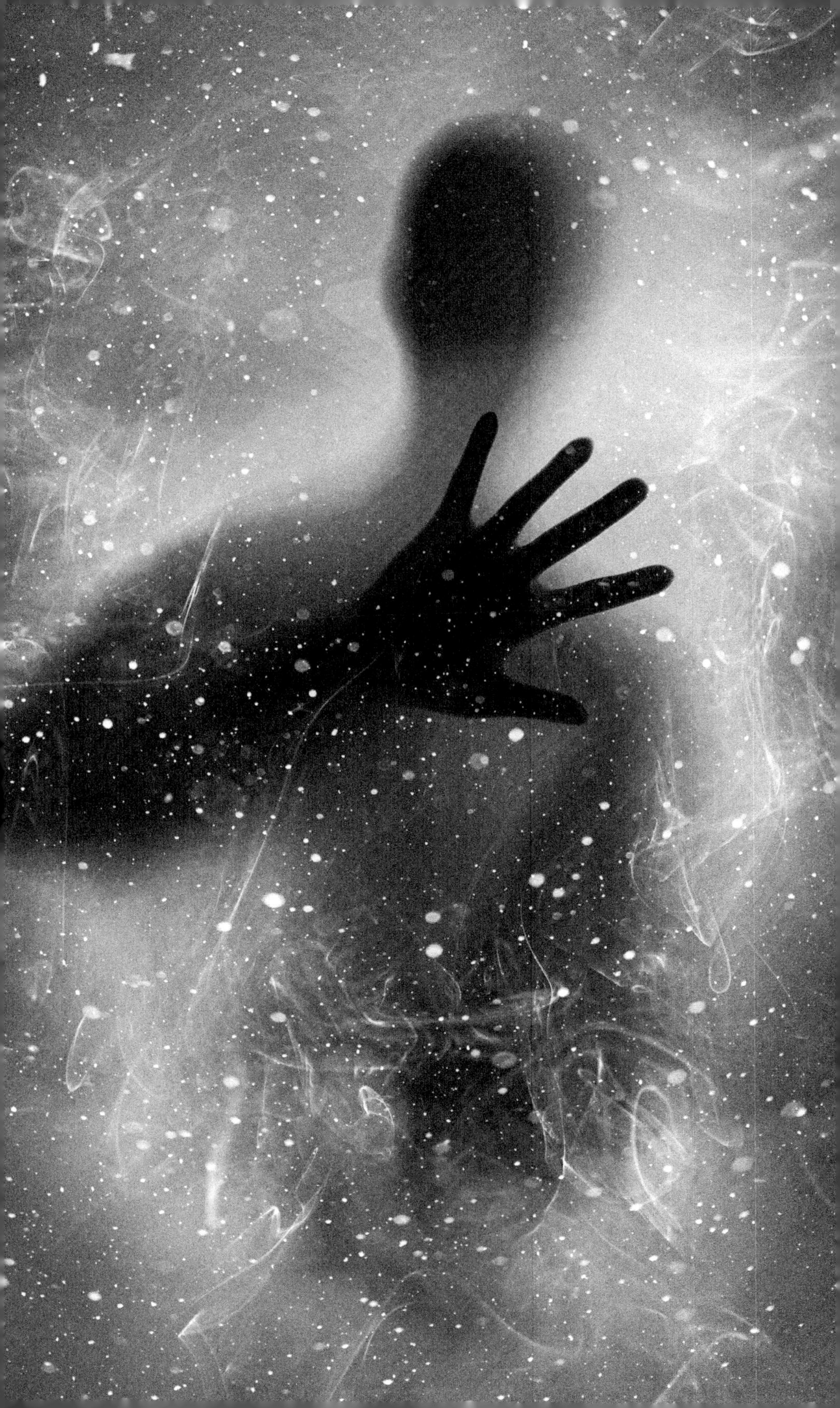

CHAPTER THIRTY-NINE

Hunter
Hell's Coming With Me - Poor Man's Poison

I thought the other side was colorless before, a murky gray of withered ash. But that is nothing compared to when Theo rips me from Astra's arms. All light is stolen, not even the ocean blue of her eyes anchoring me to the real world. Claws of black drag me from my lover's grip. Talons of wisping cigarette smoke clamping over my mouth, silencing my screams.

I wish there was a heroic story to tell. Or that I can say I overcame that cunt's clutches by sheer will, but it'd be a lie.

He tosses me around between my realm and his, throwing blasts of energy at me from all directions. Each time I re-materialize, another hit blasts me into tiny particles. And so it continues.

While proving my love to Astra was my sole focus, Theo has been biding his time. Learning to control the darkness. And that wasn't his worst - not by a long shot. I'm under no illusion stealing me from Astra, just to toss me back in her moment of need was a show of power. A ploy to intimidate me with what's to come.

Now I stand at the foot of the elevator shaft, staring up at the falling cart as it descends toward me quicker than I thought an elevator could fall. Inhaling deeply, I use all of my strength to catch it before it crashes to the ground. It has fallen almost three floors. It wouldn't have killed Astra but it sure as fuck would have been enough to scare her.

I can hear the desperate calls, begging me to let her know that I was safe. The despair and agony in her voice are like a knife to my heart and the only thing that pulls me back from the darkness of Theo's Hell.

He is playing my last nerve like the fatal wire to a bomb. You snip the wrong one and it all goes up. I swear to whatever gods made this astral place, I will find a way to destroy him if it's the last thing I do. Once I stop the brunt of the crash, my body filters through the floor and I come to a stand behind Astra. She doesn't notice my presence.

In fact, I don't think she's noticed anything other than the fact her mother is standing in the middle of the hospital lobby. Like a bat out of hell, she reacts faster than even trained marines would. She's on her feet and throwing herself from the car and a moment later, taking her monster mother to the ground in a brutal collision.

Astra's mother—Celest, as I recognize from her pictures—shrieks as Astra launches at her. Crying out, she lands on her back, her tightly coiled French updo smashing into the cold tiles of the clinical floor. The air leaves her like a tire going bust as she deflates under the weight of her enraged daughter, who rains down a torrent of brutal punches that connect to her mother's face where they'll hurt the most.

Thankfully, Astra looks nothing like her mother and after she's done with her, I doubt Celest will look much like anyone else.

Damien hurries to pull Astra away and I hold up my hand to stop him. "Let her be for a moment. Fate knows the bitch deserves it."

"You killed them!" she roars, then I rethink my decision in holding Damien back. Because Astra looks like she may just damn well end her mother in front of a lobby full of the sick. "You killed them! Papa, Luca! You killed them both and left me alone! You killed my family!"

So much grief tears through her voice that I'm knocked back a step. I wasn't expecting her mother to be here, not so soon after Astra had only just found out the truth about the fire, but here she is and I don't think my girl was ready for it. She doubles down and when her fists grow tired, she digs her thumbs into Celest's eyes, making her howl like a banshee before lifting her head and smashing it into the ground over and over again.

"Okay, grab her," I order, and Damien rushes to do as I ask.

He hauls Astra from her sobbing mother, who falls slack back against the ground, her arms sprawled wide in her daze and Astra kicks and screams with a fury I have never seen come from the living. I have known anger and I have known pain, but I have never known it as strong as this. It breaks my heart, and even though I'm already dead, I feel like I'm dying all over again when I see her crying the way she is now.

Sobbing into Damien's arms.

With trained precision, he escorts her back out to the town car and I follow. Leaving us both inside while he goes back into the hospital to clear up this mess, I pull her into my arms, and she curls up into a ball, her angelic tears splattering through my thighs and splotching the leather beneath me. "Shh, sweet girl." I soothe as I stroke back her hair.

"She did it, she killed them." She breaks, and each word fractures with her difficulty to breathe. "How could she? How could she kill them? Her husband! Her son!"

"That is something you'd have to ask her, love. I don't know why she did what she did, I can only be thankful she never took you from me when she did it."

"You wanted me to know. You lead me to those papers on purpose."

"I did. I knew you'd hate me if I told you myself. But I couldn't lie to you, Astra. I could never lie to you."

She sniffles, sucking in a stuttered breath as she lifts her head, peering to look up at me with glassy eyes that make her ocean blues swim under stormy waves. "I wouldn't have hated you. I would have finally known. That in this world full of liars, the one who promised to protect me above all else, was the only one who wasn't."

"This is our fucked up story, love. But I could never be the one who stole your trust. I told you I'd be your everything. Your moon in a sky of darkness and your stars to light your way in an eclipse. I'm just sorry this happened at all."

"How were you supposed to know my mother was a cunt?" she sneers and I chuckle, wiping the stray tears from the apples of her cheeks before they even have a chance to fall at all.

"I had a feeling."

The car door opens and Damien pokes his head inside. "Taken care off. She's being admitted and our guys are on the way so she'll keep her mouth shut. Think it's time we get you home. This time, you're resting. No ifs and buts. Tell her Boss. She planned your whole damn funeral today." Damien grunts, slamming the door shut behind him.

I turn to look at her, eyes narrowed with a hike of a thick brow when her cheeks blush and she stares at her clasped hands sheepishly. "Is that so?"

"Yeah. I tried to get everything perfect. To give you a proper send-off. I just hope I didn't mess it up."

"Love, I'm a dead man with the love of his life laying in his arms. Anything else, especially coming from you, is a freaking gift," I assure her and those tear-filled eyes light up. I stroke my thumb across her bottom lip, aching to taste her again. "I heard your call, Siren."

Like I'd just switched on the lights in a very dark room, her eyes widen and she throws a punch at my arm. I have my moments. Still pretty much transparent, but the more I'm around her, the more solid I feel. The hit jars my soul and it shudders, jump-started at the weird attack to my senses. "Hey! What the hell was that for?"

"For disappearing on me, asshole!" she hisses, a sweet frown on her thick lips. "You were literally ripped from my arms. I was worried sick. What the fuck happened?"

"You were worried about me?" I ask, kind of smug as I lean back and smirk at her. I bring up my hands to cover myself when she goes to throw another punch. "Alright, alright! I'm sorry," I placate, twisting so I can see her better. "I didn't get a chance to tell you this morning, but all those times you thought I was hurting you... it wasn't me. It was-"

"Theo. I already know. Is that what happened to you? Are you okay?" she asks, worried. I relish the concern in her gaze but a sense of dread tells me I'm not the only one that annoying asshole has been paying visits to.

"Wait, what do you mean you know?"

"I figured it out last night. Jess found some 'I hate Astra' shit in his apartment. Then there was... an incident I may have not been in the mood to tell you about at the fight club. And I smelled him." Astra shudders and I'm right there with her.

"Yeah, I found his apartment too. He didn't hurt me, but now I have a dilemma," I huff, a frustrated growl to my horse voice.

"What's that?"

"I have to figure out how to kill a dead man."

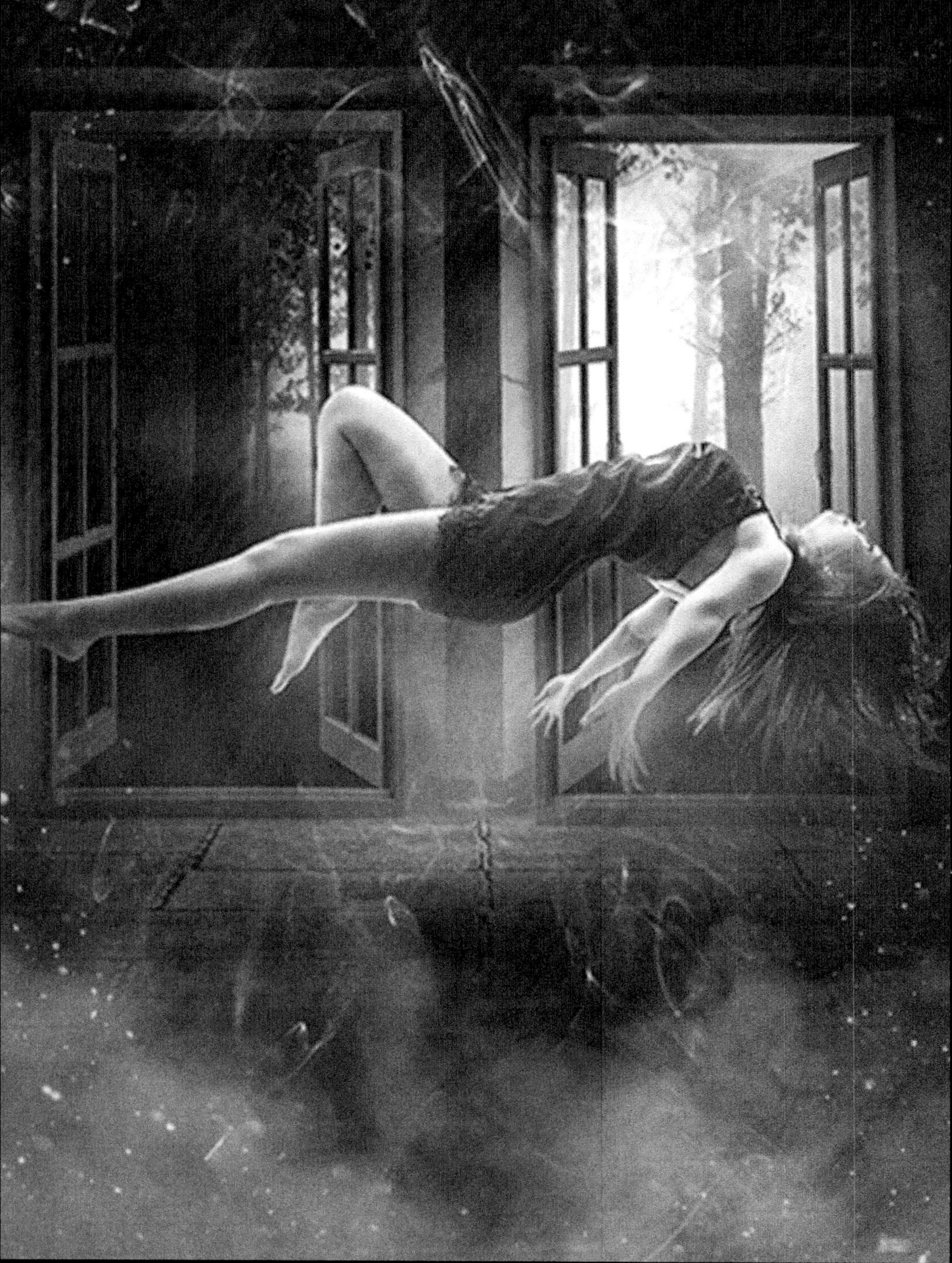

CHAPTER
FORTY

Astra
Never Stop - SafetySuit

Sighing, I toss another stack of papers into the shredding pile and drop back onto my ass. Wrapped in my thickest sweats, the music from my Bluetooth speaker circles the four walls of my spare room. It used to be my grandparent's bedroom, back when they were alive. Mold has crept into the corners, like a ticking time bomb threatening me to clean out their hordes of shit before it infects them. A task I've been putting off for years because there was no need to before. I hid behind my grief, now after facing it, I want a little bit of closure.

This time, I'm happy about the distraction.

"You should take a break, love," Hunter tells me from the doorway. A mug of coffee drifts through the air, landing softly in my hands and I smile. Hazelnut drifts into my nose and I hum in contentment. The past few days of me sifting through my grandparent's possessions have given Hunter the opportunity to test out his strength in the real world, and I'm happy to be the recipient of said experiments. These few days of rest and long-lost memories only seem to bring us closer. The day falls silent and my mind finds rest.

I'm able to feel joy in the past now, instead of being buried alive under the anguish.

God, I forgot how handsome my dad was. He got it from my papa. They looked so alike. My grandmother was stunning. Both of us shared her eyes, and so did Lucas.

"No breaks, remember? I have a penthouse and rent-free life waiting for me across the city." We share a smile, the love blossoming between us moving beyond giddy butterflies and settling deeper in my psyche. I hate to think I'm fooling myself by being shut away from the outside world, with only his presence to comfort me. But the reprieve from Theo's antics has been bliss. Not even Damien staying in my bedroom downstairs, or the excessive amount of visits from Hazel to *'check on me'* can burst my bubble. Jess does too, but her checking on me is genuine.

As long as they all leave enough takeout for me, I'm all good.

"What's this?" Hunter shifts a box with a gust of energy. It drops into my lap and I tilt my head at the unreadable scribbles on the outside. Setting my mug aside, I open the box with the same care I've been handing all of their belongings with.

Black lace slips through my fingers, sequins catching the artificial light. Underlined with a layer of satin, pristine in condition despite the cardboard box it was left in to be forgotten. I stand, opening up the length of a vintage ball gown as Hunter comes to join my side.

"I didn't know my nana owned anything like this," I breathe. The floral lace links the long sleeves to the chest, a shimmer lining with a high collar fit for the era. But the satin underneath provides bra cups into a cinched waist and further down the fitted skirt to the floor, not to mention the black, sultry appeal. I imagine that was quite the scandal back then.

Did she ever wear this? And if so, where to? For who? Questions fly around my mind, only easing when the caress of Hunter's fingers under my chin brings my attention to his stormy eyes.

I know exactly what I have to do.

"Damien! Dry cleaning emergency!"

∼

It's nightfall by the time Damien returns, his hair ruffled and usual composure nowhere to be seen. Curled around his index finger is a hanger, holding up the cream suit bag, stamped with the logo of a dry-cleaning company. Hazel sits across the dining table from me, a forkful of noodles halfway to her mouth as she quirks a brow at him.

"Fuck's sake, it was only one dress. You didn't have to launder it yourself," she tuts. Damien growls, hooking the bag onto my curtain rail, and shifts a hand through his hair to sort out the dirty blond mess.

"For your information, the dress was sorted *hours* ago. There was a security issue I had to run, as part of my *real* job," he seethes. It's entertaining watching the pair trade scowls back and forth, but even more fun when I'm also involved.

"Your job is to do whatever I tell you to." I wave my hand in the air. Hunter chuckles as Damien's face reddens to the point of combusting. Cracking a smile, I jerk my head for him to come to sit at the table. "We've left you a chow mein, come and eat, Simon."

"Astra, I'm trying to tell you, we have a problem," Damien relays with all the calmness he can muster. Two shadows appear outside the sliding doors, then two more show outside the glass pane in the front. The longer I wait, wondering if they'll attempt to break in, the more I realize they have no intention of entering. Heightened security surrounding the cottage—this must be bad.

"Okay, I'm listening. But please sit, you're hovering is stressing me out." After complying, Damien twists so Hazel has most of his back. She sneers, delicate lip curling back in annoyance at the dismissal.

"Your mother discharged herself from the hospital this afternoon. She'd been there since the attack, complaining of head trauma that didn't show up on any of the scans. They were preparing to dismiss her anyway, but she suddenly perked right up and walked out of her own accord. She knew we had men on her." I maintain his green gaze for a solid minute, then blink and reach for an egg roll.

"Okay... and what? You think she's going to come after me? The *attacked* in that sentence was her," I remind him, taking a large bite. Hazel and Damien share a look of concern, but I'm not worried. "If my mom wanted to kill me, she's had years upon years to do it. And guess what, I'm still right here. She won't make a move, especially not now I have something she wants." Shrugging, I grab a wet wipe and clean my hands, tossing the discarded wipe onto my empty plate.

"And what's that?" Damien follows my movements, lingering over me when I scoff.

"Money. Proof of what she did. She'll want to keep me sweet."

Reaching up on my tiptoes, I come up too short to unhook the hanger and look at Damien expectantly. "Little help here." Like the best ghost stalker ever, he uses the wind to uplift the hanger. Hugging the suit bag to myself, I head upstairs, struggling to keep myself from running. The back-and-forth insults have already started downstairs before I've reached the now-empty spare room. I swear bickering is like foreplay for those two.

All that remains in my grandparent's old room are a few boxes, neatly tucked into the corner, and a full-length mirror. The rest went into storage or were donated to charity since I won't have any use for old bric-a-brac. Not when a platinum AMEX with my name on it will provide everything I'll ever want and more from now on. Yet all I want is something I can't buy. Shadowing me in the mirror's reflection, Hunter's hands stroke down the length of my arms to the suit bag.

"Try it on for me, baby." And who am I to disagree? Holding Hunter's stormy gaze, I peel off my sweats. Naked and ready. Open-minded and willing to be played like his puppet. He drinks in the sight of my body with a hungry stare, and no matter how long I stand there, or how heavy my breasts grow for him, he doesn't move. The tic in his jaw is enough torture for us both so I guide the dress from its confines and step into it.

Thank God for my full-figured genes deriving from my father's side. Not like the twig-skinny clones my mother and her sisters spend too much time under the knife to maintain. My grandmother's dress hugs my every curve as if it was made for me. The satin skates against my flesh, heightening every sensation tenfold. I'm dizzy with how much I want this man to touch me, to take me, but another emotion overrides it all.

One too pressing to ignore.

"I'm going to wear this tomorrow, to your funeral," I state, chewing on my bottom lip. Closing the minor distance between us, Hunter's solid chest presses against my back. Just in time, before I swooned at the sight of his beautiful face. I will fall so hard, I'll land on my ass.

"You didn't have to fuss about laying me to rest. I don't need closure. I've got everything I want, right here." His hands skate around my middle, holding me in place. In our reflection, we slot together like a king and queen. His suit against my gown, a portrait worthy of the penthouse walls if I were vain enough to stare upon it each day. Being kept as a secret from the world, my dirty passion wrapped up into a gorgeous man that only I can see.

"That's not the point. You died for me. You lost everything you'd worked so hard for, and traded it in for being my personal phantom. You chose me, Hunter. Above all else, you choose me. Now, I'm choosing you. You mattered and you matter still. The least I can do is show the world what a king you were before that monster stole you not only from the world but from me."

"You say that like it's a bad thing." Hunter nuzzles my neck, not interested in my guilt. Or anyone's it would seem. "I don't care for people pretending they liked me one last time. Choosing you was never a choice, love. It was a necessity, just like breathing. Besides, who's even going—the hired help? Those slackers would do anything for a day off." Rolling my eyes, I nudge him away and turn in the space between his arms. Trust him to take a tender moment and turn it into a joke.

"Actually, I found some of your family members." Shock passes over Hunter's face as I reach up to link my arms around his neck. "Anyways, this isn't about you. I need to alleviate my guilt for your sacrifice. People need to know you were my hero, even if I never asked you to be."

"Whatever you need, Siren. Always." His lips press on mine then, so firmly, not even the separation of the veil can stop my heart from bursting. A thousand butterflies break free of my chest, making a beeline for Hunter's. Time slows. Barely passing at all from inside the cocoon of our passion. A fever rushes through my entire body, leaving me breathless. I open to him, allowing the slow pace of his tongue to skate over mine as it seeks to entwine our souls with the very notion.

It's like electricity pulsating in my veins.

An entwining of essences that emerge as one.

"I've decided to take a leap of faith in us," I breathe against his lips. The stubble on his jaw pushes against the veil, very gently rubbing against my cheek in a bid to get closer.

"Is that so?" He smirks like he finds me cute.

"Mmhmm. I want you. I choose you." Pulling back just enough for the swirling silver of his eyes to meet mine, Hunter regards me carefully. Hinged on my words as if he's been waiting too long to hear this. Too long to feel the ferocity of his emotions reciprocated. "Dare I say, I think I'm falling in love with you, Hunter North." The next time his lips connect with mine, there's no holding back and nothing else to say as I give myself over to the spirit who's unknowingly had my soul this entire time.

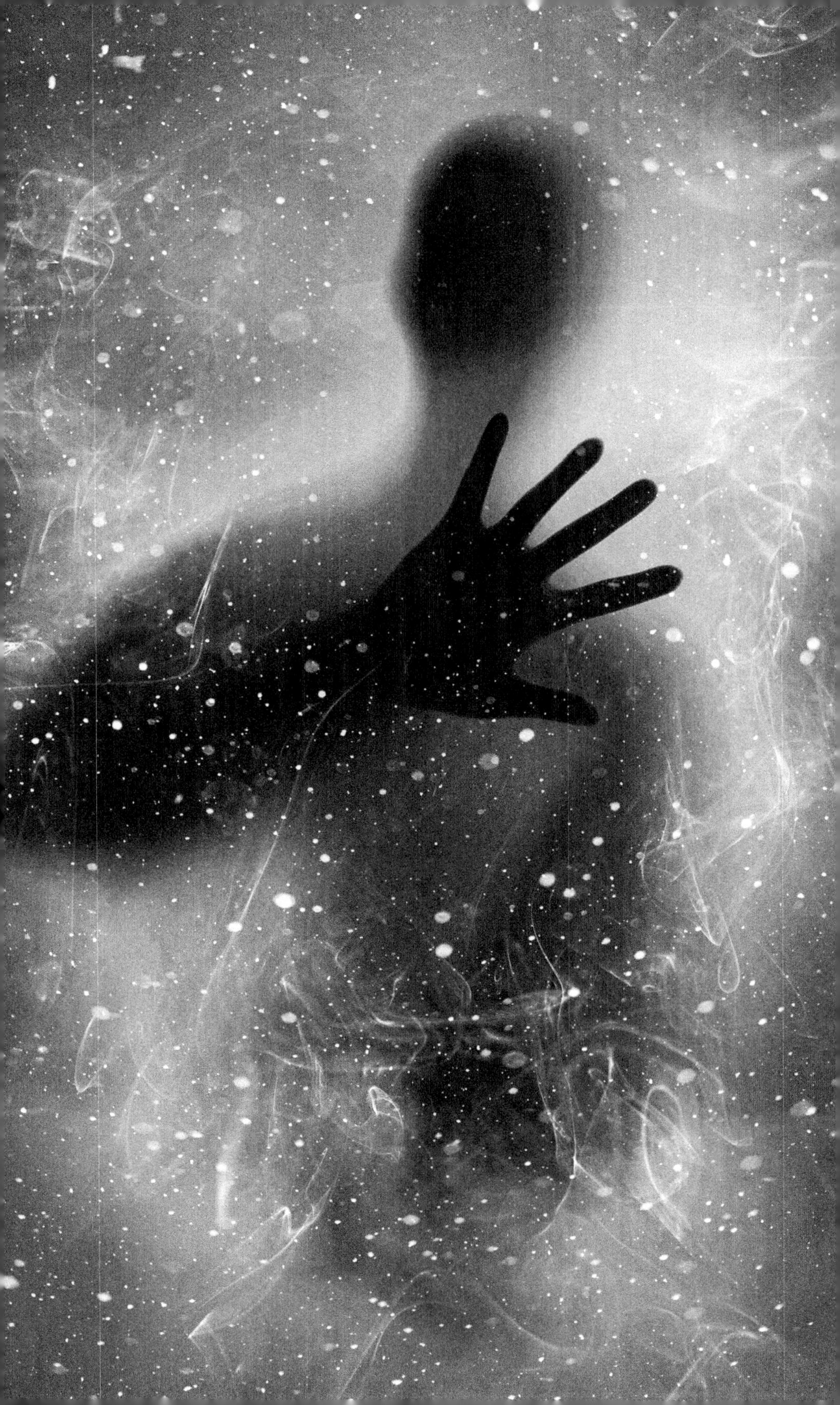

CHAPTER
FORTY-ONE

Hunter
House On A Hill - The Pretty Reckless

The smell of sweet roses mixes with the heady scent of pine and woodlands. It's a funny thing when you die, getting to finally smell yourself the way other people did in life.

But I couldn't mistake the scent anywhere. It's a perfect concoction of myself and Astra.

I stand in the darkness, staring at the hundred blue orchids that line the way up to the funeral home. The smell oozing from them potent, that they even reach me in the darkness. I never really knew how I felt about my funeral, the thought of having one even though I'm dead seemed so far misplaced, I never really gave it much thought. Now I'm not really sure how to put one thought in front of the other and head inside.

Astra did everything, pulled from me small details I never even knew I had to offer and pinned me down with everything I never even knew that I would have wanted. The fact that she went out of her way to mix those flowers with the scent of us has something strange happening to my soul. It's like a soft quivering, a waver in my dark resolve.

All I have ever known was my sweet obsession. I knew that she would have been mine one way or another, but knowing she is now as open to me as I have always been to her, is a strange sensation.

After a moment, and watching the final people that wish to show their respects head inside I finally muster up the courage to follow slowly behind. Walking up six simple steps seems to take a lifetime and I chuckle at how narrow that time frame truly is. "House On A Hill" by The Pretty Reckless begins to play softly in the distance and I still. The song I had played on repeat fills my ears with the soft hum of the angelic voice that instantly soothes me. This song always reminded me of everything. Every emotion I've ever held inside coiled into one song that just reached my soul.

I never truly knew how I felt about it.

Just that I truly love it and after not even a week at the penthouse, my little siren has already learned so much about me. She did it all herself, picking out the funeral home, handling all of the arrangements and now we're here. Actually laying me to rest.

It's been a busy week, with all hands on deck in trying to locate her mother after she went missing from the hospital. But despite everything she had going on in her own life, she refused to slow down. Refused to stop and leave all of this unnecessary shit till a later date.

I was already dead and I sure as fuck wasn't going anywhere.

But she said I had already suffered enough. That this is the only thing she could truly do for me and that she would be damned if she never did it right.

If only she knew that she had done so much more than plan some funeral.

As I enter the funeral hall, there are hundreds of people seated on either side of the room. Probably more than half of which I've never even spoken to. That's the name of the game though. Doing what I did. Working with the people I used to. I see most of my cousins sitting in the front rows, none of which I've truly spoken to in years.

Not after everything with my own parents. I spent my life building a fortune and helping the needy. I never had time for anything beyond that, beyond building my escape from misery. Don't get me wrong, I've always been there when they needed me. But other than that, we were most definitely estranged.

They all have tears in their eyes, leaning on one another and despite how much my heart wants to ache for them, there's only one person I'm interested in comforting.

Astra.

She sits beside Damien, Hazel, and Jess. Her ocean eyes are glossy as she stares forward, overwhelmed with the sea of people sitting at her back but she refuses to allow them even to become a factor. I stalk toward them, Damien noticing my presence, shifts closer to Hazel who narrows her eyes at him in confusion. I slip into the space easily, sitting beside her as I take her hand in mine. Her lower lip trembles, the pain etched into her face as a barbed wire coiled around my chest. I gulp, wanting her to see me, but she couldn't see anything other than the space in front of her, trying to hold onto her resolve.

"You did good, Siren. Really good," I praise and her lashes flutter, water welling along her lower lash line.

She clears her throat, the music dwindles to an end and a suited man stands up in the front and nods his head toward Astra. My coffin is stretched wide in front of us. The American Flag draped across it pinned down by my medals and more blue orchids. The smell of them is even stronger in this enclosed space. I'm shook, unnerved by the fact she found this out about me when not even Damien knew that I served. I was young and enlisted as soon as I could in order to get away from my father. It's something I've never spoken about and something nobody knows. Not even my cousins. I disappeared for years and when I came back, I was a different man holding the world in the palm of his hand. My huge portrait stands on a stand beside it and I gulp, brows furrowed. My soul is at war with so much turmoil which seems to flicker between the peace of this life and the anguish I left behind in the life of the living.

With shaky legs, she stands and walks toward the dais along the front. My gaze squints confused, not expecting her to make a speech for me. To stand up tall before all of these people and address them in any kind of way.

She clears her throat and stares at her feet before she brings her eyes swimming with glossy tears, up to the people sitting before her. "I know that most speeches are given over the grave. When we whisper our words to the dead and hope they carry those words with them to their eternal rest. I'm not going to do that and Hunter isn't going to be buried. I'm going to do this right here, right now, because my words aren't for Hunter. They're for everyone sitting here today who hardly even knew him."

I sit up a little straighter, on the edge of my seat as my entire focus zeros in on her. My angelic beauty, a glowing grace in a sea of darkness. I could find my way back to her anywhere with how bright she shines. My beacon in the storm, guiding me safely back to land on rocky seas.

"It's become more than apparent these last few weeks how the world saw him. Huge dollar signs and fancy suits. So many questions floated around about his network but not one person spoke to me about the man. The man who created multiple foundations for domestic abuse, saving women and children and in some cases, even men, from violent relationships alongside multiple foundations on mental health. Hunter would oversee every single case. When somebody was moved to a safe house, he'd be there to make sure he could hold their hand through the hardest time of their life. He donated so much money to schools and scholarships. Making sure that anybody who received his grant, got first-hand knowledge on how to run an empire." Her voice shakes, and I have the urge to go to her. It's a physical ache to restrain myself, but I know she will fall apart if I surround her right now. "He was a God amongst men and not one person ever saw that. So, I'm here to tell you. Anybody who knew Hunter, who got to look into those storm-brewed eyes, wasn't only blessed, but damn right fucking stupid for not seeing the hero underneath. This man died saving my life from a monster. So when you utter the name Hunter North, you better utter this." She turns, facing me, not giving a shit about who the fuck thinks it's odd that she addresses the crowd instead of my photo stretched wide beside her. "Hunter North was an amazing man. A loving man. His work will be remembered and the man will be missed. Because he was a fucking *good* man. And the world is worse off without him." She sniffles, widening her shoulders and straightening her back. "I'll miss him. I'll love him and I'll regret every single day that I never got to know him."

I inhale deeply, my fingers ghosting across the apple of my cheek when something strange feathers across it, slipping down like a strange apparition that tickles against my lower lip.

Tears.

I'm numb.

But I'm crying.

I'm crying for her love and for the beauty of her words.

Being in limbo is a mind fuck, being so overwhelmed with having no way to express it is hurting more than if I was open to the pain. I need this woman, I need her like the soul needs some kind of astral plan to survive. I get up and stalk toward her, the low hush of the murmured mourners fades and all that is left is me and her. Hands in her hair, neck craned back, I kiss her.

But this kiss is different from the rest.

This kiss is cosmic.

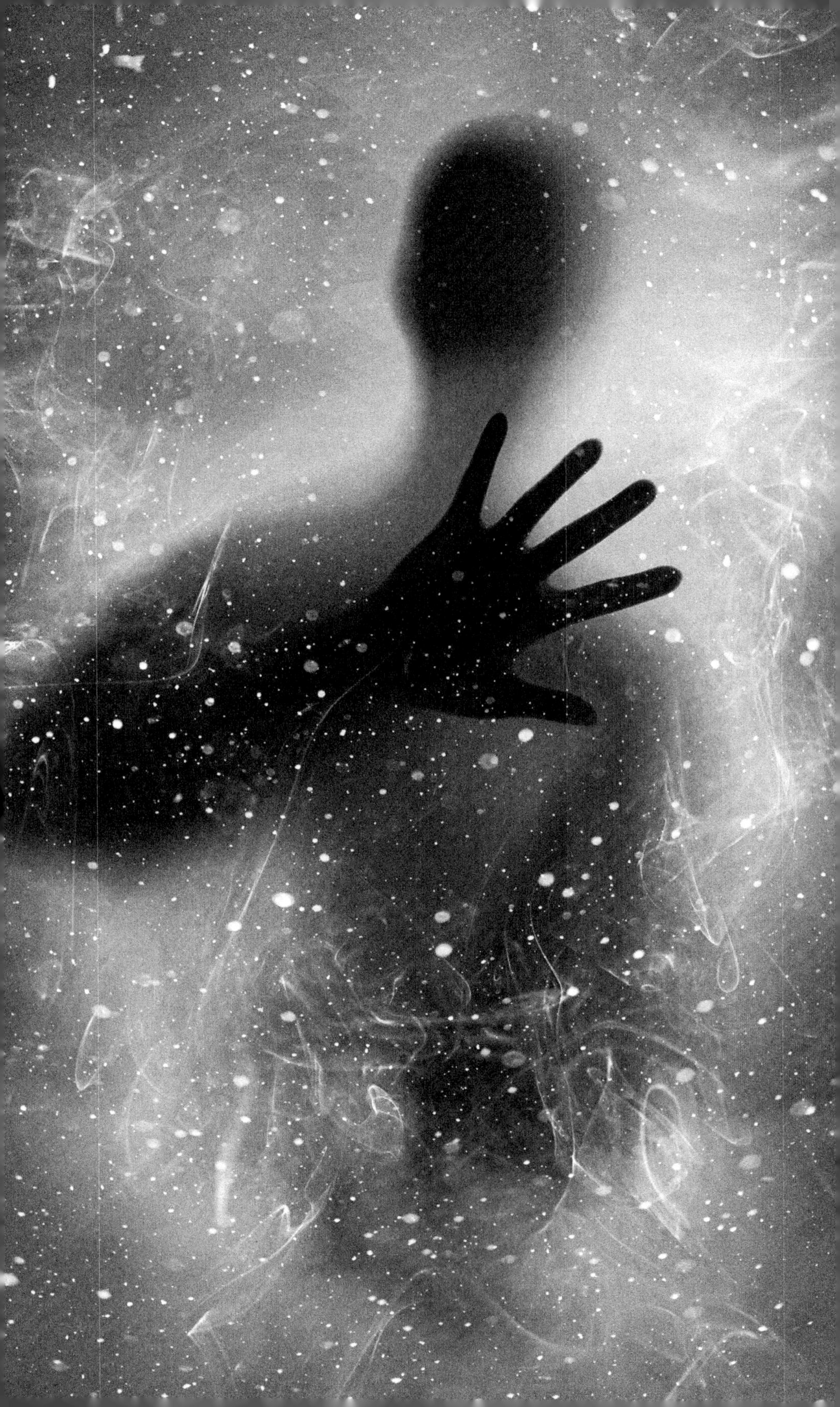

CHAPTER
FORTY-TWO

Hunter
Love U To Death - DeathByRomy

I stand by Astra's side as a silent comfort in her time of need as she greets every person who attended my funeral and forces them to look into her pain-filled eyes before they can exit. She blocks the doorway like a proud goddess and refuses to give any one of them a reprieve.

My cousin steps up next, a male tall and blond like her just behind, extending her trembling hand to clasp Astra's firmly. "Thank you. What you said? It was beautiful. I'm Julie, and this is my brother Logan. Hunter was a proud man. He never liked asking anyone for help. Never liked leaning on anybody. I'm glad he found someone who didn't give him a choice."

"Yeah, I don't know how you got that man to stop playing a fool because our cousin was like a damn pitbull, but we are grateful. I just wish he knew how much we loved him." Logan's brown eyes shimmer and I find myself reaching for Astra's hand. She holds mine tightly and I've never felt more grounded.

"Believe me, he knew," she offers kindly and Julie smiles at her softly.

"Tell them," I choke, clearing my throat. "Tell them to never stop the Fourth of July, okay? Tell them to always take the boat out. To do it to remember me," I ask Astra to relay my message.

She inhales deeply and says, "He told me about the Fourth of July. I know he would have wanted you to continue doing it. To honor him."

Logan chuckles, shaking his head as he looks down at Julie. "He told you about that?" he asks smugly.

"Did he tell you how we acquired our boat?" Julie licks her lips as her large doe-eyes much like her older brothers light up. "We'd steal them. Every year, we'd pinch them from some fucked-up asshole that had pissed Hunter off in one way or another. We'd sneak off, blow some stuff up and then get one of Hunter's helicopters to airdrop us home and leave the boat out there in the middle of the ocean." Tears well in her wavering eyes as the first one falls. "That was the only time we ever really saw him."

Astra sniffles, refusing to let her own tears fall as she places a soft hand on my cousin's shoulder. "Don't ever stop believing, he'll always be with you."

"Thank you. How did you meet him?" Logan asks, curiosity in his chocolate eyes.

Astra outright laughs. "That is one hell of a story. I'll have to tell you about it over coffee sometime."

"We'll hold you to it." Logan grins, wrapping his arm around his sister as they say their sweet goodbyes and descend the stairs.

I'm too busy watching them go. My only remaining family members. There's a longing in my chest, that I don't even notice the next person who steps up to Astra. "It's all bullshit, you know. Hunter only ever cared about himself."

"And who exactly are you?" Astra snaps back with such disdain in her voice, that even I recoil. Turning back, I baulk when I see who stands before her.

"I was his girlfriend once. Right before he called me out of the blue one day and told me to get on a plane and go back home. That he was done with me. Just. Like. That," Amber hisses. "Hunter North was a bastard."

I feel the strike before I hear it, the resounding smack that cracks across Amber's face like a whip. I hiss, shoulders drawing high to my ear as I pull a face that best represents the ' *oh fuck, I bet that hurt* ' look. Astra has Amber's head spinning, her cheek blossoming a red hot shade of scarlet.

"Don't be a bitter bitch, darling. It doesn't become you. Hunter was an amazing man, a slightly morally gray kind of man but still the best, and I will not have you stand in front of me and insult him. So do yourself a favor and walk on by before you have to be carried away," she utters, calmer than I've ever seen her. The woman who can put on a collective calmness better than anyone I know. And damn if watching her defend me doesn't get my dick fucking hard.

Amber's blonde hair falls like a veil across her face, dark eyes of fury peer through the strands before she straightens again and glares back at Astra. "Be thankful he's dead. He'd only have done the same to you," Amber offers as departing words that were intended to hammer the final nail into the coffin.

But Astra isn't having any of it. Fisting the hair at the back of Amber's head, she drags her out into the open and shoves her to her knees. Reigning over her as my loyal queen, she remains calm, unfazed like she has all the faith she needs in us that Amber's words do not penetrate her hardened heart. I smirk, watching my woman go.

Amber whimpers, putting on a stellar performance for the mini fling we had. I was hardly even with her for a month. Going through the motions of what I thought a visceral man should be doing instead of what I wanted to be doing.

Finding love.

Or in our case, obsession.

As soon as I laid eyes on Astra, I knew Amber had to fuck right off.

She was nothing to me, she was right about that. But so far from the truth in telling Astra, I would have done the same to her. Death couldn't even part us. Did she think stupid words would?

"Damien," Astra beckons and without another word, he lifts Amber from the ground.

"On it." He nods at Astra. "Come on, no one likes a sour puss. He was with you for like five minutes. I've taken shits that lasted longer than that." And then he shoves her into the arms of another guard who hauls her away crying.

It's her own fault.

"Do you see? Do you see what I mean, Eleanor? My little girl has lost her sanity, out here assaulting people." A shrill voice makes my ears bleed.

Astra's eyes find mine, and together we turn to face her mother, Celest. A woman in a loose pantsuit stands beside her, a bunch of men in white coats standing at their back.

"Rest assured, Celest. Our facilities are the best. We will help her," the woman responds so coldly, so distantly that I step in front of my girl, for what good it'll do. One of the white coats stands a head above the rest, glaring at Astra with chilling, almost black eyes.

"What facilities," I growl, drawing Damien to flank Astra's left, his hand on his gun.

"Are you insane? What the fuck are you doing here? Why would you show up knowing that the second you do, the cops will be here to throw your ass in jail for what you did to my brother and father?" Astra spits with venom, stepping through me to get closer to her mother. Her shoulders are bunched, her fists clenched, already on the defense.

I grab her wrist, halting her movement, not liking the look of this at all. I share a weary look with Damien whose nostrils flare in trepidation. The white coats stealthily move out, subtly circling us. Gives us enough room to not sense the threat that is lingering, but I do.

I fucking sense it.

"See, there she goes again. More deluded lies. Oh, my poor baby girl. It's okay, the hospital will help you right now." Celest brings a withered hand to her chest, inhaling deeply as the crinkles around her eyes deepen, showing her true age as she feigns anguish and heartfelt concern.

"What the fuck are you talking about?" Astra exclaims, her temper getting the best of her as she rips free of my hold and toward her mother with steam practically blowing from her ears.

"Damien, it's a trap," I sneer.

The men in white coats pounce the second there is space between Astra and Damien and I fly into a rage. The first set of fingers coil around her upper arm, and I lash out, bending them back. The man squeals, crying out as she lets go abruptly when the bones pop with a satisfactory snap.

Astra kicks and screams, doing everything she can to avoid the violation of having her personal space invaded by these vicious men who are doing everything they can to restrain her. One of them brings out a straitjacket the thick straps glistening under the dim light of day and when I try to punch the idiotic look on his stupid face, my fist flies straight through him.

"Damien, stop them!" I roar, the winds around me picking up in speed with my outrage.

He pulls his gun and points it at Celest and Eleanor. "Stand down and order them to stop! Or I will shoot," he demands and Celest scoffs, indifferent and utterly unbothered.

"Like you would out here, in the open, with witnesses. I am her mother. It is my legal right to have her committed. She needs help, boy. And trust me, she'll get it."

Astra kicks ass, fighting with the vengeance of the last few hurtful months that have passed. She uses her father's training and wards of each attack, all until a needle is plunged into the side of her neck and my soul turns eerily cold. I shiver, something inside of me feeling repulsively wrong when her sweet eyes flutter closed and she falls limp in their arms.

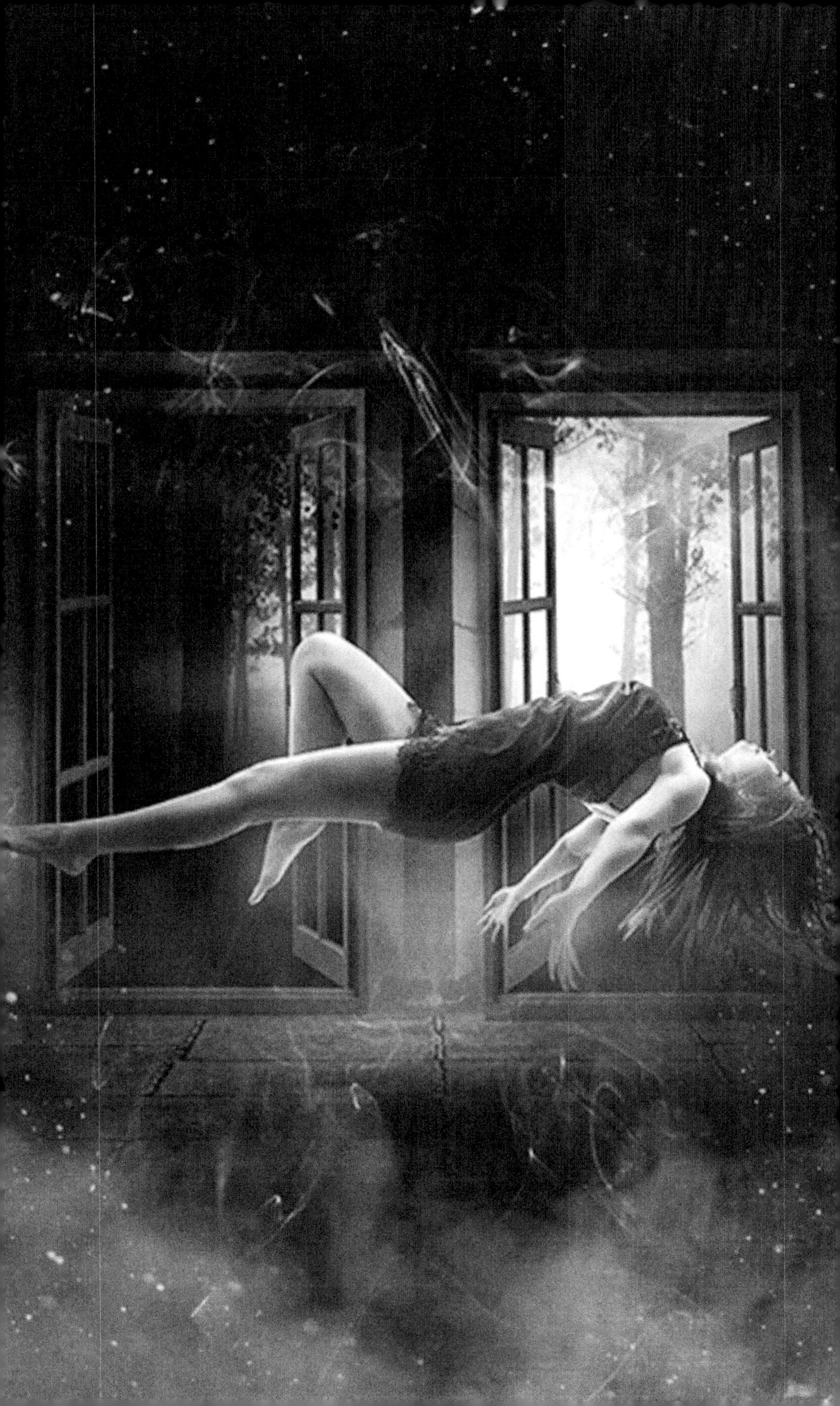

CHAPTER
FORTY-THREE

Astra
Mad Hatter - Melanie Martinez

My head feels foggy and there is such a sharp pain shooting down my limbs that makes me gasp, a small exhale that whispers past my dry lips. Trying to lift my arm, it's tugged back down by a hard restraint and I wince. The pain in my wrist throbs like a hot iron. Something cold and rough chafes against my skin and my arms fall slack in order to try and retreat from the pain. Blinking open my eyes, it takes me a few attempts because they stick, glued shut by God knows what. After a few attempts, I'm no better off when I manage to open them into a room full of darkness. There are no windows, no light. Nothing but shadows darker than the onyx abyss I'm lying in the middle of, dancing above whatever I'm lying on.

"It's okay, Siren. I'm here. I'm going to get you out," Hunter whispers. The soft presence he exudes is the only thing keeping me sane in the darkness.

I can feel his temper, his scorching wrath. But none of that fury allows his fingers to undo these vicious restraints. He fumbles, trying to unbuckle them, but throwing something is a lot easier than trying to undo something and I can feel his devastation like it is my own. Hell, maybe it is. "Dammit! I have to go get Damien. I have to tell him where you are. I'll be back, okay, love? I'll be back."

I turn my head, my neck cracks and water fills my eyes, but I'm not sure it's from panic. Something pins my head to what feels like a bed, a strap of some kind stretched taut across my forehead. Both my ankles were bound as well.

I'm cold when he leaves. Left to freeze in this well of ice.

I feel funny, this moving sensation inside of my chest that makes me feel like I've been drugged is weighing me down. Trying to remember what happened, everything comes back to me in broken flashes. The funeral, Hunter, his family, that stuck-up bitch he used to date, and...

My mother.

Bile rises in the back of my throat and a slow reality dawns. She had been there, at the funeral with strange people. I was so angry, so enraged when I saw her it consumed me and beyond ripping her face off, my surroundings were trivial. It takes a moment, a moment for my ears to open and connect with the receptors of my brain but when they finally meet in the middle, a low hum surrounds me and I realize that I'm not alone. There is someone sitting next to me. Heavy enough that I can tell it's a person, light enough that I can guess it's a woman. The song she's humming sounds familiar and I blow out a harsh breath when I finally recognize it. It's a nursery rhyme my mother made up, one she used to sing to me and my brother. It used to be our lullaby but now it's the tune of my nightmare, coming from a woman I have a crazed compulsion to hurt.

She took *everything* from me!

Through the darkness, where madness dwells, under the moon, mommy dances with her little elves.

I forgot she used to call us that.

Her little elves.

Now I'm grown, it feels like some crap she threw together without any thought other than just getting us to go to sleep. I know her now, and I can't imagine those years I used to lay in the arms of my mother were anything more than innocent delusions that made my young heart feel like she loved us. She was different then, warm. But something insidious took over the body of the mother I once knew.

Back then, before I knew the truth about her, about how fucking vile a human being she is, I used to long for the nights when she would tuck us in and sing this to us. It was soothing, coming from a mother who I had thought loved us. Not a woman who was clawing her way through life searching for things above her entitlement.

This world owes us nothing, but she has never learned that.

No matter how hard my dad worked, she always wanted more. Lived above her means, and in the end, the entire family suffered for it.

My breathing hitches, but I don't speak. I've lost my words, all syllables eluding me as I lay here and silently cry while she strokes my hair, allowing the sorrow of my past to trickle down my wet cheeks. "I know you're awake, Astra," she whispers in a low, soft voice. A vast lie to the woman she truly is. "I'm sorry sweetie, there was no other way. I needed to do this. For you, for your safety. "

I don't say anything, no words are needed to explain the things she has done to me. Hideous thoughts run through my head. The darkness around me was only a manifestation of the darkness that has long since been brewing in my heart.

I want to hurt her.

I *need* her to suffer as much as I have.

"I never meant to kill them, Astra. You have to know that. After Henry left the service, money was tight and he knew that, but he opened the tattoo parlor with Dean anyway. That place and you kids were his entire life and it was the same for me back then too. I loved him, Astra, oh God, did I love him.

"He had given me so many years of happiness and two beautiful children, but as much as I wished it was enough, it never was. I always knew there was a better life out there for us than just scraping by. Better than counting every nickel and dime, just waiting for our big break."

Her voice cracks, and I break into a silent sneer, my eyes burning like fire through the obsidian shadows and I hope more than anything she can feel the fucking burn.

"I had gotten us into some trouble. Financially. I realized how bad my shopping addiction was. How much I used credit cards to fill the hole of whatever it was that I was missing." The weight of her hand feels like boulders on my head and I try to move away from her touch, but she refuses to break the connection.

"It was me, there was something wrong with me. I had everything a girl could dream of, and it just wasn't enough. I made a plan to set the fire, to claim on the insurance. They were never supposed to be there, Astra. Henry and Lucas were never supposed to be there!"

It sounds like there's a small sob threatening to break free from what I sense to be trembling lips but I'll be dead before I show her an ounce of mercy. She did this, and ever since their death, she has turned into a money-grabbing whore and the worst mother ever.

She saw a black hole and thought it would be a good idea to play beside it, allowing it to swallow her whole instead of running for the fucking hills.

Who drugs their kids?

This bitch is a new brand of fucked up.

"After that, I couldn't live with myself. I had lost my baby. The love of my life. I had to find a way to move on."

"By forgetting about the kid you had left? Abandoning her and fucking yourself from marriage to marriage, claiming their insurance, and leaving me to clean up the mess? The debts?" I hiss, turning my head as quickly as a viper and latching my jaw around her hand. I bite down, snapping at her fingers and palm while growling like a feral dog.

The white coats.

The drugs.

It doesn't take a rocket scientist to figure out where the fuck I am.

Celest shrieks, trying to pull her hand away but I'm like a dog with a bone.

A bone this bitch wants to break. I shake my head, unhinged as I'm overcome with the urge to tear her a-fucking-part. I hate her, and I've never truly wanted to murder someone until this very moment. I wanted to watch her burn, to hear her screams as I didn't just kill her, but instead shredded her.

Flaying the flesh from her bones layer by layer to expose the rotten shit that lingers underneath.

I fucking despise her.

A sharp sting that flitters across my cheek tells me she's just slapped me, but fuck if I care. All I know is pain thanks to her. Let her hit me again, it will probably turn me on more than it will convince me to let this cunt go.

A black door painted the same shade as the black walls and black ceilings opens and a stark light floods me from beyond the other side. I recoil, eyes clenching shut as I retreat and turn my head back toward the shadows, hoping for a reprieve and praying that I won't be freaking blind once this is done. I shiver and convulse, trying to break free from my shackles, but I'm held down, hard and fast.

"Why you vicious little bitch! Do you know why I never loved you after they died? Because it took their death for me to realize just how wrong you are. A nasty little slut with a pure and utter dark seed in your black heart. I hated you, Astra, because you weren't them! I have to live with that every day. I might not be a good person, but what's done is done and I'll be dammed if I allowed you to ruin my fortune now. Burrows Psychiatric hospital is the best place for you now. That will fix all those nasty little thoughts in your head, darling. Don't you worry about a thing now."

I can hear her heels clatter along the ground, the noise fading into the distance when she leaves the door, strolls down a corridor, and takes a corner away from the cold, and the dark room she's left me in.

"Hunter!" I cry, wondering where he is.

Why I can't feel him anymore and why hasn't he come back?

I feel utterly alone, my eyes falling heavy due to the illusion of the room.

She's put me in a mental hospital, the fact they have a black box which is a form of torture that breaks somebody's psyche, tells me that whatever is about to happen next, won't be good at all.

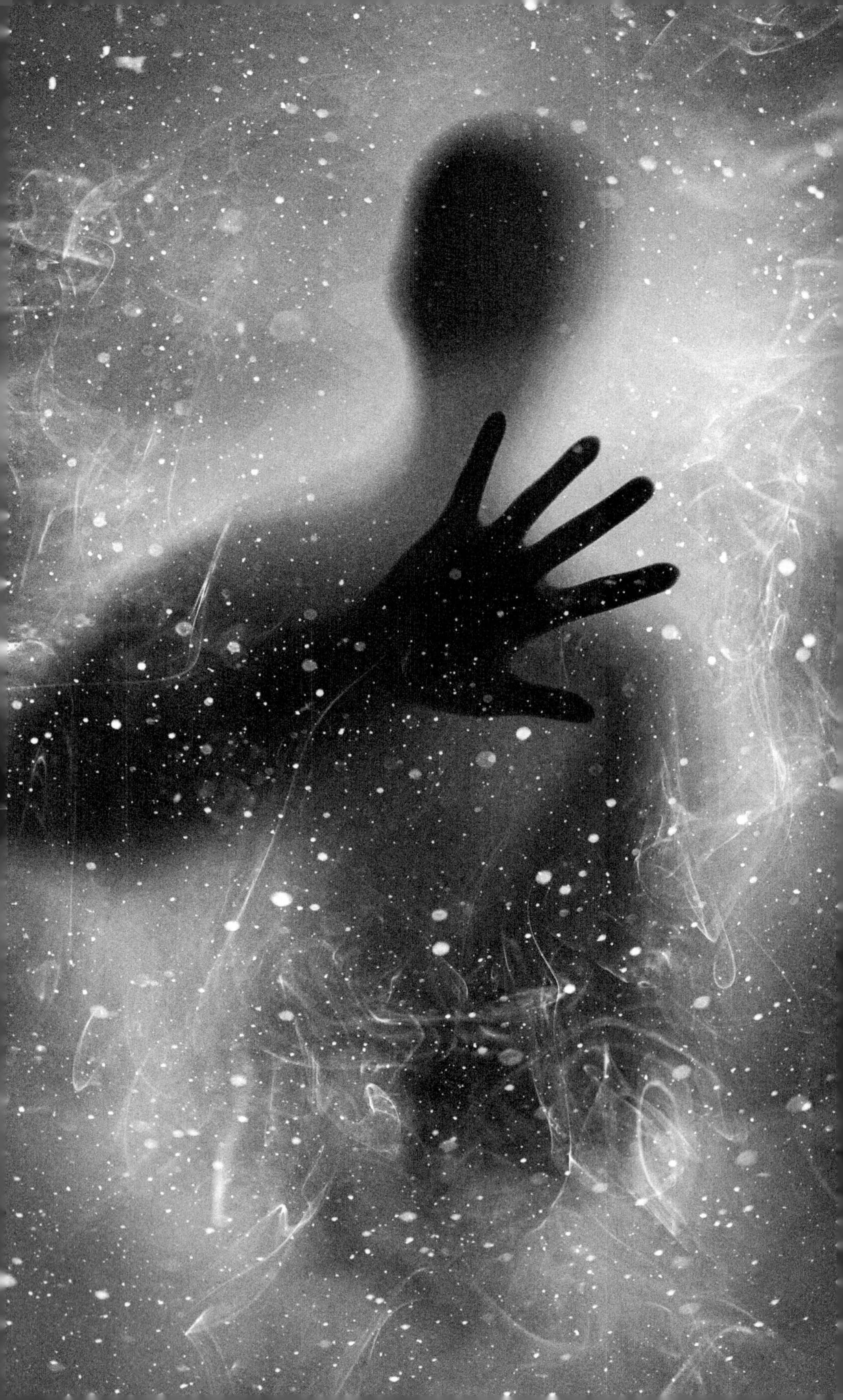

CHAPTER
FORTY-FOUR

Hunter
Drag Me To The Grave - Black Veil Brides

Getting back to Damien felt like it took forever. He is a man good at his job, so that little '*you won't shoot in a public place*' is bullshit. He very much would and most certainly has. At the end of the day, he's hired for protection. His charge was at risk. He was well within his legal rights to take fire and when he did, he took out one of the white coats. The other two got to Astra before he could though, and once she was in harm's way, he was helpless. He followed the car with a few of the other guards that were stationed for Astra and my family's protection as far as he could until he lost them.

Damn fucking funeral cars were everywhere and a mass of strangers coming to pay their fake ass respects is the reason he lost the love of my life to the crowd.

I'm furious and that kind of anger burning under my heels in the land of a place made to be paradise is fucking dangerous.

"Where is she?" he shouts as soon as I step through the walls of the Penthouse. Jess and Hazel are sitting on the large couch staring at him in trepidation. Both of them are in clear distress but I don't have time to care about their mentality right now.

Every second that I waste, is a second my girl is scared and alone.

"Burrows Psychiatric Hospital. Her fucknut mother had her committed."

"To discredit the PI's findings or to convince the judge her daughter made it all up?" he asks as he charges across the room and to the panel that has a secret security code. Once he taps it in, small little display cabinets pop up all around the Penthouse with single guns and ammo stashed inside each one.

When you're worth as much as I was, you can't take risks with safety.

"This just gets creepier. It was one thing when Astra was attacked and she told us about Hunter and Theo. It's another thing to have the man who is supposed to be protecting us talk to dead men!" Hazel exclaims, eyes clenched shut tightly like if she just doesn't look, none of this will be happening.

Damien loads his weapon and secures it into his holster, before walking back over to her and falling to his knees. With a gentle hand on her thigh, she gasps and her eyes flutter open at the contact. She stares back at him in awe and my brows furrow at the intimate connection. Damien is usually much more reserved than this.

"We don't have time to hold your hand right now. We have to go get our girl, okay? I need you to breathe for me and be here for one another alright?" he soothes, rubbing small circles on her bare thigh with his thumb.

She nods, swallowing thickly before offering him a small smile. "You're right. I'm sorry. None of that matters now, just go get Astra."

"I've got her, don't worry about us. Just be quick. She's already been through too much!" Jessica inserts, face fierce as she stares at Damien in a clear warning.

She will have his balls if he doesn't bring her home safely.

I don't even have the energy to correct him on the fact that she is very much my girl, but I appreciate the fact he gives a shit. He fell for her just as quickly as I did. Although, his devotion to her is more like a brother.

Mine?

Well... very much like a stalker.

"Grab the paperwork and get it to the right people, there is no way this bitch is getting away with this. I want the book thrown at her and then I want her past to fucking bury her! Nobody hurts what's mine and gets away with it," I sneer, catching his attention as he stands back to his feet. Nostrils flared he takes off into my bedroom to get what I asked. Hazel sniffles, fighting back her tears before she squares her shoulders.

"Right, then we need to do our part," she declares.

"Which is?" Jess asks.

"Making her happy. The world knows she deserves it. Let's just find everything that she likes. Pack it all up. I don't know. We just have to do something to take away her pain."

Clearing her throat, Jess stands to her feet pulling Hazel with her. "You're right."

"Damien, leave another guard on the girls," I shout, intent on turning my ass around and heading back to my woman when something strange coils around the apparition of my chest. I look down, seeing my essence waver, and know instantly that something is wrong.

I'm sucked from the Penthouse, tossed through time before I pop back up in a darkened corner of a large but dimly lit office. I squint through the shadows, hearing voices coming from down the hall. This office is empty, so I follow the sound with a frown on my lips and a furrow creasing my thick brows.

What the fuck just happened?

I look around, edging out of the room slowly, wondering if this will be another attack from Theo. There are multiple offices, all sectioned by huge glass doors with fancy names scrawled across each one. Plush black carpets cover the expanse of the office floor, the hallway all deep and dark woods that shine under the dim mood lighting.

Fuck this, I don't have time to expect an attack, I need to get back to Astra.

I'm just about to put all of my energy into sensing her, pulling my essence back toward its home, to the one place where it belongs, when the shrill annoyance of a voice that grates against my soul like a bad rash reaches my ears. I still, head tilting like a feline in the wild as my null heart begins to pick up at a slow and steady pace like a predator ready to pounce on its fat and juicy prey.

"I don't know what she has on me, all I know is that she knows. Right now, I've handled the situation. She is in Burrows Psychiatric Hospital. But God knows who she's told. Have you seen my face, David? The little bitch went feral when she saw me. Almost killed me," Celest whines, slender legs crossed as she leans back in a large, curved back chair. Her tirade is animated, aged hands waving in the air. "I should have aborted that child at birth. I knew she'd be nothing but trouble. Why did she have to dredge up the past? Everything was fine. The dust was settled."

"You did kill her entire family, Celest. How did you expect the girl to act? You know, you have grown into a cold, cold woman in all of the years that I've known you. There was a time when you loved your kids, both of them." David shakes his head, leaning back in his comfortable chair as he steeples his fingers together, lower lip between his overly white teeth and his brows furrow in thought. "What happened to you?"

"That woman died when everything that I loved died. She perished, David. In the ashes with the rest of her heart."

"And Astra?"

"I killed her too. The day I took away her heroes. She was never the same, David. I broke my little girl and when I lost it all, I lost myself." She hushes, the apathetic tone to her high-pitched voice, slow and withdrawn as she stares into the distance of her miserable past. "Besides," she scoffs, waving off everything else like it means absolutely nothing. "Nothing dries the tears quite like money, David. Now, can you get me out of this? Deem her insane and any of her finds as fraud or fabricated?"

A hurricane of fury consumes me. The fickle way they speak of everything my siren has been through, devastates me. This evil woman is so flippant in what she's done and her only excuse is that she thought she had already hurt Astra so she had no problem hurting her some more.

Blinded by a deep-rooted agony, I fly across the room. Finding a strength I never knew possible, I intend to wring Astra's mother's neck. Instead, I trip and fall through the desk and right into David's sitting body who quivers, right before my world spins, and I'm suddenly looking across the desk staring at a frustrated-looking Celest.

"Well?" she huffs, her regal class fading in place of her irritation. "Will I win this?"

I feel funny, almost foreign. My limbs are heavy and sluggish like I've just dove into the sea fully clothed and now have to start the long trek home. I wiggle my shoulders, aged hands flat on my softer thighs. Purple veins slither under my skin, showing me the true age of the fucker I've possessed. I clear my throat, Celest's eyes drawn to watching my Adam's apple move as I try to gather my bearings.

I have become so used to being dead, I have forgotten what it felt like to be alive.

Although I have to say being alive and possessing someone feel nothing alike.

I feel wrong, icky, and unsettled like I'm a Russian doll, inside a Russian doll, *inside* a Russian doll. Like there are three of us in here instead of two and I find myself wanting to flee from the crazy sensation.

Then my heavy breathing settles and I remember the benefits.

"Oh for heaven's sake, David. Pull yourself together I don't have all night," Celest berates and I narrow my aged eyes and hike my gray bush brows.

Leaning back in David's chair, I kick my feet up on the desk and instantly regret it when my hip begins to throb and something sharp shoots down into my knee.

Old fucker.

Glad I don't have this to come.

Wincing, I right myself, look back at this bitch who birthed the greatest thing this world has ever been blessed with, and cant my head. Turning my eyes cold and sinister, I take joy in the fact her tanned face turns ashen and uncertainty bleeds into her gaze.

She can finally sense it.

The devious change.

There's a bigger evil in the room now and I'm going to fucking love toying with her.

"What was the question?" I ask, my voice coming out croaky like I haven't spoken in years. I shake it off, my full attention on the woman before me.

"Will I have a case? We can prove she made it all up, right? You have guys for that?" she asks me slowly, then leans back in a small effort to create space between us.

"Oh, Celest. Living in your ivory tower has taught you no good. Not only will I never represent a murderer like you, but money can't always buy everything."

Her features turn quizzical as she removes one leg that is folded across the other and places both her feet flat on the floor. She shifts, sitting up a little straighter and moving to the edge of her seat. "What are you talking about?"

"I'm talking about the fact that Astra won't be in that hospital for another hour let alone the foreseeable future. I'm talking about the fact that she has even more evidence on you than you can imagine and that it is already with the police." I lift my arm, shucking back the sleek gray suit jacket to expose the watch on David's wrist. "A warrant should already be out for your arrest."

Hurrying to her feet, the look of soul-torturing horror flickers across her face as she stumbles back and away from the desk. "Why?" she stammers, tears in her soulless eyes.

I reach for the receiver, dialing security—the phone set up much like the ones I used to have in my office. Standing, I tug on the lapels of my suit and move around the desk striding toward her. Celest backs herself up against the wall. A bookcase between her and the brick causes her to knock titles down onto the ground in her haste.

Once I'm right up into her face, I lean down and whisper into her ear, "Because nobody hurts what's mine."

Then I step back, marveling at the way her chest rises and falls brokenly in her despair. She clutches her arm, the coloring in her botoxed face turning from ashen to a stark white and her breathing becomes all the more scarce. Security stomps down the hall, the ding of the elevator my only indication they're on their way.

Two large frames fill the doorway, thick men with dark hair and fitted suits hurry in. "You called, Sir?" one of them asks.

"David, don't," Celest pleads. "My chest, it hurts." Choking, her knees buckle and I step away allowing her to slump to the ground.

"There is a warrant out for Mrs. Muller's arrest. Please call the authorities and detain her until they arrive," I instruct. "And be advised that she is also having a heart attack." Then I excuse myself from the room and rush to find an empty office.

I have no fucking idea how I got inside this dude's meat-suit, but now I have to get the fuck out so I can go help save my woman.

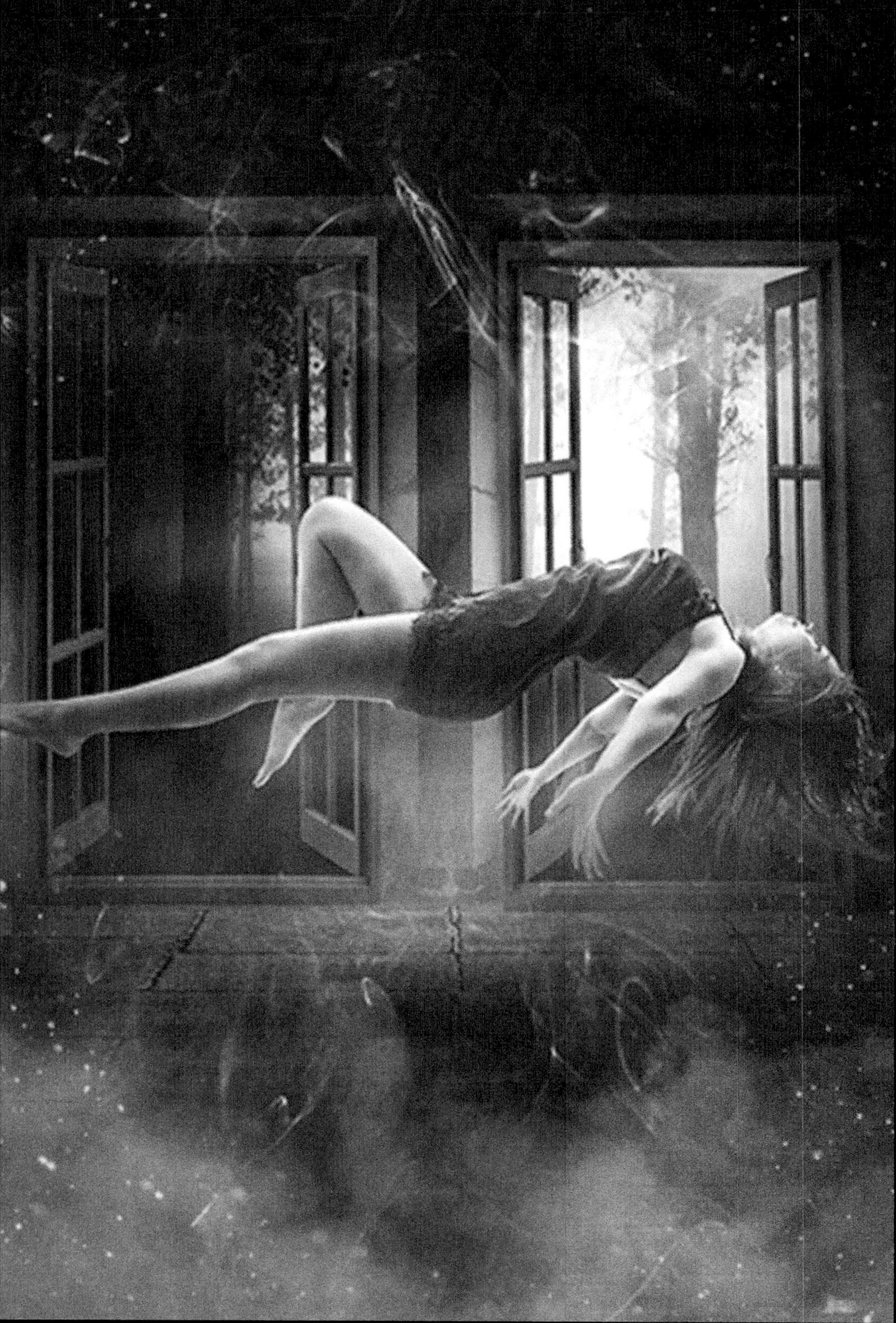

CHAPTER
FORTY-FIVE

Astra
No Saving Me - Framing Hanley

Rough hands fist my hair, pulling my head back and pulling the knotted strands from my scalp. I'm shoved under the cold water, the harsh spray fierce against my pinched face as I shy away from the brutality of the broken shower head. The orderly rips my clothes from my body, leaving me cowering to cover my naked frame from his twisted gaze as he cackles in my ear. Thrown to my knees, I grit my teeth and refuse to cry out. The sting that slashes me across my back from the tail end of his Taser wrist strap makes a welt across my spine.

Slamming my hands down into the puddle of water around me, a wave of it rushes back up to meet me. The icy chill is a refreshing wake-up call when it douses me, forcing me to suck in a harsh breath that leaves me cold.

Fuck modesty.

Nobody hurts me and gets away with it.

When I feel the air around me displace and I can sense the space he has created from lifting back his arm for another strike, I allow my hands to slide out so I can easily roll to my back. Bringing my knees to my chest, I kick out, striking him where it's sure to hurt the most. The scrawny little prick turns blue, his slender cheeks puff out and his eyes bug out of his head. But he doesn't stumble back, so I kick him again, only I'm not fast enough when he brings the Taser down to crash into my ribs and I grunt, the air gathering to leave me in a fractured gasp.

I fight for traction in the water, trying to slide myself back so that I can get away from his towering presence. He's tall but skinny, a lanky little cunt who thinks because he wears a white coat here and is seen as some kind of authoritative figure, that he can do what he wants to his charges. So much anger at the thought of other patients, *genuine* patients being harmed by this man has a tornado of destruction building in my core.

Do you know what it's like to feel helpless? Weak and defenseless against a world that does nothing but take, take and take until you have nothing else left to give? I'm drowning in misery at the stark realization of injustice in this world. No matter how much a person tries to make it better, you will always find someone like this, out to hurt those who can't defend themselves.

Overcome with desperation and fury, I clasp my hands together and squeeze them tightly, creating a wrecking ball. I bring them high above my head before I circle it and bring it down like the thunder of Thor's hammer across the man's head. He slips, falling on top of my naked body, then his slimy hand paws at my flesh in order to try and find his feet again.

Entwining my fingers within the strand of his hair, I pull with all of my might just like he did to me, ripping the roots from his scalp as he screams, crying to the water that chokes him when he arches his head and opens his mouth, swallowing lungfuls of the cold spray of the shower head.

I'm no longer cold, instead burning hot under my temper. My skin warms like the start of a wildfire and before I know the rage in my core has burst from my throat when I scream the loudest. Just like when I was in that fighting cage, I let all of my frustration and anguish collide into a bellow. I scream to the dark skies above us in this horrible little world. Reaching up, my small palms circle his face as I dig my thumbs into his eye sockets. Crimson rivers fall like the tears of death as his eyes begin to bleed but I don't stop.

Nothing can make me stop.

Nothing but the man who crashes through the door like a hurricane ready to destroy the land. In a blur, a dark shadow throws himself on top of us, knocking the orderly from my slim frame as they crash into the rotten tile walls together. The unexpected attack gives me time to scurry away, pushing my back against the frozen tiles. I use the support to get myself back up onto shaky legs. I might be alone and naked, but I sure as fuck am going to fight with everything that I have. The new man is dressed exactly like an orderly too and confusion has me second guessing my actions when I see one of them beat the life out of one of their own.

My defender shows no mercy as he pounds his heavy fist into the other man's face. Bone and cartilage crunch, the loud sound evident as it whispers through the eerie shower room. There is nothing left by the time he is done. His white uniform is saturated in red and that's when I feel it.

The change in the air has my heart skipping a beat in my chest. Time is stolen from my senses and suddenly all I see is him. Crouched down in the darkness, backed up into the corner, the man slowly rises his head. Peering up at me through narrowed slits, I see the dark storm in his eyes. It's an entity of torment all on its own and I'd know it anywhere. Through rugged breathing I rasp, "Hunter."

"Pretty Siren, did you really think I forgot about you? That I never meant it when I told you that if another man laid their hands on you, I'd kill him?" A sick and twisted smirk splits across this strange man's face and even though the features are utterly foreign, all I can see is Hunter staring back at me.

My core flutters as my tummy dips. Something so sexy and fucking hot about having my obsession possess another man and beat the one harming me to death is intoxicating. I close my eyes, my head thrown back as it lolls against the titles. Passion scorches me from the inside out. Pitch black arousal has my pussy suffering third-degree burns from the fire of hell and how badly good this feels to watch.

"Careful, wicked girl. Not even the hands of the man I possess get to touch you."

"Hunter," I rasp, the moan a plea on my lips.

"Soon, Siren. I know you need it, baby, that you need me."

"So fucking bad, I can't take it anymore. I can't take the edging, I can't take the pain. I need a release!" I cry, my deft fingers trailing down between the valley of my breasts.

A commotion starts down the hallway and suddenly I'm being pulled from the wall and tucked into the arms of my sweetest apparition one more time. The lifeless man falls to the ground in a heap, his heavy body weight clapping like the shout of thunder through the room. Hunter stands before me, insistently riding him hard. "We have to go, love. Damien is waiting out back with a car. Bend down, grab the key card, and for the love of the devil put on some clothes before I get distracted in saving you and instead possess every cunt in here just to make them disembowel one another."

The fire in my belly is doused with those words of mutilation and I'm snapped back to reality, hurrying to pick up my robe. Slick with water and hair damp and loose in waves, I follow Hunter's direction and run like the fate of the world depends on it. Taking twists and turns, I run in the other direction of the oncoming guards and straight out into the even more chilly night.

Thank fuck Damien is out back with a getaway car and double the thanks that fucking car has heating!

Throwing myself into the back seat, bloody and bruised, I fall slack into the leather, all of my energy being drained from my withering soul.

"Jesus, fuck!" Damien hisses when he sees me before throwing the car into gear and taking off into the night.

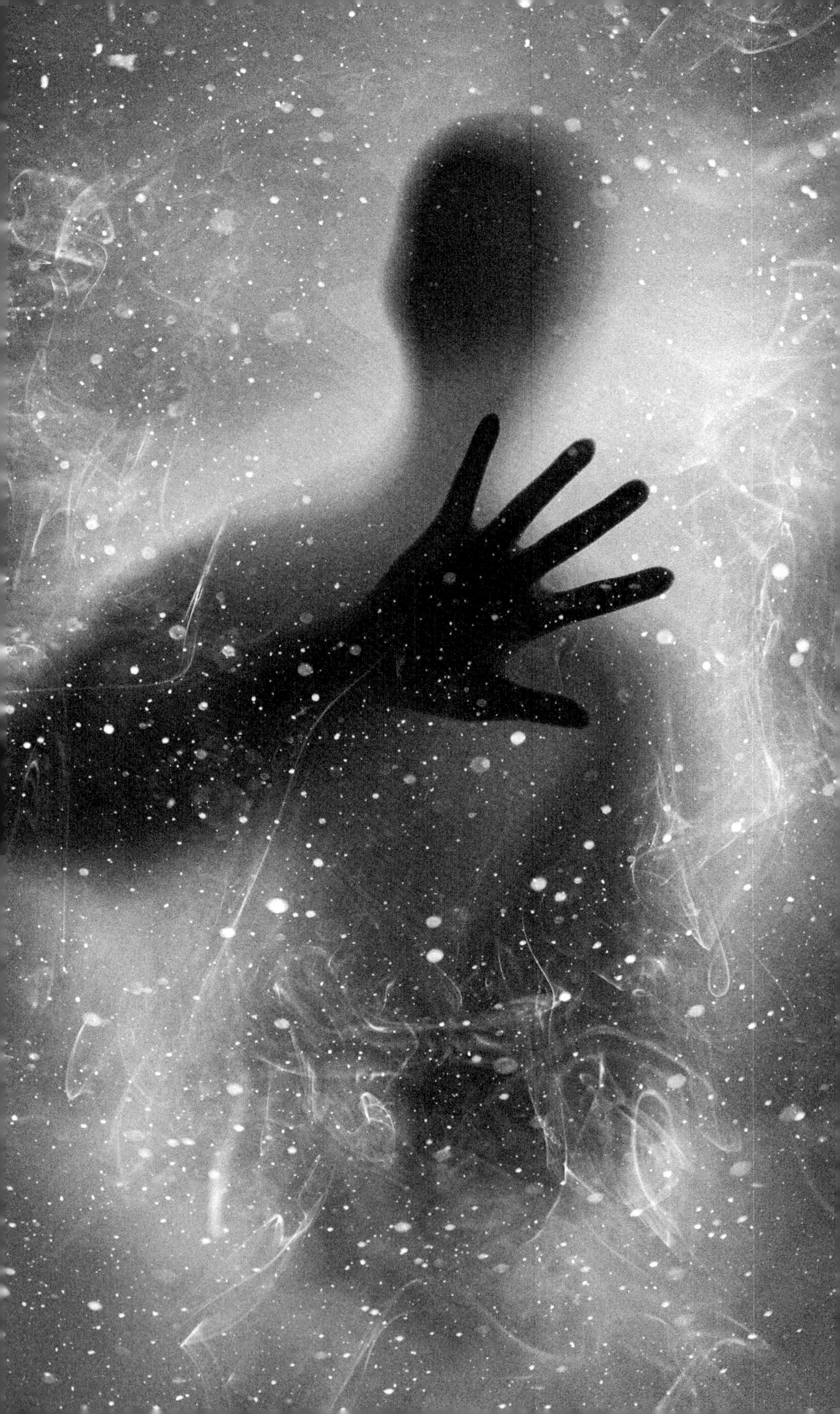

CHAPTER
FORTY-SIX

Hunter
I'm Sorry - Joshua Bassett

"Damien, she needs to rest. Truly rest without having to deal with any of the shit from back home."

"You thinking the cabin?" he asks, taking a sharp left before his green eyes find mine in the rearview mirror.

I'm holding Astra in my arms, her tender eyes closed as she lays across my phantom lap. Right now, I'm wishing more than anything that I was still alive.

That I could truly feel her and comfort her in the way that I know she needs right now. That there was no veil to part us, keeping me from feeling my skin as it glides against hers when I wipe away another stray tear.

She has endured so much. Stood in the face of adversity and I feel like I'm dying all over again every single day when something else comes to attack her, hurt her.

That someone drains her damn spirit and leaves her even more depressed than she felt after Theo attacked her all those months ago.

That was her first looking glass into a world of hate and darkness. She had the turmoil of those she loved and lost, but that was something she faced alone, without letting anyone else in.

That night though?

She hated herself for not fighting back and right now, I'm hating myself for leaving her in that nut house while I went in search of Damien.

I have never regretted dying in place of her life before and I still don't.

I regret that in dying, I've lost the ability to truly be everything that she needs me to be. If I was a better man, I'd let her go. I mean really let her go so she can live a happy and normal life, but I can't.

Even dead, I wouldn't survive losing her.

Not after I've truly been blessed in having her. In knowing what it feels like when she glances into my eyes and sucks the world around us dry, leaving me swimming in those astoundingly endless depths. The thought leaves a bad taste in my mouth.

I feel odd like my soul is screaming at me to banish the vile thoughts from my consciousness.

Caressing her cheek, I watch as she breathes. In and out, the air that kisses her lips I envy, wishing that all she can ever become consumed by is me.

I may not be a good man, but I'm also a very jealous man. Angered by every part of her that is just beyond my reach. Astra's silky skin glides against my essence, and I lose myself for a moment before I remember that Damien has asked me a question.

Looking up, I meet those emeralds that are still watching me. "Yeah. Let's go to the cabin. But can you call the girls? They need to know that she's safe."

He looks back at me sheepishly, eyes dropping to fall from mine and I narrow my eyes in return. "They already know. I sent them an alert as soon as she got into the car."

"Huh," I muse. "Do you happen to like one of them by chance?" I query.

He scoffs, shaking his head in denial. "Absolutely not. I already have one handful in my life and she came with two others. Romance would only throw me off my game and Astra is my priory." Nodding his head, it's almost like he's reminding himself of that fact.

"Brother," I start and his eyes fly back to mine in shock making me smirk. "Take it from me. Life is too short, you never know when the day you're in will be your last. Love? It's worth the world imploding around you just to experience it. If you like one of them, tell them. Don't wait like I did."

"Why did you? Wait I mean."

I look down, gazing at my love as I think over the question. Breathing deeply, I whisper, "People always leave. Loving her from afar, was safer than feeling the sting of her rejection." I've never admitted that out loud before. That a man like me ever had any kind of insecurity. "Did you know my father was insane?" I ask him, taking him by surprise. I chuckle, shaking my head sadly. "No, I guess not. I never did know how to let someone in, even when I saw them as my family."

"You did?"

"Of course I did. You were always there for me, Damien. And," I grunt, clearing my throat. "And I love you like a brother."

His eyes turn glossy and we both look away, not accustomed to so much emotion. "Anyway. He had a personality disorder. I spent half of my young life barricaded in my bedroom, not knowing when he was going to try and kill me because he thought I was replaced by the devil. In his own sick and twisted way, he always fought for the love of his son. To save him from evil. He could just never see that I was always right there in front of him and that it was him that was hurting me."

"That isn't you, Hunter. You aren't hurting her," he insists and I roll my eyes.

"Aren't I? Look at everything that has happened since I've come into her life."

"You mean, fighting off a maniac that would have raped and

killed her? Or maybe you're talking about literally saving her from possession and that dead fucker from finishing what he started?" he questions and I can hear the earnest plea in his voice, but I can't seem to take my eyes off Astra. Maybe in fear of seeing the look in his eyes, or maybe in fear of accepting he's right. "What about her mother? How about the fact you saved her from that cunt? You told her the truth and it may have opened old wounds, but you gave those wounds the bandages they need to heal. Without you, she would still be suffering that fate. Stuck in a vicious cycle because she didn't know she deserved better."

Silence falls, and my soul feels strange. Lost in my thoughts, I'm startled when a soft hand caresses the air between her palm and my cheek. But this time, I feel her more than I've ever felt her since being dead, like the veil between us was dissipating. "He's right, Hunter. You saved me."

"I've hurt you."

"And who are you to say I didn't enjoy the pain?" She smirks, a coy tease glistening in her blue gaze. "Like Damien the wise just told you, it hurt for a moment, but everything that's happened to me has only made me stronger. It's given me the strength to lay everything else to rest. That's the greatest gift anyone could ever give me. At every turn, Hunter, you're the hand that saves me. So, thank you." She leans forward, her bloody cheek shimmering the closer she grows until she ghosts a kiss across my lips and my soul quivers from the apparition.

"We're here, brother." Damien grins as the car pulls to a stop.

"Where is here?" Astra asks, sitting up to peer out of the window at the cabin that sits around us.

I'm sure it's not what she's expecting. Not some obtuse and expensive building I splurged on because a one-million-dollar cabin is just so vastly different from a two thousand, five hundred dollar cabin. Well, it's not. Believe it or not, I may have had the funds, but it was very rare that I ever spent more than what was necessary. You never stayed rich by spending it all on shit.

My cabin is made of logs and sits on a concrete foundation on top of the tallest hill that overlooks the mountains. There is one front door made of glass, one small window on either side of the cabin, and a stretch of them at the back overlooking the lowering sun from the kitchen. Huge glass windows cover the second floor, looking out from the master bedroom. Two lone chairs and a round table sit on the left side of the decking. A simple wooden bench sits on the right. Firewood is stacked up beside it, towering as high as the building itself, and low yellow lights give the entire place a golden glow that will look even more stunning once darkness chases away the lingering rays of the dying sun. At the back, on the deck that leads into the surrounding woods, is a hot tub. Other than that, I've kept the place small and cozy.

Like her home has been her solitude, this place has been mine.

And I suddenly find myself worried she won't like it. That when she notices, she might even be mad.

"Hunter," she breathes, my name sounding like grace instead of sin on those thick and plush lips of hers. "It's beautiful. Ever since I was a little girl, I've dreamed of owning a cabin. During the winter, my father used to bring us to the one my grandparents used to own. But after his discharge, he had to sell it. God, it's been so long, I can't even remember what it looked like." As she steps from the car, she stumbles forward, Damien rushes to catch her and keep her from falling.

She's still weak and I need to get her inside and cleaned up.

She allows Damien's arms to enclose around her waist as her eyes narrow in concentration. I grit my teeth, burying the demon of jealousy as it roars to life inside my chest at him being able to hold her in ways I can't, nor may ever be able to. But she doesn't need my psycho ass right now, she needs peace. "God, I feel like I did back then. When my tiny little feet would patter along the ground before pounding up the steps and into the den by the warm fire. I'd almost forgotten it altogether. It all feels so familiar."

I share a look with Damien and give him a reassuring nod as I breathe deeply. "Let's get you inside, Siren."

The three of us ascend the steps and into the cabin. Without instruction, Damien helps Astra to the couch and heads back outside for firewood. I'm on edge, watching her closely waiting for it to dawn on her that this is her grandparent's cabin. She gazes at the dry fireplace, tilts her head, and parts her lips. Slowly, she stands back to her feet and stalks toward the place where the logs chip away every few centimeters or so.

"Hunter," she whispers in uncertainty. "This is my grandparent's cabin." Once she says the words out loud, she gasps, spinning to look at me, then winces when the pain in her ribs smarts. She clutches her side, squeezing her eyes shut tightly before she turns back to the side of the fireplace that has been marked each year she grew.

Her brother Lucas too.

I rush to her side as she delicately traces the marks.

"Sit back down, Siren. For just a second." I usher her back to the couch and she slumps into it in awe, her eyes wide and glossy.

"Listen, I brought this place years ago and I mean a *really* really long time ago. I fell in love with it. There were some old photos that were left behind of a beautiful family and very young children. I envied what they had. I kept the photos because of it. Almost seemed too wholesome and sad to throw away. But I never knew this place was connected to you. Not until years later when I first laid my eyes on you and you know, kind of stalked you." I shrug like that little fact is no big deal. She rolls her eyes and I chuckle. "It came up in the paperwork later on. That I already owned something precious to you like it was fate. I never believed in destiny before that moment. Before *you*."

At first, I think she'll cry. Then she wipes her eyes and smiles at me softly. "Explains why I can so easily love a dead man. I mean? We never really had a choice in the matter, did we?"

"No, love. We never. Fate or not, though. I would have always made you mine."

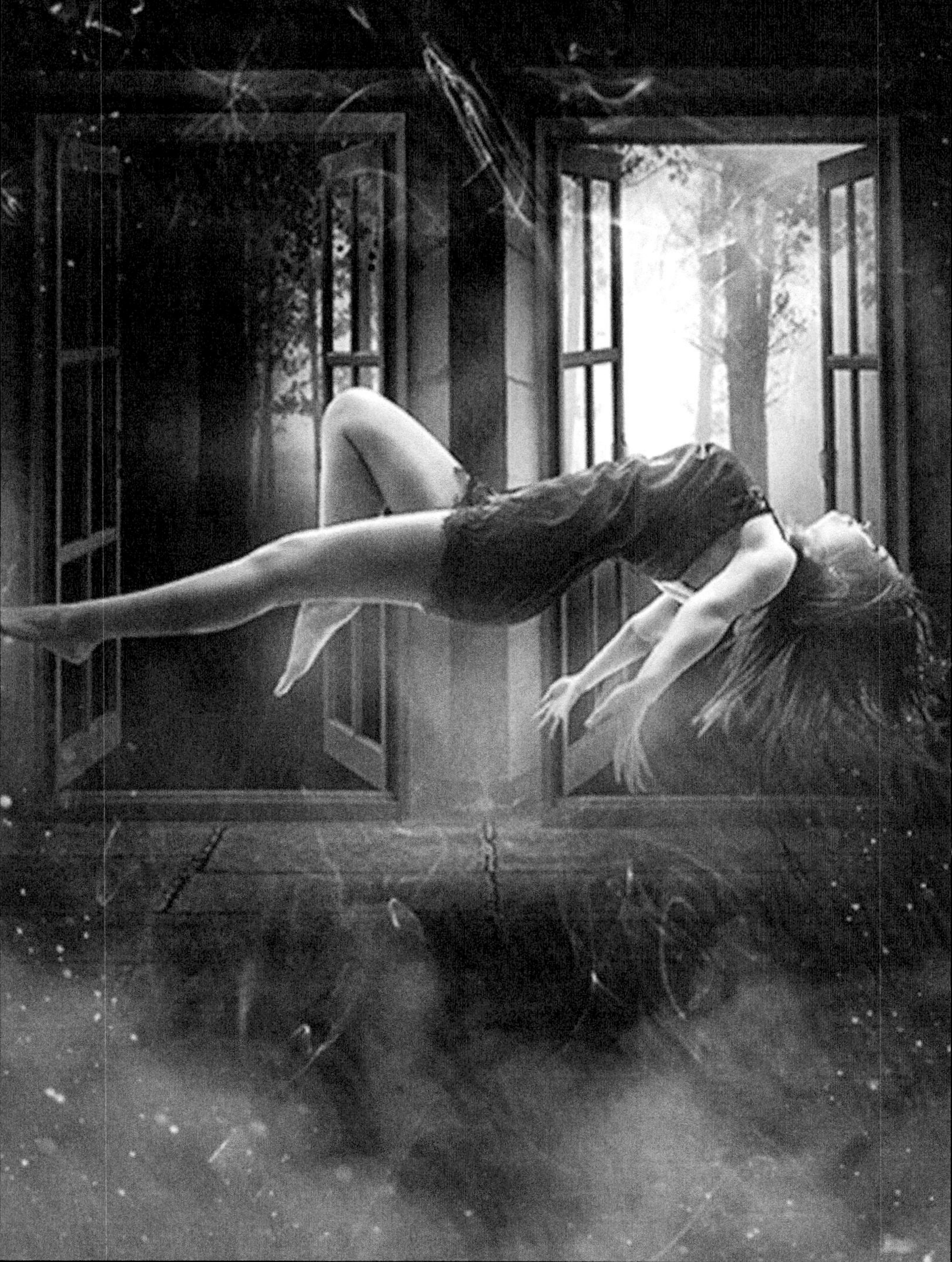

CHAPTER
FORTY-SEVEN

Astra
Naked - Jake Scott

I sigh, roll my back in the warm cotton sheets, and take a moment to slumber in bliss before I reach for my phone. I text Damien, then drop the phone to my chest, glancing beside me to see Hunter sleeping on his front. The blue apparition of him shimmers in contentment and I raise my brows in wonder. I've never seen him sleep before. Never really thought about it. I guess I just assumed he never had to.

Maybe he doesn't? Maybe it's a take it or leave it type of thing but since this is the first night he has slept beside me, he felt like he could?

Fuck, my head hurts as much as the rest of me just thinking about it.

My heart twitches inside my chest and I wind my neck at the strange feeling coursing through me.

I think...

I think it's happiness.

Swallowing, I smile softly at his defined back as my eyes trace the fine lines and sculpted curves before I get down to the dimples above his ass, his waist covered by his jeans. Sighing again, this time in irritation, at the fact the one thing I want the most for us, I'm not sure we'll ever be able to have. Stalking toward the bathroom, I relieve my bladder, then stumble over to the vanity. Washing my face, I inhale as the cool water seeps into my pores and really wakes me up.

Hunter tended to most of my bumps and scrapes last night curled in front of the fire with hot cocoa warming my hands. I remember how the amber glow flickered against his pale illusion. The shadows at his back had him almost looking human again. They fleeted across his face in such a way, they darkened his appearance and drew out his most stunning features. Eyes as dark as the begrimed storm clouds in the sky swirled, bleeding into a concoction of wild desire and dark intentions that has my breath trapped within the burning airways of my starving lungs.

The tender moment was a calm embrace to my rioting soul. Time stood still and every broken and bleeding part of me rose like the ashes of a phoenix and lit a fire in my core that had all of those jaded pieces melding back together once again.

I can't remember the last time I have felt so at peace, loved and cared for by another warming hand that delivers me a slither of happiness instead of a burden of grief.

I close my eyes now and relive that moment. The moment I truly fell for the tender care of my stalker.

Every gentle caress, every soothing stroke against my wounds chased away the pain and infused me with an intense, almost otherworldly sensation of being free from my mind and body. I gave myself to him in a way I have never given myself to anyone. He has stolen a fragment of my heart and I feel like I'll never be whole again without it returned to me. Like I'll never be whole again should I lose the man who has infiltrated my world and staged a mass takeover of everything I once thought I knew.

Opening my eyes, I look at my reflection as it smiles back at me.

My skin looks smooth, almost like I'm without the weight of my worries sitting heavily on my shoulders, so I can finally start to look my age once again. Blue eyes stare back at me brighter than they have ever since him, lips rosier than they have ever been and I exhale a breath of contentment.

Walking from the bathroom, I tiptoe out of the bedroom and downstairs. Damien is sprawled out across the couch. His tanned skin ripples, his abdomen clenches tight and coils with layers of slender muscles. I hike a brow at the thought that the pretty boy's face goes with a killer body. He's shirtless, barefoot and in nothing but gray sweat pants. Clearly he never got my text about breakfast. "I guess a stalker fell for a stalker, aye? I can feel your eyes on me, little witch, advert them before my boss kills me," he mumbles sleepily and I chuckle, descending the final step.

"As handsome as you are, Damien, I seem to like my men dead. So, unless you're dying any time soon, you're safe from my wicked enchantment." Laughing, I walk toward the couch with military stealth and slap him on the shoulder. He jolts, bolting upright with a gasp as wild green eyes snap open to land on mine making me laugh even harder. "What? You thought just because you heard me coming down the stairs you could drop your guard? Remember who taught me." The look on his face is comical and he frowns, pouting at me.

"Well, that just isn't fair. Miss Psycho, not ma'am, Astra."

"Ah, we're back to that again, are we?"

"We are now," he grunts.

I chuckle, looking up and taking stock of the cabin more so than I did when my focus was solely on him. "What the hell happened in here?"

"Your sister chicks, as they have now named themselves. They wanted to make you happy. Do something nice, after everything you've been through. They came by after you went to bed. Do you like it? I tried not to mess it up too much."

Breathtaken, I spin in a circle and take in the huge projector screen above the mantle of the fire. The orange glowing pumpkins, bats, and skull lights hang around the fireplace in a shroud. Blood red and black candles of different heights are posted around the cabin and little witch hats sit on the heads of little gray cats. Black and blue orchids are on the coffee table beside a whole set of snacks and treats and a hot chocolate machine sits on the wooden table on the right side of the couch with different cocoa options, syrups, and cream with toppings.

"You slept in the middle of my date?" I chuckle nervously as I notice the black rose petals scattered on a path toward the kitchen.

"Where else was I supposed to sleep? I just kinda laid here while they did their girly shit." He shrugs indifferently and my smile widens.

"You did the chocolate station didn't you?" I ask with a hike of my brow.

His pout thickens as he stares at me deadpan. "Maybe," he utters.

"And the snacks?"

"Well, obviously. You can't have a perfect movie night without a shit ton of snacks," he exclaims like it's obvious.

I throw myself over the couch and jump on him, digging his sides just right that he squirms and squeals like a girl, just how I intended. "Holy shit!" I chuckle. "I broke the robot!"

"Jesus, fuck! You little demon, stop! Stop, I can't breathe!" he gasps brokenly, trying to fight off my attack before he falls slack to stare at me in confusion. "Robot?" Giving me the perfect opportunity to curve my finger in the crook of his pit and hit the golden spot. He makes a noise that sounds like a bark before he huffs through his nose and begins to wiggle again.

"Yep. When you stalked me and ended up in my kitchen with all this ma'am shit, I made it my mission to knock the square out of you. I think my job is finally done. You're nice and rounded now. I can send you back into the wild." I throw my head back and cackle like a hyena.

I can't seem to help it, I'm happy today. Rounded myself, into something a little easier to handle.

"You're insane!" he cries. "Stop, I don't want to hurt you! Hunter would kill me!"

"Oh please, I'd kill you," I snort. Giving him a reprieve and falling *from the couch to lay on my back on the ground beside it.* "God, that was fun!"

"Demon," *he protests with a hiss and I wheeze a laugh from being breathless.*

"Yeah, yeah. Hey, listen-"

"- Don't. Don't thank me. It was my job all until it wasn't. Hunter has good taste in women and I have to say, I kind of even enjoy being your bodyguard. Bar the parts I was playing get away from the nuthouse. I don't have an appointment there for at least another twenty years. I think that's about how long my sanity can handle you and your crazy." *He sighs, hand slung across his abdomen as he stares at the ceiling.*

"Oh, please, I was just going to ask what you wanted for breakfast," *I joke, as I crawl back to my feet. We both know that isn't what I was going to say, but I'm glad we cleared up our appreciation for one another.* "I'm thinking pancake special."

I leave him to catch his breath as I head into the kitchen. Thankfully, the place is fully stocked and I can get to work quickly. I play "Daredevil" by Stellar through the speakers on my phone and dance around the kitchen as I mix the batter for the pancakes. A pinch of sugar is how I get them so sweet. Bacon sizzles on the stove, eggs soon to follow. It isn't long before I feel him fill the room. His essence is so powerful, I think I could feel it anywhere. I spin mid-song, my hips carrying me as I turn to face him sitting at the old oak table in the middle of the kitchen.

My heart swells, and the feeling of being back here, with all the memories of my family surrounding us and now Hunter and Damien being here too, I feel like I've stepped through a wardrobe and now I've ended up in Narnia. I even dare to say that it's perfect.

That despite the hell of last night, I'm happy.

"You're so beautiful when you're carefree," *he rasps and I smile.*

"And you're so handsome when you stalk me." *I place the bowl on the side and lean over the counter a little.* "Did you see what Damien and the girls did?" *I ask with way too much excitement in my voice.*

"I did," *he drawls in that husky tone that goes straight to my clit.*

Rubbing my thighs together, I try to settle my breathing as Damien enters the kitchen.

"I've got this, head on out to the jacuzzi. From here on out, I have marching orders. I am your humble servant and you're my charge. Now shoot, head on out. I'll bring the food out when it's done," Damien instructs, this time wearing a white T-shirt that stretches across his chest.

Not needing to be told twice, I squeal and run out into the cool autumn air. The black rose petals scatter a path all the way to the hot tub that is already bubbling away, the heat hitting me from here. More petals swirl inside, like a tsunami of black and blue that have been plucked from the stem of god knows how many orchids. My obsession with that flower grows even more. Not thinking twice, I strip off my clothes and step into the heated water in nothing but my underwear. Red wine sits in crystal glasses on a steel tray, surrounded by more rose petals.

"Careful," Hunter warns me. "If Damien sees too much, I'll have to kill him. And what a problem that would be since you like your men dead'." His brow rises, an almost playful smile on his face. There's still the element of danger though, that shows he's kind of serious and that makes me hot all over again. A man who never stops protecting me, whether from a real threat or just his own jealousy, is a primal desire in my very soul.

"Yeah, yeah. You could never kill your brother," I drawl, winking at him as his eyes narrow in accusation.

"You heard all of that?" he asks.

"Of course I did. Now get in here."

He could have stuck to pretenses and at least pretended to use the stairs. Instead, he walks straight through the tub and before I know it, I'm nose to nose with an unholy apparition.

"Close enough, Siren?" That rasp drives me wild. It's like the sin in my core, coming to life to slither through my every erogenous zone in the human body.

"Not nearly," I breathe. "I'm sorry, you know? About your dad. It must have been hard, living with that," I whisper, never looking away from his eyes. I want him to know that I heard him.

That I truly heard him.

"Life's hard, Siren. It was hard until the day that I met you, then everything else just didn't seem to matter anymore. You braved its wicked depths then calmed the storm." He's so serious, so firm. My heart stutters. "You know that's how I fell in love with you right? I've always been an intimidating man, but when I saw you in that bank? You looked straight up, stared into my eyes and huffed as you barged your way past me. Not even fully grown men stare into my eyes, love. But you did. I knew it then, in that moment, you were born to be mine."

I breathe heavily, looking into the eyes that have endured so much pain, but stood tall in the face of it all.

I move closer, feeling him with my soul. My very essence instead of my skin and bone. "Do you know when I fell in love with you?" I question. His form grows larger, infused with all of the air from his deep inhale. I'm drawn to it, the small movement that dips at the base of his throat as he swallows.

"The moment I realized that I was never alone. It wasn't when I found out you paid off my debt. Or when you bought out all of the other tattoo parlors or even the Empire. It was the night after Theo attacked me, when I emerged from the hot depths of my bath, wanting nothing more than to drown under the surface of it, I saw you standing there." Stopping, I take a moment to gather myself, still lost in those wild sleet gray eyes.

"At first, I didn't know what it was. My mind playing tricks or my conscious thinking he'd come back for me. But in that moment, in the heart of my anguish, when I saw your shadow, I found peace in the agony." My lips hover above his, my words whisper to the wind of his soul. "I think I only survived that night because I had this presence around me that was saving me even when I was giving up the will for anything else. I never understood it then, but I understand it now. I've lived for you Hunter, I've lived because of you."

"It's funny, I never thought we'd have this moment and if we ever did, I never thought it'd be under these circumstances. I don't know how this will all work, Siren. A better man would let you go. Allow you to find a man that can give you everything I can't. But I'm not a better man, and one way or another, I'll make this work. You're mine, love.

No matter the cost of my soul or my Afterlife. You. Are. Mine." Then he kisses me, and everything else settles. The world falls quiet, my soul finds peace and then my future begins to take form in my mind.

After a while, just sitting in content under the warm bubbles of the hot tub, the cool autumn air whispering past us in a swirl of orange leaves, and having moments of utter clarity, we head back inside. The whole night has been perfect and I feel like I'm walking in the clouds. That dead or alive, this could actually work.

It may not be conventional, but I know in my heart of hearts that this is what I want.

That he is what I want and nothing in this world or the next could make me change my mind.

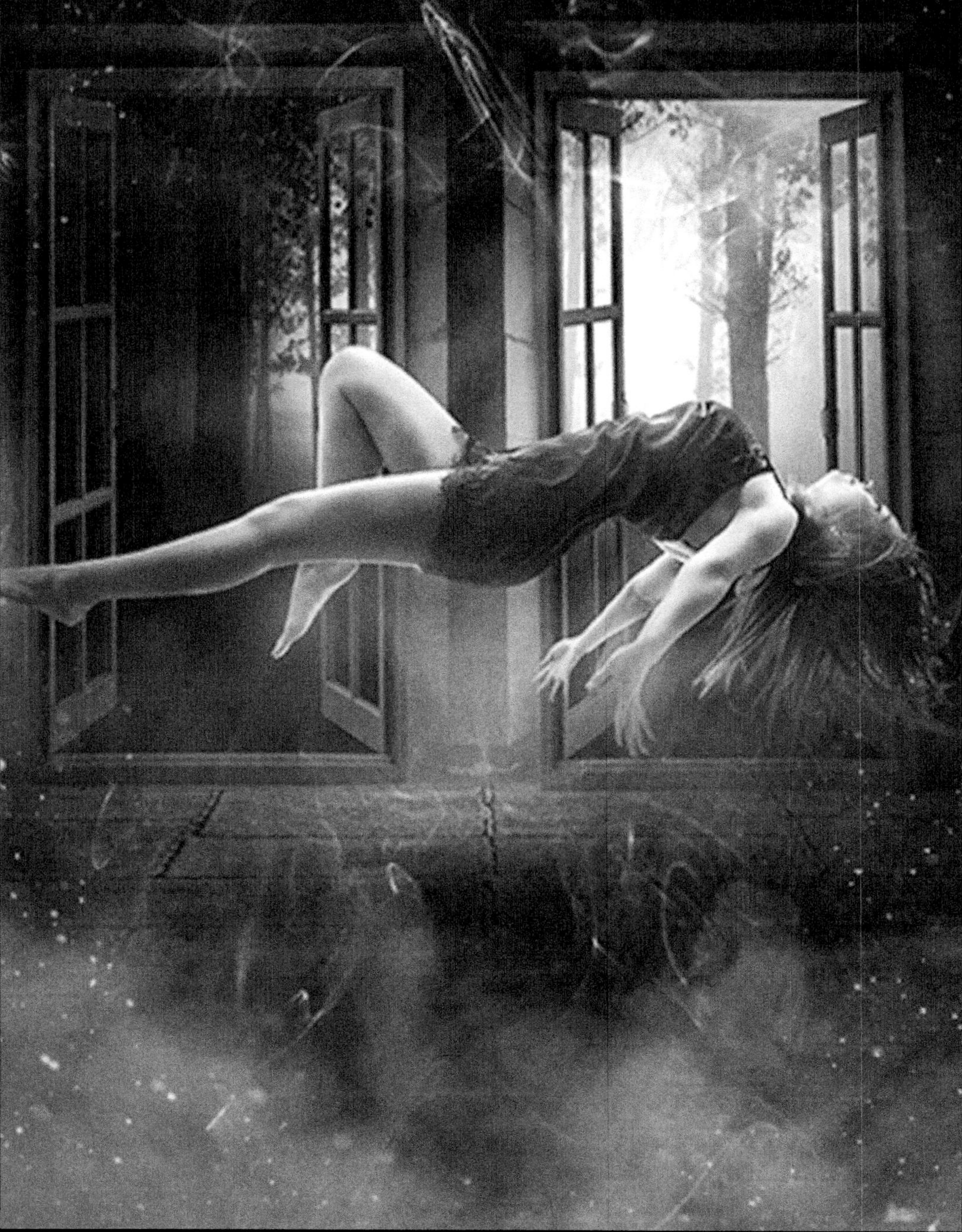

CHAPTER
FORTY-EIGHT

Astra
Ghost Town - Layto & Neoni

I don't care how much Hunter's electric fireplace at his apartment cost, you can't beat the real thing. Not when I'm curled into his side on a sheepskin rug, watching the flames rise and fall around thick hunks of wood. I have to rely on my imagination, picturing Hunter outside in nothing but jeans, slamming an ax down on the trunks to supply the firewood, but who am I kidding? He probably just had Damien order it from a factory somewhere.

"Hey, I resent that," Hunter jerks. "I happened to chop this firewood myself. Got the splinters to prove it and everything." Hunter holds up his right hand for me to inspect the pale sheen to his once perfectly porcelain skin, tinged in a beautiful blue.

"My poor baby," I soothe, stroking his palm through the veil's layer. "Manual labor can be a bitch like that." Hunter knocks my hand away and leans back into our embrace. Despite the high messy bun, my hair continues to drip from our time in the tub, creating a wet patch down the back of the large T-shirt—one of Hunter's favorites—as provided by Damien, that reaches my upper thighs like a nightshirt. Underneath, a pair of his boxers that hugs my ass while the warmth of the fire takes care of the rest.

"Neither of you are even watching this," Damien mumbles, switching off the projector. He's right, even though the girls went through so much trouble to set it up. Even though they still think I'm sitting here talking to myself, we just aren't into it. We're more into talking to each other. Jess is more in tune with the spiritual side, so she's the easier one to persuade. Whatever is happening to me - I'm happy. Hazel on the other hand, total non-believer and I don't have the time to convert her.

Damien leaves the controller in case Hunter and I change our minds and returns to putting away the last of the dishes. He keeps promising to head upstairs and is clearly stalling for some reason. Not that it matters. I have everything I need right here, and not even the clang of crockery can dampen that. If anything, it's one less job I have to do.

"Do you ever stop thinking, Siren?"

"I might, when you stop reading my thoughts." I tilt my head and purse my lips. Hunter laughs, a deep, throaty sound I could listen to all day. For some, it's rainfall they find solace in but for me, it's this. The rare rumble of Hunter in his most carefree state. And it's me that makes him that way. Knowing when he's wrapped up in my protection, always on high alert, I can still catch him off guard feels like everything. I'm starting to wonder if perhaps I'm not the only one who needed saving...

Crash.

Twisting around the leg of the couch, I frown at Damien. Shattered porcelain covers the kitchen tile at his booted feet, and he's staring downward, not moving a damn muscle.

"It's alright, Simon. Life happens, shit breaks. Just sweep it up and try again." I try to resume my position but Hunter is no longer there. I find him across the room, summoning his energy to carry the pieces of the plate over to the trash. A frown is etched between his eyebrows, something about his stance putting me on edge. "Guys? Are we all good?" Rising to my feet, I tug on the hem of the shirt, just to give my hands something to do.

"Go upstairs, Siren. I'll be there shortly," Hunter orders. His voice has dropped to its lowest octave and the hair stands up on the back of my neck. Call it intuition, but something tells me not to argue for once.

Taking one step towards the staircase, Damien's head whips in my direction. Black coats his eyes, from corner to corner without a trace of vibrant green anywhere to be seen. A scream rushes from my throat before I can stop it and I'm moving. Heavy footsteps pound behind me, heightening my terror as I curve around the steps. Something shatters in the spot my head just was, the wall stained red as glass rains all around.

"Hunter! Do something!" I scream, running as fast as my legs will carry me to the master bedroom.

"I'm.... trying," the reply is gritted out just before I slam the door closed and hastily lock it. Taking a few steps back, I spot my cell on the bedside table and reach for it, before stopping myself. I just left one mental hospital. I'm fairly sure *'my bodyguard doesn't look right and is trying to kill me and my ghost lover can't save me'* will secure a one-way ticket into another.

The choice is taken from me as a single pound against the wooden door is my only warning before Damien kicks the entire door down. Bursting free of its hinges, I have to roll over the bed just to clear myself from the squishing zone. Rushing for the window, I fight against the aged lock to start shoving it open when a hand claws into my hair and rips me from my feet.

"Damien…" I hedge, pushing my back against the glass. "We all good, buddy? Don't worry about that plate. I didn't much care for it anyway." I decide to keep to myself that it was, in fact, my grandparents and probably over sixty years old. Maybe worth a fair bit too, but when he's glaring at me like I've pissed in his coffee, what's some crockery between friends? Employees?

Whatever.

"Astra! That's not Damien!" Hunter's strangled bellow sounds from somewhere within the cottage.

Yeah, no shit!

Pain laces his voice and I suddenly don't give a fuck about who's stalking tiptoe by tiptoe around the bed, a lion circling his prey. Straightening, I stare into the black eyes narrowed on me, Damien's top lip peeled back and the stench of cigarette smoke emanating from him sickens me.

"Theo," I growl. "What have you done to Hunter?"

I heard him, but I couldn't see him. He wasn't beside me, protecting me, and the thought that I couldn't protect him hurt a lot more than the thought of being hurt by a possessed madman.

His head tilts in an animalistic way, his head seeming disjointed at the neck. An echo rattles inside Damien's chest, the deepest rumble of a growl from another world.

"You mean…" the raspy voice sneers from Damien. "Your boyfriend can't save you after all?" His mouth slats in a taunting smirk, and damn if I refuse to let him see me running scared. Sure, internally there's a little girl screaming and hugging her tattered teddy, but I won't let him see that side of me.

I ran once.

I will *never* run again.

My light will be snuffed out on my terms, not begging for mercy under the hands of a vile human in life and an even more vile spirit in death.

Reaching behind me, I manage to pop the lock on the window and shift at the same time Damien does. Throwing the glass plane upwards, my body is halfway out when a pair of arms lock around my legs. Clawing at the wooden slats outside the cottage, the slated roof terrace so close, my nails crack. My fingers cramp. My teeth grit, but I never stop fighting.

Kicking backward wildly, none of my efforts slow Damien. *Theo.* Damien already possessed the strength needed to drag me back inside screaming, but with Theo, I never stood a chance. All too soon, I'm tossed on the bed like a rag doll and Damien is leering over me, unadulterated rage twisting his features.

"What the fuck," I spit, shoving the weight of his chest from lowering to crush me, "did I ever do to you, Theo?!" Large hands close around my wrists too easily, slamming them on either side of my head while my legs are pinned by his bony shins. "You're a fucking lunatic!"

Somewhere in the back of my skull, a tiny alarm bell rings. No matter how many horror movies I've devoured, I've never learned the art of antagonizing the captor. A hard, brutal forehead slams down on my mouth, and instantly blood pools across my tongue. *That'll teach me for talking.*

"What did you do to me?" He tilts his head again, his smile growing freakishly wide. I bet Damien himself doesn't realize his lips can spread so far, and here I am, immobile with it hovering over me. Then he starts to laugh. A mechanical sound, echoed by the shadows drawing closer.

"What did you do *for* me, is the real question. What did the world do for my mother, other than pile shit, upon shit, *upon shit* on her plate? Hmm?" With each word he growls down at me, the vice-like grip on my wrists tightens. I whimper when it becomes too much, my bones threatening to snap just for the relief of his grip.

"Luck doesn't find people like us. Those at the bottom of the food chain. We never even stand a chance. And you? You just liked to humiliate me every chance you got, didn't you?" On a roar, Damien jerks his hands to my waist and tosses me aside. A scream escapes my throbbing lips and I sail through the air like a feather tossed into the spiral of the wind and crash into the wardrobe.

"Astra!" Hunter yells, still too far away.

Where the hell is he?

I drop to the ground, pain exploding through my spine but I don't waste a heartbeat. My arms are moving before my head has even processed the tattered rug I used to play on. Luca and I stayed up every night, playing card games by candlelight until we were caught.

I vowed to beat him one day, but that day never came.

Water clouds my vision and I blink aggressively, forcing those tears to fuck off. There is no time for memories. The groove of the door's threshold dips beneath my elbows, my breath wheezing in and out as I catch sight of the stairs.

I'm coming Hunter, just hold on.

I'll save you this time.

It's the only vow that pushes me forward. That drives me to never give up, and never back down.

"And then she came along." The mechanic rumble echoes just as an impossibly heavy weight sits on my back. "My angel. My saving grace." The air rushes from my lungs, my insides on the verge of bursting free from my body by any means necessary. Somehow, between choking on my tongue, I manage a few words in the hopes to distract him.

"W-who... Jess?"

"My pure, kind Jess. She could have been the answer. I was trying to change for her, to be the man she saw in me. But you just couldn't keep your fucking mouth shut." Damien's weight shifts and then slams down on me again. Agony rips through my left side, betraying the ribs that give way and crack beneath the strain.

"You never gave me a chance. You suffocated me with your judgment and put doubt in her mind. I knew I wasn't worthy, but I didn't even have the time to try!" This time when I try to scream, no sound comes out. My fingers and toes uselessly scratch against the exposed wooden flooring as the desperation to drag myself out from beneath him reaches a fever pitch. But apparently, Theo isn't finished with the woe is me story.

"I had to do something to get you out of the picture. So I watched. I waited. And who should I see but Hunter North, the billionaire, lurking in the shadows? All the while he was watching you, I was watching him."

A strangled scream bounces around the walls, the harrowing sound ripping through my soul.

Hunter.

He's close, yet so far away and it's then I realize he's not in my world at all. Theo's sent him somewhere and an icy shiver races down my crushed spine.

The daunting notion that I can't save him, and he can't reach me is like acid in my soul.

"Good to see things never change." Theo chuckles through Damien, his body leaning forward to mutter in my ear. "You're his perfect distraction and his biggest downfall." Cigarette smoke coils into my nostrils, making me gag through my panting wheezes. Remaining close enough for his breath to shift the hair around my face, an underlying noise can be heard. So small, so distant, I have to use all my focus to make out what it is. A word being rasped from Damien's very being.

Bite.

My head shifts the tiniest amount, my tongue too thick to moisten my cracking lips. Black eyes gleam down, reveling in my turmoil.

Bite!

It comes again, and I simply oblige. Craning my neck, my teeth sink into Damien's cheek and jaw. I clench when he jerks, despite the fresh wave of pain exploding from my ribs. Despite the dark tendrils that seep from Damien's back and close in around me.

Blood pours, and we both scream in termination. The flesh of Damien's cheek begins to peel back and I loosen my grip, unable to continue until his bellowing roar bursts free of Theo's clutches.

Do it!

Shivering, crying, and utterly furious to be in this situation, I comply. Something cracks, whether my own teeth or his jaw, reverberating around my skull until Theo can't take it anymore.

All at once, the weight from my back is relieved and I'm in the air again, thrown against a wall and held in place by the black tendrils seeping from Damien. The snarl on his bloodied face has tripled, the darkness of his eyes like pure onyx.

"What makes Hunter North better than me, huh? Even the richest man in the country had to sneak around, stalk and obsess. Yet you're not fighting for freedom from him, are you? So why me, bitch? Why was I never good enough?"

The smoke binds my wrists and ankles, then drifts upwards to clutch my neck. And squeeze. Spots instantly dance in my vision, my head so light I'm not sure it's still attached. Liquid seeps from my eyes and in my peripheral vision, droplets of red pattern over the T-shirt at my breast. Damien stalks forward, a cruel smile growing on his unsuspecting mouth.

"I can feel your hatred. Your loathing smells like heaven to me. Don't worry, *Siren*." Theo mocks Hunter's nickname for me and I growl. It's the best I can manage. "This won't be quick. I want him to hear you scream, to feel your pain. It's all I've ever wanted. After all, it's the only reason I followed you out of the Empire that night with a butcher's knife in my pocket. You stole my future from me, so I repaid the favor." He pulls me from where he had me pinned, and we twist and twirl in a fight against wills, and then the shattering of glass splinters around me. Moments before my back hits something solid, it lasts a mere second before the weight is gone and a harsh breeze is whooshing around my head.

My hair billows, smacking back against me and hindering my sight as Theo hangs me out of the top window of the bedroom in the cabin. By the second, my back moves up the frame. My lower back and tailbone the only thing stopping me from falling from such a height, I'd break my neck. My heart somersaults, my stomach bottoms out and the only thing running through my mind is...

I'm going to die.

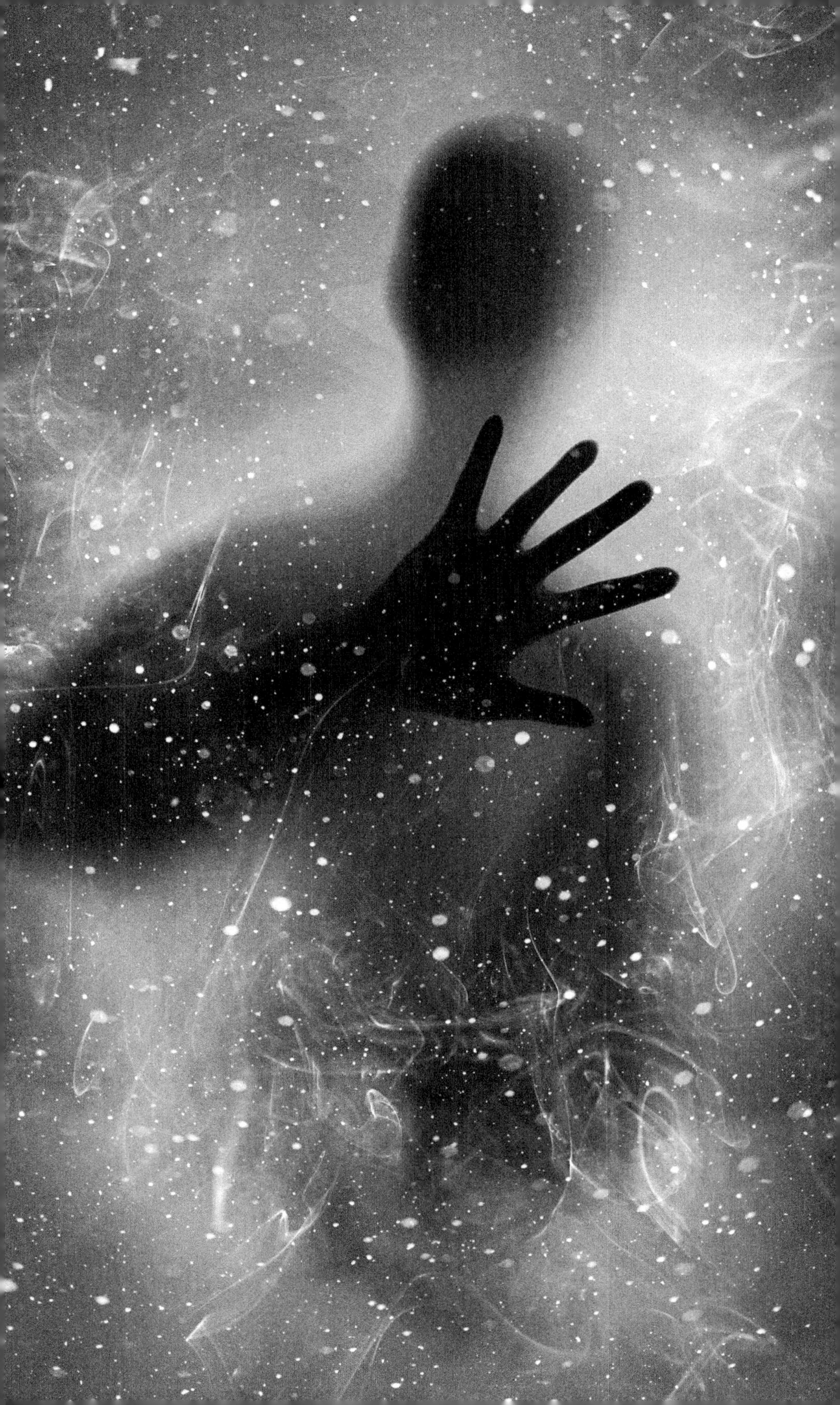

CHAPTER FORTY-NINE

Hunter
Bring Me to Life - Evanescence

Consumed by shadow.
    Lost in smoke.
    Each way I turn, the force of a thousand daggers rips through my soul. Each time I have to wait for the fragments of my being to put themselves together before trying again, but giving up is never an option. Not when I can hear Astra's cries for help. Her agony flares in me as powerfully as my own.

I thought I could understand this world. How to bend it to my control. But Theo already had a cemented bond to the darkness before he died. He embodied depravity in its purest form, and in killing him, all I did was free him of his physical form.

Droplets rain down on my skin, seeping through the clouds to splatter across my recently rejuvenated skin. I squint to see them, just making out the deep crimson that fills my soul with dread. I need to hurry, before it's too late.

Instead of moving further onward, I halt. Rushing blindly through the smoke isn't working. Theo has a hold on Damien, his attention is distracted, so there must be a better way than to keep running into his pre-set traps. Closing my eyes, I shift my chest up and down as if I were breathing. Centering myself to do what I do best - stalk.

A pair of sparkling ocean-blue eyes ignite in my mind. Ranging from specs of sapphire to the purest cyan, Astra's eyes hold my entire world. From the turbulent seas to the cloudless skies, she's my anchor. My soulmate. For her, I have and would do anything, and on that single thought, the cabin bedroom comes into view.

Dark wisps leak from Damien, pinning my girl to the ground, hanging her like a rag doll from the high-arched window. Rage slams into my chest and just like that, the landscape disappears back into smoke.

Fuck.

Hunter, you don't need to control Theo's astral plane, you only need to control yourself.

Leaving my hands down by my side, I release my fingers from the fists that had snapped closed moments ago. Free my mind of everything except her. Her hold to me, hold her love for me. We could move mountains with the strength of our bond, and save worlds with the power of our passion.

We can do this.

"I'm here, love. Reach out to me. Hold onto me," I murmur with nothing more than blind hope she'll actually hear me.

"Always," the reply comes within an instant, and my chest lifts. Beneath my soot-covered shirt, a light begins to glow. Like a bulb that gradually builds in intensity, it brightens, sending tremors through my body. Electricity sparks along my veins, jump starting my non-beating heart for her. Only for her.

This time when the cabin comes into view, I don't release the hold on our love. I dive into it. Even when the blood seeps from her eyes, I imagine washing her cheeks clean. Even when her bottom lip wobbles, I long to kiss her fears away. All that's dividing us is the spirit of an unfulfilled asshole who's possessing my bodyguard.

My best fucking friend.

My *brother*.

Throwing my head back, my bellow is filled with yearning as the light explodes free. My body disintegrates into specks of light, dithering in the wind. Hovering on the edge while the tendril around Astra's neck tightens and her head lolls to the side.

Not yet, Siren.

You *live* for me, that was the deal.

Gathering my subconscious, I thrust myself forwards, bursting free of the veil that hinders me. Damien's face turns, his fully black eyes spotting me as I propel into his back. This is my brother, the only man I've ever allowed to get close to me after my father. Without stopping, without barely thinking, I bulldoze Theo through Damien's front in a spectacular display of light and ash. The essence of my being so pure and blue, it burns the darkness and toxicity of Theo's right out of the confinement of a light soul such as Damien's.

The charred remains of a broken soul fall softly to the ground.

Still, inside Damien, I stomp on the crisp flecks until the smoke clogging the room dissipates too. Only then do I shoot out of Damien, hearing the weight of his body collapsing to the ground as I catch Astra before she falls like an angel falling from grace out of the window.

She falls limp in my arms, her eyes flutter shut.

Red welts and bruises form around her throat.

"No, no, Siren. Not today. Not like this." I smooth the hair back from her moistened face. Sweat beads her pale forehead, her cheeks smeared with too much crimson that I can barely look beyond it. My entire focus is on the fan of her lashes, willing her to open those beautiful eyes.

"You die on your terms, remember. Not some petty asshole that couldn't take a hint. You've always said that. That's always been what you wanted, Siren. Fight it! Fight it and come back to me!" Fuck, I want to bring him back just to obliterate his soul all over again. Damien groans behind me lying on the shattered glass. Rolling onto his side, he throws up over the ashy flakes from a rotten soul and that's good enough for me.

Easing us both down onto the ground, I cradle her body, rocking back and forth. So many words come to my lips, but none make it past. Nothing I can say to describe the desperation crawling at the inside of my throat.

Instead, I focus on *feeling*.

The heat prickles my skin. The electricity in my veins. Everything she has made me feel since she first put the tattoo gun on my skin. From that day, I was marked by her. Both internally and externally. Only her hands would touch me, even when she had no idea of the effect she had on my mind, body and soul.

Two lost, lonely twin flames looking for their other half.

Both too stubborn to put their pride on the line and speak up. Well, I'm speaking with the light still thrumming from my spirit now, filling Astra with so much energy, she has no choice but to gasp and buck in my gentle hold.

"Hunter?" she breathes just before blinking those stunning eyes open. The eyes that strip me down and force me to bare my soul. I choke on a half sob, pushing my face into her neck so she can't see me like this. Let her remember the stoic stalker, not the man crumbling at her feet and begging to be righted.

"I thought I'd lost you," I mutter. Only now does the weight of my inner worries slam down on me. What if she went to another astral plane? What if Theo tainted her soul and sent her to a version of his hell like the one I've just escaped? There are too many unknowns, other than when she's here with me. Like this, we have each other. It may not be the same as the press of skin to skin, the feel of her clenching around me as I drive her into ecstasy, but it's everything I need. More than I ever hoped to have.

"I'll always find you, Hunter. Just as you will always find me," Astra soothes and despite the situation, she raises a hand to brush her fingers through my hair. The severity of her words is lost on me as I crumble, crying for this incredible woman I just can't be without.

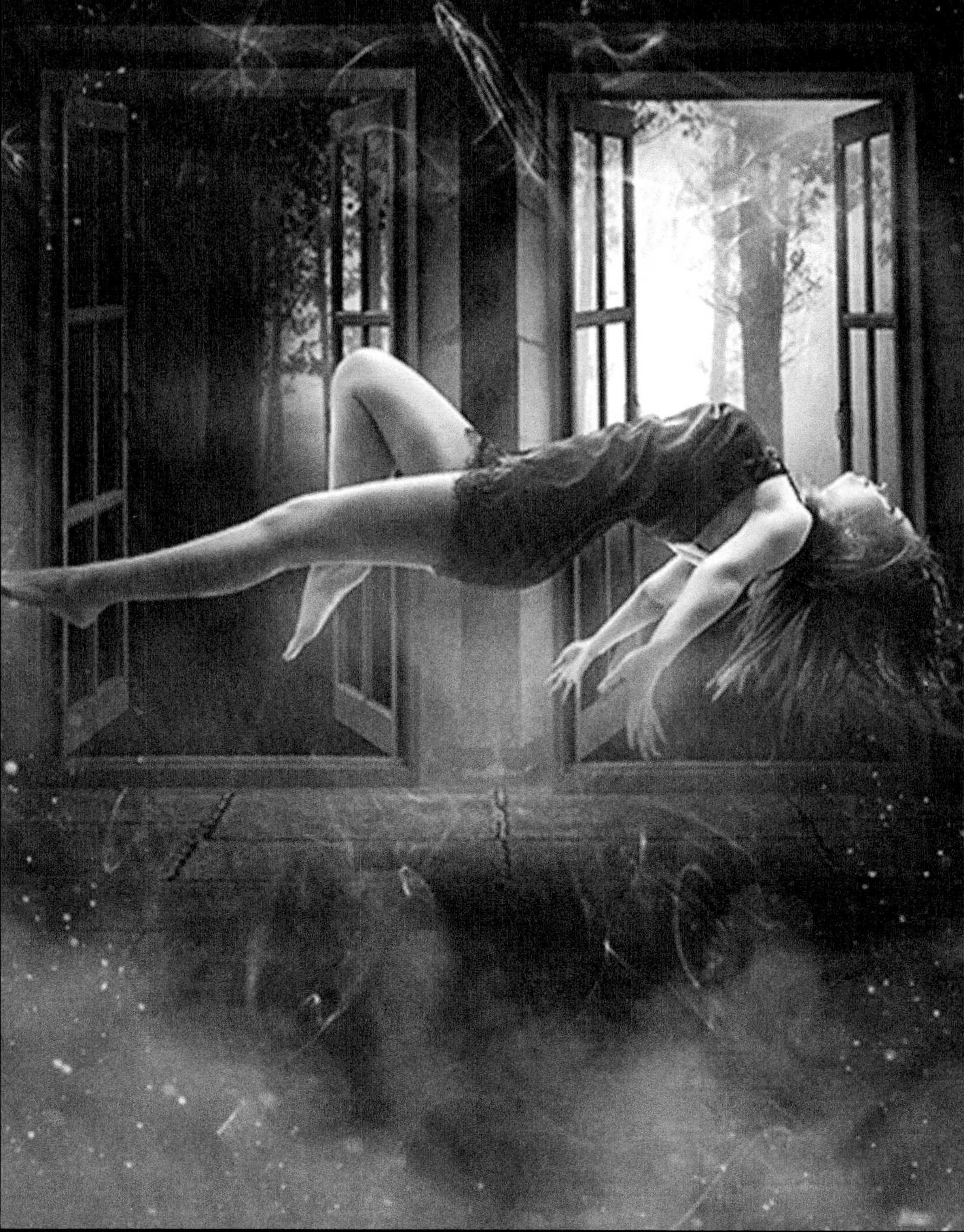

CHAPTER FIFTY

Astra
If Today Was Your Last Day - Nickelback

"Are you sure you want to do this?" a graying man with kind eyes asks from across the desk. I ease the pen from his hand and sign my signature on the dotted line in response.

I've had plenty of time to think over the back end of the past few weeks, nestled in the safety of Hunter's arms. I'm sure if any trace of Theo remained, he would have shown himself by now. So, with the knowledge he was well and truly gone, it was time to turn my thoughts back to my own life. Not the bitter memory of a man who wasted his own. Theo thought he could overpower me. From our first meeting, where I vividly remember calling him out as a gold-digger, and it spiraled from there. He lied to himself, thinking Jess would save him, but the truth was, he was just mad that there was someone out there with tits that could see right through his bullshit.

Was his life wasted, if hating me is what spurred him to wake up in the morning?

I can't say.

I've been pondering my own mortality, and to what end it would seem fulfilled. Hunter hasn't uttered one word of regret about dying for me, and in doing so, he's given me an outlook I hadn't considered. What makes life worth living if the host is happy? And without him physically by my side, will I ever be truly happy?

Pushing the documents back to my attorney, he stands to shake my hand and I bid him a lovely afternoon. First I head to the tattoo shop. Walking around, I take in the place that I've built from the ground up. All in honor of my father. The aesthetic is chic goth, there are portraits of tattooed nuns sticking their middle fingers up with their tongues hanging out.

Sexy little devil worshipers posed in lingerie and standing in pentagrams suggestively with quotes like

'I ride the horns of Satan.'

and

'I was born in Hell... As the Devil's Mistress.'

Nostalgia thickens in my throat as I blink away the memories. *Fuck*, I'm proud of this place. It means everything and it was built on the wings of my heroes.

Ghosted from the memories of my daddy.

Sniffling, I wipe my nose and do a slow walk around, taking in every single inch of my own personal little Empire. Then I head over to my station, set up my stencil, place it smoothly on the skin and tattoo my final tattoo for a while, breathing in the scent of the ink and blood, making my soul happy.

When I'm done, I lock up, place my hand on the cool glass and thump my forehead against it. Peering back through the shadows. With one last sigh, I close my eyes and turn back to the street.

The sun is out, gracing an otherwise frosty, winter's day with the blessing of its shine. Not a cloud hinders the blue sky that will descend into darkness a mere few hours from now. Pulling my scarf tighter around my neck, I push my hands into the deep parka pockets and stroll back to the Empire.

James, the waiter, opens the door wide with a welcoming smile and hastily closes it behind me to keep the warmth in. I scrape my winter boots on the doormat, inhaling the heavenly smell.

"Is Pierre trying out the new seasonal menu?" I ask as James removes my coat.

"A special treat for you, Miss. Your company is already waiting in the booth, and trust me - they're famished." I grin, dismissing James with a warm smile.

"This suits you," Hunter appears like a wisp in the air. He's gotten better at understanding my cues for when I need some space and when there's nowhere else he should be than by my side. In the Empire, I've forbidden him to float away for a second. Not even to debrief Damien on some upgraded security system we don't need. No, here, we reign his life's work together.

"Hey, girl! I've been calling you! What's taken so long?!" Jess flaps her hand to hurry me into our usual booth faster. My heart blooms at the sight of them both, sitting so casually in my restaurant. It's been a rough few months, the rockiest in our friendship by far, but we've pulled through with a happy medium. I gave up trying to convince either of them about Hunter's presence. I'm the double near-death experience wacko that talks to herself and they're still the same, reliable friends as always. Encroaching on my space forces me to be social, and I love them for it.

Hazel's eyes are staring into the distance, drawing my attention to Damien withdrawing into the shadows. My heart tugs that he's still refusing to talk to me. That he feels at fault and won't forgive himself for that night at the cabin. If only I had more time, I could work on setting things straight, but I know it won't be long before Hazel gives in to her stubborn crush.

Spotting me for the first time, she blushes.

"Oh, hey! Yeah, hurry to fuck up. We're starving and the chef wouldn't serve anything until you arrived!" I laugh as a bottle of pinot is placed in front of us with three wine glasses. A sharp double clap sounds from inside the kitchen, no doubt from Pierre, and within a second, three waiters are rushing to the hatch. They're in full uniform, despite the Empire not being open for a few hours and I roll my eyes.

No matter how many times I tell the staff they don't need to impress me, it seems Hunter's rules are hard to forget. Approaching with two bowls in each hand, James is among them as they place down an array of plates for us to feast our eyes on. Smoked salmon, duck confit, scallops and so much more.

If it's exquisite and delicious, it's here.

"Holy yum," Jess groans, hugging her fork to her chest after filling her mouth with steak tartare. She's halfway through her wine and food before remembering the question I was hoping to avoid. "So where have you been, Miss Billionairess?"

"Stop calling me that. You know I hate it." Hunter chuckles and I discreetly nudge my elbow into his side. "If you must know, I had a meeting with my attorney."

"Is someone suing you already?" Hazel blurts out and Jess elbows her. "I mean, is everything okay? It's not a hassle with your mom, is it?"

"No, nothing like that. She got the message after I kept blanking her prison calls. Did get two lovely letters though. The first telling me I was a devious, selfish bitch, and the second apologizing for the first whilst asking me to put funds into her commissary account."

"Let her rot," Jess mutters around another mouthful. "She had plenty of time to come clean. Not to mention all those years you've grieved, not understanding what happened. Two consecutive life sentences is a slap on the wrist for double murder and fraud to me." Shrugging, I prod my fork around the plate, suddenly losing my appetite. Not through hatred, but almost the opposite. The ability to release myself from the overriding hatred that has consumed me for far too long.

I lost my heroes, all because my mother thought this world owed her more than it already gave. Even if she claims her intention wasn't to hurt them, that it was all an accident, her poisonous heart is still the reason they were ripped away from me. But no amount of moping has brought them back and I have to believe they're watching over me, smiling in approval at my recent epiphany.

Hunter is quick to notice the shift in my mood, raving about kicking the chef to the curb if his food isn't up to standard. Beneath the table, I place a hand on his thigh and placate him with a warning look. Only he would be so quick to fire a man he had flown over from Paris, just for the reputation of a legit French chef. Steeling myself in his cloudy gaze, I lick my lips and turn back to the girls.

"I'm thinking about going away for a while," I announce. The two pairs of brown eyes lift to mine at the same time Hunter leans into my ear.

"You have?" he asks and I tighten my grip on his thigh.

"Where are you going?" Hazel perks up, dabbing her mouth with an embroidered napkin. "If you're closing the tattoo shop, that means I'm also technically free too if you want company. Madagascar is on my bucket list!"

"Ohhh same, I just want to sit around and let the lemurs jump all over me!" Jess adds and I can't fight my grin.

"Not Madagascar, although there's nothing stopping you guys. You can take the private jet and I'll see to it you have everything you need. I think I need to venture off on my own for a while. Explore new things, possibly find myself again, you know? After everything that's happened."

"I stopped listening after the private jet." Jess winks and nudges my shoulder. "You do you, baby girl. We'll be right here when you return." My breath hitches in my throat as it tightens, my chest overcome with emotion. "But don't take too long. I understand you need time, I really do, but you're our girl and this is your home. We need you to complete this trio and this city needs you for your badass ink."

I smile at them, my heart warming at the love and joy I see bright in their chocolate eyes.

Hunter tries to soothe me with words but it's the two girls digging into their meals that have my attention. The ones who have been there for me through everything. My darkest days, my foulest moods.

Never failing to perk me up with their smiles and coffee refills from Joy's.

Throwing my arms around Jess, she chokes on her food and gulps down the rest of her wine. Then she shifts to accept my embrace, her voice unsure.

"You all good, Astra?"

"I just love you, that's all. Both of you. I don't say it enough but I appreciate everything you guys have done for me over the years. No matter what, I need you to know that and I need you to protect each other. Promise me."

"Okay, now I'm really worried. What's going on?" Jess pulls back. Wetness touches my cheeks and I quickly wipe away the tears that had escaped and dropped on the cashmere of my sweater. Jess watches me with unreserved horror and then bursts out laughing.

"How times have changed, huh? One minute we're sitting on cushions on the floor of your cottage, waiting for the electrician to come and fix the dodgy lights. Now you're professing your love for me and wiping your nose on cashmere." She's not wrong.

"I'm serious, promise me." I look to Hazel, making sure they both see how serious I am.

She gulps and nods her head, flicking unsure eyes to Jess.

"We promise," they whisper in unison.

"Hazel, you will become the best tattoo artist ever. Jess will find her love and passion and it will *not* be in a man. And me? *Fuck*, I think I'll finally know what it's like to be happy. We're going places, girls. Onwards and upwards." I blink away the tears refusing to slink into the emotion and widen my smile. As I finish the last of my wine, I signal for Hunter it's time to go. "I've got places to be, but seriously, take the jet. Take Damien too, I'm sure you could show him a good time." I bob my eyebrows at Hazel and she blushes a fierce shade of red again. "Watch out for him while I'm gone, alright? He's become really important to me. I want you to remind him of that, okay? Remind each other."

Jess outstretches her hand and I take it, giving her a comforting squeeze. I've never been big on over-sharing and she's never been the type to force me, even when the concern shimmering in her gaze wants her to pry.

Not this time, I shake my head with a sad smile.

These last few months have been nothing but heartache. A mind fuck that has torn me apart and left only the ruins of destruction, but not because of Hunter. This started long before him. I was lost, adrift in a sea I couldn't surface until he showed me the truth. The person I can be, if only I release myself from the turmoil I wear like a cloak of protection. Now I understand what my soul knew all along.

What it really wants.

Blowing them a kiss, I walk away from the girls who have been my everything up to now. Their giggles reach me all the way to the elevator, and when Damien shifts to follow me, I stop him. "I kind of love you, Simon, you know that? What happened wasn't your fault. Hunter was right, you do make the perfect brother. Now go, I'm giving you the day off." Devastation and love, kindle in his green gaze but I don't give him a chance to respond before pressing the button that shuts the doors. Needing a moment to just breathe, I fall slack against the wall and relish in the feel of it firm against my back.

All the painful thoughts of the past few months dwindle. Even the ominous words of that police officer who threatened me dissipate. After all, worries like that won't touch me where I'm going.

Hunter activates the button to the penthouse and winds an arm around my waist, pulling me into his transparent side.

"Now what was all that about?" he growls and I just smile in contentment.

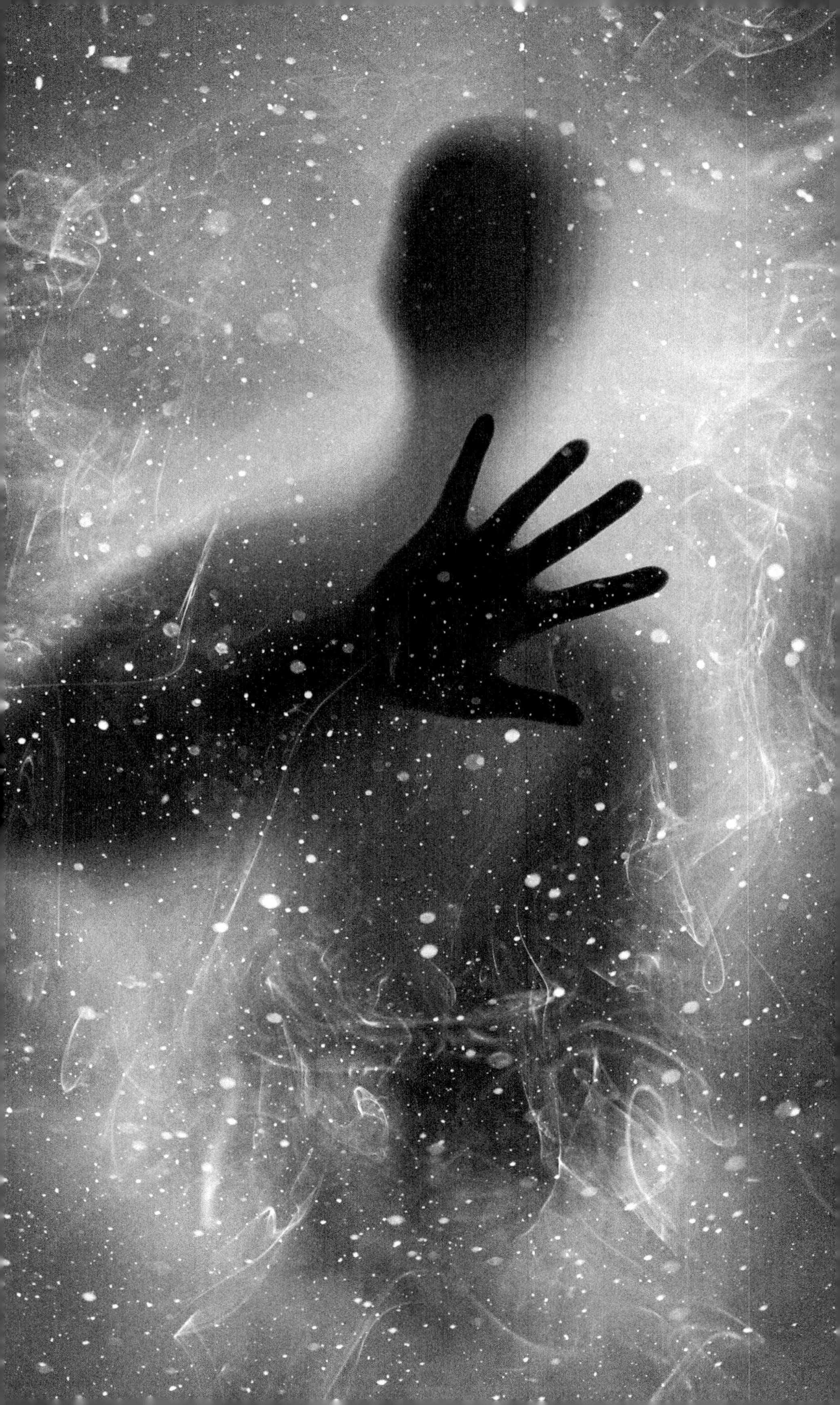

CHAPTER
FIFTY-ONE

Hunter
War Of Hearts - Ruelle

I lay beside Astra, holding her in my arms. She hovers, my aspiration keeping her from falling into the mattress. I almost can't believe that we're here, right now, in this tender moment of utter paradise. This had all started with an obsession, a need that was so compulsive it was like I was living in somebody else's body.

I never truly believed that she would see me, let alone end up falling in love with me in return. All I knew was the darkness, the black hole that had spent countless years chipping away at my heart and soul until I thought I had lost it, all till I met her and she brought my cold and heartless self back to life.

This isn't the end of our love story, it's the beginning, and here, in this moment, my greatest wish had just come true.

She was finally mine.

Dead or alive, I did it.

I captured the heart of my dark queen and I was never letting it go.

No matter the cost.

I'm overfilled with so much energy, I feel electrified. The electrons of my thundering soul send little shockwaves through my very essence. Astra leans into my touch, her soft cheek leaning against the phantom of my right pec. Thick lashes flutter, a dreamy sigh leaving her plush lips as I can feel each and every breath she takes against me.

God, she's been through so much.

And here she is, still fucking standing.

I've broken a thousand times at the devastation and heartache in her ocean gaze. How the Nordic blue waters would become overcome in her grief, overshadowed in a raging hurricane of turmoil.

Those she loved, those she *trusted* had failed her, exploited her.

Let her down and threw her to the wolves. Standing by as the world hurt her over and over again.

Pride wells within my chest even as foreign tears prickle the backs of my aching eyes when I look down at her. The thoughts of her pain force me to relive the anguish in her soul. But that look has faded over the last few days. The turmoil I am so used to seeing in her brightly troubled eyes has waned and utter joy and fulfillment stare back at me. I don't know when her storm settled, but I am hoping it was around the time I decided to weather it with her.

If this is all I ever have, the feel of her in my arms, then I'll remain a very happy fucking soul.

Screw heaven, the only time I've ever found anything even remotely close to it, has been every second she's laid in my arms or been standing at my side.

"Hunter," she breathes, and my soul trembles.

"Yes, love?"

"I need you to do something for me." The low tone of her voice is soothing, a gentle purr that rolls from the back of her throat, meshing with the perfect silence that falls like a veil around us. The only sound to be heard at all is that of our sensual breathing.

Pushing a silken strand of hair out of her eyes, I place my finger under her chin and lift her head so I can gaze into those pretty complexities of hers. "Anything, Siren. You know that."

"It won't be easy," she whispers and I narrow my eyes in displeasure.

"Sweetheart, I came back for you from the other side of death for you. Do you really think there is anything I couldn't give you? Even if I have to tear the worlds apart to get it?"

"I know you would, but, Hunter, this is harder than the veil that parts us."

I pull back, my gentle lift of her jaw turning into a firm hold as I grip her chin and crane her neck back at a better angle so my gaze can flicker across her face, fleetingly, taking in her pinched and apprehensive features as those bright eyes of hers darken to something akin to fear.

"Astra, talk to me, love. You know you can ask me anything."

Another stretch of silence falls, and my anxiety only grows. Shifting up the headboard, she curls into my lap. I leave it be for a moment, allowing her to soak into the comfort she is clearly seeking from me and by the time she's ready, she inhales deeply and then moves to sit up straight beside me.

Turning, she looks me in the eyes and says, "I want you to kill me."

I said that I was unfeeling on this side. That I felt it here, in my chest a niggle of annoyance that told me I should feel more than Utopia but it was nothing more than a memory of what life had been before grace had welcomed me.

Right now though, all of that flies out of the window when my heart skips a trillion beats and falls out my ass. My stomach bottoms out, sinking to my knees as I stare at her utterly dumbfounded.

I say nothing.

What the fuck can I say to that?

"I want to be with you, Hunter. I'm tired of this pain, of this anguish, and this darkness in my soul that eats at me. Every day it grows and it leaves me with nothing but a deep agony in my heart." I blink, then blink again, drowning in her swirling abyss of a sick kind of hope. "I only know peace when I'm with you and I don't want to die any other way than in your arms. I can't ask anyone else to help me, baby. It needs to be you."

Still lost for words, my breathing grows heavier as my mind spirals.

I died to save her life, how can I be the one to take it from her now?

"I know, it's selfish. *Evil*, probably. But I don't know what else to do. I'm suffering, Hunter. I'm suffering here, alone, and without you." There is a desperation in her voice, a plea for me to understand. It's cut raw with an undercurrent of torment like she is hating herself for asking me this. For putting me in this horrible situation. "I'm sorry. I'm so sorry, I know that it's unfair. But I can't, I can't go another day with only the promise of you, but never truly having you. I love you, Hunter. I love every sick and twisted dark part of you. Please, don't leave me in this vile world alone," she sniffles, her tears free falling down her smooth cheeks, stained rosy-pink from her grief. "Don't leave me alone in the darkness," she whispers and it breaks my thundering heart.

Only one thing slips past my numb lips, and it's brewed from a promise. A promise to give her the world, and everything in it. I swore to her that she could trust me. That in this world of darkness, I would be her guiding light. The stars that pave her way. Breathing in deeply, I utter the words, "I'll do it."

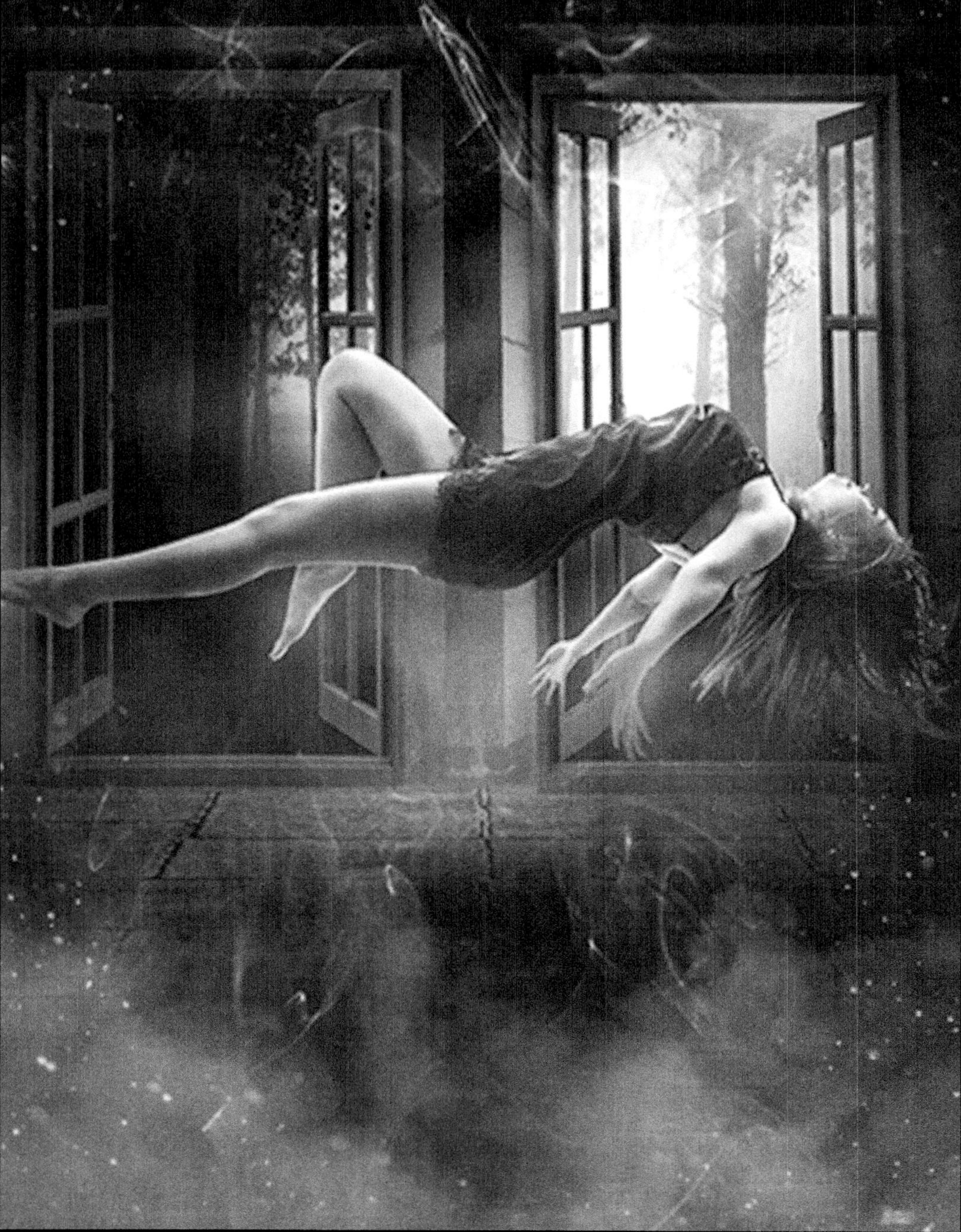

CHAPTER
FIFTY-TWO

Astra
Heaven - Julia Michael

My back arches and my head lolls within the satin sheets as I'm touched everywhere. My entire body is worshiped with soft kisses and delicate caresses that has my heart racing and my limbs trembling. Eyes closed, my lips part as each shallow breath whispers past them in search of their twin flame.

I feel like I have spent my entire life waiting for this moment. That every waking second has been leading me here, to this... to *him*.

I have never given much thought to how I would die.

But I also can't think of a better way to die than what is killing me right now, in the arms of the man that I love.

Hunter moves above my naked body, his skin slick against mine like the satin feel of baby oil, not leaving an inch of my feverish skin untouched from his sensual praise. I try to watch him, to follow the trail he leaves in his fiery wake, but I can't. I'm lost for a silent moment in time as my heart and soul leave my body to float within the clouds of contentment. There is a space between myself and my emotions, almost an ocean-wide space in fact. I can't describe the feeling as anything other than utter brilliance, a peace that consumes my soul and departs my mind from my consciousness. I'm high, my extremities numb and my head fills with nothing but air.

"Look at me," he whispers, his cool breath feathering across my abdomen forcing me to shiver under the attention. "Look at me while I kill you, my beautiful, beautiful, Siren."

He places a gentle kiss on my chest, the place right over my heart. The fresh ink is dark and black, the font bold and delicate as it reads the words, *If I can't get close to you, I'll settle for the ghost of you.'* I needed it on my flesh, etched into the strands of my soul before we did this. Before I finally said goodbye and hello to a new world. Pulling back, he reads the words as devastation flickers in his eyes. The pain and anguish there is so raw, I almost choke on it. I sense the grief, I can feel the misery. It's as brutal as it is moving. It feels like he has just witnessed mass devastation and his heart just can't handle it and the vise of all of that is seen through the storm in his eyes that suck me in and refuse to let me breathe.

My eyes blink open, my chest heavy as my heart thunders beyond the cage of my ribs. I look down, glossy eyes finding his and I become enraptured, unable to look away from the deep abyss of emotion seen swimming in his dark, dark gaze. "I love you, Astra," he utters, the words a quiet storm whispered into a soft breeze.

I reach out a tender hand, gently threading my fingers through his tousled hair and kneading his scalp. He leans into my touch, his own eyes fluttering closed as I reply, "I love you too, Hunter North. Till death parts us and even then, I'll still be loving you."

He crawls up my body, the tips of his fingers gliding across my ribs, causing me to shudder under the hefty weight of his slender frame built of nothing but muscle as he presses me deeper into the mattress beneath him. I'm a fool in those dark complexities, swimming in the essence that is *all* him. Hunter was the air and I was the breeze, together, our love made the world tremble.

I could feel every inch of him as if I was burrowed under his apparition, living inside of his soul. This is the place I called home. The only place I have ever truly wanted to be. He has shown me so much, given me more than he could ever imagine.

"Are you sure about this, love?" he rasps against my lips. The cool air fluttering across them has a small moan slipping free and I dreamily nod my head in a thick daze.

"It's you, Hunter. All I want is you."

His right land trails languishingly up my center, over the swell of my breasts until he wraps his large hand around my throat. At first, it's a gentle placement, a slack hold as he drowns within my gaze. He looks at me like a man falling from a cliff, and like I'd be the wings that saved him from hitting the earth. He looks at me like I've saved him from purgatory and I wish that he could see that I felt the same in the way that I stare back at him.

He saved me from the demon of depression I hadn't known was killing me slowly after the death of my family.

He has gifted me the stars and given me something no other person ever could.

Peace.

My soul finally stopped hurting. Everything settled, the pain fell idle no longer hanging me from its knotted noose when I was in his presence.

All at once, he thrusts his hips forward, and the thick head of his hardened cock breaches my walls as his hand clenches in tandem, around my throat. I can't breathe, with each unhurried stroll of his hips, he rocks into me, hand tightening slowly by the second. Hunter never intended for this to be fast, he wanted it to be meaningful.

I can feel the slick sliding off his cock as he moves inside of me, filling me so wholly, that I don't know where I end and he begins. He consumes me, replacing everything that was once lost and so utterly cold with the warmth that I assume he would have surrounded me in had he still been alive. As my air dwindles and my eyes grow languid, my body sluggish, I hold his stare, even as darkness encroaches. I refuse to look away, to blink the perfection of him into oblivion.

He is so handsome, ungodly so. His brows furrow in tragic despair, his bottom lip quivers as he tightens his hold once more and a struggled choke threatens to slip free, but I swallow it down as best as I can. It comes out like a small squeal, a plea for air withered by my resolve.

I won't make this any harder for him.

His head drops, staring between us as the first drop of his tears rains down like acid and burns against my abdomen. I lift my hand, stroking the side of his cheek and forcing him to look at up at me. I need to give him my strength, implore my desperation for this to happen.

My need to be with him moved beyond time and space, and every second I was held back from truly falling into his embrace, was another second my heart shattered into a million pieces.

"Siren," he sobs. The sound so broken, so severe the tears welling within my eyes overflowed like a steady stream of a waterfall. They fall down my cheeks, his hips moving all the faster as he encourages my release. "I'm sorry," he breathes. "I'm so sorry."

"Lo-ove you," I croak, using the precious tendrils of air I still have available. "P-please. Ne-need to be with you." My eyes roll back, I gasp. My soul is on fire as it burns through the cage of my flesh.

It can sense that the end is near and it itches to be freed to find its flame.

Together, we cry.

Together, we make love for the first time as euphoria encloses around us. Like a delicate petal of a budding rose, second by second we wither and fall, flat against the earth until nothing but our core is left exposed.

"You can do this. It's time to take me home, Hunter." Still caressing his cheek, wiping away the tears that drop onto my silken skin, I use my other hand to wrap around his. The one firm on my throat. I show him my insistence, forcing him to tighten his hold until all I see is four of him dancing in my vision, a thick black outline moving back and forth as his soul wavers.

My lower belly tightens, and my body seizes as I begin to convulse from under him. I shake as his devotion to me is unrelenting. He cries even harder, as the perfect lines of his face pinch and contort in a brutalizing kind of despair. A kind of despair I feel in my soul just as it's about to leave my body.

He pinches my clit, and just as I take my final breath in the world of the living, I orgasm in a collision of worlds colliding. The explosion was so fierce, it sends a torrent of fire blowing through my core. My mind explodes in ecstasy. My soul skyrockets from my lifeless corpse and all these months of edging have finally become worth it when the second my soul steps from my body, Hunter is there grabbing my apparition and picking me up with dominating hands.

My legs wrap around his waist, as he slams me into the wall, entering my clenching pussy before my mind can even process what is happening. I'm dead and the life I knew is over. The air around me turns cosmic like I'm literally drifting through the galaxies. Color fades from existence and all I'm left with is a blinding blue light. The world is utter darkness around me, all until I look down at Hunter.

He glows a brilliant blue, his aura a stark contrast that compels me to notice how he looks so human here, now that I'm on the other side. His skin is golden and tanned and those dark eyes turn even darker in comparison to how they looked when I was alive. My heaving chest is the same transparent blue he first presented to me as. My mind riots, unable to track all of the sudden changes.

I'm in awe, utterly breathless as he pounds into me with wild abandon. "Do you know how long I've waited for this, Astra?" My name is like honey on his lips. "How long I've craved this? You're all mine, baby girl, and now there's no escape. I'll follow you wherever you will go, my sweet death mate."

Something happens, it's like the world spins around us too fast for the eye to see. Color beings to restore, like a cup of paint spilled on an outline of a beautiful sketch. Slowly, the world around me begins to settle in place, and it no longer feels isolated.

I gasp, clawing at Hunter's back, blood beading under my fingernails, not sure how to function with these raw sensations that plague me all at once. I feel like I'm standing on a live wire, and my very veins can feel the static of electricity that rushes through me.

"Fuck, I love you," Hunter grunts, lips pressed to my neck as my body turns back into human texture. He sinks his teeth into my throat and I cry out from the twisted pleasure of it throbbing in my wanton clit. "Scream for me like my dirty little bitch, Siren. Come all over the cock that has been waiting on his queen to sit upon his throne for over a goddamn year. We're done waiting. Fucking scream, love!" Then he thrusts one last time, my back pushed up against the wall. A firm thumb pressed against my clit with his mouth latched around my nipple and a finger circling the rim of my puckered star. He pushes his finger inside my ass, and the moment he does, he shoves his cock so far inside my cunt I bellow his name to the gods. My clit pushes against his thumb, grinding against his pelvis as I roar my release.

My soul explodes.

Literally coming apart in tiny little molecules of clear blue glitter that drift through the air before the particles weave together, reconnecting and I'm under him whole and utterly soul-fucked once again.

"That, love, is how you fuck the love of your life dead," he breathes and I chuckle struggling to stop myself from falling from grace, blissed out on euphoria.

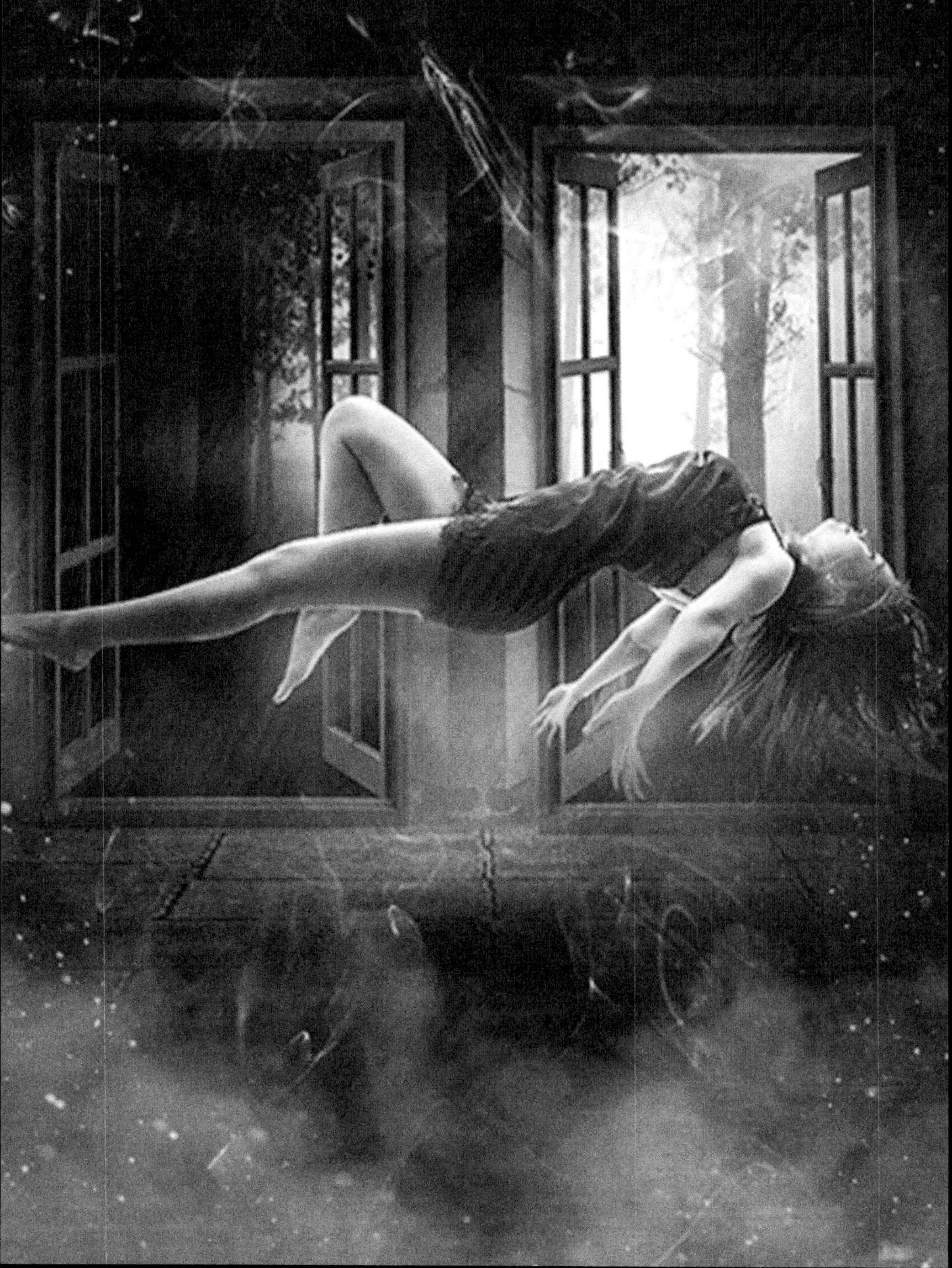

EPILOGUE

Astra
Afterlife - Hailee Steinfeld

C olors burst before my eyes, flashing in the brightest vibrancy. My king smiles the purest of grins, his straight teeth gleaming between his full lips. A panty-melting display, if I were wearing any.

Drawing to my feet, my entire body is instantly encased with soft and tiny prickles. Shimmering gold particles settle on my skin, collecting together to form a luxurious gown that clings to my body. Plunging low to my sternum, completely strapless with a scandalous waist-thigh split. Almost as if the dress molded around my tattoos to show them off in the most alluring way. Tendrils of my hair shift, stroking against my nape as they are drawn upwards and secured in an updo. Fitting for the ethereal sense that this is the first day of my forever.

"Shall we?" Hunter offers his arm. Also formed from the particles, a classic, smart shirt shimmers against his upper body, sleeves rolled back at the elbows. White slacks hug the length of his legs, his shining dress shoes back in place. But none of that compares to his face.

Sculpted by the gods themselves, no one has the right to be this sinfully beautiful. A jaw carved from ice, eyes derived from the rawest granite. His shaggy hair has been combed back from his forehead, not a strand out of place. And still, even that's not what's striking me the most. It's the sheer glow radiating from his skin. The aura of contentment seeped into my own. He's so genuinely happy for the first time that I could just burst at the seams with joy. He told me once that life on the other side was like a forced kind of paradise, and that he felt like he was waiting for something, he just never knew what.

Well, it was this.

Placing one foot in front of the other, I lean on his arm, savoring the sweet yet woodsy scent coiling around us both.

Our smell. Our *ecstasy*.

A world materializes before us. Much like the one I just left, the inside of the cabin my grandparents once owned forms from wood panels layering on top of each other and further still until the roof is built. Mountain ranges span beyond the windows, bordered by decking fit with a porch swing beside the hot tub. Memories hang on the walls, framed in gold, displaying moments of my life that I cherish the most. The setup the girls had made, wanting me to relax with all of the Halloween decorations and the plush couch just as I left it, except every inch of the space is now bursting with light, shining like the focal point of my soul.

Another happy time.

Guiding me outside, the lake at the base of the mountains beckons me. A layer of stars, a dazzling sea of dreams all coming true. I thought death would be dark, reeking of depravity, but this isn't any version of hell I've speculated on. This right here, is my heaven.

Drawing me down the hill, there's an exciting hitch to my movements until I'm flat-out running. Hunter and the screams of my laughter chase me, the golden dress whipping around my legs. My toes grace the cool water just as he collides with my back and together, we sink beneath the surface. Taunting lips lock with mine before we rise, no need to rush for air in our realm. No need for air at all in our destiny.

Lost to the ripples, hands swish, bodies sway. Tongues dance, whirling with movements as old as time. We're one. Where I end, he begins, in spirit and soul. The other half of me, the man who's been watching from the shadows.

The one who saw me, no matter how hard I tried to be invisible.

Breaching the surface, the endless sunshine beats down. My smile stretches ear to ear, my waist gripped in Hunter's hands as he rocks us to and fro. My solid, unbreakable man. It stuns me how even from death, Hunter gave me a reason to live. Provided me with a purpose, even if it was to leave the ties of mortality behind. I see it now—how tied down I was, how nothing felt right since... *well*, no point going back there now.

This is my fresh start. My new beginning.

"We should probably dry you off, Siren. Looks like I'm not the only one desiring your attention." Following Hunter's eyeline back up the hill, any heartbeat I may have had halts in my chest. Four figures stand beside the cabin, their backs to the sun, and their features are indistinguishable.

But I know those heights. Those stances.

I've seen them a million times in the fleeting crossover before my dreams become nightmares. Before the grief drowning my soul crashed over my treasured memories like a tidal wave. It's a state I became used to living in, but now the dam is threatening to break and take the last of my strength with it.

"I-I thought... you said you were all alone on your side..." I take a tentative step back in the water, not allowing myself to believe this is real. Hunter steps into my back, blocking my retreat.

"It was because I had no one to connect to. I was waiting, but I wasn't waiting for the afterlife, I was waiting for you. This astral plane has been built by you, Siren. Your heart is your anchor, Astra.

You've tried desperately to protect it, but your love runs deep enough to keep it long-lasting, even if you never knew you were doing it. My heart was connected to you... My soul. And yours? It was connected to all of us." My knees give out, my weight relying on Hunter to hold me up. Braced in his arms, he aids me out of the water, the droplets trickling from me step by step until I'm completely dry, my hair pinned back still perfect in the updo.

Every step is weighed down with apprehension, and anxiety spiking in my chest. Reaching the crest of the hill, their looming silhouettes become too much. I scrunch my eyes shut tight, unable to build myself up for the heartache. I've wished too hard, and waited too long.

"Hey, buttercup," the melodic voice greets me and my eyes shoot open with a gasp. Like a figment from the past, he hasn't changed one bit.

Blue eyes like icy shards that have no right to look as gentle and kind as they always did. Black hair cropped short, the beard I always complained tickled my cheek. Army fatigues cover his body, reminding me of the day he returned home after being discharged. The same dog tags hang at his neck—a man so honorable, so noble, stolen from me far too soon. But he's here now, right here as real as can be.

"Papa," I weep, running into his arms. More close in around me, the familiar smell of lavender that my grandmother's bed linen smelled of coiling around us all.

"Careful there, Rikki. That's one hell of a grip." He chuckles, using my childhood nickname from *H2O: Just Add Water*. I break down, and absolute devastation and joy clash in a brutal tsunami that has tears strolling down my cheeks. Frail fingers and withered limbs wrap around my torso, my grandfather's grip tighter than I remember.

"Damn, sis, you sure know how to make an entrance. We felt you enter the atmosphere like a freaking comet." A hand ruffles through my long dark hair and I don't even complain. Peering up at my brother, I kick his shin playfully. His boyish smile beams down at me, trapped forever young against his youthful face.

"I learned from the best. Remember the time you got the marching band to parade you to your first detention? No one has ever been so proud to have been caught distributing porn magazines before."

A mix of laughter and disgruntled groans sound as I pull away, my grandmother's mouth pouting the way it does when she's trying to hide her disappointment. And I fucking love that after all this time, she hasn't changed a bit. None of them have. They're my flesh and blood, and we're finally together again.

I realize now that we all live in a limbo after death if our souls aren't ready to move on. Hunter moved on when he had me, I'm sure that my grandparents did the same. Luckily, my brother and father had each other from the moment they died. They never knew what it was like to walk the world alone and I'm overjoyed with the truth of that.

"How about I cook up your favorite, barbecue sticky ribs with my secret sauce?" My father quirks his brow. The four of them turn, and it's only then I see two more cottages have formed behind them. Similar to ours, although the one Luca and my father stride over to hosts a huge BBQ on the deck, and the last cottage is shrouded in lavender hanging from the trellis.

Three cabins in a row, housing those I love more than anything. I'm, overwhelmed with the knowledge that we'll get to stay together for eternity. Turning to find Hunter hanging back, I beckon him into my arms.

"Do ghosts even eat?" I ask and he smirks.

"It's your world beautiful, we can do whatever we want." Lifting my hand, Hunter brings the back of it to his lips and presses a soft kiss there. I'm enraptured by his relaxed smile and the way my core is already craving him again, so when a band of metal eases onto my finger, it takes me by complete surprise.

Shimmering in a royal blue band with all the love in the world, diamonds stare back at me. Split into four, forming the shape of an orchid, my heart bursts at the wedding ring that is too perfect to be real. But nothing here is. It's all created by the will of our love, the very essence of our souls intertwining into our new reality.

When you die? The paradise that awaits is man-made, a new world at the tip of your fingers to make your wildest dreams come true.

"You asked me once what it was like here," Hunter murmurs. His eyes dance with silver sparks, filled with more life than I've ever known him to show. Half an hour ago, I had thought that I knew what he meant. That the missing piece was just us, I never knew it was all of this too. "I said it was peaceful, but something was missing. I knew it then, but not even I was selfish enough to ask you for your ultimate sacrifice. It had to be your decision, your choice. Now I can answer your question properly. My afterlife, Siren, was missing you."

MORE HALLOWEEN READS FROM EMMALEIGH

Check Out Wicked Hallows

What happens when it's Halloween and you decide to try and summon a sexy demon from Hell but get a dead serial killer instead?.......

Prologue
Welcome To The Circus - Five Finger Death Punch

The night was supposed to conceal our demons, keeping them hidden from the pure minds that would hang us for the morality that dwelt in their darkened hearts.

It was the one place where you would find your monsters lingering in the ominous shadows.

That was what we were told.

Every day of our lives, the things soaked in crimson were the things we should be wary of. That the ugly and the depraved were the sins we should burn with holy water, and every malicious thought should be purged from our minds and soul with an iron cross.

But when you play it right, the night was also the void that let our personal demons out to play with nobody to bear witness to such an incredible dark art of wickedness. Society couldn't condemn you for the sins cloaked in the veil of a lethal abyss.

We have been taught to think anything unholy was wrong.

But that was a lie and anybody still accustomed to such warped ways had my pity. We all held it within us.

A parasite that was waiting for the right time to consume your withering bones and installed you with the strength of a monster fit to rid this world of all its evils.

The night?

Had always been my favorite thing, no matter what side of it I got.

Just as the night covered my arms in darkness, so did the blood that ran in rivers down my wrists as crimson plasma splattered against my lips.

I stared back at the wall, seeing stars in the mayhem, and smirked to myself.

Why was blood so pretty?

Hmmm.

I ran my toes along the silken ground and smeared the essence that surrounded me as I went. Humming the theme song to *Stranger Things*, I licked my fingers clean before I kicked the body at my feet. Then, like a demon possessed, I threw myself onto the corpse and rained down maddening punches, licking the air that seemed to become electrified in my psychotic state. Everything tasted sweet and glorious, but I *needed* more. I let out a throaty sneer, putting *Scary Movie* and their what's uppp scene to shame as I lost myself to the rejuvenating euphoria that came with bloodshed at utter carnage.

Nobody talked about what a beautiful thing death was.

How final and complete.

Could a human brain even comprehend the magnitude of such a thing?

How we were here, until we weren't.
Until the lights went out and then we were where?
Nowhere and everywhere?
Well, I have a secret for you, sugar.

There was nothing after death. Nothing but torment from the thing that killed you.

Like so many others, that asshole's happily never ever would feature my twisted mug and my sexy as fuck sinister smirk.

As I carved the heart from her chest, I held it in my hand. Her pale face stunning under the light of the moon, breaking through the cracks. With eyes as dark as chocolate glossed over in a yellow sheen of crystalized balls, she stared back at me. It didn't feel like I thought it would. The heart was hard encased with squiggly edges—with curves and crevices that hide away all of the little valves that once kept this useless thing beating.

Now, I was eye to eye with it, holding it before my very face with a steady hand placed over my own heart. I just couldn't seem to feel the connection.

The horror.
The fear.

Which I presumed a normal person would. All I held was unbridled curiosity that coursed through my veins like burning embers of a great fire. I needed to know more. I needed to breach the barrier of inquisitiveness that kept me up at night. I needed to make some kind of sense of how I was alive, with a heart that beat under my palm and that was the only difference between me and the dead bitch beneath me.

Anyway.
Enough about me.

Welcome to the slaughterhouse, the place born of bloody desires and a curiosity that would most definitely kill the cat.

Happy Halloween!

MORE HALLOWEEN READS FROM EMMALEIGH

Chapter 1

Ophelia
Monsters - Shinedown

Dark fog coiled around me as I kneeled into the cold, sodden soil which seeped through the fabric of my jeans. The rounded moon sat like a beacon of silver light that washed over me, highlighting parts of the grim and ominous graveyard in Hallows Point. Baleful clouds circled overhead, breaking apart the abyss, and forming sinister-looking images within the sky that had my pulse thundering under my skin. Throbbing with an acute awareness at the column of my throat with such force, it began to ache as if I had been stabbed with a needle.

I shouldn't be here.

I shouldn't be toying with the dead.

It was disrespectful, not to mention creepy as fuck.

The souls in these graves had either been blessed by the heavens or cursed by the devil himself. There was a feeling that burned into the back of my neck, deceptive eyes watched me from the shadows. It was in my head, I was alone here. I knew that. I knew that I shouldn't be here at all and the smart thing to do would be to pack up my shit and leave.

But I just couldn't help myself.

I wanted to know... *needed* to know.

How real such wicked words uttered on that one special night called All Hallows Eve could truly be. We all played into the feeble tales of such an unholy night.

Played the games of Bloody Mary and watched out for the Candyman with razor blades in his cut-throat sweets.

But what about the rest of it?

What about the demons of the dark?

My heart beat frantically, more wild than the stallions riding their way through autumn, churning those golden leaves. I could feel my pulse thumping against the taunt skin at the column of my neck as I tried to build the courage to play with all things spooky.

This was a stupid idea, but there's no backing out now.

If I wanted my next book *Summoning Hell* in the *Shits & Giggles Of Purgatory* series to be another hit for me, I needed to do the research.

I needed to know what it felt like in the dead of night when you're alone, but never without company. When the darkness concealed your worst nightmares and you convinced yourself that something lingered there, in the shadows, waiting to destroy you with all the sick and twisted things you thought you had kept secret but were unable to in this very moment of a very bleak night.

The untamed pace of your horrified heart, that wanted any excuse to take you out of the game altogether instead of sitting idle and experiencing these acute feelings of terror.

Because being nothing was more than being a pathetic human riddled with so much fear, it forced you to give in to those so-called irrational emotions that plagued the simplicity of a human mind.

I felt that way now, like I was moments away from succumbing to my self-induced terror and falling by the wayside onto some unknown person's grave.

I jotted everything down in my notebook.

Every little twitch and eye flicker and every little flutter and small seizure of fright.

Detailed every sensation and thought that was running havoc through my chaotic mind.

Everything from the chill skating down my spine to the tremble in my hands. The book beside me flickered in the wind as the pages flipped in a hurried arch, as if a gale force wind had just blown upon it with harsh and unforgiving lips. I gasped, jumping back, bringing a quivering hand to my chest as the air around me burned like ice in my lungs, "For fuck's sake, pull it together, Ophelia." I slammed my hand down on the old leather bindings and huffed at the night. I found the book on some website that referred to themselves as the *Olden Truths Of Wiccan Ways*. I purchased the only thing they actually advertised on the site, actually. The description read that this was the only copy in existence and that only the one of pure blood could wield the spells within it.

Sounded like some shit marketing if you asked me, but I had to set the scene.

After I wandered through the graveyard aimlessly, I chose a spot at the back. It was barren, with dried, rotten and withered leaves laid along the ground. I wasn't disrespectful enough to do this over somebody's actual grave.

Sheesh.

A Weeping Willow tree that overhung, brushed against the backs of my hands. The trunk was huge and spiraled into the earth beyond the canopy of weeping Catkins.

The foliage seemed to glow a neon kind of deep and dark green, under the scarce light of the moon that reflected back at me as a dull kind of silver, now hidden from my vantage point at the moment. I rooted through my bag and pulled out the three blood-red candles, then set them down, embedded into the soil at the three trips of a triquetra. Then I sprinkled black salt around the iron pentagram buried under the dirt at the base of the tree.

"Jesus fuck. Feeling like you're about to have a damn aneurysm as the dead rise to eat your flesh definitely needs to be explained in the book, " I uttered with a small whisper under my breath like the abyss would hear me and come for my soul if I uttered the words too loudly. "The things I do for my readers." My breath is harsh and chilled. A billowing white burst of cloudy smoke whispered from my lips as I shook my head and lowered my eyes back to the book, sitting by my knees.

I ran my deft fingers over the engraved cover. Gold foiled embroidery bordered the edge, curved and entwined like the symbols of a triquetra. The binding is one long and slithered snake twisted around another. Thick lips that looked to be coming out of the cover itself more than being added in some way, sat in the right hand bottom corner, and the title *Wicked Words Spoken On All Hallows* was scripted in such a deep and dark red above it, you could hardly read the words at all. I took a moment to appreciate the unique beauty of it before I flicked it open and found the page that I needed.

Anima Summoner

A spell that translated to Soul Summoner in Latin. The ingredients were the blood of the caster, a desire for the darkness, and the idea of the subject you wished to raise. In my case, a smut God from way down under. I pulled the knife out next and held open the pages with my knees, as I fought against the speed of the wind that funneled into small tornadoes around me and unheaved all of the dirt on the ground. My mind spiraled into what the fuck territory, but I had to see this through. I needed to experience absolutely everything if I was going to write it so accurately, my words would feel the way I was right now. My hair whipped around my face, the sharp strands barbed as I shook them away and pulled the blade across my palm. Blood dripped, small rivulets splotched against the soil, soaking them in the crimson tears of my very essence. I hissed, the pain not entirely unpleasant but unnatural as the sting spread through me like veins of fucked up desire and heated my very core.

But we don't speak about that.

"Hear me, come to me, something wicked this way comes," I began to chant, the words raw and powerful as they tore from my throat. I felt it rushing through me, almost like the thought of this working alone was enough to empower me with a vicious tone that bespoke determination. It was enough to make a damn fool of myself inside a creepy graveyard too. "Hear me, come to me, something wicked this way comes." The tone of my voice increased in volume as it dropped to a deadly low octave, a low hum that sounded like the purr of an engine. "Hear me, come to me, something wicked this way comes." I glared up into the night as I willed all of my strength and focus into summoning this demon God. I risked a quick glance back down at the pages and read the next incantation like a damn pro.

Maybe I was a witch in my past life?

Huh.

"Come to me, wicked demon. A soul from the dark, a sinful heathen. I call to you, this Hallows Eve, to give you life and grant you a reprieve. Stain this earth red with my blood on your corpse, wreak your havoc as this night runs its course. I call to you now so let it be, rise from the ashes, and answer to me."

The sound of an explosion shattered my ears, but nothing seemed misplaced. Thrown back, I hit the ground hard and groaned as I rolled to my side and brought my knees up so I could lift myself back up onto them. "What the fuck was that?" I asked at the very same moment lightning struck and I shrieked like a siren getting whacked by the ship of sailors she was hoping to devour.

The sky flashed a neon-colored blue as the bolt of lightning that struck beside me shimmered in an angelic glitter-like purple. It was beautiful, you know if it wasn't trying to kill me dead.

Guess I was in the right place to keel over though, aye?

My chest burned as my throat turned dry, painful as I swallowed past the thick lump lodged within it. Sweat beaded along my brow, dropping onto my lashes as I batted them away and tried to settle my breathing that branded me like a hot iron. Thunder clapped across the heavens like a roar of demented deaths calling for the night and I shuddered, then folded within myself as I fell to my ass and lifted my knees to my chest in a cradle.

Unholy Satan, that was not supposed to happen.

What was supposed to happen?

Fuck knew.

But mother nature scaring the shit out of me at the exact moment I decided to do some in-the-field research for my next book was not one of them. I trembled as I spied something that looked like gray-stone poking through the soil. I crawled toward it and swiped away all of the moist dirt and recoiled when I saw that it was a headstone.

A very neglected headstone.

Shit, fuck, Halloween cunt!

Here lies Blake Colton.

Not exactly poetic and heartfelt.

I did this on somebody's grave.

Damn.

"Oh shit," I breathed, as I stumbled back and forced myself up on unsteady legs. "Sorry dude, no disrespect!"

"None taken. But couldn't you have knocked first, given a guy the heads up? I mean, come now, love. I'm not even wearing my best face," a deep, brooding voice husked from the darkness as a man bled from the shadows and stepped through the overhang of the willow tree. I swallowed thickly, unsure if I should tuck my tail and run, or play dead to the man who stalked toward me with half a chiseled face of the exposed bones shaping his skeletal form. It weaved back together, regenerated, and connected to look like the side of his face thankfully covered in normal flesh.

Pain started in my neck as my spine locked up in terror. Everything within me seized in fright and disbelief, but the horror didn't stop the word from slipping out. "*Demon,*" I breathed while the final piece of his flesh coiled and weaved back together and showcased an Adonis of a man before me.

He was striking, eyes darker than onyx with cheekbones as chiseled as Spike's from Buffy. Tanned flesh glistened under the rays of night, his entire body covered in tattoos. Not the kind that left no space on the skin, but the kind you ached to run your tongue over in the heart of one sinful and never spoken about again night. His chest and abdomen were on display as he wore a leather jacket that fell from his shoulders. My warped pussy fluttered as I clenched together my thighs.

He stood without shoes, toes twined within the soil, with black jeans hung low on his carved hips. The V that was sharper than any blade dipped between the waistline and stole my focus for a moment. There was something else that added to the sinister air around us though. Something that added to the feeling slithering all across my skin.

Blood.

He was covered in blood.

By the time I recovered from the sight before me, it was already too late.

He was there, in front of me with harsh breath that kissed against my skin and a vicious hand that coiled within my hair until he yanked me back far enough that he could expose my throat to him. Greedy eyes assessed me and everything fell silent. The only thing to be heard was the thunder of my hammering heart louder than the actual thunder that clapped around us.

His lips were a fraction away from mine as my hot air blew against them softly and he growled, "No demon, love. You did just bag yourself a serial killer though. Want to tell me how you brought me back from the dead? Because I'm pretty sure when my lights went out, they never came on again."

When his lips touched mine, nothing else mattered. The world fell away, broken piece by broken piece as it was taken by the breeze that took all of my sinful secrets to the void and I hoped they stayed far away from this sinful man.

ABOUT THE AUTHOR - EMMALEIGH & MADDISON

Emmaleigh and Maddison are best friends living in the UK. They met through their love of books and all things crazy. As doting mothers and wives, writing Haunted By Desire has provided a much needed escape from the real world to write this sinfully good story you can't live without. As authors, we relying on each other and our loyal readers for support, so thank you! We couldn't do it without you! We hope you've enjoy our story as much as we loved writing it and who knows what the future holds...

Facebook group - https://www.facebook.com/groups/761268698283302

About the Author - Emmaleigh Wynters

Emmaleigh Loader is a stay-at-home mum of three - her two boys and her brother-in-law - and a wife, who lives in the UK.

Her favorite things are storms, the sea, and anything witchy! She finds winter beautiful and enjoys the beauty of the sun. She loves anything dark and adores loving alphas and strong women. She's an avid reader, and despite living with disabilities, pushes herself to be someone who her family, husband and sons are proud of.

Follow my socials:

https://linktr.ee/EmmaleighLoader

ALSO BY EMMALEIGH WYNTERS

Fantasy/Paranormal

Standalone:

Don't Read Between The Line's

Wicked Hallows

Death's Wish - TBA

Devoured By The Lines TBA

Also by Emmaleigh Loader

KING'S WOLVES MC

SAVAGE

OUIJA

STRAIGHTJACKET

STITCH

TOOTHPICK - TBA

A FALL FOR DESIRE:

The Last Time You Break Me: A Fall For Desire

NOVELLAS:

Who I Crave To Be

Daddy's Calling - TBA

IMPERFECTLY BEAUTIFUL

RISING FROM THE ASHES

Emmaleigh also has a series of notebooks.

The Witches series.

The Fantasy series.

(All Can Be Found Under Emmaleigh Loader On Amazon)

Merchandise:

Open Book: The VillainsThat Feed Our Soul Quoted Notebook.

Knife And Blood: The Villains We Need Notebook.

Girl In The Mind Library: Don't Read Between The Lines Quoted Notebook.

Black Unicorn: Savage Quoted Notebook.

Skull And Butterfly: Ouija Quoted Notebook.

Skeleton Couple: Stitch Quoted Notebook.

<u>All notebooks will be live March 2022 on amazon. Other products with the merchandise designs will be available soon as well.</u>

Printed in Great Britain
by Amazon